Jim Costello is a sixty-three year-old married Scotsman who, during his varied and interesting life has 'reincarnated' himself several times. His experience has included psychiatric nursing, the Royal Navy, gents outfitting, the civil service, and political campaign organiser and fund raiser. As election agent and a senior party executive he has worked with many well known Cabinet Ministers, MPs, MEPs and Members of the House of Lords.

After life in politics he retrained as a driving instructor. He spent several happy years helping countless people of all ages attain that elusive passport to increased personal freedom, and stay alive in the process. Unfortunately, the driving instructor industry became overcrowded, making it harder to earn a decent living, and it was time for another change. His next job was with a major bank, working with customers who needed help with financial problems.

During his lifetime Jim has accumulated a variety of skills including verbal and written communication, public relations, market research, marketing, press and media, campaigning, and fundraising. He has always had a love of the sea and his other interests and hobbies have included backgammon, creative writing, science fiction, fish keeping, gardening, photography, and rabbits. His current house rabbit is a loveable little hooligan called Toffee.

Find out more at www.jimcostello.co.uk.

ADONGIVA

JIM COSTELLO

SilverWood

Published in paperback 2012 by SilverWood Books, Bristol, BS1 4HJ
www.silverwoodbooks.co.uk

ISBN 978-1-906236-76-2

British Library Cataloguing in Publication Data
A CIP catalogue record for this book is available from the British Library

Set in Sabon by SilverWood Books
Printed on paper sourced responsibly

I would like to thank my long-suffering wife
Jane
for putting up with the countless hours of listening to the tap, tap, tap
of my keyboard
and the constant researching on the internet with
my regular companions Messrs Google and Wikopedia.

CHAPTER ONE

Monday 25th August 2025

"Question – Is this really the answer?" said Hiram Montgomery, staring into the glass of whisky he held in one hand. *"Answer – you know the answer already, you stupid Scottish pea brain."* He sneered at himself in the mirror.

It was normal for Hiram to conduct abusive arguments with himself when he was 'down', and he had been down for some time.

"OK, clever Dick, and the problem is what? *You know damn well. Sarah died and you feel guilty. You'd upset her, and when she died you hadn't apologised enough."* Tears flowed. "Stop feeling sorry for yourself, you worm. You've cried enough." He had cried buckets in the last few weeks. He'd wept so much he should be de-hydrated. Perhaps he had re-hydrated himself with whisky? "I am not crying for me. I love Sarah and miss her. I want her to walk through the door. *If she did she'd give you hell. Look at this pigsty.* I don't care. I deserve to be punished. I want her here. I can't live without her, don't want to live without her. *You feel guilty because you were a constant disappointment with your faults, mistakes and wrong decisions. You could never get anything right. No wonder she decided to die on you.* She did not decide to die. It was a blood clot that killed her."

He had relived that night repeatedly, thinking what he could have done different. They had been watching TV and she had dozed off, as she had so many times. He had sat a few feet away, until bed time, when he tried to wake her. He called several times then shook her. He tried harder, to no effect. He would never forget the moment of realisation and the wave of panic. He remembered continuing to shake her, even after he knew. It had taken a long time to accept that she was dead.

Finally he had walked to the phone and dialled 999. He told the operator his wife had died and when she asked what emergency service he wanted, he'd said, "It doesn't matter, just send somebody. They'll know what to do."

He hung up and waited. Two policemen arrived, then others; paramedics, doctor, detectives. They asked questions but seemed to be mumbling. People stared from close up. Looking back Hiram remembered feeling stupid, literally. His brain and body had slowed to a snail's pace and everyone else rushed around him like rockets. A doctor gave him something and then he didn't care for a while.

When his mind was clear they told him that Sarah had died because a clot had formed in a blood vessel, travelled to her brain, and killed her quietly, peacefully, and painlessly. The police had called it an act of God. Hiram had blamed God for a lot of things over the years. He imagined that when he died he would be dispatched to Hell by his maker, for his constant blasphemy. Now Hiram felt, God was at it again; screwing up his life by lulling him into making a wrong decision, or by throwing a spanner in the works. He thought that if God was human, he would be considered a sadist.

"Question – if God controls the universe and everything in it, does he actually enjoy dispensing famine, disease, earthquakes, crashes; and taking wives away without warning. *Answer – God only knows.*"

The funeral had been an ordeal for Hiram. His mask was paper-thin and people kept saying to let the grief out. He had kept himself mentally rigid, for if he opened the flood gates he would be an inconsolable wreck. For weeks he felt surrounded and suffocated. Friends and relatives took to drowning him in a sea of sympathy and cups of tea. He wished they would all go away and leave him alone. Finally they did, and he could grieve in peace. He sobbed like a baby for days and nights. After the sobbing he drove himself insane with grief, loneliness, anger, self pity and despair. He neglected himself and did not eat properly, alternating between starving, and gorging on junk food washed down with alcohol. He did not wash, clean dishes, tidy up or put anything away. He was aware of punishing himself and damaging his body, which sometimes he rationalised as a crazy attempt to force Sarah back and sort him out. He knew that was ridiculous but was powerless to stop. If she did return she would give him hell, and he yearned for that more than anything in the world. All that happened was a deeper slide into a binge of self-destruction.

He had always enjoyed a drink but since Sarah's death he was going for the world record. An ocean of booze passed over his lips, through his system and back to the sea. He bombarded himself with assault after assault on his anatomy. "Question – Are you drinking to forget? *Answer – If so, it isn't working, because you always remember.* Question – Is it an attempt to self destruct? *Answer – Probably. I deserve to be destroyed.* Question – Are you punishing yourself? *Answer – Yes. I need to be punished.* Question – Are you angry with yourself? *Answer – Yes. I am alive and Sarah is not. That is not fair. It has to be put right.*"

He posed more questions. Was he drinking because he was dependent on it? No. He could give up if he wanted. Was he drinking because he liked it? Yes. It was good stuff and he liked the taste. Correction, he *usually* liked the taste. At that moment the thought of another drink turned his stomach, probably because his taste buds, like the rest of him were wrecked. He had not enjoyed it for days, but had kept going despite his growing knowledge that this banquet of self mortification was destroying him, costing a fortune, and preventing his recovery, not that he wanted to recover.

Now he was in his living room at ten in the morning, scotch in hand, when he should have been at work. He felt ashamed, and filled with self-loathing If he had a gun he would shoot himself. "You'd put a dog out of its misery, wouldn't you?" If he had sleeping pills he would down the lot. He knew there was no gun or sleeping pills in the house. There was gas or electrocution, or swallowing aspirins, but he had read that this was not sure-fire and painless. A common method was to step in front of a train but he'd always regarded this as a selfish act because of the inconvenience to others. There were pills around the place, but he was not sure what they were. He did not fear dying but didn't want pain or unpleasantness. Knowing his luck he would probably just disable himself and have to be looked after by strangers.

Right now he should be putting all this behind him and getting back to work at Everards. The store couldn't keep his job open forever. Everards was a department store, and he was chief clerk. When he had telephoned to say his wife had died Mr. Fothergill, the Store Manager, had said to take as long as necessary.

As the sun warmed his shoulder through the window Hiram knew he had reached a crossroad. It looked like a lovely day out there, where people were going about as if nothing was amiss. Sarah's death had been a catastrophe for him, but the world was still turning and people carried on as before. He could stay here and rot, or he could get his act together and re-join the human race.

What would Sarah have said if she could see the way things were now? The house was a mess; no clean dishes or clothes, and an empty fridge. His wife had been, on occasion, a dragon. If nagging had been an Olympic sport, she would have been a medallist. He would have been in the dog house right now, and he longed for that. Every time he thought of her, his heart ripped. He loved her deeply and needed to tell her, but couldn't. Tears streamed, as so many times before. Please come back, he cried. Deep down he knew she was gone, and it hurt beyond description. He knew what he had to do, and right away. He could have poured the whisky down the sink, but that would have been pointless, as there was more in the cupboard. Logically, he would have to pour the lot away and that would be stupid. This extremely good malt whisky had stood for years waiting for a suitable occasion, which never came. He walked to the sideboard and poured the whisky back into the bottle, went up stairs, showered and dressed in clean clothes. It felt good to brush his teeth again and feel their cleanliness with his tongue. He gathered washing and sorted light and dark, as Sarah would have done, filled the machine, added powder, and switched on. He collected glasses and crockery from every room, filled the dishwasher and turned that on. Next, he tidied up around the house, took the vacuum cleaner on a tour, sprayed polish and flicked a duster.

Finally the house was fit for a 'Sarah Inspection' but it was four in the afternoon and he was famished. After a curious meal from assorted tins, without alcohol, he slept more soundly in the empty bed than he had since his first night alone.

The next day, continuing the process of restoring order, Hiram decided to take Sarah's clothes to a charity shop. This would draw a line, but it was easier said than done. As soon as he opened the wardrobe and saw the skirts, dresses and tops, memories overwhelmed and his legs buckled. He sank to his knees and cried.

After a while he tried again. With tear filled eyes and aching heart he folded the clothes reverently, one by one. Sometimes perfume would waft and stab him through the chest, and it took longer than anticipated. When he had finished, several plastic bags covered the bed, but the morning was gone. He had not seen the news for weeks and felt the need to see what was happening. Over a cup of tea, he switched on the television. The first story made him laugh. Two pensioners from Plymouth were preparing to sail the Channel in a home-made concrete boat. Hiram was not sure whether this was funny because he had not laughed for a while, or because it was reassuring that Britain was still the home of eccentric individuals who cared not for public opinion.

The next item said that the new jumbo space shuttle, carrying stores, equipment and multinational crew of ten astronauts and engineers would dock with the space station the following day. Hiram was shocked at how the space station had changed since he had last seen it. Before Sarah's funeral he had watched regular reports of rockets taking bits up to the station 'core'. Since the funeral he had seen nothing, but he had obviously missed a crucial phase. The space station had sprouted a large dustbin-shaped chamber at one end and another arm, leg, or whatever they called it, jutting out half way along its length at a ninety degree angle. There was now a 'permanent' crew of fourteen.

Next Hiram watched an MP flap his jaws. "The Government would not be hurried. There were experts to be listened to… blah, blah, blah… public consultation process… blah, blah… proper consideration of all the facts… blah, blah… it was truly regrettable… blah, blah… all in good time… blah, blah, blah…"

Hiram had listened carefully and although not stupid, had no idea what the man was talking about. Next a newscaster was saying a double rollover lottery prize winner was running out of time. Hiram switched off. That was enough news for now and he trudged upstairs to finish the clearing up.

When he entered the bedroom and looked at the open wardrobe he howled with pain. There was nothing left to remind him of her. His belongings huddled at the other end, as if comforting each other. He wanted to put everything back, but knew if he did, he would change his mind again later. He had to be decisive and take the stuff to the charity shop before he changed his mind again. He loaded the car and drove the nine miles to Upper Radcliffe, the nearest town with charity shops. There were two to chose from but he decided the Cancer Research shop, which would have been his first choice, was too difficult because of the double yellow lines outside and five bulging plastic sacks to carry from the short stay car park. The shop in the side street was something to do with a local hospice, and had a single yellow line so he decided to give the stuff to them. He explained to the woman behind the counter, and saw the pity in her eyes.

The following day he decided to tell the store he was coming back but got as far as the phone and decided he was not up to it. Instead he would sort the jewellery. There were valuable pieces, some of sentimental value, and some cheap colourful baubles but he could not say which was which. Sarah would know in an instant. Perhaps he could take the lot to a jewellery shop and ask them to sort it out. He imagined the jeweller eyeing him up and made a note to wear a suit, so he didn't look like a burglar. Then again, if he was too smart they might think he was a fence. A sports jacket would be better. This was more difficult than he imagined, so he gave up for the present. It would be easier to sort the papers. Sarah liked to accumulate magazines, and cut out recipes, coupons and offers. There were receipts and coupons passed their use by date, in various rooms. He would go through them and throw away those of no use. Then he could start on the filing cabinet. Sarah had files with details of investments, insurance policies and bank accounts etc. He did not imagine there would be anything of great value but it had to be sorted.

He gathered the bits of paper in one pile and the magazines in another. He started with the magazine pile. Now Sarah was gone he had no use for recipes, decorating and gardening tips, Christmas ideas, or bargain breaks. He gave them a cursory glance and dropped them into a black plastic sack. He then turned to the 'old receipts' pile and was tempted to dump the whole lot without examination, but thought he should check first in case there was one for some electrical thing that was not too old. He thought keeping the receipts for groceries was rather crazy especially if the goods had long since been consumed.

He read each receipt to make sure it was not important, then screwed it up and tossed it in the bin. His aim was good and they all flew easily to the target. Next was an old lottery ticket. "Question – why on earth keep lottery tickets after the draw date? *Answer – No idea.*" It crossed his mind to check it but decided against. He never won anything, and Sarah always checked. He would have remembered a whoop for joy.

He screwed the paper and tossed. The aerodynamics of lottery tickets must be poorer than receipts. It bounced off the rim and landed on the floor. He continued reading, screwing and tossing until they were all gone. Every projectile found its mark. When the job was done it was time for another cuppa, then upstairs to tackle the filing. This did not fill him with enthusiasm. On the way he picked up the screwed ticket and held it over the bin, when he thought, "This was the only piece of paper to miss the bin. Question – Is it was trying to say something? *Answer – Very funny, you louse.*" He said the answer aloud. He was addressing God. "You want me to go and switch on the telly, get to the teletext pages, turn to the lottery and look up the numbers, don't you? You want me to expend energy just to confirm what I already know. I have not won a sausage and we both damn well know it. I'm not falling for your tricks this time. Go play with somebody else for a change."

He dropped the paper in the bin and made his tea.

Thursday 28th August 2025

Hiram woke in the morning feeling out of sorts and tired. He'd had a disturbed night, because of a dream about being scolded by Sarah over carelessness with money, and important papers. He ate breakfast without enthusiasm in front of the television. The morning news depicted the space station as a hive of activity. Experts, who seemed to be vying with each other to speak the fastest, were describing preparations for the biggest space walk in history. In a few days time eight or nine astronauts would be outside the space station doing great things with spanners and bits of metal. Next, Members of Parliament were either deploring the government's lack of action, or defending it. A young couple from Newcastle said they could not buy a house for love nor money. Hiram was puzzled. It was clear that this and the previous story were connected but he could not figure out how. He had obviously missed something important during his solitude, and had some catching up to do. He made a mental note to buy a newspaper.

The rest of the news was filled with uninteresting stuff but he felt he should listen and try to keep up with the world. Greenpeace activists were demonstrating about a motorway near Wales. The European Parliament wanted to standardise the size of something. The final item said one single winner of the biggest lottery prize since the mayhem of two years ago, when several record payouts had been made in quick succession, had not yet come forward and this was the last day to make a claim.

Hiram thought people were stupid. If he had won a lottery prize he would not be hesitant in coming forward. His thoughts were interrupted by a loud 'hiss' outside the house. He saw the dustbin lorry stopping at the corner opposite. The noise had been the air brakes. He knew the lorry would turn right, go to the end of the road, turn and make its way back, to pick up the bins outside each house. He had forgotten it was rubbish day and he hadn't put his out. He needed to gather the plastic bags in the bins around the house, dump them in the wheelie bin and push it to the pavement for collection.

He started in the kitchen, tied the plastic bag handles in a knot and left it by the front door. Upstairs he collected the bags from the bedroom, bathroom and the study. The last one was full because of yesterday. He tied the bag handles as he rushed down the stairs, but as he bent to pick up the bag in the hall, one of the bags under his arm burst and littered the floor. He hadn't time to get another bag or he would miss the collection. He decided to leave the mess and get the other bags out.

When he returned to the house he looked at the bits of paper and sighed. He got two more bags from the kitchen, thinking that the first bag had been too full, or tied too tightly. He gathered handfuls and stuffed them in the bags. The very last paper was the screwed-up lottery ticket. Hiram plonked his behind on the stairs and gazed at the ball of paper.

Finally he looked skywards. "Question – are you taking the piss?" He was speaking to God. He did not expect an answer. "This is the third time I have tried to get rid of this bloody piece of paper. We both know I haven't won, so why are you tormenting me? You want me to go to the trouble of looking it up, just so you can have a laugh." He got ready to throw the paper. The bag's mouth waited, like a chick. Another thought occurred to him. God could be trying a double bluff. Suppose he had really been given a winning ticket by The Almighty, who knew it would be thrown away. Now that would be funny.

Without another word he climbed the stairs, entered the study, switched on and typed. Up came the page. He clicked the results checker. There was a box for him to enter the numbers of his ticket. He unravelled the crumpled ball and typed the numbers. A new window opened. It said 'Congratulations you have won a prize. Please telephone this number for verification'. A number flashed.

Numbly, Hiram grabbed his mobile and tapped the number. A woman answered and asked for the numbers, the date, and the number in the small box in the corner. After a few more questions, Hiram became aware of something different in her tone. "One moment please," she said. There was a tremor in her voice, and that was the last he heard from her.

He waited for what seemed a long time and he considered hanging up and redialling to complain when a man came on the line. He sounded stuffy and asked for the same information Hiram had already given, which irritated him.

Eventually the man said, "Congratulations, Hiram.... may I call you Hiram? I can verify that the ticket would appear to be genuine and have now registered your claim. We now need to arrange for you to deliver the ticket, complete a form, and collect your prize. Do you know how much you have won?"

Hiram shook his head then realised the man couldn't see. "No," he said.

The man said that the total prize fund was £45,225,200, and with the number of participants and other winners the prize jackpot was £25,550,000.

Hiram's feeling of numbness deepened. "Question – are you telling me I have won twenty five million, five hundred and fifty thousand pounds?"

The man replied, "Not exactly, the prize has been accruing interest at the rate of 4.5 percent per annum, calculated on a daily basis. The prize now stands at £26,103,986.68."

Hiram was speechless.

"Why has it taken you so long to come forward?" asked the man on the end of the telephone line. "Do you realise the 180 days in which to claim expires at five-thirty today."

Hiram said, "I have only just come across the ticket."

"I see," the man said. "Hiram, you must make an appointment to come and give me your ticket. Today is the last day for a claim but as it is now officially registered, we can allow seven days grace to complete the formalities."

"Where do I have to bring it?" asked Hiram.

"You must go to one of our Regional Centres. I'll give you the address."

Hiram grabbed a pen and wrote as the man recited a Watford address and told him the time of his appointment.

"One more thing," said Hiram quickly before the man hung up. "No publicity. I don't want any fuss."

"I'll make a note of that Hiram. Rest assured you will remain anonymous until you decide otherwise."

After Hiram had pressed the button to end the call he stared at the paper with the Watford address for a long time. His mind was a jumble. He couldn't allow himself to accept the fact he was now rich, because that might make him happy and he had no right to be happy. Sarah was dead and he was alive. For years he had strived to be financially successful, to provide a comfortable living for his wife, and buy her nice things, which is how, with his Scottish working class upbringing, he measured success, but instead he had struggled and been in debt more than once. Now he had more money than he could need, but it was too late. He felt angry, ashamed and riddled with guilt.

He sat for a long time, lost in his thoughts until eventually he realised almost two hours had passed and his backside was numb. He glanced up to see that in the time he'd been sitting there, the postman had been. There were envelopes on the doormat.

With a sigh, Hiram picked them up and turned them over. Three were statements from mobile phone, electricity and gas companies. The last had his name and address hand written. He slipped his thumb under the poorly-glued flap and eased it open. It was from the Colo-Rectal Surgery Department at St. Andrews General hospital asking to arrange an appointment for test results. He was surprised by this. Last autumn he had seen his GP and been referred to St. Andrews. They had taken samples, diagnosed an infection of the bowel and prescribed pills. At another appointment in February, more samples confirmed that the medication had worked. They said he would receive another appointment soon, to get the 'all clear'. It was now September and he had forgotten about it. Either the hospital was very busy or somebody had only just remembered about him. He had a mind to complain, but then he decided he couldn't be bothered. If they had taken this long they could wait until he was ready. After all, if it was important they would have contacted him sooner. He went back to the computer and planned his route to Watford, allowing an extra hour for road works.

CHAPTER TWO

Tuesday 3rd September 2024

The computerised patient's records system introduced at St. Andrews General Hospital two years ago was finally being rolled out, and had now arrived at the Colo-Rectal Surgery Unit. Professor Cann saw nothing wrong with the old system, but accepted that change was inevitable. Using the hand-held computer tablets rather than cardboard folders was easier than he had imagined, and he had to admit there were many advantages.

However sophisticated they might appear to an outsider, computers remain dumb machines that can only do what they are told, with whatever is fed into them. There is an oft quoted phrase "rubbish in, rubbish out". It was simply too big a task for every item in the mountain of paper and cardboard files that existed previously to be checked for errors, discrepancies and anomalies before being converted to digital format. Any 'rubbish' that should not have been there was simply converted into computer data. One particular item of 'rubbish' was assimilated on the day the new computer system and its rapidly expanding database had a momentary 'hiccup'. The item, not having a proper file of its own, was sorted into a convenient nearby file, which just happened to be the one containing the medical history of Hiram Montgomery.

Friday 29th August 2025

The trip to Watford was straightforward. Arriving early, Hiram sat outside and waited. He did not want to be early, or even be there at all, and would have preferred to have the cheque posted. Now he was here, he didn't want to stay longer than necessary, or talk more than he had to. He parked, took a deep breath, and entered.

He completed a claim form, met three suits who studied his ticket, read the form, beamed, congratulated, proffered champagne, laughed and joked, offered advice. Hiram endured it all, wishing only to go home and be alone again.

Finally it was over. On the ground floor there were no cheering crowds and nobody looked up as he walked to his car. Two and three quarter hours later he parked on his drive in an empty street. He had just arranged to have over twenty six million pounds transferred to his account, and no-one here was any the wiser.

Saturday 30th August 2025

Despite being fabulously wealthy, Hiram Montgomery felt no different. He woke unhappy and exhausted after a restless night, looked at the adjacent empty pillow and got up without enthusiasm. He showered, dressed, trudged to the silent kitchen and as he pulled the cereal packet from the cupboard realised he was not crying. Was this was good? Was he was getting over her, or getting used to her absence? Should he feel guilty about not crying? Should he make more effort to cry, to keep her memory alive?

After breakfast he decided to arrange a return to work, but then wondered if he could get through a whole week without crying. Perhaps he could do part-time, to ease in gently, even if it meant less pay. The lottery money gave him breathing space before he needed full wages… then, all at once, it dawned on him that he didn't actually need wages at all. In fact he need never go back to work again.

This revelation shocked him. He was amazed he had not thought of it before. "I need never work again." He repeated the words a few times, then scolded himself. "Don't be stupid! You can't stop working. That would be lazy, and wrong. Question – why? *Answer – God gave us talents. To not work is slothful and therefore a sin; but against what exactly?*"

If you don't sell your talent or the sweat of your brow for wages, you could use them for something else. He could do the things he had always wanted to do if he had the time or money. He was not sure what they were, but there must be some. Everyone has to retire sooner or later. "Question – are you ready to retire? Does being retired mean you are too old to be useful? *Answer – not necessarily. People have been known to retire early and enjoy years of leisure. It is important to feel useful, and without a sense of purpose it is harder to maintain self esteem.*" In Hiram's case, self esteem had never been a strong point.

That decided it. He phoned the store.

Fothergill sounded pleased to hear from him and asked how he was. Hiram said he was feeling better and would like to do two or three days a week, for a while before being full time again.

Mr. Fothergill paused for a few moments then said, "Hiram, you're obviously not ready yet. Take as long as you need. Don't rush back."

An alarm bell seemed to go off in Hiram's mind. Perhaps they did not want him back. He said, "Actually I could start on Monday, full time."

"Well only if you are sure, Hiram. Pop in and see me before you start, for a chat."

As Hiram hung up he was worried. "*Question – what did he mean? Answer – perhaps they had found someone else to do his job, or that they could do without him. Maybe he was going to be sacked, or be prematurely retired. Or maybe it was just showing support and there was nothing to worry about.*"

If he was going to start on Monday, he had better get the house in order and do some shopping, as he wouldn't have time during the week. Hiram had always been prepared to admit that women were more efficient, competent, and sensible than men at running a household. In future he was going to have to do all the jobs that Sarah had done. Pre-marriage he was a typical semi house-trained bachelor. He could either go back to that slovenly life style and not so healthy diet, or he could maintain the standards to which Sarah had educated him. That's what wives do: train their husbands to be civilised.

Monday 1st September 2025

Hiram had settled back to normal work routine without difficulty. His first day back meeting had just been so that Fothergill could check that he was alright. During the week colleagues found reasons to visit and show they cared, but there were too many identical conversations. Eventually he felt like putting up a notice that said *Leave me alone*.

The work was the same as it had always been: invoices, forms, requests, memos. Hiram had stumbled into this job some time ago. He had applied for the post of Junior Clerk for what he called a 'temporary recuperation' after the pressures of his previous job, and to de-stress after the humiliation and indignation of redundancy, and until he found something better. Everyone, including himself, regarded this job as far below what he should be doing, and a complete waste of his accumulated years of experience and talents. However before he found another job, he was promoted to Senior Clerk, after which the Chief Clerk retired and he was promoted again. This was considered meteoric, and eyebrows were raised. Several years later Hiram was still plodding along. He wouldn't say he enjoyed his job, but it had paid the mortgage. Now, he thought with disbelief, he didn't have to worry about the mortgage ever again.

Tuesday 16th September 2025

The doctoring profession is the same as every other in that it has members who can be categorised as brilliant, good, average, poor, and why on earth are they doing that job? Some are mature, level headed, sensible, and some are not. Doctor Peacock was a recently qualified doctor who had been variously described by other members of staff as having the bed side manner of a domestic appliance, arrogant and self obsessed, a loose cannon and a twit. Sister Rachael Cowan was having a nightmare morning because her ward was short staffed, decorators were converting it into an obstacle course, and now Professor Cann was expected to be in several places at once. They agreed to let Doctor Peacock deal with the 'clear and go' cases, as they were too simple to mess up, and it would take some pressure off Professor Cann.

Sister Cowan saw the schedule had eleven negative test results, and found Doctor Peacock. "Find these patients, read the results then get rid politely and quickly, as there is nothing more to be done for them. OK?" She had intended to pop her head round the door periodically, but when everyone wants you, it's hard to stick to a plan.

As he walked to reception Doctor Brian Peacock was feeling pleased. This was his chance to prove himself, then people would realise he was an asset to the department. He collected a terminal, placed it on the consulting room desk, and looked round to make sure everything was neat. He didn't want patients thinking he kept an untidy office, even if it wasn't his. In the waiting area he called the first name. An old lady stood, he ushered her to the room, called up her record, scrolled to the last page, read out the test results and asked if everything was all right. It was. He stood, wished her well, she thanked him for everything they had done for her, and she left.

Doctor Peacock thought to himself that this was easy. Dispensing good news and being thanked by grateful patients that he and his team had snatched from the jaws of death was something he could get used to.

The next few cases were equally simple. Some were chattier than others but he processed them expeditiously. He made good progress and was sure Sister Cowan would be pleased. As he was becoming bored, and did not need much concentration, he was able to hone his doctor image during the consultations. His hero, Doctor Hector Truelove, featured in a TV hospital drama which he never missed. Each week Hector Truelove saved patients from death using ingenuity, talent and skill. The male colleagues were in awe and the female staff and patients in love with him. Brian Peacock could see himself fitting into such a role quite easily.

As he listened, or pretended to, he concentrated on inclining his head at the correct angle and nodding wisely, like the saintly Hector Truelove. Sometimes interlocking his fingers and bowing his head whilst considering the facts, he wished there was a mirror behind the patients so that he could check his effectiveness at portraying a brilliant and clever physician. He had scored through nine of the eleven names on the list when he came to Hiram Montgomery.

A man in the back row stood up. He did not look well, with eyes only half open, as if peering into sunlight. In the consulting room Brian opened the record. The treatment summary box said, "Results – all clear."

"Good news, Mr. Montgomery," he said as he scrolled to the final page, without looking at his patient. He spoke loudly. "Your test results show no further sign of the infection and everything seems as it should be." The next line was a prompt message, "Check medication completed." Brian looked up and asked Hiram if he had completed the course of tablets. Hiram nodded and Brian typed "Yes." He was about to stand and usher the patient out when he noticed the scroll bar at the right of the screen was short, suggesting more notes below. It would be from top to bottom if there was nothing else. He scrolled down and saw more information below the date and time stamp. Every note or report on a patients record had the date and time it was entered, on the last line. Normally there would be only one item on each page and subsequent items would be on following pages. He thought it strange that this was not the case here, but brushed this thought aside and carried on reading.

"It says here you had a severe pain in the posterior." Brian looked up for confirmation.

Hiram had a terrible night and was not feeling good. He felt tired and just wanted to go home and get some sleep. He said, "Not the posterior, more the abdomen really."

"I see," said Brian, not seeing at all. He looked at the screen again and read aloud. "The treatment has reversed the tumours to their dormant state, allowing temporary remission, and period of calm, before the next episode." Brian looked up to see if this meant anything to the patient because it did not mean much to him. The fact that there was no mention of tumours above the date and time stamp should have rang alarm bells but a modicum of common sense was necessary for this to happen.

Hiram looked how he felt, puzzled. "I don't understand," he said.

Brian repeated what he had just said.

"They didn't tell me about tumours before," said Hiram.

Brian shook his head and looked down again, wondering why patients didn't listen when something was explained to them. "It says here after a period of peace lasting from four to eight years the condition will return and become unbearable. Resumption of current treatment is unlikely to be effective, and the patient should die of intense pain in the rectum." Brian had started reading quickly, but slowed as the awfulness penetrated.

He should have been thinking, "There is nothing in the previous notes to suggest that this could be true, and the patient appears to be hearing this for the very first time. I think I should double check."

Instead he was thinking, "Patients only hear what they want to hear. He has admitted finishing his medication and it says in the notes that the treatment has successfully reversed the tumours. When he first came here he was in pain and now he is fine. The notes say he had a severe pain and now there is going to be a period of calm for between four and eight years."

He took a deep breath and spoke slowly. "It says in the notes that resumption of the current treatment is unlikely to be successful. With medical advances, by the time the tumours flare up again there could be a new treatment which solves the problem." Brian did not believe this but offered a reassuring smile to the patient.

If Hiram had been mentally alert he might have said he did not believe this, and demanded a second opinion. Unfortunately he was mentally and emotionally fragile, and physically exhausted. Yesterday evening he had been thinking about Sarah and he could not see her face. A moment of panic had overcome him, similar to that on the night she had died. It was as if she had died all over again. He racked his brains for a mental image of the woman he had been married to for years, and couldn't find one. He rushed to a photograph and stared at the face, concentrating on every line, curve and shadow. He was afraid she might disappear again and couldn't bear to think of her fading away like a hillside mist. He had spent most of the night looking at photographs. Some made him smile and others brought tears. He had not had a drink for a week but as he sat through the night surrounded by memories he had four large whiskies. He did not intend getting drunk, and indeed felt disgustingly sober all night, just more and more maudlin. By morning his 'hangover' had less to do with alcohol than a cloak of sadness, and lack of sleep.

Now, as he sat listening to his death sentence being unveiled, he did not find it hard to believe. He was simply being dealt another lousy hand in this stinking poker game of life. However no matter how low you feel or how little you value yourself, somewhere deep inside is a spark which refuses to accept the inevitability of death. The questions emerged. "Is there anything that can be done? Are you sure about this? Is it worth getting a second opinion?"

Brian Peacock had no doubt that if the hospital laboratory said Hiram Montgomery was dying, then it must be so. Doctors do not make mistakes, at least not in the episodes of Doctor Hector Truelove, and he was carefully following his hero's example. The last question did not please him but he concealed his exasperation. Patients should know their place. Doctors were the experts and patients should accept without question what was said to them. He said, "The answers to your questions are No, Yes, No, but before we jump to conclusions let's read the rest of the notes." He returned to the screen and continued, "Because of the

24

unusual nature of this complaint and its very rare occurrence, an extract is appended from the original book entitled *Kilwinnings Encyclopaedia of Rare and Exotic Medical Ailments*."

Brian had never heard of the book and looked to see if his patient was impressed. Hiram was expressionless. Brian said proudly, "You have a rare and exotic medical ailment Mr. Montgomery."

Hiram replied, "That is no consolation."

"Quite so," mumbled the good doctor as he carried on reading. "So rare is this illness, it has never been reclassified in modern nomenclature but retains its original name. St.Augustus's Fire. It was named after the Jesuit monk physician who identified it in 1896, and because of its principal symptom which is a feeling that ones bottom is on fire. It is a little known fact that on the internal walls of the lower abdominal tract and rectal passages is a net of hair like fibrous filaments which ceased to have a purpose when man stopped eating leaves, grass and bark. In an extremely small number of cases, thought to be less than .001 percent of the entire population of the world these harmless fibres inexplicably flare up and cause excruciating pain as they attack the adjacent tissues. The ailment can be controlled in the first instance with a course of drugs which reverts the fibres to their dormant state. When the second attack occurs, approximately four to eight years later, the previous medication will prove ineffective. The patient is expected to die within weeks, as the organs in the lower abdomen are systematically destroyed."

How a monk in 1896 was supposed to have discovered such a rare condition without modern technology defied credibility, but this seemed to escape both men.

Brian Peacock felt pleased for two reasons. He had learned of a rare illness which he could use to outdo any doctor engaging in one-upmanship. Secondly he had successfully silenced Hiram Montgomery by demonstrating who was boss around here. All he had to do now was shoo the man out. He stood up and extended his hand. "We will see you again in four years time, Mr. Montgomery."

Hiram didn't move. He had already been feeling low before he arrived and the doctor had merely told him that the manner of his death would be in keeping with the life he'd had up till now. Not exactly a bundle of laughs.

"Is there is anything else we can do for you, Mr. Montgomery?"

"Not unless you can bring my wife back from the dead. She died recently and I am still getting over that," said Hiram.

If Doctor Peacock had any common sense he might have considered getting a more experienced person to help with someone in mourning, and not thinking clearly. However common sense was not Doctor Peacock's forte and he had other patients to see. "I am afraid we have not yet mastered the art of bringing people back from the dead, but we are working on it." He was pleased with his joke which he thought diffused the tension rather well. "In the meantime, please don't hesitate to make another appointment if you experience any other problems. All being well we will not see you again for many years, and rest assured when you return we will do everything in our power to make you comfortable."

This was Brian's diplomatic way of saying, "Time to go, now that we have stopped your pains, but come back when you are dying properly."

Hiram looked up. "Thank you for being so frank, doctor. I appreciate all you and the other staff have done for me. I just need a moment to get my head round this."

Brian wondered how Hector Truelove would deal with this. After a moment's thought, he walked round the table and placed his hand gently on shoulder. "Now listen to me," he said adopting a deep and manly voice which he thought sounded mature, compassionate, professional, kind but firm, and rather sexy. It was a pity he did not have an audience of nurses to gaze on his wonderful performance. "Life can be unfair. Whatever fate throws at us, we have to deal with. I want you to get out there, Mr. Montgomery, and grab life by the throat. Live every day as if it were your last." This was pure Hector Truelove. "Life is like a one way tram ticket. You get on, travel one way, and then get off. It is a single ticket and you cannot return or go past your stop. Do you understand what I am saying?"

Hiram looked puzzled. "I think so, doctor."

He clearly didn't understand so Brian pressed on. "Live life to the full. Grab whatever happiness you can along the way. Don't put off till tomorrow what you can do today, for tomorrow is not guaranteed. Now do you understand?"

Hiram nodded, but felt stunned.

"Good. Now get the hell out of my office." Brian liked that last bit, it was sort of John Wayne-ish. "Go out there, Hiram Montgomery, and enjoy what time you have left. Don't waste a second. Time is too precious to squander." He brought his portrayal of Hector Truelove to an emotional, stirring climax, and he loved it.

Hiram finally stood up. They shook hands, smiled grimly, and Hiram left without another word.

CHAPTER THREE

Hiram sat in his chair and tried to gather his thoughts. Since Sarah's death, he carried a mountain of grief on his shoulders, which made everything exhausting and slow. He had acquired a heap of money that, with her gone, he did not need or want. The money reminded him he had failed during her lifetime, and now it was too late. Just to make sure he could not look forward to a happy future, he now learned he did not have one. He was going to die, and to keep him focussed on this, he had been told it was going to be damned unpleasant.

How much could a man take before his brain exploded?

It occurred to him that it was getting darker and he checked his watch. It was five-thirty and he had arrived home at lunchtime. Is this how his life was going to be? Sitting in a chair, listening to his creaking brain crawling through piles of curled up memories, looking for a place to sleep?

Just then, the telephone rang. It was a girl called Sophie, from his telephone banking service, who wanted to talk about the large amount of money in his current account. She suggested three interlocked 'intelligent' accounts which monitored the balances and automatically transferred funds between them. This would ensure his 'pocket money' account was never empty, his 'regular bills' account always had sufficient funds, and the remainder was kept in a savings account.

As he hung up Hiram felt relief. He had been ignoring his huge balance because of the emotional baggage attached. Now young Sophie was setting up a mechanism to do it all for him. As long as he didn't go wild, he need never worry again about bills.

Abruptly, he wondered why he was worrying about bills. With four years left to live, if he didn't go wild he would hardly have made a dent in his fortune by 'check out time'. What was the point of not spending it, before meeting his maker?

After dinner Hiram was deciding whether to put on some music, watch the television or go to bed early when the telephone rang again. He recognised the voice of Shaun Glendower. Shaun, a long time friend, was a gentleman in every sense of the word: kind, and generous in thought, word and deed. Many people had asked Hiram how he was, and his standard reply of "I'm fine" kept conversation to a minimum, and avoided further probing. However, when Shaun asked, Hiram did not feel the need to hide his feelings and said, "Slowly getting back to normal. I went through a rough patch and was very low at one point. I am sure you know how it is."

Shaun did indeed know how it was, having not long since lost his father. He expressed his sympathy then said he would be in the area soon and wondered if he could call. They could have a meal and a drink. Hiram agreed.

As he hung up he thought about the others in his address book. He had avoided everyone including family and neighbours since the funeral, but now he should mend bridges. Actually he had not burned bridges or fallen out with anybody, although he might have upset one or two by not answering calls. His 'crime' had been to lower his portcullis, raise his drawbridge and retreat to his dungeon. Now it was time to make peace. He found paper and a pen. He needed to make a list.

Friday 26th September 2025

During the last ten days Hiram had invited neighbours in for drinks. They seemed glad that he was on the mend and if they had been annoyed or upset that he had ignored their attempts to make contact, they did not show it. They had asked how he had been doing and seemed pleased he was back at work; the house was clean and tidy and he appeared to be coping. They did not ask awkward questions. He said nothing about the lottery win, or his appointment with the Grim Reaper. By the end of the evening, unaware of these two items, they departed and he was glad that hurdle was past. He had also telephoned his family, scattered over the country, and made arrangements to visit. They seemed pleased to hear from him. His calendar was starting to look busy.

At five-thirty Shaun arrived and as soon as he was settled with a cup of tea, Shaun asked a few tentative questions about how Hiram was coping without Sarah. Hiram found it therapeutic to talk about the past few weeks and the trough of depression into which he had fallen, and climbed out of by himself.

After an hour and a half Shaun knew that his friend had gone through hell, but was definitely on the mend.

Hiram had prepared a casserole. A bottle was opened and as they ate, they talked some more. Over biscuits and cheese Hiram said, "I have good news and bad news, which you must promise to keep strictly confidential."

"You know I am the every essence of discretion. Let's have the good news first."

"Remember the news recently about somebody winning a double rollover?"

Shaun nodded. "Vaguely."

"It was me," Hiram said. I won over twenty six million."

Shaun's knife stopped in mid air. "If you don't mind me saying, you don't look like somebody who won the lottery. Shouldn't you at least be smiling?"

Hiram explained how he felt burdened with guilt and feelings of failure for not having this money while Sarah was alive.

Shaun listened patiently as Hiram poured out his thoughts. He had to use all his skill of logical argument to gradually peel back each layer of Hiram's ingrained prejudice against himself. It wasn't that easy, after years of self-mortification, but finally the message got through and a hint of a smile reached Hiram's lips. Shaun knew he had found the switch to the light bulb over Hiram's head. "Feel better?"

Hiram nodded with a slightly bigger smile and said, "I don't feel so bad. You're right... I wasn't shamefully extravagant, just not good at managing what little I had, and perhaps being a bit dumb sometimes."

"Now that you have forgiven yourself, do you think you might be able to spend some of your fortune without feeling too guilty?"

"I'll give it a try," replied Hiram.

"Just don't go from one extreme to another. Spending it on junk you don't need would be just as stupid as not touching a penny of it."

"I agree. I will set myself an allowance, using just the interest, then capital will last forever."

"I think you need a financial adviser," said Shaun. He put down his fork and eased a card from his wallet. "Here's my guy's card. He's excellent and you don't have to take his advice but he could ensure you have enough for whatever you want, as long as you want. He will also help prevent those money-grabbing pigs in Downing Street taking more than necessary."

The casserole was gone, the bottle empty, so Hiram made two steaming mugs of hot coffee. Shaun took a sip and said, "So what was the bad news?" He was unprepared for what came next and sat in horror as Hiram recounted his discussion with Doctor Peacock. "Are you sure about this? There is no mistake? Is there nothing that can be done?"

Hiram shook his head. "The doctor who saw me said his team are experts. He showed me the article in a publication called *Kilwinnings Encyclopaedia of Rare Diseases*." Hiram's recollection was based on his memory of that day, which was sketchy. He hadn't seen the publication, merely an extract on a screen. Since then he had replayed it in his mind, to recall the words, and each time he read into them, and between them, as much meaning as he could. He was trying to make sense of it but each time he exaggerated. The fact that the young doctor was inexperienced and foolish, and that the suggested illness was highly improbable, had escaped him. As far as he was concerned there was no doubt, and he was able to describe it with details he had added during his recollections.

Shaun was shocked. Hiram tried to console him by saying that by the time the illness flared up again there would probably be a cure. Neither of them believed this.

Eventually Shaun regained his composure and asked, "What happens now?"

Hiram shrugged and said that he had no plans, except soldier on as normal until it was time. He did not elaborate on 'time'. They both knew what he meant.

Shaun said, "By soldier on, do you mean carry on as before?"

"What's wrong with that?"

"Nothing, if the future is to be as brilliant as the past. I'm not criticising the time you had with Sarah. You made each other happy, but you admitted there were problems, and you never had two pennies to rub together. Now you are rich you can't carry on marking time in a dull job. Why don't you quit, and enjoy what you have left? You realize you are fortunate?"

"Excuse me if I don't agree."

"You know you're going to die, and roughly when. That's a tough deal, but it means you know how long you have left to finish what you want to do. Most people think they have time for procrastination, and then realize it's too late to do what they were putting off. Ring any bells?" Hiram nodded. Shaun continued. "I don't mean to offend but right now you need a friend to give you a kick up the backside. When your 'time' comes, as you put it, it's no use saying 'God, give me more time.' He will say, 'You had plenty, but you wasted it'."

Hiram smiled grimly. "The doctor told me the same. He said life is like a one-way tram ticket. You get on, take a short trip then get off. You can't go back."

Shaun understood perfectly. "Did he tell you to enjoy the scenery, or talk to the other passengers?" When he saw that Hiram understood the point, Shaun went on, "You have time to put it right, my friend. With eight years left, try looking out the window. Time and life are too precious to waste. Do whatever you want, but do it now."

Hiram smiled. Shaun made it sound easy. He wished he could do whatever he wanted.

As if sensing the thought Shaun said, "Everyone has a dream... something we want but never get round to. What's yours?"

The briefest hint of a smile touched Hiram then he said, "Nothing really."

Shaun had spotted it. "When I mentioned dream your mind dug up a memory, then swatted it, like a fly."

"It was nothing" said Hiram.

"Tell me now, or I'll beat it out of you with a lead pipe," demanded Shaun. The thought of Shaun using a rolled up newspaper far less a lead pipe was ridiculous, and they both laughed.

"OK, but you will think it stupid."

Shaun shook his head.

"It's a boat. I have always wanted to have my own boat."

Shaun had not considered anything so mundane. "What sort of boat?"

"I'd like a floating home." Hiram waved his hand. "This house has

32

four bedrooms, living room, dining room, kitchen, utility room, en suite, bathroom and toilet, and garage. With a boat this big I could sail anywhere.

Shaun raised his brows. "That's a fair sized boat. Sounds expensive, but then again, you are a man of means. I think you should do it."

"People would think I was crazy," Hiram said.

"So what, let 'em. If anybody says you're nuts, say 'I don't give a damn'."

"You make it sound easy."

"Everything is easy, once you know how," said Shaun.

"Do you think I should give money to charity?"

"Do you want to?"

"I suppose I should."

"Why? Because you think it's expected, or to help the less fortunate?"

"I would like to share my good fortune."

"That is a good enough reason."

"You must think I am thick."

"Not in the slightest. I think you are a bit battered, having had several life changing events in a short time. I suggest you take your time and don't make hasty decisions."

Hiram nodded. "I should give some money to family and friends."

Shaun waggled his finger. "Only if it's what you want and not because you think it's expected."

Hiram agreed and added, "I would like to give you something."

Shaun frowned and said that he had not been a friend all these years, on the off-chance of a slice of lottery win. They had been friends longer than the lottery had existed, and would remain so regardless of finances. Hiram was sorry if he had offended but Shaun brushed it aside. He urged Hiram to be careful about appearing to buy friends. Some would remain friends for friendship and others for the money. He would need to identify the difference. He continued, "Rather than give me money, which is kind but unnecessary, go buy your boat. Thereafter I will be offended if I don't get an invite to visit my very good friend, the multi-millionaire, Hiram Montgomery."

They both grinned, and drank the last of their coffee.

"What is the boat to be called?" Shaun asked.

"You gave me the idea when you said I shouldn't give a damn what other people thought. As a fellow Scot you know how we run our words together and sometimes omit the rude word from our expression of displeasure, lest it offend any ladies present, and to allow the listener to insert his own favourite expletive, whatever that might be," Hiram said. "The 'Adongiva'."

Shaun laughed. "I like it," he said "That is brilliant and very apt."

Monday 29th September 2025

On Monday Hiram handed in his notice. One month later, he was presented with a carriage clock, and became a man of leisure.

Hiram had five brothers and two sisters; Martin, Ronald, Marlene, George, Gerald, Lara and Stuart. Over a number of weekends he visited all of them and his mother, covering hundreds of miles in the process. These journeys took him to Surrey, Bristol and his native territory in the lowlands of Scotland. He considered that although time consuming and exhausting, it was absolutely necessary because it would be his chance to say goodbye. He even travelled to Aberdeen to see an old friend who had been a colleague in a previous job. They had been made redundant together and had a long-standing joke that if either won the lottery, they would share it. During these visits Hiram told them he had won a decent amount on the lottery, but would not say how much other than that he wanted to share it. He had never been tight fisted, and would have liked to be more generous but he now had plans for his winnings. To stop them from comparing notes he said as they had always held a special place in his heart he would like to give them a bit extra. He asked them not to disclose the amount in case one of the others felt they were not getting their 'fair share'. He then presented a £196,000 cheque, which delighted them, and secured their silence.

He did not tell any of them his bad news but said he was going to do some travelling, and would be out of touch for a while.

Monday 27th October 2025

After just twenty minutes with the financial adviser Shaun had recommended, Hiram knew Roger Campbell of Taylor, White, Campbell and Associates was clever, talented, and capable. He gave advice on bank rates, minimising tax, and managing finances for maximum advantage. He admitted his fees were expensive but said that if Hiram took his advice, he would be far better off. He said he was also able to provide legal as well as financial advice because the firm had grown to include a team of experienced lawyers. They agreed to meet regularly to discuss progress and keep everything under revue.

To secure his fresh start, get the past behind him and ensure he changed his life, Hiram put his house on the market. He spent a lot of time exploring internet sites on ship design and naval architecture, boat building companies and yacht manufacturers. He learned that the size of vessel he wanted was a 'Super Yacht' and that 'entry level' starts at about eleven million. Many of the companies who ruled supreme in this field were based in Italy, but Hiram wanted a British boat, mainly because of patriotism, and because he wanted British workers to benefit from his money.

His starting point for designing his yacht was a two or three mast sailing schooner in lightweight modern materials, with state of the art navigation and safety equipment and a powerful engine and propeller for independent propulsion. He remembered a conversation he had once had on holiday with a merchant navy officer who said the biggest single running cost was wages. To avoid a huge wage bill he toyed with designs for equipment to raise and lower the sails by crank handle. He spent hours dreaming of devices to enable one man to do the tasks of many. He had seen a ship's hawser being looped on a dock bollard, or being removed before departure, with more than one man involved in the operation. He designed a mechanism to allow one man to remotely do this without even touching the rope, and was amazed it had not been thought of before.

As he played with his ideas, they evolved. The ship and components went through stages of metamorphosis. Some things were dropped and others made more elaborate. He had always enjoyed drawing and sketched a figurehead for the bow. Not a beautiful mermaid, buxom lady or sea captain, but the head of a highland cow. Sarah, despite the fact that she was a Londoner, had always loved these hairy beasts and he had promised her that if they won the lottery she could have one as a pet. Now he could finally afford her 'Hielan Coo'. This figurehead seemed fitting, and appealed to his Scottish nature. It had a magnificent pair of wide horns, shaggy face and almost comical enigmatic smile as if it knew a secret it was not prepared to share. The ship continued to change shape, sometimes broader, sometimes taller. As Hiram's knowledge of construction and handling problems grew, he gradually went off the idea of a sailing ship. The sails and masts became the superstructure and funnels of a motor yacht.

Sadly the figurehead had to go. It just did not fit the image of a fast elegant super cruiser, but he vowed to keep it, as an amusing decoration, to hang on an inside wall, perhaps in the bar. His research on the internet resulted in a short list of boat building companies. Three were eliminated at the telephone discussion stage but the fourth man he spoke to, Oliver Russell of Cardhu Russell Boat Builders, impressed him. He listened attentively, and seemed to know what he was talking about. He offered sensible suggestions, and they talked for over half an hour. An appointment was arranged to go over the ideas in more detail.

CHAPTER FOUR

Thursday 4ᵗʰ December 2025

It was the type of day Hiram hated, when a fine mist hung in still air, soaking everything by stealth. He much preferred water that had the decency to rain properly, allowing shelter under an umbrella. After his marathon round trip of his family and friends, the two hours and forty-five minutes drive from his home near Derby to Hamble Point on the Solent was but a short hop and his spirits were buoyant as he arrived at Cardhu Russell Boat Builders. His dream was finally getting off the ground. A line of yachts on trolleys, graduated in size, stood to one side. Behind, two ships were being worked on by men in boiler suits. One was a fishing boat and the other a cargo ship, shrouded in scaffolding.

The receptionist offered coffee then ushered him to an office. Oliver Russell was a well-built man with ruddy complexion and thick dark hair. He smiled a lot, but was clearly no fool. His penetrating stare bored through Hiram and after just a few minutes it was obvious he knew his business and able to cut to the chase with surgical skill. He studied Hiram's notes and sketches then said, "Before we discuss this, I want to talk about you, your lifestyle and what you expect after this is built, if ever. What part of Scotland do you come from?"

Hiram couldn't see the relevance of his background, to building a yacht. In addition, what was that 'if ever' bit? However with Oliver's confident air of command, and Hiram being brought up to respect authority, he responded, "I was born and raised just outside Edinburgh. I lived in Derbyshire for many years with my wife, who died recently. I have just won over twenty six million on the lottery and I have always wanted my own boat."

Oliver looked at him levelly. "I am sorry to hear about your wife. When did she die?"

Hiram replied that Sarah had died on the eleventh of June, in her armchair in front of the television.

Oliver said, "Dreadful for you, but nice for her. I know how fragile life can be. My wife Joanne died on April 13th, in a car accident. I kissed her after breakfast and by lunchtime my life had changed forever. I didn't get the chance to say goodbye."

Both men sat for a few quiet moments, forcing respective genies back into bottles.

"I went through a dark place… anger, despair, guilt, shame. I felt like killing myself," Hiram said.

"I've been there," said the other man. "I tried drinking myself to death."

"I tried that. People say it gets easier with time, but it doesn't."

"It's like walking around with a sack of bricks on your back. It doesn't get lighter. You just get used to it and accept it as your burden. Part of you doesn't want it to get lighter. Those bricks are your memories."

"Ain't that the truth. You know the hardest thing? I come home and cook a meal for one in silence, in an empty kitchen. I usually cook slightly too much, and by the time its ready, I don't feel like eating."

"For me it's the empty wardrobes. I thought it would be better if I gave her clothes to the charity shops, but it has not helped. The empty space reminds me of her every day. There are still bottles of nail varnish and smelly stuff on the dressing table. I can't decide whether to ditch or keep them."

"I have a box of heated rollers on my bedside table." Hiram said. "Curling tongs and hair dryer."

The men looked at each other and smiled grimly at how these small inanimate objects could so affect them.

Oliver opened a filing cabinet and produced a bottle of Cardhu 36 year-old and glasses. Hiram was impressed. "Does your company own the distillers or do they own you?"

"Sadly it's neither. My ancient ancestry is Scottish but the name is just a happy coincidence, and it's damn good stuff."

Hiram nodded his agreement. Oliver poured two very respectable 'wee drams' and said, "Here's a toast to the memory of our lassies."

They downed their glasses in one movement. Oliver asked about the lottery win, and about Hiram's background. When Hiram had finished Oliver tapped the drawings again. Hiram told him he had always been in love with the idea of going to sea, and living afloat. "Why didn't you?"

Hiram explained that all his life he had been surrounded by people who had not shared his dream. Everything he had done till now was what others had wanted, or expected of him. He had never had the time, opportunity or the money to explore his dream. Now he was a free agent, of sufficient means. He could do what he wanted.

Oliver nodded, and then said, "OK, now the rest."

Hiram was about to say, I don't know what you mean, when Oliver raised an eyebrow. Hiram knew there was nowhere to hide from those all-seeing, all-knowing eyes.

He lowered his gaze as the sadness returned. All his life Hiram had dealt with problems by using the technique 'Out of sight, out of mind'. Now he had to turn his thoughts to Doctor Peacock, St. Augustus's Fire, and the fact that the time he had left could be as little as forty-six months, before his backside was consumed by 'the ring of fire' as he elegantly christened it. He told the story in detail. When he finished the other man whistled through his teeth.

"I am amazed you are still sane," Oliver said.

"What on earth makes you think I am?" asked Hiram with a smile.

"I can understand wanting to fulfil your dream as quickly as possible, given the circumstances, but why this?" Oliver tapped the paper again.

"I told you I want to live on my own yacht and go to sea."

"There are better ways."

"Such as?"

Oliver went to the window and beckoned. "See that yacht?"

Hiram looked at the row of boats he had seen when he had arrived. "Which one?"

"At the back," said Oliver.

When Hiram had first arrived there had been a mobile crane standing behind the yachts. It had now moved and he could see another yacht beyond the others, about one and a half times bigger than the largest. The gold and black lettering proclaimed *The Snow Queen*.

"You have heard the expression 'the dog's bollocks'? Look and drool. It is one hundred and fifty percent fabulous."

"It looks very nice. What's so special about it?"

"Nice!" Oliver exploded. "You use the word 'nice' to describe that? It is a 98-foot-long fast motor launch with carbon fibre hull and superstructure, offering comfort and high performance with open plan saloon and dining area of leather upholstery and cherry wood surround. The fly bridge has ample seating, below which is a dinette, bar and Jacuzzi. In the water it's 28.10m long, 6.10m beam, but with just a 2.10m draft. It has four guest cabins with eight berths and three crew berths. There are two Merlin Sea Snake turbo diesel 1400 hp engines with top speed of 28 knots and cruising speed of 22 knots, plus excellent manoeuvrability. The fuel capacity is 9000 litres and the fresh water tanks hold 3000 litres. Do you see those fins behind the booster screw? They are computer programmable, variable pitch, hydrofoil blades, rotatable for maximum lift, giving power boat speed, and automatic anti-roll compensating stabilisers. Calling that 'nice' is an insult." He shook his head. "I've added an auto pilot with Sat Nav and GPS, accurate to half a metre. It has surface and bottom finding radar, and a communications suite with Sat phone and radio. It is under five and a half years-old but immaculate. I paid a decent price but with the additions, I could ask for four and three quarter million. As I have taken to you, I can let you have it for three and a half, and have it ready for sea in two weeks. What do you think?"

Hiram scrutinised every inch and said, "It's beautiful, and sounds fabulous. I would love a look, but I don't think it's for me."

"How could you not fall in love? Isn't it what you're looking for?"

Hiram replied that it was magnificent but despite being big, powerful, luxurious and technologically superb, it was still just a leisure craft and not a permanent home.

Oliver stared. "You gonna give up dry land all together?"

Hiram said given the time he had left it was doubtful if he would ever be coming home. He had been influenced by a visit to the Royal Yacht Britannia, now a permanent tourist attraction in Edinburgh.

It was Oliver's turn to smile. "The reason it's a tourist attraction is because it was pensioned off for being too expensive. If the nation couldn't afford it, you sure as hell can't."

"I did not mean I want something as grand as that, after all it was used to transport the Royal Family and entourage across the globe and entertain Heads of State with formal banquets. It had a large crew of Royal Naval officers and seamen, and The Band of the Royal Marines. I am not that ambitious. I remembered reading that The Queen wanted to recreate the ambience of a comfortable country house, in the decoration and layout. That sounds good to me."

"It sounds more than good," said Oliver. Abruptly the smile disappeared. "If I were to build a ship, from scratch, that combined that" – he jerked his thumb at the window – "and this" – he tapped the papers – "it would take my workforce two years. Without being insensitive, your alarm clock is ticking."

Hiram was crestfallen.

Oliver carried on, "I am sorry to sound cruel but honesty is what you need right now. You would be lucky to find what you are looking for, without building from scratch."

"I realise that now," said Hiram. "I guess I need to think again."

Oliver saw Hiram sag and thought, *the poor sod has only a few years left and I am pouring cold water on his dream.* "You could however go for a conversion. Find a redundant ship the size you want, gut and refurbish. It's cheaper and quicker than fresh build."

"What are the chances of finding a ship? You just said we would have to be lucky."

"I know a man who can improve our chances," said Oliver smiling again. He produced an address book, flicked the pages, and motioned Hiram to sit as he picked up the telephone. "I have a friend at M&S who owes me a favour. I was saving it for a rainy day, but I guess your rain is as good as mine." He winked as he dialled, saw the blank look on Hiram's face and said, "Please don't tell me you thought I was talking about Marks and Spencer." Hiram's face showed that this had been his first thought.

Suddenly the penny dropped. M&S Shipbuilding were huge. Hiram remembered a news story about M&S working on one of the biggest, most powerful, technologically advanced, and most expensive warships in the world. An admiral had said that this ship could out do every air traffic control centre in Europe by tracking all take offs and landings across the continent. It had 'real time' communication with two rings of satellites and no ship, aircraft or submarine could get close enough to be a threat without being first detected at safe distance. He recalled that this vessel could command more firepower than the combined might of the all the Second World War navies."Surely M&S is too big for small fry like me?" Hiram protested.

Oliver shrugged. "They have a civilian division which builds tankers, cargo ships, ferries and the like. They recently dipped a toe in the leisure market to build yachts, motor cruisers and pleasure craft. I happen to be a close friend of their chief and – " he interrupted himself, and asked to speak to Bertrand Cavendish.

After a few moments he spoke again. "Hello Bertrand. It's Oliver. How are you? I am well, and busy. How are things, and your better half. And the children? That's marvellous. Well done her. Give her a hug from me and tell her I think she is brilliant." So the conversation went on then Oliver said, "Bertrand, do you remember *Corunna*?" Oliver's frame shook with forced laughter, and he held finger and thumb in a circle for Hiram's benefit. "I saved your ass big time and you said you owe me a humongous favour." He laughed again. "It's time for me to call in that favour buddy, and it's a big one." Oliver looked at Hiram and winked. "I have a friend here, by the name of Hiram Montgomery, who is in a spot. He needs a yacht, and we are talking big. A super yacht, in fact. He needs it quickly. I can't explain right now, but I wouldn't ask if it was not important. We need a conversion to turn a decent-sized boat into a floating mansion? Can I count on you my friend? Thank you. I really appreciate it. Do you remember the *The Maltese Princess*? I have added new equipment, a facelift and renamed her *The Snow Queen*. I don't mind saying, it is a cracking piece of work. Hiram loved it, but it's not big enough. He needs a permanent home. I'm talking lounge, drawing rooms, bar, dining room, space for entertaining, luxury bedrooms en suite, kitchen, pantry, wine cellar, lots of storage, sauna, Jacuzzi, steam room, fitness suite, games room with full sized billiard table, crew quarters, car garage, boat dock with pleasure boats. What do you think?"

He waited a few moments. "Excellent. Hiram has done drawings and notes of his own. I'll send them over with *The Snow Queen* plans. For someone who knows bugger all about boats and ship technology he had come up with some interesting ideas. Some are off the wall but others are good. You're a star, my old friend. If you pull this off, it's me who will owe you the favour. I'll get Hiram to make an appointment. Give my love to the family, and once again my very grateful thanks."

Hiram sat open mouthed, partly because of Oliver's description of the ship, and partly because the other man had agreed to it. He said, "That was some boat you just described. Are you sure I can afford it? I have only got twenty six million and I can't spend it *all* on construction. I have to keep something for running costs."

"Don't worry. Bertrand will work out what you can afford and tailor the plan to fit. Right now all you have to think about is that your dream boat is to be built by the most reputable shipbuilding company in the world. Let me show you round *The Snow Queen* to help you focus your thoughts."

Monday 15th December 2025

Eleven days after his chat with Oliver Russell, Hiram's car Sat Nav led him on a three hour journey to Lascelles Avenue, just north of Portsmouth harbour. The tall featureless wall topped with razor wire and CCTV cameras which had stretched for over a mile, suddenly had a gap in it, and a large sign which said 'M&S Shipbuilding Ltd'. He turned into the drive, which had two lanes separating staff to the left and visitors to the right. The visitors' entrance was blocked by a large metal blade protruding from the tarmac. It slid out of sight and he drove over it, to see it rise again in his mirror. A similar blade blocked his path. Three uniformed men approached with practised precision; one with a clipboard, the second pushing a long handled platform on casters bearing an upwards pointing camera and spotlights and VDU screen on the handle. The third carried a contraption like an upright vacuum cleaner but with two prongs instead of a cleaning head. It too had a VDU on the handle. Both men appeared oblivious to all but their screens. Clipboard man stood while the other two walked either side of the car. The platform swept underneath and the pronged gadget swept over and around the vehicle sampling for odours from explosive or volatile substances, and electronic, electrical or magnetic fields.

The man with the clipboard asked Hiram's name and ticked his list. "Once inside follow the blue signs until you reach M&S Leisure. Reception will look after you." He smiled and returned to his hut, followed by the other two. The front blade disappeared and Hiram moved forward once more.

He followed the blue signs and soon found himself in a car park in front of a two storey building. He found a space near the building and got out. As he locked the door a movement caught his eye. He looked at the corner of the building and exchanged stares with a camera. Inside a receptionist flashed a smile, asked him to look at the dot and pointed to a black glass rectangle at the end of her desk. In the centre was a circular lens and as he looked, the frame lit up. The girl tapped keys on her desk, took something in her right hand and something in her left. Her hands came together then she handed him a laminated plastic identity badge with his photograph, name, date, time of arrival, and a ribbon to hang it round his neck. He was most impressed. He put on the badge but declined her offer of coffee, then sat in a chair in the reception area.

A few moments later the lift doors opened and out stepped Bertrand Cavendish, a tall handsome man whose appearance exuded money, success and confidence. "Welcome to M&S Leisure. My name is Bertrand Cavendish, Principal Officer." He shook Hiram's hand and ushered him into the lift. As it rose silently Hiram was fascinated by two paintings. The only illustration he had seen on the inside of lift doors was graffiti. Wooden sailing galleons tilted gracefully on a pea green sea with white wave crests and seagulls wheeling. As Hiram studied the paintings, Bertrand studied Hiram. After the initial call from Oliver Russell, when he had agreed to see Hiram, a second call had provided further information. Hiram had asked Oliver to keep his medical condition confidential, because he did not want special treatment out of pity. Even as Oliver agreed, he had no intention of sticking to it. From the beginning the two men had made a connection, perhaps because they shared recent bereavement. Whatever the cause, Oliver wanted Hiram Montgomery to achieve his dream in his time remaining. He therefore told Bertrand everything and asked him to ensure it happened.

Bertrand had agreed in an instant. He had a comfortable and successful life, and had no doubt that but for Oliver Russell it could have been very different. Years earlier, as a rising star, he had been sent, as part of a diplomatic mission, to solve a technical problem for the Spanish Navy. After correcting the problem the Minister for the Interior, Ricardo Desvaldo, invited them to the society wedding of his nephew, to thank them. To cut a story short, Bertrand had a momentary error of judgement during the reception when he allowed the Minister's beautiful daughter kiss him. It was a fleeting thing but seen by Marcella's fiancé who aspired to be a crime boss. But for Oliver Russell's intervention the fiancé would have arranged Bertrand's visit to the hospital, or the mortuary.

Oliver ended up in hospital, and persuaded Bertrand to keep quiet, thus saving himself great embarrassment, humiliation and possible loss of his job, marriage and even his freedom. Much later, Bertrand and his wife were blessed with daughters, now fine young ladies. Oliver married and Bertrand was best man at the wedding. Bertrand was promoted to senior engineer, then Head of Department. When M&S Leisure was created he became Head of Division. He was eternally indebted to Oliver for being in the right place at the right time, and for putting himself in grave danger, the result of which was that life had turned out well for both of them – and he was now more than willing to repay his debt.

As he looked at Hiram Bertrand thought about the winding paths of life. When did Hiram's story begin? The death of his wife, the lottery win, his illness, his dream of owning a boat, a Spanish beauty kissing an engineer, or when their paths were laid by The Almighty, before they were even born? Oliver had often talked about fate. Bertrand argued that we make our own fate. As he considered Hiram and what had brought them together, he wondered.

The lift doors opened and Bertrand led Hiram into his office. The room was large and expensively furnished with desk at one end, armchairs, coffee table and fireplace at the other. The picture windows overlooked the harbour, on the far side of which were huge air ship hangers next to the water. One door was open, revealing the bow of a ship. These giant buildings were actually roofs over repair docks. The aroma of fresh coffee danced a fandango in Hiram's nostrils and he gladly accepted a cup. He sat opposite Bertrand and stared at the desk. It was vast and clearly designed for very large sheets of paper. At one end a laptop waited and at the other a telephone dozed, while in the middle sat a cardboard folder.

When they were settled Bertrand said, "I understand you are a great friend of Oliver Russell."

"Not really," replied Hiram. "We met for the first time the other day, and he was very helpful. Unfortunately he is so busy he is unable to accommodate me. He is a lovely man and kindly gave me your name. I am grateful to you for seeing me at such short notice."

Bertrand smiled. Hiram had passed the honesty test. It was an M&S custom, when first dealing with a new supplier or customer, to put a little test: a seemingly innocuous question, to which the answer was already known. The purpose was to see if the person was not averse to telling a little white lie, perhaps exaggerate their important, influence or connections. Bertrand concluded that Hiram was honest, and possibly a bit shy. "Oliver has sent your notes, his ideas, and what you liked about *The Snow Queen*. I think I know what you are looking for. Before we discuss that, how much do you know about M&S?"

Hiram was not expecting that. He thought quickly about his discussion with Oliver, and his memory of the news. "M&S Leisure is a subsidiary of M&S Shipbuilding Ltd, one of the most important and influential ship building companies in the world. That you could deal with a small fry like me is flattering, if a little scary. Your company has built some of the biggest and most prestigious ships in the world including tankers, merchant ships, liners and warships for many countries. I have seen stories about amazing ships that have blown my socks off."

Bertrand roared with laughter. "I am sorry to hear that. I hope we have not blown your socks off today?"

"Well I am gob-smacked by the high-tech security." said Hiram.

Bertrand explained that security had to be tight because work was sometimes of a sensitive nature. He said they'd had a long time to make sure everything runs perfectly. He liked the man in front of him, finding him very open and genuine, if a little out of his depth. "It is most kind of you to say we are important and influential. We are not the biggest, but we don't think that's as important as our reputation. M&S Shipbuilding was born on the first anniversary of Armistice Day. Our company motto is 'Treat others as you would be treated'. From that first day all employees had to swear an oath of integrity to the principles of the company before work. A copy of that declaration is over there." Bertrand pointed to a framed parchment on the far wall.

"Since the beginning we adhered to our founder's principles: fair trading, flawless products and services, and guaranteed satisfaction. When others fought to steal customers, stab competitors, and do shady deals, we held back. Other companies grew bigger, faster, and over time, came and went. We remained constant to our oath and gradually as our reputation grew it became accepted that in this world, there is one company you absolutely depend on. Instead of 'all's fair in love and war' we treat people with dignity and respect. Instead of 'let the buyer beware' we say 'if you are unhappy, tell us and we will fix it at no cost'. We don't cut corners, but are obsessive in our quest for perfection. We never advertise, and our books are full. We are choosy and refuse customers if we don't like them. Some have thought our policy means we are gullible, but have learned their mistake. We make sure we are fair to ourselves, as well as others." Bertrand steepled his fingers under his chin and regarded Hiram across the desk. "I am telling you this for two reasons. Firstly we are not the biggest ship building company but the contacts and good will we have developed over the years make us one of the most influential, and therefore powerful. Secondly our attitude towards customers, regardless of name, rank, wealth, power, never alters. We both know the only reason you are here is because I agreed to see you as a favour to a friend, but having seen you I have made a decision. I cannot have a customer of mine tiptoeing around like an imposter or stowaway. I am prepared to take you on if you hold your head high and look people in the eye. Do you agree my terms?"

Hiram sat straighter as he said, "You can't blame me for being over-awed. However, I will not let you down."

Bertrand smiled again. "Good. Now let's get to work." He opened the folder on the desk in front of him.

Hiram recognised *The Snow Queen* brochure, and his own notes.

"I've read your notes and some of your ideas are interesting, particularly the remote control docking derricks. Once we have developed this, it should be patented. Other ideas of yours have already been done better. I read Oliver's notes on your opinions of *The Snow Queen*, and that he told you conversion will be cheaper and quicker than new build. I took the liberty of casting around for suitable 'donor' ships, and came up with a candidate." From the folder he pulled a photograph and plans. "The *Aurora Dancer*, a support ship in the oil industry, has been sitting for two and a half years in Aberdeen harbour. It is perfectly sound, but no one currently has need of it. This is what it looks like now and this is how I suggest we convert it."

As Hiram studied the papers, Bertrand said, "It started life as a hospital ship in 1964 but converted in 1981. It's made of steel, with a number 1 diesel main propulsion engine with type CPP propeller, total BHP of 1200, 1 spade rudder and additional Aquamaster Azimuth Thruster. Maximum speed eleven knots, economic speed ten knots and idling speed four knots. Its 62.6 metres long, 10.2 metres abeam and has a 5.1 metre draft. The net registered weight is 299 tonnes and gross weight 999 tonnes. Fuel capacity is 101 tonnes, water capacity 123 tonnes." He pointed out the changes he proposed to make and how it might look afterwards.

Despite his inexperience, Hiram was able to follow the gist and was delighted. "Wonderful," he said. "How much will it cost?"

Bertrand pulled more papers. "The asking price is £437,500, and this is the estimated conversion cost, and prediction of possible running costs, including crew, provisions, supplies, fuel, and a contingency fund." He turned the piece of paper round for Hiram to see.

Hiram was impressed by the detail, and the bottom figures. "I can afford this," he said hardly able to contain his glee.

Bertrand nodded. "I shall make an offer."

Hiram poured a coffee and wandered to the framed parchment. Bertrand called over as he picked up the phone. "Is this the name of your ship?" He nodded at Hiram's notes. Hiram nodded back. Bertrand read aloud but mispronounced Adongiva as if it rhymed with hay-loan-sleeve-ah. He asked, "What does it mean?"

Hiram thought how Bertrand would react if the ship had an irreverent or arguably rude name? Without abandoning the sentiments, he decided a Bowdlerised explanation would be prudent. "Roughly translated it means I boldly go forward, regardless of the reservations of others," said Hiram.

Bertrand nodded approval. "What is the origin?"

Hiram silently cursed and thought that this proves you should not tell lies unless prepared to tell more to cover up the first. Hoping to end the matter he said, "An ancient and little used dialect of Gaelic."

Bertrand said "I like it... old as the mists of time and yet timeless. It fits well with a ship seeking new adventures on the high seas."

"Boldly go where no man has gone before," said Hiram.

"That's from *Star Trek*, isn't it?" asked Bertrand as he dialled.

"Yes" said Hiram, turning to the parchment.

It was yellowed, torn where it had been folded, and looked ancient.

He read silently, imagining assembled employees proclaiming the words before starting work. "Be it known by all around that I (full name) a God-fearing and industrious person, desirous of mutually profitable association with M&S Shipwrights and Ship Builders, do hereby sincerely promise and swear by Almighty God, that I shall ever abide in thought, word and deed with the tenants contained in the articles of Principle and Integrity hereinafter delineated." Hiram thought that this sounded like some sort of Masonic ritual, but before he could continue he heard Bertrand's voice explode behind him.

"I don't believe it!"

Hiram looked round as Bertrand sat forward. "Why didn't you ring me? You knew I was interested. Who? Hell's bells." Bertrand looked at Hiram, shook his head and spoke again. "What do they want with it? Yes I know that's what it's for, but I had plans for that ship. After all this time, no interest and suddenly this lot appear and snap it up in twenty-four hours." Bertrand sighed heavily and said, "Oh well, back to the drawing board. No, I appreciate it's not your fault. Thanks again, Peter. If anything turns up you will let me know."

Bertrand put the phone down "I guess you worked it out."

"Someone else has just bought the ship?"

"It was moored for over two years with no interest. I make an enquiry and a Korean mining firm appears out the blue, gives it one look, and buys."

Hiram felt he shouldn't be disappointed. He was not used to things going without a hitch. "Are any of the other ships you looked at any good?"

Bertrand twisted his face. "I discounted them for various reasons. This was the one, and at a bargain price." He sighed. "I guess we have to cast our net further." He looked at Hiram. "How do you fancy a trip to Russia? It will cost about five grand to get us there and back."

Hiram was aghast. "Why would I want to go to Russia?"

"Let me tell you a story. At the height of the cold war Russia and America were locked in a battle for supremacy, spending billions to best each other; the nuclear arms race, the war of the intelligence services, and the space race. USSR needed to prove their air force, army and navy were bigger and mightier than USA. They built many ships, all shapes and sizes. Now the Cold War is over and Russia is in a mess. They still cling to the facade of a super power but have crippling problems. They spend millions on space exploration whilst people in remote parts starve and freeze, and tracts of hinterland are contaminated with toxic waste. The Russian Navy has many surplus ships in mothballed fleets. They officially deny this and if you asked to buy one, the door would slam in your face. You would be denounced for insulting the Soviet Union. However they do sell them off, by the back door. We can have one, if we play by their rules. I just happen to know the guy in charge of one of their mothballed fleets."

Hiram wondered whether there was anywhere that did not come under the influence of M&S Shipbuilding.

Bertrand explained. "Have you heard of Ivanovitch Petrovsky? He's a Russian commodore who is probably the greatest expert in naval architecture the world has ever seen. There is probably no shipbuilding company, naval institution or university of any significance that does not have his books on their shelves. I have several signed first editions that are priceless. He is to naval technology what Sir Christopher Wren is to architecture."

Hiram was suitably impressed.

Bertrand went on, "Ivanovitch Petrovsky is not only a genius with encyclopaedic knowledge of maritime methodology, he's a highly decorated and respected naval officer."

"If he is so great, why is he in charge of a mothballed fleet?" asked Hiram.

"When I said he was respected, I meant by his peers. However there are powerful people in the Communist Party who despise him. You see the trouble with Ivanovitch is that he is a larger than life character who doesn't care about upsetting politicians and party officials. When I say larger than life I mean in every way – over six feet seven, built like a grizzly, a wicked humour and big appetites. He is a reprobate who does not believe in moderation when it comes to vodka and womanising. Unfortunately his conquests have included wives, or daughters, of his bosses."

"I imagine that is unwise in the Soviet Union," said Hiram.

"Correct. What saves him is that his great uncle is one of the most senior naval officers in the Kremlin. Ivanovitch knows that the old man can't last for ever and when he goes his enemies will kick his head like a football."

Hiram was aghast. "Why doesn't he get out while he can? Defect to the West or something."

"He's too important. Lord only knows what secrets he carries in his head. They could not afford to lose control of that information. Besides, they like trotting him out for special occasions, when it suits them. That's how I met him, at a United Nations conference on Maritime Safety. If he tried to leave, they would stop him. We have all seen stories of Russian defectors who thought they were safe in the West, but came to an untimely end." Bertrand continued, as if to change the subject, "I could make contact and arrange to go buy one of his ships."

"Just like that?"

"Not quite. Remember I said we have to play by their rules. Are you agreed?"

"If it will get us what we need, then definitely."

Bertrand dug out a mobile phone and explained that the infrastructure in Russia was not good enough to be sure of a successful landline call. Ivanovitch had told him his satellite phone was always with him, and more reliable. Bertrand dialled and waited. He waited some more, and then his face lit up and he raised a thumb.

"Hello, Ivanovitch, its Bertrand Cavendish from England. How are you, my old friend?"

Hiram was amused to hear that Bertrand had developed a Russian accent. He listened to the one sided conversation with interest.

"I am very well. She is well. They are both doing fine and becoming young ladies, so you can stay where you are you scoundrel." He laughed enthusiastically then said, "That's fantastic news. I am very pleased for you. Well done; richly deserved and long overdue." Bertrand frowned "Does that mean a better posting? Oh. I See. Oh well, at least it's a bigger pay packet and a larger pension eh?" After a pause, he carried on speaking, but the accent had slipped a little. "Actually, I am telephoning to ask if you could help with a problem. I have been consulting your books which have been most helpful but there are points that I would like to clarify. Incidentally, you remember Patrick? He said he was interested in your book *Ship Identification and Recognition*, and that your books on Target Acquisition and Ship Recovery Procedures were of great interest. I digress. The project I am engaged in is the conversion of an existing, redundant, ship into a luxury yacht. If we could meet, your advice could assist me greatly in getting my project to sea, as it were."

Hiram listened to Bertrand nattering and wondered why he had suddenly brought up the subject of Patrick, whoever he was. Irrelevant chat did not seem the best use of a satellite phone call to Russia. It crossed his mind that the stuff about ship identification, target acquisition and recovery might be code, but he dismissed this as paranoid. Bertrand was speaking again. "You mean this weekend? It's a bit short notice, why the rush? Oh, I see." Bertrand looked worried, and the Russian accent had disappeared. "Is he all right? That's not good. I see. Do you think there is going to be trouble? Oh right, we will definitely come. I will get on to it." Bertrand did not look happy. "Hiram and I will see you on Friday. Oh yes, of course. Saturday it is then. I look forward to seeing you again old friend."

Hiram thought he could guess the conversation, but asked. "What's up?"

"Good news and bad news. "Ivanovitch is now a Rear Admiral."

Hiram nodded congratulations then said, "I take it from your conversation, he is not being moved and still in charge of the mothball fleet?" Bertrand nodded. "He wants us to go over this weekend?" Bertrand nodded again. "I take it his uncle is not well?"

Bertrand said, "He is in hospital with a chest infection, which is not good for a man of his age. Admiral Uri Redrikov, Commissar 2nd Fleet Marshal of all USSR Fleets is the second highest ranking naval officer in the entire Soviet Bloc. If he does not survive it's very bad news for Ivanovitch, but apparently he has had several such scares in the last few years and has survived them all. The promotion was the old man's idea, 'to help keep the wolves at bay'. Ivanovitch wants us to do the deal, before he is no longer able to do so."

Hiram spent a few moments taking it in. "So he knows why we are coming. All that stuff about his books was code, right?"

Bertrand nodded. "Ivanovitch knows my middle name is Patrick, that I was talking about myself and what I want. However, so does everybody else. Nobody just hops over to Russia to clarify a few reference books. The KGB are probably analysing a recording our conversation as we speak."

Hiram looked anxious. "That's bad."

Bertrand smiled. "Not necessarily. I told you if we play by their rules we will be left alone."

"Can we get over there in a few days?"

Bertrand raised an eyebrow. "You haven't met my secretary. She is a witch. She can turn phone calls into travel arrangements, hotel bookings, or whatever you desire, at the drop of a hat. Pack for a few days including thermals, a good coat, hat and boots. It will be damn cold over there at this time of year."

CHAPTER FIVE

Friday 19ᵗʰ December 2025

Heathrow to Moscow by Aeroflot took six and a half hours. After a brief layover, Hiram and Bertrand flew to Murmansk and arrived two hours later. They were picked up by Peter, a colleague of Ivanovitch, who drove them to the base. Ivanovitch's office was not as grand as Bertrand's but there were computer terminals and drawing boards. Map tables sat at one end of the room, dining furniture in the middle and a desk at the other. Bookshelves lined two walls, with filing cabinets and wooden cupboard covering another.

Bertrand had described Ivanovitch as a giant among men. He was not kidding. Ivanovitch towered above Hiram. He had thick white curly hair and a weather beaten face. "Welcome to my office, and to Russia," said Ivanovitch in baritone voice. "Be seated, my friends. You must be Hiram. I am pleased to meet you." As they shook hands, Hiram thought Ivanovitch's grip could crush his hand in an instant.

Bertrand reached into his briefcase and pulled out a bottle of scotch. Hiram recognised the label and was amazed. He had once read about this very special, rare and expensive 45-year-old single malt with a price tag of over three thousand pounds.

Bertrand said, "Ivanovitch, I have brought you a token of my regard, which I hope you enjoy."

Ivanovitch studied the label and whistled. "My God, this might be expensive in your country, but have you any idea of the value over here? You could buy a good car or small house for the same money. It's too generous."

"Listen," said Bertrand, "I value my friendship with the greatest naval architect in living memory. I have dined out on you and I know you appreciate the finer things in life. Drink it with pleasure."

"I am overwhelmed," said Ivanovitch. "I shall save it for a special occasion. We will have a vodka or two later, when we have concluded our business." He turned to face Hiram. "So, you want to buy one of my ships, do you?"

Bertrand replied on Hiram's behalf. "I can give you an idea of what we want." He pulled a folder from his briefcase.

"No doubt," said Ivanovitch with a wave of his hand. "We will get to that presently. First, I want to hear from Hiram. Listening to the horse's mouth helps pin point the heart."

Hiram was not expecting this, assuming Bertrand would be doing the talking. He thought about how to summarise his ideas succinctly. "I would like a *dacha* for the sea, designed for long periods afloat. Lavish, ostentatious or flamboyant style is unimportant to me. I am an ordinary guy with a dream and have come into a bit of money. I don't need the best of everything but it would be nice if the yacht was quite fast, big and comfortable, with a modicum of luxury."

Ivanovitch studied the man before him, then opened the folder. Bertrand made an attempt to speak but Ivanovitch silenced him. He read Hiram's notes, *The Snow Queen* brochure, Oliver's report, the *Aurora Dancer* plans and Bertrand's notes. He closed the file and said, "OK, I know where you are coming from and where you want to end up." He drummed the fingers of his right hand on his chin and closed his eyes. "I know the very ship. It's a fine 36.5 metre transport called *The Vashoya Calishka*. It was used to move senior officers in hotel standard accommodation. The ship is designed for global travel and extreme weather with air conditioning throughout and keel coolers for the engines. It has two diesel Dragonfly 1500hp engines with shaft drive. Overall length is 41.5 metres, beam 11.15, and 3.2 metre draft. It is very fast, highly manoeuvrable, and has lots of space on several decks. The accommodation consists of twelve two berth passenger cabins with en suite facilities, plus separate crew quarters. Though it has been idle for years, it is damn near perfect. You could almost use it without further conversion, other than changing the Russian signs, dials and controls. If you wanted to add modern technology and amenities it wouldn't be difficult. We'll take the chopper and look her over. Do you have any questions before we go?"

Hiram said *The Vashoya Calishka* sounded impressive and asked about the price, embarrassing Bertrand. He had planned to broach the subject of cost with subtlety after seeing the ship.

Ivanovitch smiled, amused by Hiram's unsophisticated approach to what would normally be discussed more clandestinely. "Let me tell you about my place of work. We are currently on a large deep-water natural bay on the north coast of Russia and protected from the sea by two curving peninsulas of hard rock. There is no civilisation anywhere near, apart from a remote village called Rumyantsev Snezhnogorskia. The ships moored in the bay are the Northern Fleet Reserve, 2nd Division, but are often referred to as the 'Rumyantsev Snezhnogorskia Fleet' because of their location. I am in command of this fleet. There are some in the Kremlin who see me as a rusty, old admiral in charge of a rusty, old naval junkyard. They largely don't interfere and I can do pretty much what I want. These ships are an embarrassment to the government for a number of reasons. There are too many ships for current deployment. As technology improves, they become more obsolete each day. In addition, they are slowly rusting away and you can only cannibalise so much. The government cannot sell them on the open market for fear of accusations of mismanagement and incompetence."

Bertrand was shocked at Ivanovitch's frankness. He guessed that this office had been swept for bugs.

Ivanovitch continued, "The ships here are out of sight, out of mind. I am sometimes asked to select a ship for missile, torpedo or gunnery practice. Apart from this, I am free to do as I choose. Should the hypothetical situation arise of someone wishing to buy a ship, which is unlikely given that no one knows they are here, I could charge what I like."

Bertrand could not help but smile. Everyone in the naval industry knows of these ships, just not the location.

"However, no one has ever made such an approach and naturally I would have to consult my superiors following such a preposterous request." His expression indicated that he was not telling the truth. "In the case of the 'Vashoya Calishka', I would have to take into account its original cost, age, condition, the likelihood of its future usefulness, and so on."

"Roughly speaking what would that be?" asked Hiram.

"Let me see." Ivanovitch scratched his head. "The ship cost the equivalent of a hundred and fifty two and a quarter million pounds when first commissioned. It had a number of defensive systems, military communications hardware and one or two other little things that I won't go into. These have all been cleared away, reducing the value a bit. It is not a new vessel and has seen active service, albeit only for a short period. It has been moored in open water for some considerable time and subjected to the elements, which can be rather harsh in this part of the world. Given all this, I value the ship at..." He counted on his fingers. "Lets round it up to twenty five million."

"Your arithmetic is impressive, but I'm not sure I can afford to buy such a ship, get it back to Britain, convert it and then run it," said Hiram.

Ivanovitch slapped his forehead and said, "What was I thinking? What is the date today?"

Hiram was puzzled but replied, "18th December."

Ivanovitch smiled. "You are fortunate. This is the very day I had put in my diary to give one lucky customer a half price bargain, which would bring the price down to twelve and a half million."

"That is a fantastic price," Hiram said, "but still on the high side."

Ivanovitch said, "Let's wait until we see the ship. After all, we might see minor damage or wear and tear which will reduce the price even further."

"Wait a minute," exclaimed Bertrand. "Let's not get completely out of hand here. I know what you are trying to do, Ivanovitch, and it is very kind and exceptionally generous. But Hell's bells, we don't want you to get into trouble over this."

Ivanovitch leaned forward conspiratorially and said, "I am already in plenty of trouble, my friend. Trouble is where I have spent most of my life. As far as I am concerned, this is purely business and I am simply doing to my political masters what they have been doing to me for years. As long as I collect enough money to pay off the small army of parasites I have to feed, they turn a blind eye to whatever I do here. Personally, I don't give a shit if I give the ship away for nothing."

They left the office and walked to a small helicopter. Hiram had never flown in one before and he was excited. Once they had boarded the aircraft, been strapped in and given headsets, the helicopter rose rapidly. Hiram sat next to a window and had a good view of the base and the surrounding ocean. The sea looked dark and menacing. Around the buildings was a simple chain-link fence with one gate.

Ivanovitch said, "There is no need for elaborate security here. The water is so cold survival time is counted in seconds, or minutes with a survival suit. The land around the base has a name you would find utterly unpronounceable, but I can tell you it translates to 'the slow train to the back door of hell'. It is essentially a vast featureless plain criss-crossed by rivers of tar. The crust, frozen solid by the icy winds, varies in thickness and, from time to time, hot gas breaks through and sprays tar. Anyone nearby would be enveloped in a hot black mist that quickly congeals and sets in the cold air. The incapacitated unfortunate would sink before it freezes over again."

The helicopter wheeled away and turned out to sea. The natural bay was an almost perfect circle of two rock peninsulas curving towards each other and overlapping with enough space for a ship to pass through. Within the bay, over a hundred ships lay at anchor in straight rows. There were sleek greyhounds and broad shouldered mastiffs. Some had turrets whilst others had rings where guns had been. A few seemed intact with dishes, spheres, domes and radar arms. Most of the ships had empty spaces where equipment or whole sections had been removed.

They were about half way across the bay when Hiram spotted an unusual vessel at the end of one row. "Wow! What is that?"

Bertrand looked over and saw a ship the likes of which he had never seen before. It was a catamaran with a massive dome across the bows, like a giant tin helmet. "Good lord, Ivanovitch, what in heaven is that?"

Ivanovitch looked discomfited. "It's nothing. Ignore it please."

He clearly did not want to discuss it and Bertrand decided that politeness should outweigh curiosity. The dome ship soon passed from sight and the helicopter descended as it approached a particular ship.

The 'Vashoya Calishka' appeared to be in good condition, but out of place among the grey ships. It had a black hull, white two-deck superstructure with smoke stacks to the rear, a short fore deck, and a landing pad aft. Before they landed, they circled and Ivanovitch pointed out how the different parts could be converted into useful areas befitting a luxury private yacht.

Finally, they settled on the deck and began their tour. As they looked around, Ivanovitch slapped a wall here or equipment there and said, "Oh dear, we will have to knock something off for that." This was amusing for Bertrand as there was clearly nothing wrong with any of it. It took two and a half hours to cover every compartment, deck and amenity. When they had finished their tour, Bertrand was satisfied that the ship was what they wanted and Hiram was like a dog with two tails.

Back in the helicopter, Ivanovitch asked Hiram's opinion. Hiram was practically speechless with joy. Ivanovitch said, "Given the problems we saw and the repairs necessary, I think we should reduce the price to five and a quarter million. What do you think?"

Bertrand shook his head. "Ivanovitch that's crazy. Are you sure your superiors are not going to go mad?"

"It's a deal then," said Ivanovitch, extending his hand.

As they flew back, Bertrand said he would organise a crew to fly out in January to get the ship back to England.

Ivanovitch shook his head. He explained that his men were Russian sailors, albeit shore-based in this godforsaken posting. It would be better if he organised a training exercise for a few handpicked men to take the ship for a 'run round the coast' to give the engines and men a workout. They would sail round the Norwegian coast, as far as the North Sea, then head for home. What could they do but run to the nearest port for assistance if the ship happened to suffer from a crippling engine fire whilst off the British Coast?

"You will never get away with that," exclaimed Bertrand. "Everybody knows that Russia doesn't tolerate other countries assisting one of their ships in trouble. Remember that submarine catastrophe when they allowed their sailors to die rather than ask for help?"

"You don't have to remind me," snapped Ivanovitch. "I lost friends on that boat. Don't forget that this is a face-saving exercise to offload an unwanted ship without having to admit it. They know what is happening and as long as everybody sticks to the subterfuge, all is well. The 'Vashoya Calishka' had an identical sister ship which was cannibalised for spare parts before a fire gutted her. A while ago, the Russian Air Force needed a target for a new weapon. Before I gave them the sister ship, I took photographs of the damage. I'll put them in the 'Vashoya Calishka' file which means I can sell the ship to you for the scrap value of two million pounds, which is all I need to pay off the bribes."

"Won't they think it's strange that the photographs of both damaged ships are identical?" asked Bertrand.

"No. I only need to keep photographs of ships kept for use, not those that are destroyed."

They flew close to the dome ship and Ivanovitch watched as his two companions looked down. Hiram looked at Ivanovitch who said, "Why do you find it fascinating?"

"It looks like something from *Star Trek*," said Hiram.

Ivanovitch smiled. "You're a *Star Trek* fan?"

"I sure am!"

Ivanovitch grinned briefly. "That's the *Ul'iana Borisovskaia*. Some years ago, a 'genius' in the Russian Academy of Naval Studies designed a ship, which I thought from the outset was plain dumb. Two space rockets were mounted in conventional hulls. Between the hulls and dome was room for tanks, artillery and troops. The ship would be able to race across a sea at a speed too fast for interception, allowing the army to get on location with total surprise and minimum resistance. A naval exercise some years ago, involving many ships, turned out to be a humiliating disaster. A rocket throttle jammed open and spun the ship in ever-increasing circles. The fleet had to scatter to avoid collision. Most men inside were cooked or shaken to death. The few survivors were left deaf and crippled physically or mentally. The event has come to be known as 'The Spinning Turtle' and anyone who was there avoids discussion about it. I expect one day we'll be told to take it out and open the seacocks. But until that day, we ignore it."

After the helicopter landed on the snow covered square, the men got off and walked to the middle building and up to the Admiral's office on the first floor. As they sat at the dining table, the staff brought in an ample lunch of fish salad. Over coffee Ivanovitch said, "So Hiram, which *Star Trek* are you a fan of?"

"Do you know much about *Star Trek*?" asked Hiram.

"I am an avowed trekkie," replied Ivanovitch, much to the surprise of his guests.

"Wow! I didn't know that *Star Trek* was big in Russia," said Hiram.

"My dear boy, *Star Trek* is big the world over. I visited a *Star Trek* convention in Japan," he beamed.

Bertrand shook his head, knowing he was about listen to a conversation he would find boring.

Hiram said, "I was a total devotee from the very first episode of the original series. I loved the first *Enterprise* with James T. Kirk, Doctor Spock, Bones and Scotty. I am a big fan of *Star Trek: The Next Generation*. I never really got into *Deep Space Nine* but I enjoy *Voyager*. I have the complete collection of *The Next Generation* DVDs and all the *Star Trek* films."

"So do I, and I have a huge library of *Star Trek* books, some in English and some in Russian," said Ivanovitch.

"I have the *Star Trek Encyclopedia* and other reference books on the films and various other things," said Hiram.

Ivanovitch got up and beckoned Hiram to the cupboard. The doors opened and lights illuminated a display of *Star Trek* models.

"Wow, a Klingon Bird of Prey, a Romulan Warship and, of course, the *Enterprise*." Other memorabilia included identity badges, a tricorder, phaser and signed photographs. As Hiram stood in awe, Bertrand buried his head, but his curiosity as engineer and designer quickly got the better of him. He found the models interesting and detailed.

Eventually they returned to the table. "I take it you are not a trekkie?" said Ivanovitch as he picked up a pad and pencil.

Bertrand said, "I have seen *Star Trek* films."

"Which ones?"

Bertrand shrugged. "Just *Star Trek* films."

The other two smiled and held the same expression that exuded both pity and compassion for this uneducated soul.

"I have watched the odd episode on television," said Bertrand to redeem himself.

Ivanovitch nodded and turned to Hiram. "I understand your fascination with the *Ul'iana Borisovskaia*. I suppose it looks like something from *Star Trek*, except that it should have a central hull under the dome to make it look more like the real thing."

"Real thing?" said Bertrand. "*Star Trek*, and the space ships therein, are fiction."

"We know that," said Ivanovitch, "but there is nothing wrong with building a ship which copies fiction." Bertrand did not look convinced.

Hiram said, "What about railway engines like *Thomas the Tank Engine* and hot air balloons like *Winnie the Pooh*?"

"OK, I accept that," said Bertrand, "but you couldn't have a ship exactly like the *Enterprise* because it would be bow heavy, and the front of the central hull would be permanently underwater."

"You're right," said Ivanovitch. "The *Enterprise* is designed for space and anything built for water would have to be different, perhaps like this." Ivanovitch turned a pad of paper he had been scribbling on during the conversation. When Bertrand and Hiram saw what he had been drawing, they were stunned.

Ivanovitch had designed a trimaran reminiscent of the *Enterprise*, with a wide, low central hull streamlined at the bow but broad in the beam. Above the bow was a large disk with windows on several levels, suggesting a number of decks. Behind the disk, the central hull had a flat stern deck where a small helicopter sat. Two slim hulls, each with a single streamlined superstructure, ran along either side of the central hull and extended some way behind. These hulls were connected to the central hull by cylindrical tubes with windows along their length. On the stern decks of the two-side hulls were funnels shaped like airplane tailfins. Near the top of these fins were horizontal 'wings' bearing radar and communications equipment. It was superbly drawn and the cumulus clouds above and choppy white crested waves were a work of art.

Bertrand was stunned by the draughtsman-like technical detail and the artistic beauty of the ship on a rolling sea. He just beat Hiram to the question that sprang to both of their minds. "How in God's name did you draw that so quickly?"

Ivanovitch gave a knowing smile and said, "If people think I am one of the best ship designers in the world, they are wrong. I am *the* best. Sorry if that sounds immodest, but you have to admit that was fast and not too bad."

"Good lord, Ivanovitch," said Bertrand. "You truly are a God."

"Not just at designing ships, but a brilliant artist too," Hiram added.

"Don't be silly." Ivanovitch was a little embarrassed at this adulation. "Let's have a drink to conclude our business." He got up and retrieved a bottle and glasses from a cabinet. He filled three delicate, miniature wine glasses, raised one and said, "*Vashe zdorovie.*"

Hiram followed. "*Sláinte.*"

"Cheers," Bertrand said.

They emptied the glasses with one swallow. It was cold, smooth and silky to the palate but hit the throat like lava. Hiram gasped as the fire descended from his mouth to his stomach.

They placed the glasses on the table and Ivanovitch refilled them before getting on with the business at hand. "Two things," said Ivanovitch. "We will discuss payment for the ship in a moment but first you must now tell me one important thing you have so far declined to mention."

Hiram looked blank.

"Why are you in such a hurry to complete this transaction?"

Bertrand glanced quickly at Hiram then away to avoid eye contact with Ivanovitch.

Hiram hesitantly replied, "I just want to get in the water as quickly as possible."

Ivanovitch sighed. "Don't bullshit a bullshitter, my friend. I am about to do you a colossal favour. Is the truth too much to ask?"

Hiram thought, *Why does everybody need to know I am dying? How can these people see my secret? Am I so transparent? Or are they really so clever they can interpret the tiniest sign? I don't want special treatment out of pity. My God, I am getting special treatment. Look at the price he is quoting.* Hiram took a breath and told Ivanovitch he was dying.

Ivanovitch sat motionless and, when Hiram did not elaborate, he said, "Go on."

Hiram told him the full story. He talked about Sarah, his trip to the doctor and the conversation he'd had with Shaun.

Ivanovitch said, "I thought I'd heard most things but I've never heard a story quite like that, and I am very sorry to hear it. We must do what we can to make your dream come true and ensure that you enjoy your ship as quickly and for as long as possible."

"I don't want pity or special treatment."

Ivanovitch clasped Hiram's hands between his massive palms. "I am doing this out of friendship. It has been a pleasure to know you and I would deem it a great honour to be allowed to assist you."

Hiram noticed that Bertrand looked embarrassed. "You knew?"

Bertrand said, "Oliver told me. He knew he was breaking your confidence but wanted to ensure you got top priority. I assure you, I have not treated you differently than any other client and this has nothing to do with pity. My favour to Oliver was seeing you quickly. Once we had spoken, it was just business." This was not entirely true. He probably would have passed the case to an assistant, but had been influenced by Hiram's plight.

Hiram didn't feel angry by the betrayal and was satisfied by the explanation.

"Now to business," said Ivanovitch. "I suggest that you take these bank details." He fished out a piece of paper. "You will get a call when the ship is off your coast and once you have transferred the money, I will order the ship to dock. My men can assist you with familiarization before I bring them home.

Bertrand said, "Are you sure it will be alright at your end? We don't want to create trouble."

"It will be fine." With that, Ivanovitch picked up his glass. The second vodka did not shock like the first and the third was rather good.

After lunch, they discussed ideas for the conversion. Hiram asked if he could keep the sketch of the *Enterprise*.

Ivanovitch signed it and handed it over, then asked if Hiram had a name for the ship. Hiram turned to the first page of his notes and pointed. Ivanovitch looked then grinned.

Bertrand said, "It's ancient Gaelic and means 'boldly go forward, regardless of the reservations of others'."

Ivanovitch looked to see if he was being humorous and realised that he was not. "You sausage, he's yanking your wiggly bit."

Bertrand looked puzzled as Ivanovitch said, "I suppose that's what it means, but expressed more succinctly."

Bertrand suddenly got the joke and laughed at his own gullibility, then admitted that it was a good name. Ivanovitch said it was in keeping with the *Star Trek* theme. "Boldly go where no man has gone before."

Soon it was time to leave and Ivanovitch said Peter would take them back to the hotel, then to the airport in the morning.

Sunday 21st December 2025

The return flight was much more pleasant than the previous one. The plane was half empty and the air conditioning was working. They had an eight and a half hour layover in Moscow, allowing time for sightseeing and last minute Christmas shopping. They took a taxi to Red Square for the obligatory photos in front of the Kremlin. Afterwards, Bertrand bought Matryoshka dolls for his daughters and an antique religious icon for his wife.

Moscow, whilst less glitzy than the decadent capitalist cities in the West, had its share of festive merriment. The market square had rows of stalls selling Christmas decorations, toys, jewellery, food and drink, and an outdoor skating rink.

As they wandered round, Bertrand talked enthusiastically and marvelled at the sights. He suddenly grew aware that Hiram was becoming quieter. "Hiram, have I upset you?"

Hiram shook his head.

"Sorry, buddy, but if we are friends and something is troubling you, I want to help." Bertrand could see Hiram's lip tremble and the moisture on his eyes. "Hey, what's wrong?"

Hiram wiped his tears. "It's all this," he said with a gesture.

"Moscow?"

"No, Christmas," said Hiram.

Bertrand looked round and saw laughing people and a Christmas tree with hundreds of lights and quickly realised.

Hiram said, "This will be my first Christmas without Sarah. I have always loved Christmas and everything about it, more so since sharing it with Sarah. Now I'm dreading it and don't know how I am going to get through it."

Bertrand clasped his forehead. "I am so sorry. I've been going on about having enough food and drink to feed a platoon and getting the biggest tree ever, and all the time you have been in agony. I am so sorry."

Sick of the constant sympathy, Hiram could no help but shout. "Stop apologising! It's not your fault. You are successful and deserve Christmas with your family. I am going to be alone, but that's not your problem."

The two men stared at each other for a moment before Bertrand asked, "What are you going to do?"

"I am trying not to think about it."

"You mustn't be on your own. You should go and stay with your family."

"Perhaps I will." Hiram knew this was untrue. He had every intention of hiding away until it was over. He sighed and decided to come clean. "I don't want to be happy over Christmas, enjoy myself, smile or pretend everything is OK, because it isn't. For years I longed to be able to give my Sarah the best ever Christmas, but couldn't afford it. Now I can, and it's too late. I don't deserve food, drink, fun and nice things to share. I am alive and she is not, and it is not fair. It's bloody not fair." He couldn't control himself and tears flowed. Bertrand's heart turned over and he too wept. They hugged each other for support.

Bertrand said, "It's nonsense to say you don't deserve happiness. Sarah's death was a tragedy, but would she want you to be miserable, guilt ridden and incapable of enjoying life? If she loved you, she would want you to be happy. Am I right?" Hiram nodded.

Bertrand continued, "There is going to be more Christmases, wedding anniversaries, birthdays and other memorable days which will remind you. Are you going to hide from them too?" Bertrand could see he was getting through. "Whilst it's important to grieve, it's equally important not to be so obsessed that you cannot move on or remember without falling to pieces. You have to allow yourself to touch those memories despite the pain, which will get easier in time."

Hiram could see the logic but still had doubts. "The last thing people want is the ghost of Banquo, pouring cold water on their festivities."

"We are not talking about 'people'. Your family care about you and will understand if you feel down. What is the worst that can happen? Do you think they are going to be annoyed if you are weepy over Christmas? What will upset them more is you being on your own and not allowing them to support you. Do you think they will be able to enjoy a morsel knowing that you are alone and underfed in a darkened room? Turn it around, how would you feel?"

That thought settled it for Hiram. "You're right. I have been too wrapped in my own misery to think of others."

"No one could blame you for feeling sorry for yourself after what you've been through. I hope I have been helpful."

"Enormously. I'll spend Christmas with family. In that case I had better do some shopping!" Hiram said to lighten the mood. "Will you help me?"

"It will be my pleasure, my friend."

After a busy afternoon, they returned to the airport. During the flight to Heathrow they did not talk much but drifted in and out of light sleep. Even when he was awake Hiram kept his eyes closed and thought about everything that had happened so far.

Finally, they arrived at Heathrow, collected their bags, said their goodbyes and arranged to meet again at M&S after the New Year.

Monday 12ᵗʰ January 2026

Hiram arrived at M&S on the tenth of January feeling content. Christmas had been as Bertrand predicted. He had decided to accept the invitation from his brother Martin. Apart from a couple of sad moods, the holiday was pleasant and his family had assured there was no reason for him to feel embarrassed.

In Bertrand's office, they exchanged New Year greetings and stories over coffee. Bertrand had the Adongiva folder open but, before they began to discuss work, the telephone rang. He answered and looked surprised. "I wasn't expecting him for a few days. Put him through." He put the phone on loudspeaker.

Ivanovitch's voice said. "Hello, Bertrand. Is Hiram with you?"

"Yes he is. Did you have a pleasant Christmas break?"

Ivanovitch replied that he had, but his voice sounded heavy. "Listen carefully. I have important news and limited time so don't interrupt. There has been a change of plan. Firstly, forgive my rudeness. I hope you both had a good Christmas and a Happy New Year. Just after the New Year I received some very bad news. Two days later I received worse news. Yesterday, I received the worst possible news." Bertrand and Hiram exchanged looks. Ivanovitch continued, "My great uncle, the former Commissar 2ⁿᵈ Fleet Marshal of all USSR Fleets, died on January first. His successor is Vladimir Constantine Voshputen and he is the worst man to have that office, He is a hard line zealot and cold-hearted swine with a reputation for vindictiveness. I doubt that he hates anyone more than me."

Bertrand clasped his head. "Oh my God, Ivanovitch. You must flee before it's too late."

"It's already too late. You haven't heard the third bit of news." Ivanovitch sounded sad. "My death warrant has been issued."

"Oh my God, Ivanovitch. You must escape!" gasped Bertrand.

"There is a situation in Russia today that is impossible to escape from. When Stalin wanted enemies to disappear he 'sent in the cleaners'. This idea has been resurrected and improved, to a level of supreme clinical efficiency. Nowadays, when 'The Sterilisers' are sent to collect enemies of the state they not only get rid of the person, they destroy every indication that he ever existed. When they 'sterilise' a place there are no witnesses. The person, their furniture, books, files, pets, family members and anyone who happens to be around at the time even if unconnected, are thrown into a truck. The contents of the truck are then tipped into boiling acid and literally disappear. Everybody knows what 'The Sterilisers' do, and this ensures absolute silence. They even go to the person's old schools, colleges, previous work places and other building where records are kept, and remove all references to the 'non-person'. Anyone wishing to live will not see or hear anything."

Bertrand struggled to control his disbelief. "You are too well-known to disappear. There are places around the world with your books on their shelves,"

Ivanovitch spoke softly, "It will be said that they were written under the name of the fictitious character called 'Ivanovitch Petrovsky'."

"There is video of you at conventions and conferences."

Ivanovitch said, "There is film of Santa Claus, Robin Hood, Count Dracula and E.T. although they never existed."

"I can't bear it!" exploded Bertrand.

"Bear what exactly?" asked Ivanovitch. "My being boiled alive in acid or that after today I will be a fictitious legend?"

"Both. I can't understand how you are so calm!"

"There is nothing to be done. Fleeing is not an option."

"You run a navy base, for God's sake. They may control the ports, but you could get away in a fast boat."

"How far do you think I would get?" asked Ivanovitch. "The temperature of the sea is fatal. They would detect and sink me before I left territorial water. I would rather die in this warm office with your excellent malt whisky. I was going to save it for a special occasion, but my last day alive is pretty special, don't you think? Besides, I have no intention of letting those reptiles boil me in acid, and have prepared a demonstration for them."

"What do you mean?" asked Bertrand.

"You mentioned that this is a naval base. It's not much; everything was hastily assembled, and old ships come here to die. Part of our job is to strip armaments before cannibalizing parts. In the Soviet Union, post-cold war, many things were done badly. Effort was made to show off to the world, but behind the scenes many activities are sloppy or haphazard because of lack of cash, expertise or interest. Some time ago, we stripped a battleship, stored the ammo in a bunker and, in due course, a convoy took most of it away. Typically, there were not enough trucks. They promised to send more for the ten shells left but never got round to it. Yesterday, after the call from a friend in the Kremlin telling me that 'The Sterilisers' were due today, I organised cash for everyone on the base and ordered them and their families out of the area for a month of leave. I spent the afternoon moving those shells and they are now standing around the base. Each has a billiard ball-sized nuclear warhead, which can vaporise the mid-section of an aircraft carrier. Imagine what they could do to this dump."

Bertrand and Hiram were stunned as they listened to their friend describe what was about to happen.

Ivanovitch continued, "When they arrive they will see the base is deserted. They will enter this room and see me sitting here with my glass of whisky. I will say I have been expecting them and that I bear no grudge as they are just doing their job. I will invite them to join me in a drink, but I have no intention of letting them taste this nectar. I have already had half the bottle and can say it is to die for. Once they each have a glass, I will rise to join them in a toast. Unfortunately, the chair I am sitting on is on a pressure switch. When my weight is lifted the switch will activate a transmitter, which will send a signal to the radio controlled mines taped to each of the ten shells. The base will light up and be visible from space. American satellites will report a nuclear explosion on a naval base near the Cola peninsula. Let's see the government hush that up."

"Ivanovitch, what have you done?" croaked Bertrand.

"Enough of that, it's nearly time and I'm afraid I have more bad news. Hiram, I had to order the 'Vashoya Calishka' back to another base twenty miles from here. If my men were caught, they would be spitefully arrested for selling a warship to the West. After a show trial, they would be executed and their families would suffer, and I cannot allow that. Bertrand I am sorry we will not meet again, our friendship meant a lot to me. Hiram, although we only met once, I am glad we met. I hope the rest of your life is as happy as possible. I'm sorry you cannot have the ship I promised, but you don't go empty handed. After I finished rigging the triggers yesterday, I designed your yacht. It was a pleasure to do something different from normal and I'm pleased with the result. I printed the drawings and asked one of my men to come and collect it. You will have it in a few days. I have signed and dated each page so that when I am dead they will be worth a fortune."

"I would never sell them," exclaimed Hiram. "They shall be a prized possession."

"Nice of you to say so, Hiram, but they'll be worth something so don't spill coffee on them. Do you remember that artist's impression of the ship that looks like the *Enterprise*? After I finished your yacht, just for fun, I started doodling on the computer using my very powerful maritime CAD programme. Visualizing what the deck plans might look like in such a ship, I put some designs together. I refined, fiddled and twiddled, tweaked and polished for over six hours. It was a rare treat for me to just explore my imagination and pointlessly play around. And you know? The designs are not bad. Of course, it's just fantasy. It would be about triple your budget to build a yacht like this. The designs are simply a fun memento – a gift from one trekkie to another. Very soon it will be over, but I don't want you to be sad. Raise a glass in memory of my eventful life, which I don't regret. Promise me to enjoy the rest of yours. Aha! I hear car doors slamming. I believe my visitors have arrived. They aren't being subtle. They think they've come for a harmless old man, not a Siberian tiger. I must go boys, see you in heaven. May your God smile on you."

Hiram and Bertrand heard a click then the dialling tone. Any second now the man they had been speaking to and the room they had sat in would evaporate. They remained motionless as they waited. There was no explosion, flash, rumble or commotion, just the ticking clock, like a heartbeat. Simultaneously, they checked their watches. It might have happened already. Bertrand was the first to breathe. He walked to the cabinet, took two glasses, reached for the Stolichnaya then changed his mind. Instead, he opened the lower doors and picked the Stolichnaya with the black and gold label. Hiram knew this bottle was expensive and pure – a fitting choice to commemorate the life of the Admiral.

Bertrand poured two large measures and returned to Hiram, who took a glass. "A toast to Admiral Ivanovitch Petrovsky, the greatest man

I have ever known. May his memory last forever, and he rest in peace."

"*Vashe zdorovie*, Admiral Petrovsky," Hiram replied and they emptied the glasses.

Neither Hiram nor Bertrand felt like working the day of Ivanovitch's heroic suicide. They agreed to meet in a week when the plans arrived. They spoke again, however the very next day, when Hiram telephoned to voice his anger and disgust at the pitiful television coverage of two news stories from Russia, which were reported as unrelated minor items. The first item concerned an accidental nuclear explosion which had taken place at a disused naval base in an uninhabited area of northern Russia. It was said that a small number of naval personnel had been killed while decommissioning obsolete weapons, but there was no danger to anyone else as the radiation had been blown seaward and quickly dissipated. The second story reported the sad death of retired naval officer and renowned maritime expert, Ivanovitch Petrovsky. The report stated that he died peacefully at home after a lengthy illness. Hiram was furious and Bertrand had to spend some time calming him down and persuading him that trying to convince the world that the news stories were lies, would only stir up a heap of trouble. Most people who go around talking of cover ups and conspiracies, are dismissed as cranks. When Hiram returned on the 19th of January, they talked briefly about the Russian stories. Talk about the nuclear accident had lingered in the news for three days, but Ivanovitch was never mentioned again.

Bertrand pointed to two large tubes. "I have taken the liberty of scanning them. I suggest you store them at your bank. Treat them as you would an original Monet or diamond necklace."

Hiram agreed and asked if Bertrand had a chance to examine them. Bertrand said that he was a damned good ship expert, but was bowled over by the designs Ivanovitch had created in a matter of hours. Ivanovitch may well have been using the most powerful design programme in the world but even so, there was no escaping the genius. There were designs for two ships; one based on the *Enterprise* sketch he had done during their meeting and another, more realistic option. Bertrand explained that the ideas they had discussed had been incorporated into a clever design with clean lines, simplicity and elegance, and everything you would wish to include on a private luxury yacht was fitted into an ingenious use of space. The cabins and other compartments gave the impression of spaciousness, extravagance and style, but the sizes, shapes and juxtaposition ensured there was no wasted space.

When Hiram asked about the *Enterprise* ship, Bertrand said it was even more splendid and awe-inspiring. He reminded Hiram that although they could spend days looking at it, they should remember it was pure fantasy and not going to be built. He said Ivanovitch's estimate had been right and that a figure between thirty-five and fifty million was accurate. He suggested they leave the designs until they had time to enjoy it and instead concentrate on the plans for the real Adongiva.

Bertrand turned to a large computer screen and pressed a remote control. A plan of ship's deck materialised. Bertrand pointed a fat pen at the screen and a dot appeared. "The ship would be 42.53 metres long, 9.33 metres on the beam and have a draft of only 1.89 metres allowing navigation up river. It would have a displacement of 225 tons, cruising speed of eighteen knots and top speed of twenty-two, which is quite nippy." He moved the dot and discussed other features, sometimes zooming in for a better look. When they had finished examining the first deck, another appeared and they talked about that one.

One by one they discussed all the decks, which contained everything Hiram had wished for. Ivanovitch had created a magnificent jigsaw and put it together perfectly. Ivanovitch had not just sent deck layouts. There were also technical drawings and pages of notes. It was a masterful, scholarly and comprehensive work.

Hiram was delighted and asked if Bertrand had worked out the cost. Bertrand produced a sheaf of papers and said the estimate was just less than seventeen and a half million. Hiram scanned the information with a widening grin. Bertrand said that over the next few days he would have meetings with his design and construction team leaders. He suggested that Hiram go off and relax and he would arrange another meeting in ten days time to sign contracts, after which construction would commence.

CHAPTER SIX

Sunday 25th January 2026

Sir Richard Pickles arrived at the Freeman Plaza Hotel just after nine, early for his ten o'clock meeting with Benjamin Wainwright. This gave him time to *reconnoitre*. He wanted a coffee table with two chairs, far enough from the other tables to talk discreetly without appearing secretive. It should be partially screened but not overtly hidden. His planning was meticulous. Once he found the ideal table, he instructed the waiter to bring coffee and biscuits the instant his guest arrived. He carefully positioned his folder and laptop to look as if they had been put down casually, but not carelessly. He always liked to operate with several available options that all led to the same inevitable outcome. Today, fast moving events had given him little choice and he was on edge, but he had to appear supremely calm and in control.

As Pickles waited, he ran over events of Friday's dinner. The timing had been fortuitous. Three days prior, he had overheard a bit of gossip at his golf club which he brushed off as being of no significance. At the dinner, however, by pure luck he heard a few seconds of a conversation which when added to that first piece of news suddenly made it extremely important. The timetable he had been secretly working to for a very long was about to be dramatically cut short and he had to act fast to avoid being left behind. Yesterday, he had compiled a list of men with several things in common – they could be trusted to keep quiet, they were very rich, able to produce twelve million pounds at short notice, and would trust him with it. Also, they needed to be free today. The first three on his list were not available. Number four, Benjamin Wainwright, had planned to be sailing today but agreed to cancel and meet for a chat.

Everyone knew Sir Richard Pickles as a highly respected entrepreneur with a reputation for making large sums of money even larger. When he requested a meeting you had to be mad, or bereft of funds, to turn him down.

At ten precisely Benjamin surfaced, spied Sir Richard and ambled over. As he sat down, the waiter produced coffee and biscuits. Sir Richard's glance said, 'Well done. You will get your tip'. Once the waiter left, they exchanged small talk to break the ice. As they talked, the two men weighed each other up. Sir Richard guessed that Benjamin knew perfectly well that the polite banter was false and that they were not really friends, simply business acquaintances. He also guessed that Benjamin although having his guard up would be curious to know what this was all about, and what was in it for him. Sir Richard said, "Tell me about UKSA?"

Benjamin was surprised. This was not on the list of possibilities in his mind. "UKSA, The United Kingdom Space Agency was set up nine years ago and was considered a controversial folly which would wither or be dropped in time. When the European Space Agency, NASA, Russia, India and Japan agreed to form the Earth Space Agency, our team decided their contribution should be a space-monitoring centre in the UK. Since then, UKSA has refused to fade away and speculators have been buying up everything they can get hold of in anticipation of the acquisition. Of course, we're still waiting for this great white elephant to materialise. The disruption to the economy because of this land rush has been getting worse and the government is coming under pressure to do something about it. If I remember correctly, there is some sort of deadline coming up in the autumn, but I can't remember what for exactly."

Sir Richard nodded his approval of this summary. "Where is the space-monitoring station to be built?"

Benjamin was surprised by the question. It was common knowledge that an area in Sunderland had been earmarked. Property prices were rocketing, causing great unhappiness among locals unable to find homes. The bill was rushed through Parliament and many concessions were required in order to secure an agreement between the parties, including agreement to compulsorily purchase at the full prevailing market price. The problem now facing the government is that anyone with land or property within the area before the purchase date is announced is guaranteed to multiply the value of their investment many times over.

After Benjamin replied, Sir Richard said quietly, "Wrong. Tell me about the alternative sites."

Benjamin took a few moments to dig out the memory. "North Scotland was dismissed because of inaccessibility and geology. Cumbria because of the proximity of nuclear waste sites. Cornwall was eliminated because of something that I can't recall. And that just left Sunderland. Everyone knows that."

"In that case, everyone is wrong. None were ruled out. When scientists, experts, the media and the public jumped on the bandwagon, the government kept very quiet. The hullabaloo died away and conclusions were reached. The government got away with perpetrating a trick of smoke and mirrors. They produced an extremely complex and lengthy publication, giving the impression that a decision had been made. It hadn't, and still hasn't."

Benjamin was totally stunned. "Are you sure?"

"I have meticulously checked every record available and I assure you, no decision has been made. To be fair, the document is extremely clever and designed to confuse the experts." Benjamin felt filleted.

Sir Richard continued, "I organised my own private research, commissioned geological surveys at enormous cost, and spoke to experts from every discipline. I have no doubt that Sunderland is not the site."

Benjamin almost slid off his seat. Eventually he managed to whisper, "Where?"

Sir Richard leaned forward. "For many years, I have been buying relentlessly and now have a portfolio of many thousands of properties of every conceivable type and size. It has consumed the bulk of my personal fortune, which as you know is considerable."

Benjamin wagged his finger. "You couldn't have. You are too well known and, with your reputation for making money, a sustained programme of buying everything in sight by the great Sir Richard Pickles in one specific area would have attracted attention and aroused curiosity. I would have read about it in the newspapers."

"Do you really think I would do it in my own name? I set up six separate companies to do the research, purchasing and property management. Believe me, I am buying up Cornwall on a industrial scale, but I am doing it under the radar so as not to arouse curiosity, as you put it."

Benjamin was bouncing with excitement. "Cornwall!" he exploded.

Sir Richard looked round to see if anyone had reacted to this noise. There were a few people scattered around but no one seemed to pay any attention. "Have another cup of coffee," said Sir Richard to calm his excitable companion.

"So where do I fit in to this grand scheme?" said Benjamin quietly.

"There is a large tract of land I have been reeling in for a while. It's big with hills, forest, farms, two rivers and a stretch of coast – and is owned by The Duke of Corian." He paused to see if this meant anything. It did not. "The Duke is an odious man with the charm of a cornered snake. He wants to sell but keeps upping his price. It's worth seventeen million pounds and he agreed to sell but at the last moment raised the price by two million. After preparing the contract, he raised again to twenty. I told him to go to hell, but had no intention of giving up. He promised that if I agreed to this latest price he would not raise again. I have twenty million ready for the deal and am seeing him tomorrow morning."

"So why do you need me?" asked Benjamin.

"I would rather dip my penis in a tank of piranhas than trust that man not to cheat again," said Sir Richard. Benjamin winced at the image. "I am going to offer him twenty million, which just about cleans me out as far as spare cash is concerned. I need a little extra in my pocket, just in case. If he tries it on, I shall offer him a final take it or leave it deal. I intend to own that land by tomorrow morning."

"What do I get out of this?" asked Benjamin.

"If you loan me twelve mill' right now, I guarantee to double it within two days."

Benjamin nodded at this attractive proposal, and then frowned. "Wait a minute, if the government is going to announce in the autumn, why the rush?"

"The timetable has suddenly changed. Most people move in limited orbits. I have eyes and ears in many orbits, to give me an edge. Unrelated information has been bubbling to the surface recently. I knew the government was up to something, but I couldn't figure what."

"When is the government not up to something?" Benjamin smiled.

"On Friday I hosted a dinner, which I routinely do to fish for snippets, sow seeds, or just keep communications open. There was the usual assortment of government ministers, civil servants, city types, and celebs." Sir Richard explained the chance timing of the dinner and how, by pure luck, he happened to overhear a fleeting comment by Patrick Southwood, the Permanent Deputy Under Secretary in the Cabinet Office. "His words exploded in my ear like a bomb. When added to other facts I had acquired, I saw jig saw pieces fall into place. The government is attempting to catch everybody on the hop by announcing the UKSA decision on Monday."

"I see," said Benjamin. "So by tomorrow afternoon, it will be too late for you to do any more planning or buying because word will be out and property in Cornwall be among the most expensive in Europe."

"Quite," said Sir Richard, not too happy about the look on Benjamin's face.

"It's not like you to get yourself hemmed in like this, old *friend*." Benjamin emphasised the word 'friend' to let Sir Richard know that he knew the word had been used earlier simply to ease the path of this business transaction. "From what you have told me, I suspect you don't really need to rush to Cornwall because you already have more than a sufficient amount of property to make a gigantic killing. You simply don't like people to get the better off you. Old Duke of Hazard, or whatever he is called, tried to stitch you up and you are determined to buy his land so that by tomorrow afternoon he will realise the master has bested him. Vanity, Richard, vanity." He wagged his finger. "I'll tell you what I will do. I will lend you the twelve million today, for a thirty-six million profit."

Sir Richard's face fell. "That is monstrous. To double your money is an extremely good return, to triple is piracy."

"Not triple it, Sir Richard. I said thirty-six million *profit*. That makes quadruple return of the original stake. Take it or leave it."

Sir Richard looked pale. He was about to say, 'You are as bad as him'.

Benjamin carried on. "We both know that after you have paid Snake Features and paid me, you will still make a huge mint."

Sir Richard knew this was true and he did not have the time to argue. They shook on it. "We'll use GAFDST," said Sir Richard, opening his computer. Benjamin was delighted by this news because it ensured that his money was completely safe.

GAFDST, or Guaranteed Assets Frozen for Delayed Secure Transfer, was the most secure way of transferring money in the world. There were other ways but this was the Rolls Royce of systems. More secure than Fort Knox, 100 percent guaranteed safety. A distinctive feature of GAFDST, pronounced 'gaff dust', is that the system's computer is required to 'peek' into the account to check availability and freeze the amount required so that it can guarantee payment at the date and time agreed. Without this, the deal cannot take place. Safeguards ensure no bank security details are compromised. As the wealthiest people on the planet, including heads of state and bank presidents, use this system regularly for moving billions, absolute trust has to be beyond doubt.

For several minutes, Sir Richard and Benjamin took turns typing in their relevant information. Finally, Sir Richard said, "We have established that sufficient funds were available and now need to be frozen until the moment of transfer." More buttons were pressed and he said, "OK. It's done. The contract is ready." He spun the computer.

Two windows were open. The window on the left said, 'To agree the transfer of twelve million pounds from the bank account, stated in the other window, to the bank account of Sir Richard Pickles, on Sunday 24th January 2021 at 11.15am. Please press the yes button now.' Benjamin had pins and needles in his left hand and flexed his fingers and thumb a few times. He pressed the 'yes' button and another window opened on the left. 'WARNING. By answering the security question in the right window you are agreeing to a legally binding and unbreakable contract. If you are sure you understand the consequences, answer the question now.' The pain in his hand had moved to the upper arm and was really uncomfortable. He rubbed but it didn't help.

Sir Richard waited expectantly for Benjamin to tap the final buttons to complete the deal. Benjamin looked at him with a strange expression, as if seeing him for the first time. He groaned in pain and tried to stand but just succeeded in toppling backwards in his chair. Sir Richard stood up and looked at the other man who was by now gripping his chest. People gathered round and Sir Richard instinctively turned the computer so that they could not see the screen. Someone said to call for an ambulance, but Sir Richard was in shock. *What about the deal?* he thought.

After what seemed like just minutes, two paramedics rushed in and started treating Benjamin. He was given an injection and an electric shock with portable paddles. An oxygen mask was placed over his nose and mouth and he was placed on a stretcher. Sir Richard alternated his stare between the prone figure and the waiting computer screen, knowing the message would not wait for long. As the green boiler suits rushed away, the computer was warning that the deal was about to abort. Now Benjamin Wainwright was gone, and so was the deal.

The paramedics had asked if he wanted to go in the ambulance, but he declined. He asked which hospital Benjamin would be taken to so that he could ring the man's family. He said he would come later but, as he spoke, he knew it was unlikely. It was 11.50am and he needed twelve million pounds by tomorrow. He rang Benjamin's home, explained what had happened and where he had gone. He turned to his computer, which mocked him by asking if he wanted to start another transaction. He typed 'no', logged out and went through more names in his head. Annoyed that his deal had disappeared, Sir Richard found it hard to concentrate. He knew the people he had thought of were not the sort to sit and wait for a call. Locating and meeting was going to be difficult, even by his standards.

The waiter gathered the cups. "I hope your friend is alright." he said and minced to the bar where a second waiter was standing. Sir Richard did not have a problem with gays, but the high camp fluttering of wrists and wiggling of hips was distracting and Sir Richard could not help but eavesdrop on their conversation. His waiter spoke of the recent drama, flicking sympathetic eyelashes at Sir Richard.

The second waiter changed the subject and asked if the other remembered the news about the recent twenty-six million pound lottery winner. He said the man was upstairs meeting his financial adviser and he bragged about serving them tea and biscuits.

Sir Richard's ears became radar dishes as the waiters continued. His brain went into overdrive. He gathered his belongings and wandered over. "I couldn't help overhear you mention that the recent lottery winner is here." They eyed him suspiciously. He wore his most disarming smile. "By amazing coincidence, I am dining with him this evening. I didn't realise he was staying here. I'd like to pop up and ask if he wants a lift. There is no point in us taking two cars, is there?"

"I suppose not," said the second waiter.

"What room is he in?" The suspicion returned. Sir Richard smiled harder and put hand on shoulder, much to the chagrin of the first waiter. "I promise I won't let on." He winked.

The waiter was a sucker for an expensively dressed, handsome man with a hand on his shoulder and the room number popped out. "That's great," said Sir Richard, appearing to turn. He looked back and said, "How stupid. I forgot his name." The suspicion was back. Sir Richard's smile was hard enough to break his jaw.

The waiter said, "Mr. Montgomery."

"I know that, I meant his first name."

The waiter relaxed and said, "Hiram."

"Of course, I remember now. You have been most kind." Sir Richard sped away with a grin. He was still the Master of pulling rabbits from hats.

Hiram had just finished studying Roger's figures. He was about to suggest breaking for lunch when there was a knock. He opened the door to a familiar face from the television. Not expecting a celebrity at the door, it took him a moment to martial his thoughts. Sir Richard extended his hand. Roger Campbell was equally surprised when he saw the face. Handshakes were exchanged and introductions made.

Sir Richard spoke to Roger and said, "I know Taylor, White, Campbell and Associates by reputation. Your father would be proud of you. He was a good man and I was sorry to hear of his death. I shall include your firm in our list of accountants in future." Roger thanked him and they sat. Sir Richard declined coffee and offered congratulations to Hiram on his lottery win. He then explained that he had come to do business with an associate who had suddenly taken ill.

He decided that if he was going to gain the trust and cooperation of this stranger he had better be completely open. He spared no detail as he explained about UKSA, the space monitoring station, the land speculation in Sunderland, his investigations and campaign to buy as much of Cornwall as possible in preparation for the announcement. He told them about the Duke of Corian, and the dinner party. He concluded by asking if he could 'borrow' twelve million for a few days, with a guaranteed profit of thirty-six. As he had already agreed this with Benjamin Wainright, he thought there was no point in haggling over a few pounds when time was pressing. When Sir Richard finished Hiram and Roger were speechless. Hiram was still taking in the mass of detail and Roger had never heard such an offer before.

Roger recovered first. "You're offering thirty-six million pounds return for a few days investment of twelve?"

"That's right," said Sir Richard with a breezy smile.

Hiram turned to Roger and spoke as if they were alone. "Normally, if a stranger asked to borrow a huge chunk of what I have, saying he could triple it overnight, I would assume he was a crook. I have always understood that if an investment sounds too good to be true, it usually is. Tell me, Roger, would you trust him?" Sir Richard smiled broadly, and Roger looked embarrassed.

Sir Richard said, "Go ahead, Roger. Answer him truthfully. You are his financial adviser. Advise him."

Roger organised his thoughts. "Sir Richard Pickles is internationally known as a shrewd, talented entrepreneur who turns companies round and makes fortunes. People watch him if they think he is on to something. There are people who don't mind destroying others for profit, but Sir Richard isn't one of them. Investments sounding too good to be true usually are, and opportunities to make lots of money fast hardly ever happen, but they do occasionally. If anybody could spot the difference it would be Sir Richard Pickles."

Hiram said, "Well, that's an endorsement! I have never in my life had as much money as I do now, and I know how I want to use it in my time left. If I were going to live a long time it would make sense to be prudent. As it happens, in a few years it won't make much difference either way. You, Sir Richard, said that this is an unrepeatable once in a lifetime opportunity. You, Roger, said you would trust this man as much as anyone. What have I got to lose? We are all going to die sooner or later, and it's only money. What the hell, let's do it."

Sir Richard looked horrified. "What do you mean *in a few years?*"

Hiram told him about his medical condition. Sir Richard was stunned but did not let that distract him too much from the business at hand. He explained that GAFDST would be used for the payments, and described what it was and how it worked.

"In other words," said Hiram, turning to Roger for clarification, "even if the business with the space thingy falls through and everybody else gets ruined, GAFDST guarantees to pay me what I was promised by recovering the loss from Sir Richard? So I can't lose?" The other two men nodded.

Sir Richard brought up the programme on his computer, but before he began to type a thought ran round Hiram's head. "Wait." Sir Richard stopped. Hiram continued, "You said this was once in a lifetime opportunity to be exploited fully, and that to do otherwise would be to squander good fortune." Sir Richard could not deny this. "You, Sir Richard, are pushing for maximum benefit from this venture. You did not have to come here today. Even without the Duke of thingy you will still be considerably richer than when you started. This extra deal is really icing on your cake, and I guess you already have lots of icing on all your other cakes. This is icing on top of the icing on the biggest cake in the history of cakes. I am not criticising, judging or begrudging your prize. You have earned the right to it by being clever, far-sighted, connected and industrious. Nevertheless you did come here, knock on my door and present me with this deal. Am I not right to follow your example and get the maximum benefit? I have always been hard up but I now have millions by chance and about four years to live. I can fulfil a dream to own my own yacht, but not for long. I visited Russia and met with the greatest naval architect in history who gave me plans for two yachts. One I could afford and the other just an expensive pipe dream. You, Sir Richard, can allow me a chance at that pipe dream. I shall follow your brilliant example and ask not for thirty-six million profit but forty-eight. I will never get another chance and have to take it. Sorry, but there it is."

"You were doing very well until you apologised!" Sir Richard exclaimed. "Carpe Diem does not mean seize the day if others don't mind. It means seize the bloody day. If you want my money you shouldn't ask, you tell me!"

"OK, I am telling you. I want forty-eight million," said Hiram. Roger looked in amazement at this surreal conversation. Sir Richard was coaching Hiram on how to get more money out of him.

Sir Richard continued, "I did not get where I am by asking permission to make lots of money. In your shoes, I would have done the same thing. Forty-eight is OK. You should always haggle."

"I am not good at haggling," said Hiram.

"You are doing fine. You got forty-eight million, what more do you want?"

"Forty-nine," said Hiram. Sir Richard stopped. "It's not for me. I am thinking of him." He gestured at Roger. "I can't quadruple my money while he gets nothing. He deserves something, a broker's fee."

Sir Richard looked at them both. "I daresay, he is not cheap, but so be it. You're a nice man, Hiram. Forty-nine million pounds it is." Roger's bottom jaw fell open. Sir Richard spun the computer and told Hiram what to do.

As Hiram typed, Roger said, "I don't know what to say."

"Well you could say *thanks*," said Sir Richard. "He just got you a one million pounds broker's fee." Roger thanked Hiram profusely.

Hiram turned the computer back. "It has now frozen twelve million pounds in my account, ready for the transfer.

Sir Richard typed again. "Final bit. Answer the question from your bank and it will give a transaction release code to GAFDST."

Hiram typed again. "It says transaction contract completed."

Sir Richard looked ecstatic. "At 7am tomorrow, twelve million pounds will move from your account to mine. By lunchtime, I will have concluded my business and in the afternoon the Prime Minister will stun the nation. Thousands who bought property in Sunderland will scream in pain. I feel sorry for them but there is nothing I can do. By Wednesday or Thursday, the government will issue compulsory purchase orders for land and property in Cornwall. Everyone with money to spare will fight to buy anything in the South West corner of Britain in a 'name your price' situation. At precisely 4.30pm on Friday, a sum of sixty-one million pounds, your original stake plus forty-eight, will transfer from my account to yours."

"You will have the money that soon?" asked Roger.

"No, but the GAFDST guarantee ensures that Hiram gets paid regardless. I have been a member for years and my credit rating is solid. They will give me time to collect the money from HMG before sending the bailiffs."

"What happens if it goes wrong?" asked Roger.

"I will be transformed from a very rich man to very poor one. GAFDST will pay my all investors in full, and I will be ruined. Every stick of my considerable properties around the world, my companies and assets will be seized and sold. I may go to prison and, when I am released, I shall simply start again. It's only money after all." He smiled cheerily. "I am staking everything on not being wrong." He slid a memory stick into the computer, typed briefly then handed it to Hiram. "This is a copy of the contract." As he closed his computer and gathered his papers Hiram asked if he would like to join them for lunch. He said he would love to but right now he had to fly to Cornwall and be with The Duke first thing in the morning. "Watch the Parliamentary Channel tomorrow afternoon. It will be interesting."

CHAPTER SEVEN

Monday 26ᵗʰ January 2026

Bertrand had just ended a phone conversation with Mike O'Donoghue, Chief Engineering Projects Manager, and was not happy. After last Monday's meeting with Hiram, he had written an action list and called his CEPM to discuss key personnel. Although a seventeen and a half million pound yacht was not the biggest or most prestigious project, he was determined to make it as perfect as possible and wanted his best people on it. Two were on another project due to finish any day and a third was on compassionate leave but back the following week. Bertrand had already started on budget and material lists. This morning, Mike told him the other project had overrun its deadline but was sure they would be finished by Thursday at the latest. The man on compassionate leave had returned and a meeting was arranged to put him in the picture.

Bertrand poured himself a coffee and sat in an armchair, savouring the peace and quiet before the day's activity. As he listened to the ticking clock, he thought again about the phone call from Oliver Russell who called him on Saturday 'just for a chat'. Oliver never rang 'for a chat'. He was articulate and could talk for England, but only rang when he had something to say. Oliver had spoken of a bizarre dream he had two nights before. It had been so real he could not get it out of his mind and felt he had to tell Bertrand about it. He said there were seven large cogwheels lying in a row on a vast open area, all connected and turning slowly. Marcella Desvaldo, the daughter of the Spanish Minister of the Interior, stood on the edge of the smallest wheel, about twenty feet wide. Oliver was standing on the next wheel, thirty feet in diameter.

The next wheel was the same size as the first one and Hiram

Montgomery stood on its edge. Next was a very big, slow wheel with Bertrand on it. Adjacent to Bertrand was a wheel with a familiar face, although Oliver was sure they had never met. He was obviously rich because of his expensive suit and the wads of cash he periodically counted. Next to him was a perspiring, overweight man who talked incessantly to no one in particular from behind thick files. The last wheel bore two men, one in a laboratory coat and the other in silver firefighter uniform.

The interlocking wheels turned in alternate directions and, because of the different sizes, at different speeds. On one side, a huge crowd silently stood After many turns, the wheels turned Oliver and Marcella so that they could touch. She handed him a stick like a conductor's baton. The audience murmured approval. As his wheel moved, Oliver realised that he would be able to hand the stick to Hiram and saw it had become a thick wooden truncheon, pointed at one end like a crude carving of a boat. Hiram took it and polite applause issued from the audience. Hiram's wheel turned and carried him to where Bertrand reached out. Hiram handed him the boat, which was now about two feet long and brightly painted like a radio controlled model. The audience murmured approval and clapped enthusiastically. Bertrand slowly turned on his large wheel and, as the rich man sailed across his front, he had to use both hands to hand over the boat that was now three feet long and no longer a toy. It had all the detail you would expect from a replica yacht in a museum. The audience almost got to their feet as they clapped louder than before. Now all eyes were on the rich man as his great wheel slowly moved him to the far side.

Oliver thought the overweight man behind with the files must be a politician. He wore an old-fashioned three-piece pinstripe suit and never stopped talking but seemed oblivious to everyone. The rich man pushed the replica boat towards the politician. It was now five feet long and on a large wheeled trolley. The ungainly politician grabbed the bow and pulled it. By the time he had manoeuvred the trolley and parked it by his side he was sweating profusely. Everyone cheered wildly. The politician stood proudly by his prize, mopped his brow and managed to fit in a few more speeches by the time he reached the far side. The man in the white coat got ready at the edge of the wheel. The politician pushed the trolley, which was massive and now supported a magnificent replica of a beautiful yacht over fifteen feet long. It took all his energy to haul the trolley across his front and shove it on to the other wheel. The man in the white coat grabbed the front, pulled it past him, and wheeled it in a tight circle to his right side, where the silver suited man waited. The cheering reminded Oliver of the spectators at the cup final.

As this last wheel turned slowly, the silver suit sprayed the boat with something and performed actions no one understood. He repeated his movements as the wheel carried its occupants inexorably into a dense fog. The wheels continued turning, the participants strained to see, and the audience sat in silence. Suddenly, a fanfare made Oliver jump. Out from the mist rolled the white bow of a large, sleek and streamlined ship. The audience leapt to their feet and cheered ecstatically. A brass band marched and a fly past roared overhead in a heady carnival atmosphere.

When Oliver had finished describing the dream, Bertrand could tell from his voice he was emotional. "I wish you could have seen it," said Oliver in hushed tones.

Bertrand could not keep his amusement to himself. "I was there, apparently."

"I know it was only a dream but it was so realistic, I would swear it actually happened."

"I've had dreams like that, What do you think it meant?" Bertrand was sure he knew the answer from previous conversations with Oliver, and that the cogwheels represented great wheels of fate, but he felt he should he let Oliver explain.

Oliver said what Bertrand expected, and more. He said the players were on courses pre-set before birth to fulfil their destiny. He admitted that he was puzzled by some of the characters in his dream. He understood dreams to be graphic illustrations of the subconscious mind rationalising waking hour experiences but if this were true, why would he dream of people he had never met? He had no idea who the rich man, the politician, the laboratory technician or the firefighter were.

"Perhaps he had met them but could not remember," Bertrand suggested.

"Maybe, but unlikely. I think the dream was trying to tell me that the Adongiva is more important than the individuals." He felt that there was something special about this ship and it had to be built without delay, whatever the cost.

Bertrand thought this was absurd, but simply said, "In what way?" Oliver said, "I'm not sure. All I knew is that it's important."

Bertrand suspected Oliver felt guilty about passing the ship to him and wanted it to be built quickly because Hiram was dying. He knew Hiram and Oliver had made a personal connection, possibly because of their shared pain of recent bereavement. Bertrand was also determined to get the ship built to the highest standard in the shortest time. This was because of his debt to Oliver, because it was in keeping with the high company values, and because he too had taken Hiram to his heart and wanted to fulfil his dream before it was too late. Despite this, he felt it important to keep a grip on reality and not get carried away. He said, "Let's be honest Oliver, we know this ship is important to Hiram, and why. However, in the great scheme of things a vessel like this would not normally be regarded as unusually important. My company has built grander, more expensive, and more sophisticated ships in the past and will do so in the future. If this order had never happened we would not be worse off and, regardless of the Adongiva, the world will continue."

"You are wrong," said Oliver. "I can't explain, but I can tell you that this is bigger than all of us – a world changing event."

Bertrand laughed loudly. "Oh for heaven's sake, Oliver, that is ridiculous. You are too involved. Forget it and move on. I am looking after this now and I will ensure Hiram gets his yacht to enjoy for as long as he can." Bertrand told Oliver about Russia and the plans by Ivanovitch Petrovsky.

At the end of the conversation Oliver said, "Mark my words, Bertrand, you will remember this conversation."

Bertrand had replayed those final words in his mind over and over since Saturday. After finishing his coffee, he stood up from the armchair and walked back to his desk. He was just deciding which of several people to speak to when the phone rang. It was Hiram. He asked how everything was going. Bertrand always told his clients the truth and there was no point denying they were slightly behind schedule. He explained about his team leaders not being available but that they would be getting on track any day. Hiram said he was glad of this and asked for a temporary stop for twenty-four hours.

This was not what Bertrand was expecting. "Why?" Hiram said he might be changing his mind and instead going for the bigger, Star Ship

Enterprise version.

Bertrand was stunned. "I thought we agreed you couldn't afford it."

"I think I might be able to in a very short time," said Hiram.

Bertrand was flabbergasted. "Don't tell me you have won the lottery again."

"No," said Hiram. "However, I have had an investment opportunity which has literally fallen into my lap."

Bertrand sensed danger. "What do you mean?"

"I met someone at the weekend who presented me with a unique opportunity to increase my money dramatically."

Bertrand closed his eyes. "Hiram what have you done? Who is this man? How much have you invested?"

"It's confidential but, suffice it to say, I am about to become considerably richer."

"You nincompoop!" exploded Bertrand, not his usual manner with clients. "You have probably been conned and lost your money. I can't believe after all the work so far, you have just thrown it away. Have you any left?"

"Steady," said Hiram. "It is all above board. My financial adviser runs a most respected company and the man in question has the highest reputation. I am not completely stupid. I have fourteen million left but, by Friday, I should receive four times my investment guaranteed by GAFDST."

Bertrand was surprised to learn that GAFDST was involved. M&S had used it many times. "I'm sorry, I should not have spoken like that," said Bertrand, "but increasing your money like that is not normally feasible or realistic. Are you sure it's legal? It's not gun running, or smuggling drugs or illegal immigrants, is it?"

Hiram laughed and said he was sworn to secrecy until the balloon went up, but suggested that Bertrand watch the news this afternoon, especially the parliamentary channel. "The Prime Minister is about to rock the nation with an announcement that will change the lives of thousands."

With Oliver's dream already in mind, Hiram's words struck Bertrand like lightning. The Prime Minister! Hiram was now involved in something political after just dealing with someone with lots of cash. "Are you still there?" asked Hiram.

Bertrand breathed hard. "What is the Prime Minister going to say?"

"I promised not to say, just watch it."

Bertrand said he would and that they would talk later. As soon as he hung up he called Oliver. "Your dream has grown legs."

Bertrand found it hard to concentrate on work that morning because of the questions spinning in his head. *What was going on in Parliament? How was Hiram involved? Who was the mystery man? How did Hiram know the Prime Minister? How did mystery man and Hiram meet? How long has this been going on? How do you quadruple an investment in a few days, legally? How did Oliver know? How can you dream about something before it happens? What if it is a big mistake? What if the man who spoke to Hiram was a con man and there is no announcement? What was he going to say when Hiram comes back and says forget about either ship because he is poor again?*

Just after 1pm, Mike O'Donoghue arrived at Bertrand's door with Andre Keelan, Senior Management Technician from Information Technology, Electronics and Electricals Division. They sat round the table and drank coffee. Mike O'Donoghue looked at the television murmuring in the corner and the green benches steadily filling with MPs. "I didn't know you were a fan of those elephants' bottoms in the cradle of democracy?" he said. Bertrand returned the smile and said that there was something he wanted to keep an eye on.

"I can't be bothered with them," said Andre. There were two blue cardboard folders on the table. He stared as if willing them to spring open and reveal their secrets.

Bertrand checked what Mike had told Andre and filled in the rest, including the Russia trip and the plans by Ivanovitch Petrovsky. Bertrand's eye was drawn to the television and he picked up the remote. "Sorry, gentlemen, but I must hear this." He increased the volume as the House of Commons Speaker called on the Secretary of State for Trade and Industry, who was sitting next to the Prime Minister. Bertrand did not consider himself cruel but he had no charitable words for the PM. Many words came to mind but they were all uncomplimentary. *Slimy, smarmy, pompous, arrogant, self indulgent, indifferent, deceitful, untrustworthy and odious* were among the politer ones.

However, the Prime Minister did have character and personality, albeit unpleasant, which is more than one could say about the Secretary of State for Trade and Industry who was devoid of charisma. His bulk, constrained in pinstripe suit, and the round spectacles on his red face made him look bloated. He had fat, slug-like lips below a knob of a nose. *This is Oliver's politician*, Bertrand thought.

He and the other men strained to understand the monotone bumblebee drone. "The Honourable Members will recall those occasions I have been asked to clarify previous legislation which, although passed by this house, is in places badly drafted and therefore ambiguous or confusing." Members could not recall those occasions because what had just been said was a lie. The mumbling continued, "I, therefore, bring to this house a statement of clarification to rectify the situation and assist the Honourable Gentlemen. The first bill which I hope to clarify is the 'Transportation of Animal Carcasses bill of 2003'. Honourable Members will recall that in Clause 295 of the bill, paragraph 17, sub-section 12, it states…"

Bertrand, Mike and Andre were all intelligent and well-educated but what followed left them open-mouthed. It was convoluted gobbledegook and they did not understand any of it. They looked at each other in disbelief as the sweating man lumbered on for several minutes without saying anything comprehensible.

He continued, "I am sure most Honourable Members would agree that was a trifle difficult to understand." This produced ritual cross bench guffaws.

The Secretary of State lurched forward once more. "My department has produced clarification of this sub-section which states…" What he said next, although understandable, was as dull as dishwater, explaining the specifications around transporting animal carcasses.

"Why are we watching this?" asked Andre. Mike looked equally puzzled.

Bertrand said, "I suspect that this devious government has padded the statement with drivel to lull the Members to sleep then slip the important stuff in when they are off guard." Bertrand hoped this was not just wishful thinking and kept fingers crossed. He was praying that there was something more important to come and that Hiram had not been conned into parting with twelve million pounds because of animal carcasses.

His prayers seemed to be answered. The government had trawled previous bills to find verbiage and then sandwiched the business of the day between parliamentary junk. This allowed them to fend off enquiries from curious backbenchers by saying it was a tidying up exercise. MPs were used to devious tactics and not easily fooled, so the chamber was busier than normal for a Monday afternoon.

Mr. Monotone rumbled again. "The next item for the attention of this house is Clause 297 of the UKSA Space Monitoring Station Enablement Bill 2004, paragraph 65, sub-section three. This Clause states that after due consultation and discussion, and taking into consideration all pertinent information, the Department would, without further recourse to this house, make a decision on which of the four territories, defined in appendix 17 of the Bill, are to be used for the construction and location of the Space Monitoring Station and associated accommodation village, storage and transport facilities. It is my duty to inform the house that such decision has now been made and that I have much pleasure in informing the Honourable Members that the territory to be used for the said space monitoring station and associated accommodation village, storage and transport facilities is outlined in proposal number four in the list of four proposals detailed in the said appendix, which the Honourable Gentlemen will recall is headed 'Cornwall'. An instruction has today been issued by my office to the Crown Agents for the issue of the appropriate warrants, enabling compulsory purchase of all necessary land and property for the above mentioned facility, in accordance with clause 304, paragraphs 21 and 22 of the Bill."

There was absolute silence in House of commons, as well as in the room where Bertrand, Mike and Andre stared in shock. Mike whispered, "What did he just say?"

Andre croaked, "They can't do that. How can they announce a new decision about something decided years ago? It was decided years ago, wasn't it?"

"I thought so," said Bertrand, still unable to believe what he had heard.

Andre shook visibly, turned green, covered his mouth and rushed for the toilet.

Mike and Bertrand exchanged glances and Mike said, "Methinks he has overstretched himself and made a terrible mistake."

Bertrand nodded. "Did you invest?"

"Thought about it, very glad I didn't." They heard Andre retch but this was drowned out by uproar on the television. Bertrand had seen MPs shouting before but never like this. Nearly everyone was screaming and waving fists. The cabinet ministers were motionless with shock and betrayal by their leader who, unmoved by the mayhem, looked smug.

The Speaker stood. "Order, order," but was ignored. He persevered until he was heard to say that if the Honourable Gentlemen could not control themselves he would suspend the House for an hour to allow tempers to cool. Gradually, the commotion subsided and MPs started to sit, but two Members stood nose to nose and bawled insults. It was playground bluster but puffed chests made contact and one staggered. MPs rushed forward.

Mike grinned. "Go on my son, hit him."

The altercation was over but it was enough for the Speaker. "I suspend the activity of the House for one hour to allow the Honourable Gentlemen to recover their composure." With that, he left the chamber. MPs ambled aimlessly, looking more like lost sheep than the legislators of the nation.

As Bertrand switched off the television, Andre emerged. "Feeling better?" Andre nodded and apologised. They resumed their seats and Bertrand asked if Andre had lost much.

"We put the bulk of our savings into a large property in Sunderland. We paid more than it's worth but everything there is inflated. Like everyone else, we assumed the government would buy it and we would make a profit. I could swear that a decision had been made years ago."

The other two nodded in agreement. "Gentlemen, we have just seen the greatest 'hunt the lady' trick in the world," said Mike.

"In heavens name, why? What could the government gain from wrecking peoples' lives?" groaned Andre.

Mike shrugged. "Does anyone understand why the government does things? Perhaps it is a botched attempt to cover incompetence? Perhaps it was to divert property speculators so that they could get the land cheaper? Perhaps they are just wicked cretins who like screwing people."

"This isn't getting us anywhere. You got off light, Andre." said Bertrand.

"How the hell do you figure that?"

Bertrand said, "You lost your life savings, which is tough, and right now you are thinking that despite years of hard work your retirement plans are on the floor. However, you still have years of lucrative work, your home, your wife and family, health and time to rebuild a nest egg. Other people out there are facing complete meltdown and their lives are wrecked irrecoverably. Does that apply to you? Or is your situation survivable?"

"When you put it like that, you're right. It's only money after all." Suddenly, his face fell. "My brother-in-law is one of those you mentioned. He owns a transport company and they mortgaged everything to buy a derelict quarry, which is basically a waterlogged hole, in the middle of the supposed Space Monitoring Station. It was potentially worth a fortune but after today, they're going to be penniless, homeless and jobless."

Mike shook his head. "They're not alone. Thousands are affected and, by this evening, property values will have dropped through the floor in one area and shot through the roof in another."

Andre looked accusingly at Bertrand. "Did you know about this?"

Bertrand shook his head. "When I asked you to this meeting to discuss a new ship, I had no idea. This morning I got a call from the client asking to put the plan on hold for twenty-four hours. He said watch the television because a bombshell was about to drop, but he gave no details."

"How did he know? Judging from the faces of cabinet ministers, they didn't know."

"All I know is that he met someone yesterday who offered him the investment opportunity of a lifetime, and he took it."

"So what happens now?" asked Mike.

"We wait for the client to ring back. I think we're going to shelve this plan and start work on this one," Bertrand said as he took the bottom folder and lay it above the other.

"That suits me," said Andre. "I've got to go home and tell my wife the news."

Mike looked aghast. "You mean she doesn't know that you've invested your savings in a property worth ten pence?"

"Of course she does." Andre smiled grimly. "It was her idea. I want to make sure she doesn't blame herself." The other two nodded as he headed for the door.

"I'll ring you as soon as I hear from Hiram." Betrand said as the telephone rang. "That may be him now." The other two waited as Bertrand picked up. It was Oliver. Bertrand shook his head indicating it was not the fortune-telling millionaire and Mike and Andre departed down the corridor.

CHAPTER EIGHT

Oliver sounded as shocked as everyone else and said he had been convinced it had been decided ages ago. He had not invested but knew people who had. Bertrand and Oliver talked about the scenes in Parliament then Oliver talked about his dream. He confirmed Bertrand's thought that the politician in his dream had been the Secretary of State for Trade and Industry, a person mostly regarded as a background non-entity. He still did not know who the rich man was. Bertrand was unsettled that Oliver's dream featured a man whom he had barely been aware of and others yet to be discovered. Oliver was more convinced than ever that his dream was prophetic and important, but Bertrand refused to buy into that.

Tuesday 27th January 2026

Hiram rang Bertrand to ask if he had seen it. You would have to be a mountaintop hermit to not be aware that the nation had been shaken. Throughout the evening, the television had been full of news, commentary and discussion.

There were prophecies of hospitals being inundated by suicide attempts. Politicians, finance experts and scientists howled for the head of the Prime Minister and people from all walks of life were filled with rage, desperation and despair. It was interesting that no one was interested in the Secretary of State for Trade and Industry, confirming his image as an unimportant marionette of the PM. Experts scoured parliamentary records and found, to everyone's amazement, that no decision had previously been made on the location. It was described as a monstrous, obscene and duplicitous trick, immoral and dishonest, and a criminal act of deception. It was said that everyone had been duped or, more correctly, had duped themselves by jumping on a bandwagon and the government had allowed, if not encouraged, them to roll in the wrong direction.

Hiram told Bertrand, in the strictest confidence, the story of Sir Richard Pickles working out the truth, buying up Cornwall, and needing a final investor. He told him about his deal and how he was now able to order the three-hulled *Star Trek* Adongiva. Bertrand suggested he wait until Friday, when the money was safely in Hiram's bank account. Hiram reminded him that with GAFDST the money was as good as his. Bertrand agreed and said he would get the wheels rolling immediately by seeing 'The Big Mac'.

He explained that the M&S empire classified work by size. Less than twenty-one million was 'small'. Any division could initiate these without reference to the MD, and simply submit a monthly report. Projects between twenty-one and fifty-six million were 'medium' and the MD expected early warning to avoid simultaneous projects straining their resources. Over fifty-six was considered 'large' and the MD insisted on notification at the outset.

As the preliminary estimates for the new Adongiva ranged between forty-seven and sixty-three million pounds, it could be 'medium' or 'large'. It was therefore essential to speak to Terence Biggins McCallister, the MD affectionately known as 'The Big Mac'. Bertrand assured Hiram this would make no difference to the speed or manner in which the ship was built. Hiram said he was flattered that his ship could be regarded as an M&S large project, albeit near the bottom end of the scale. Bertrand suggested they meet again on Monday by which time he would have all his experts lined up and the initial work underway.

By two-thirty that afternoon, Bertrand was being ushered to the inner sanctum of The Big Mac. Terence Biggins McCallister gestured Bertrand to sit. They exchanged pleasantries before moving onto the subject of M&S Leisure Division. As usual The Big Mac had done his homework and was aware of the recent work in Bertrand's patch. He mentioned a couple of jobs and congratulated him on the growth of the division since its birth. With the preliminaries over, they got down to business.

"What have you got for me?" Bertrand told Terence about the request for a super yacht. Terence was surprised that a pleasure boat could be big enough to merit his attention and assumed it was for an entertainment celebrity. Even top footballers don't go for something this large. Bertrand corrected his boss and said it was not for anybody famous, but an ordinary man. Terence was intrigued.

Bertrand continued, "Hiram Montgomery is a man who's had some very bad luck and very good luck in a short space of time. To cut a long story short, he decided to fulfil an ambition by getting us to build him a floating home on which to sail the world before he dies."

Terrence Biggins McCallister didn't like long stories cut short because important details get left out. He asked, "What do you mean by bad and good luck?" Bertrand explained about Hiram's wife's sudden death, which he was not fully over. He spoke of the lottery win. Terence listened in astonishment about Hiram's medical condition. With possibly only four years to live, Hiram had decided to blow the lot on his dream of a yacht on which to sail away, and probably die on. Terence was speechless. Bertrand told how Hiram had gone to Cardhew Russell Boat Builders and Oliver Russell had sent him to M&S Leisure. He said as time was of the essence, a conversion was thought better than a new build but the first choice had fallen through. He recounted the Russian trip and meeting with Ivanovitch Petrovsky, the purchase of *The Vashoya Calishka*, and how this had been cancelled because of his enemies.

Terence was surprised by this. "I thought Ivanovitch Petrovsky died of natural causes." Bertrand said that this 'official' story by the Russian Government was not true. He explained 'The Sterilisers' and how Ivanovitch died.

Terrence Biggins McCallister sat back in his chair. "My God, Bertrand Cavendish, I thought I lived an interesting life, but you put me in the shade."

"The story is not over," said Bertrand. Terence felt he could not be surprised by anything after this, but he was wrong.

Bertrand told him that Ivanovitch Petrovsky and Hiram shared a passion for *Star Trek* and that, as a consolation for not getting *The Vashoya Calishka*, Ivanovitch had spent the night before his death designing two ships. "One is a conventional luxury yacht and the other is what Ivanovitch described as 'a bit of fun from one trekkie to another'. The first is sensible and affordable, from Hiram's position, and the second is, or was, pure fantasy well beyond his budget. Hiram had decided to commission the first yacht."

By now Terence was positively bubbling with excitement. "You have original designs for two ships by Ivanovitch Petrovsky and they are his last work just before he died?"

"Hiram has the originals in a bank. I have scanned copies in my computer." Bertrand tapped his laptop and Terence stared as if it were a holy relic. "The story gets better," said Bertrand. "Yesterday's hullabaloo regarding the UKSA Space Monitoring Station is part of the story."

The Big Mac looked punch-drunk. "No kidding. Go ahead, surprise me. I think my poor brain can take anything now."

Bertrand explained the Richard Pickles deal and how Hiram was now rich enough to build the Ivanovitch fantasy design and this was why Bertrand had arranged this meeting.

"If you wrote it as a book, no one would believe it. The truth is stranger than fiction," said The Big Mac.

"If you want strange, I will tell you spooky," said Bertrand.

Terence shook his head. "How could this story get any stranger?" Bertrand told him about Oliver's dream. The Big Mac's expression changed. "Show me the ship."

Bertrand opened the folder next to his machine and turned to the artist's impression by Ivanovitch. Terence McCallister stared at the drawing as if hypnotised, minutely studying every detail. Eventually he closed his eyes. "I think I have found what I have been looking for, for quite some time. Your friend, Oliver, said he believes in fate. Do you, Bertrand?"

"I am trying not to, but it is becoming more difficult by the minute," said Bertrand, sensing increased tension.

"Do me a favour," said Terence. "Wait with my secretary while I make a call."

Bertrand felt rebuffed. A few moments ago, he had been told he was an asset to the company. Now he was being dismissed while a discussion not for his ears takes place. Terence picked up the phone and without looking up said, "Tell her to keep you amused. I don't care whether she gives you tea, a dirty joke or a blow job. Just wait until I call. And leave the folder behind, thank you."

The lady who The Big Mac described as secretary was actually his personal assistant called Lady Cynthia Jane Kettlestown Brown, although she preferred Cynthia. She adored her boss, although she knew he could be a trifle vulgar in the company of colleagues. As Bertrand Cavendish walked through her door she recognised the expression that indicated her boss had said something insulting, which she was more than familiar with. She had heard worse in the barracks of her husband, Lieutenant Colonel 'Tommy' Kettlestown Brown. She also knew that Terence and some of his senior colleagues had referred to her as 'the thinking man's top drawer tottie', which she found amusing and accepted as a compliment. She smiled sweetly. "I think we can rule out option three, don't you? Milk and two sugars, isn't it?" As she poured a cup of tea she said over her shoulder, "Have you heard the one about the two spider monkeys and the rather ugly camel?"

Bertrand alternated his gaze from Cynthia to the light on her phone, which indicated that her boss was talking. Twenty minutes had passed since she had given him tea. He sighed theatrically, which she ignored. Eventually she looked up, smiled, and offered another cup. He declined. Finally, the light went out and he stood. She looked at the phone and, as if prompted, the light reappeared. Bertrand felt exasperated. With one finger, she motioned him down and he obeyed. Another twenty minutes went by, and then another ten. Finally, the door opened.

"Cynth, cancel my appointments for the rest of the day. In fact, move everything back one week. I want to be free for a few days. Contact all board members – Thursday morning, emergency meeting, nine sharp. Tell those on holiday to get back and the Company will meet the cost, both ways if necessary. I want everyone. No excuses. Tell them an agenda will be emailed shortly." If Cynthia was surprised at the instructions, it did not show. She always exuded unflappable calm and control.

The Big Mac beckoned Bertrand and quickly disappeared. By the time Bertrand entered, his boss was behind his desk and without looking up said, "Wood in the hole." Bertrand dutifully shut the door and sat down. For The Big Mac to cancel his diary and call an emergency board meeting, something of immense importance was up. His boss put down his pen. "What do you know about tanks?"

Bertrand had no idea what he was being asked about but knew

a quick intelligent answer was expected. He said, "Do you mean air tanks, water tanks, fuel tanks, oil tanks, storage tanks, ballast tanks, buoyancy tanks, floatation tanks, septic tanks, fish tanks, think tanks, or Bob Hope's signature tune, 'Tanks for the Memory'?"

Terence frowned at the humour and raised a hand. "Try military tanks."

Bertrand replied, "Tanks – armoured, tracked vehicles, first used in World War 1, were slow, cumbersome, unreliable and dangerous to occupants and targets alike. Nevertheless, they dramatically changed warfare. They have undergone many changes over the years and modern tanks are extremely sophisticated and efficient. Large and heavy, but fast and manoeuvrable. They're well-armoured platforms for large calibre armaments with automatic self-levelling laser sights. They give good protection from nuclear, chemical and biological attack, or small to medium calibre firearms rockets, cannon and anti-personnel mines. Latest generation includes American Abrams, British Chieftains and Challengers, Russian T95s, and French Leclercs."

The Big Mac held up his hand. "Enough. As usual your knowledge does not disappoint and you've mentioned the word I was looking for – heavy." The Big Mac leaned forward. "There are Light Air Transportable Land Rovers, trucks and artillery pieces, but no air transportable battle tanks. Moving them by land requires tank transporters. Going abroad means ships, which takes time and organisation and ruins the element of surprise. It has long been a dream of military planners that one day tanks made of light weight material could be carried by plane, or even helicopter, but still capable of going head to head with another tank. Imagine the panic and destruction you could inflict by dropping Challengers behind the frontline."

Bertrand was perplexed. His boss would not have wiped his diary if there was not something momentous about to happen. He was keen to find out what, but tanks had nothing to do with the business of M&S. Terence smiled at Bertrand's impatience, but he was not prepared to rush his explanation. He had to prepare the ground. He continued, "In the 1960s America asked several companies to come up with material for LAT battle tanks. Since then, those companies have been wrestling with the problem, without success. Armour for modern warfare is heavy, and despite improvements it remains heavy."

Bertrand suppressed a sigh, gritted his teeth and listened. "One company has been more successful than the others. Have you heard of Anderson Plastic?" Bertrand shook his head. "It's a Swedish Company, about fifty years old, who manufacture clever, unusual, specialist plastics for various industries. The Department of Defence, desperate to develop new alloys, asked several American firms and a couple of foreign companies they could trust to keep a secret. Most of the firms have dropped out and there are only two or three competitors left. The head of Anderson Plastic is a man called Hans Kristian. Please, spare me the jokes. He and I have spoken many times during the fifteen years since they first surprised the Americans by producing a hard, lightweight plastic, better than metal."

Terence took a deep breath and continued, "They were asked to produce a life-size replica tank that could withstand heavy calibre machine gun fire. They did this and the Americans destroyed it with cannons. They were asked for a version impervious to cannons, and watched it destroyed by rockets. After a succession of similar tests with escalating firepower, they are now working on a version which could take an anti-tank shell."

The Big Mac looked visibly frustrated. "They are thoroughly hacked off at this constant shifting of the goal posts and are convinced the Yanks really don't want to give a foreign company the contract. The fact that they have not been told their work is no longer required is proof that none of the American firms have come close to achieving what they have done. There have been serious attempts over the years to steal the secret of the material they call 'Hard Plastic', but they have security that makes Fort Knox look like a tent. They even developed a cladding for their buildings that generates random patterns of thermal, magnetic and electrical energy impossible to penetrate by even the most sophisticated spy satellite. After every firing test they painstakingly collect every piece of debris to avoid analysis."

As The Big Mac continued, Bertrand still could not understand why his boss was telling him all this. "The Americans have told them that if they can produce a material ten times stronger than steel and a quarter of the weight, they can supply armour for the next generation tanks. Anderson Plastic is not convinced they can trust the Americans, but they have spent too much money to stop now. They don't yet have a material that matches that specification but they currently have something about six times the strength of steel and less than half the weight."

"Wow," said Bertrand. "That's impressive, but why are *we* interested?"

"Patience, dear boy. We're nearly there. Anderson Plastic continues to work in total secrecy, developing their material of warfare for future generations to enjoy. In the meantime, they would like to recoup some of the billions they've spent by launching a civilian version. Six years ago, Hans asked me to keep my eyes open for a project suitable for a prestigious launch of Hard Plastic. Think of all the inventions that have altered civilisation – the wheel, metal, the automobile, aeroplanes, telephone, computers, microchips, and space travel. Anderson Plastic is convinced that their Hard Plastic is destined for that list. They believe everything currently made of metal could, in the future, be made from Hard Plastic. Think about the rewards of being a part of this from the start."

Bertrand considered the potential gains from being involved with such a project. "They were quite specific in what they were looking for. When the items we daily take for granted – televisions, radios, video, hi-fi, phones, washing machines and so on – first appeared, only the rich could afford them. But in time prices fell and now everyone can. It is the same with all innovations and inventions. A great construction project using Hard Plastic would be too expensive, and this ruled out civil engineering. Likewise, it must be something not too mundane. Even a brilliant invention that everyone needs will, in time, be taken for granted. One of the most important criteria was that it had to be something that would make people stop and say 'wow'. When I showed Hans the image of your ship, his first word was 'wow'."

"Hold on," said Bertrand. "You are forgetting something. We're not dealing with a large corporation or government with limitless funds. Hiram Montgomery is an individual with finite resources. You said your-self this new material is very expensive. He will not be able to afford it."

"Don't you think I have already thought of that? Hans Kristian and I have discussed a solution. Sadly, Hiram will not be with us for very much longer."

"Good God," Bertrand exploded. "You told him Hiram is dying? That was confidential."

If The Big Mac was bothered by his subordinate's tone, he didn't show it. He calmed Bertrand with a hand. "Hiram is dying. He is buying a yacht on which to cruise and then die on with dignity, and considerable comfort. This is an unarguable fact and, like it or not, relevant. Once he is dead, or too ill to manage, what happens then?" From what you said, he has no offspring to which he can leave it. There is an amicable and mutually acceptable solution."

"Go on," said Bertrand, feeling protective of his client.

"The cost of the Adongiva constructed from Hard Plastic would be approximately four times the cost of a conventional ship." Bertrand whistled and shook his head. Terence ignored him. "We will put it to Hiram that he pays the price you and he agreed, and the difference is met jointly by Anderson Plastic and ourselves. When the ship is built, he uses it as planned for the rest of his life, more or less. When the time comes for him to depart this mortal coil, his share reverts to us."

Bertrand was sceptical. "Why should he pay for something that will never belong to him? What benefit is there for him? What's in it for us? Why should M&S invest a huge sum in a plastic boat from which we will get no benefit for at least four or possibly eight years? We will be seen to be sitting waiting for his demise, like vultures? What did you mean by 'more or less'?"

The Big Mac stared stonily. "You have raised several important questions, but firstly don't ever question my integrity with regard to a customer again. I have always upheld the principals of our company and will defend Hiram Montgomery's right to the same respect and service we give all customers. Is that clear?"

This was the first time Bertrand had been rebuked by The Big Mac, and it brought him up short. He apologised.

"Apology accepted. Your attempt to protect your client from exploitation is commendable, but unnecessary. You asked what was in it for Hiram. It is all very well buying an expensive yacht but you have to be rich to keep it going. Hiram may think he has the resources to run the ship for the remainder of his life, but what if he is wrong? We are not going to let our investment deteriorate or go bust for lack of funds. He will have his fabulous dream, as he intended, for as long as he wants. But by going into partnership with us, he will have a safety net if his plan fails. The terms of the agreement will be fair and beneficial to all parties."

Bertrand felt slightly relieved. The Big Mac continued, "You asked about the benefits of co-ownership. In practical terms, he will be no worse off. He will still be able to go where he wants, invite who he wants and do what he likes apart from sell it, unless he wants to sell back to us. What's wrong with that?"

"When you put it like that, it seems like a good deal," Bertrand conceded.

"You asked what I meant by more or less. It's not uncommon for retailers to do deals with customers by giving them a discount in exchange for letting potential customers visit and inspect the conservatory, fitted kitchen, driveway or whatever. For a certain number of weeks each year, people will visit his yacht and possibly stay a few days to see it in action. We are not talking huge numbers of hoi-polloi running amok and throwing rubbish. They could be admirals, defence chiefs, captains of industry, and very rich celebrities. It's hardly likely to make a big impact on his life, is it?"

Bertrand felt more relaxed as Terence continue to answer his question. "You asked what was in it for us. Your assumption that whilst Hiram is alive there is no benefit for us is incorrect. The ship would be a showcase to prove to that Hard Plastic is the future. People will see for themselves that it is light, tough and practical. We aim to make a serious mountain of money. Anderson Plastic and M&S have agreed that, for an initial ten-year period, we are the only outlet for Hard Plastic for all maritime purposes. Can you imagine the financial gains? It is up to Anderson Plastic how they release Hard Plastic in the aeronautical, automobile, manufacturing and construction industries. However, for the foreseeable future, the sea is ours."

The full realisation began to settle on Bertrand. "There have been notable duffers and blind alleys in the history of inventions – Betamax video recorders, the Sinclair C5, and others. However, if it works as you suggest M&S could grow so dramatically, I can't even imagine it."

"Exactly," said Terence quietly. "The stars are the limit. I made two phone calls just now. The first was to Hans Kristian. He had not found another project for Hard Plastic and right now he and his team are on their way here. The second was to inform Conrad Meredith and to get his agreement to proceed. He suggested the emergency board meeting, at which he will be calling for a unanimous vote."

Bertrand was surprised. Conrad Meredith, President of the company, was an eighty- five-year-old recluse who rarely attended meetings. If he wanted a unanimous decision, that is exactly what would happen.

"Bertrand," Terence continued, "I want you to ask Hiram to come here now. We need explain this development to him."

Bertrand raised an eyebrow. Hiram was his client and it was unusual for The Big Mac to muscle in.

Guessing Bertrand's thoughts Terence said, "This is still your project and under the auspices of M&S Leisure, but from here you share control with me. This project is now too important for me not to be involved. That's not negotiable. We will make all major decisions together. OK?"

Bertrand realised this was a rhetorical question. The Adongiva project had just accelerated to maximum speed and he was being offered a share of the glory. If he refused, it would continue without him. He nodded meekly.

Hiram lay on his bed, pondering. Seven months ago, his life was ordinary and uneventful. He was never going to be rich or famous, but he had a loving wife who cared for him and an easy job which provided a steady income until retirement. If his life expectancy was average, he could be around for at least twenty or perhaps forty more years. Now everything had changed, and so quickly it made his head spin. Everyone dreams of winning the lottery but don't expect to. He had done it. His wife was suddenly dead. He had more money than he ever imagined or needed, but no one to share it with or spend it on. He was only just beginning to accept the possibility that it could bring him some joy, without feeling guilty about it. Last week he was just rich enough to buy a very nice yacht. Now he was so rich he could commission the building of a fantastical ship which would look like the Star Ship *Enterprise.*

His old world seemed miles away. He had always believed you must work hard and save for your old age. Now he had lots of money, but he wasn't going to have an old age. He had sold his house deliberately so that he was not fixed to an abode. His previous existence recognised owning property as a measure of success. Now, he lay on his bed in the middle of the day in a side street guest house two miles from an large ship building company about to start building his super yacht.

There was a time bomb inside him and in as little as forty-eight months he could be dead. If anyone asked why he was bothering to do anything other than lie here and wait to die, he did not have an answer. He felt tired even though he had done nothing all day except eat breakfast, order an expensive yacht, eat a sandwich, and lie there contemplating.

He felt tired of everything and wanted it all to go away and to go back to how it had been a year ago. A year ago, he had no money and no aspirations, but right now it seemed preferable to feeling strapped into a roller coaster. "Question – Why am I bothering with this damn boat? *Answer – You've always wanted one.* Question – Why this big? *Answer – The original was more modest, but things gathered momentum and got out of hand, as usual.*" He could have settled for a cabin cruiser moored next to a top class hotel where his permanent penthouse suite overlooked the water and attentive staff catered for his every whim.

Instead, he had decided to build and live on a big luxury super yacht capable of sailing round the world. "Question – Am I really going to sail round the world? *Answer – That had been the idea, but now the plan is becoming confused.* Question – So what was the latest plan? *Answer – Not entirely sure.*"

Hiram was surrounded by experts who seemed to know what they are doing and, once again, he was not in control of his own destiny. Roger Campbell was a money wizard who had taken over the financial side, which was not a bad idea given Hiram's history. The last time he looked, his assets were increasing by £5,900 per day. Roger had pointed out that the ship running costs would be a substantial drain on funds and Hiram's idea of putting several million aside, to use the interest, would not work. He said the world was full of rich people prepared to buy the finer things in life, and suggested running the ship for a quarter of the year as a 'top end of the market' luxury mini cruise liner, offering an all inclusive holiday for those with deep pockets.

He said to imagine large, well-appointed en-suite cabins with sea view balcony, well-stocked complimentary drinks cabinet, fresh fruit and flowers, large flat screen HD television, hi-fi, computer with internet access, satellite telephone, etc. There would be a lounge bar, billiard room, and restaurant with an excellent chef. Guests could enjoy the function room, fitness suite, sauna and Jacuzzi, swimming pool, fast launch for ferrying and water skiing, jet skis and other rich man's toys, together with a hairdresser, beautician and fitness coach. Wallets would only ever be required for exchanging currency for shore trips. The ship would be a floating a hotel for the *crème de la crème*.

He said his calculations, based on educated assumptions, put the annual cost of fuel, wages, provisions, parts and other items at £1,750,000. He suggested six double suites with guests paying £2,000 per head per night, and full occupancy during a one hundred nights 'season' would yield £2,400,000. This would pay the running costs and show a profit of £650,000. Hiram said this sounded too good to be true and couldn't imagine people paying that sort of money. Roger produced several brochures for top hotels where people do pay these prices for the height of luxury and self-indulgence. He said he had contacts in the hotel and travel business that could help put the plan together. Hiram said it all sounded excellent and, although the ship was expanding and becoming grander than envisaged, the idea of having the costs paid for by a short season seemed irresistible.

Bertrand Cavendish was in charge of the construction of the ship. Hiram wanted to control the details and be involved in the discussions but felt overawed and was aware of his lack of expertise. He wished Sarah was with him. She could be forceful and had always been a better negotiator than him. He just wished that she was with him, full stop.

A noise made him jump. It was his mobile phone. Bertrand said The Big Mac had asked to see him this afternoon. He told Hiram that this was not usual and therefore an honour. He agreed to come along.

Daylight was fading when, just after five, Hiram spoke to the guard at the main gate. The guard's breath steamed in the cold air as he said to follow the Land Rover rather than go to the Leisure Division he had visited previously. A white Land Rover pulled away as he entered the gateway and he obediently followed it. A few snowflakes drifted in the air as the Land Rover pulled up before a large office block and Hiram stopped behind it. Another guard hurried down the steps as the Rover sped away. The guard said Hiram should go inside whilst he parked the car. Inside another official escorted him to the floor above, which was beautifully decorated with wood panelling and large paintings of serious men in suits. A tall elegant lady introduced herself as Mr. McCallister's PA. She took his hand and, with elocution that matched old BBC presenters, said she would take him to his office. Hiram's first thought from her attire, jewellery, coiffeur, and bearing was of a lady-in-waiting from Buck House. In the room, Bertrand stood next to The Big Mac.

Terence Biggins McCallister wondered how he was going to open the conversation. *What do you say to someone who has recently lost his wife but just won the lottery, been told in about four years he will die an agonising death, but who has since quadrupled his fortune?* The Big Mac gave Hiram the nod and grim smile reserved for funerals. Hiram returned the silent signal and then shot Bertrand a look that said 'I told you not to tell anybody'. Bertrand looked shamefaced.

Terence opened the drinks cabinet and poured very generous measures into whisky tumblers. "This is a fine, old single malt reserved for special customers. May I say, Hiram, welcome to M&S and here's to us, and to the Adongiva." They tilted and drank deeply.

Hiram enjoyed a good scotch but the excellence of this surprised him. "That is exceptionally good."

"It dammed well should be at that price." The others chuckled which pleased The Big Mac. The ice had been broken and it was time to get to business.

He started by saying he had read the folder and all that had happened so far. He said Hiram's ideas were interesting, that Bertrand had told him about the Russia trip and the meeting with Ivanovitch Petrovsky just before his death, and that he knew many who would have given anything to have to have met the great man. He told Hiram he was very fortunate to have originals of Ivanovitch's last works and he should make sure they are safe. TBM said the plans for the three-hulled ship were so spectacular and unique that this vessel will turn heads and draw attention. He said you don't have to be a trekkie to appreciate the sleek good looks of this unusual hybrid – the progeny of a cruise liner and space ship.

He went on to say that since the first time man took to the water, in craft of all shapes and sizes, the building materials have changed many times with advancing technology. The Romans, Vikings and Chinese warlords used timber. The British navy favoured solid oak when fighting the Spanish and the French centuries later. Steel ships ruled the waves during two world wars. Today, boats are made from fibreglass, carbon composite and other lightweight materials.

The Big Mac could see that Hiram was not sure where this was going but was controlling his impatience. He repeated what he had told Bertrand earlier that afternoon, about the American Government asking Anderson Plastic to produce lightweight tank material, why they have decided to launch a 'civilian' version four times stronger than steel and a third of the weight, and how the Adongiva would be perfect. Hiram listened without reaction.

"Just think, Hiram," said The Big Mac. "When cars, ships, planes, buildings, bridges, space ships are all made from Hard Plastic, you'll go down in history as the owner of the very first sea going vessel made from it."

"Going down in history is not high on my list of things to do right now," said Hiram.

"Perhaps not, but can we make the ship in Hard Plastic?"

"What difference will it make?"

The Big Mac looked Hiram in the eye. "Good question. It will be light and ride higher in the water, carry more weight without affecting handling, be faster but more economical and, because of its strength, will be safer in an emergency."

"Sounds good, but how much?"

The Big Mac said that Anderson Plastic had invested billions in research and development, and any prototype is expensive. He said the market price of a Hard Plastic Adongiva might be over £210,000,000. Hiram looked pained. The Big Mac raised a hand and said M&S were proud of their reputation for ethical, fair trade policies. He said Hiram would be doing a favour by allowing his ship to be a guinea pig for the new material. Anderson Plastic and M&S had therefore agreed to share the cost, and that Hiram pay only what he had originally agreed.

Hiram nodded but remained silent. The Big Mac went on, outlining how Hiram would use the ship as his own for part of the year and let potential customers of M&S and Anderson Plastic visit. Hiram told them of Roger Campbell's plan. The Big Mac said an agreement could be reached.

"It sounds too good to be true. How much of this is influenced by my life expectancy? I told Bertrand I don't want pity. What happens when I die?"

Terence Biggins McCallister admired people who, despite delicate problems, spoke their mind. He looked at Hiram squarely and said,

"This is no Santa Clause generosity, or borne from pity. This is hard business and we intend on making a mountain of money from future sales of ships, parts and accessories. You will act as roving ambassador and shop window. Bertrand told me of your condition for which I am sad and I wish there was something we could do. The fact is we are where we are. Who knows what lies ahead? I am sure I speak for everyone when I say we hope you live a long and happy life. However, when you pass away, your share reverts to M&S. I understand you have no dependants and I think this is a fair and reasonable return for the money we are investing. Do you agree?"

Bertrand and his boss held their breaths as Hiram stared into space for an age. Finally he said, "Yes."

"Great," said The Big Mac. "I will get a contract drawn up for you to run by your legal people."

Hiram found this amusing, as his 'legal people' solely consisted of Roger Campbell.

CHAPTER NINE

Wednesday 28th January 2026

After breakfast, Hiram packed his suitcases and loaded his car, and settled his account at the guest house. He drove in silence, listening to the crunch of tyres on snow and thought again about the meeting yesterday. After he had agreed to the building of the Adongiva in Hard Plastic, The Big Mac asked Hiram where he was staying. Hiram told him about his B&B, saying it was basic but pleasant.

The Big Mac said, "That will not do. You are an important and prestigious customer. I insist you stay here."

Hiram had looked round. "That's very kind but this room is not terribly big. If I set up a camp bed it might put your other visitors off."

This made The Big Mac laugh. "Behind this block is the Senior Staff Club with rooms for VIPs. They are comfortable, and the bar and restaurant is excellent." Before Hiram could refuse, The Big Mac telephoned to arrange it. He replaced the handset and frowned. "I had forgotten about the Argentinean Brass staying here in connection with a Frigate order. Change of plan Hiram." He picked up the phone again. "Prepare a cabin for a VIP. I don't know, could be a few months. That's right. That's what I said. He will move in tomorrow morning. Hiram Montgomery. Thank you." The Big Mac came off the phone and saw Bertrand's expression. "Caesar was moaning about the cabins being a waste of money, expensive, and under used. He can't have it both ways. Hiram is important and we need to keep him sweet. This is a good use of a facility and I don't consider it extravagant."

Hiram said, "What am I missing? What are the cabins? Who is Caesar? Why do I need to be kept sweet?"

The Big Mac said, "We have six secluded log cabins reserved for our most important visitors – heads of state, admirals, diplomats, and so on. Caesar Meredith is Finance Director."

"*Acting* FD," Bertrand corrected.

The Big Mac said the FD, after a riding accident, was on sick leave and Caesar, who was standing in, was enthusiastic as guardian of our finances and enforcer of parsimony."

"He is a pain in the rectum," added Bertrand.

"Why do you need to be kept sweet? We simply want you to be happy. We have already stated the importance of Hard Plastic being launched to allow us to harvest millions, if not billions, in future sales. That makes you important."

"Yes, but comparing me with heads of state, admirals and diplomats seems over the top," said Hiram.

"Not at all," said The Big Mac. "Caesar Meredith was complaining that we don't use the cabins enough and you are going to be my guest until your ship is built. Further more you shall have free use of the Senior Staff Club and facilities and a staff pass so that you can come and go as you please."

"I don't know what to say," said Hiram. "This is extremely generous. I don't want to cause any fuss or trouble, or get mixed up in M&S internal politics.

The Big Mac replied, "Don't worry about that. If anyone gives you trouble, tell me and the problem will disappear. I only ask one thing in return."

"What's that?"

"Enjoy yourself. Bertrand will continue to be your main contact and he will facilitate anything you want. I hope you will live your life to the full and get great pleasure from your dealings with us and from your ship. When the time sadly comes, I want you to die happy knowing that you have fulfilled your dream and achieved what you wanted to."

At the gate, the guards walked awkwardly in the snow. It was thicker here than at the guest house. The clipboard guard said, "Good morning, Mr. Montgomery." He had addressed Hiram as *Sir* on previous visits. He continued, "Inside the gate, stop on the left."

Inside another man opened the passenger door and, blowing a cloud of steam, said, "Good morning, Mr. Montgomery." He fixed a pass to the windscreen and came round to Hiram's side. He said, "That will get you through the staff entrance and you needn't come through here again. Please wear this at all times on site."

Previously his badge stated the date and time of his visit and he had to hand it in on leaving. The man handed Hiram a key, a booklet and mobile phone.

"This is the key to Cabin 1. The book explains everything you need and the facilities. The cabins are behind the Main Administration Building. Would you like me to arrange an escort to take you there, Mr. Montgomery?"

Hiram said he had been to the Main Administration Building the night before and thought he could find his way. The man said the mobile phone could be used to contact any staff member using the quick dial numbers listed in the book, but if he pressed zero the switchboard could answer most questions. The man then saluted and disappeared back into the control building.

Hiram followed the road to a barrier of box hedge with a sign reading 'VIP Guest Lodges'. The open iron gate revealed a row of wooden cabins, each with its own lawn and driveway. It was a picture perfect postcard oasis of tranquillity, hidden from the world outside. He pulled onto the drive which had a sign saying '1', got out and looked round. At hedge level, he spotted a discreet CCTV camera keeping watch. He gathered his cases, walked to the door and inserted his key. He expected a voice to say, "Hoy, what are you doing here? This isn't for the likes of you, clear off."

He opened the door and stepped into a short hall with a door on his left leading to a well furnished living room. He could feel the heat from a crackling log fire. Pictures adorned the walls and a mantle clock made a slow, soft, heavy, tick. It looked like a place in which to kick off your shoes and feel at home.

He nudged the front door with his bottom and stepped through. The door on his right led to a large bedroom with king sized bed. Extra blankets and a dressing gown were folded neatly. There were built in wardrobes, a dressing table, a trouser press, bedside lockers with table lamps, a clock radio and a cable which looked like the charger for the mobile phone. There was a television mounted on the wall opposite the bed and a remote control on a locker.

114

He dropped his cases and explored the en-suite. He opened the cabinet which was filled with designer toiletries. At first he thought they had been left by a previous occupant until he saw that they were pristine. There was toothpaste and brushes in wrappings labelled 'hard', 'medium' and 'soft'. There was so much stuff he was amazed that anyone would provide this for guests, or that they would expect to be given it. He decided to check out the kitchen. It was small but well stocked with a kettle, bread and sandwich toasters, a microwave, a fridge freezer and plenty of cupboards. He opened the fridge in amazement. It was full – eggs, milk, butter and margarine, cheeses, cold meats, bottles of tonic, and small brown and white loaves. The cupboards were equally well stocked, not for cooking meals, but certainly for making snacks. From the kitchen, an archway led to a dining room with a table and chairs. Another archway connected to the living room. He opened the doors of one of the wooden units. It was not the usual complimentary mini bar but held full size bottles of every popular alcohol, mixer, soft drink and beer. You could have a hell of a party with this lot.

Just as he was about to unpack his cases, a bell softly sounded. At the door was a uniformed guard who paid Hiram his compliments and asked if he would care to join Mr. Cavendish and Mr. McCallister in the Administration Building for a meeting with Dr. Hans Kristian. Outside was an electric golf buggy. The guard said, "Sir, may I suggest you wear your badge and take the mobile phone, which you should carry at all times." As they rolled towards the gate, the guard pointed out a smaller gate in the hedge which Hiram could use for the Senior Staff Club without using the road.

In the Managing Director's room in the Administration Building, Bertrand and The Big Mac were talking to four men. "Ah, Hiram," said Bertrand. "This is Doctor Hans Kristian, owner of Anderson Plastics." Hiram looked at Hans Kristian and thought he was the tallest man he had seen. He was at least 6'6", with white hair and a bony face but a kind smile and a twinkle in his eyes. They exchanged hellos. He was then introduced to Gustaf Bjorne, Design and Construction Analyst, Doctor Gottfrid Halsten, chemist and inventor of the principle ingredient of Hard Plastic, and Professor Nils Olof, the ergonomics, safety and training expert.

"What part of Scotland are you from, Hiram?" Hans asked. Hiram told him he was from Edinburgh.

Hans pointed to The Big Mac and Bertrand and said, "They are English, you are Scottish, and we are Swedes, or as you Scots would say turnips."

Hiram chuckled, but the English were puzzled. He explain that this was a play on words because traditionally in Scotland the vegetable called a turnip is what the English called a swede, and vice versa. Hiram asked Hans how he knew this and Hans replied that he once had a Scottish girlfriend.

They chatted for a while. Hans Kristian told Hiram he thought the drawing of the Adongiva was remarkable and that he must be honoured to have a design by the late Ivanovitch Petrovsky. Hiram agreed and said he felt privileged to have met him before he died. Gustaf said he had met Ivanovitch once and was sorry he had not had more time to talk to him for longer.

Eventually, The Big Mac said, "Gentlemen, I think it's time we made a move. My Division Principal Officers and department heads are in the meeting room." They followed him next door where people sat around three sides of a large table. Two men in one corner fussed over a video camera on a tripod. A television and large screen computer monitor and two remote controls lay on the table in another corner.

The Big Mac occupied the centre chair on the empty side of the square. He welcomed everyone to what he considered an important meeting with potentially far-reaching consequences for the company. He asked everyone to ignore the film crew who were there to record the meeting. He said the entire construction of the Adongiva was to be recorded for posterity from this moment until the launch of the ship.

He introduced Hiram as the customer who had come to M&S with an order for a super yacht that sparked off the sequence of events which had led to this point. Hiram looked round at the smiles on everyone's faces apart from one. He assumed this was Caesar Meredith. The Big Mac then introduced Hans Kristian and his team. He asked the others round the table to introduce themselves. The meeting group was informed that, although the Adongiva had been upgraded in status to a major cross-division project, it was still officially under M&S Leisure Division and Bertrand was in charge.

Bertrand then took over and spoke about how Hiram had come to visit M&S, and their visit to Russia to meet Ivanovitch Petrovsky. They were surprised to hear that the great Ivanovitch Petrovsky was a *Star Trek* fan. Bertrand explained how they had agreed to purchase a ship but when the deal fell through, Ivanovitch created a design for the Adongiva that was based on the Star Ship *Enterprise*. He picked up one of the remote controls on the table. The computer monitor came to life with the artist impression that Ivanovitch had drawn. Bertrand pressed a button and the detailed design drawings appeared. Several people leaned forward with their eyes wide and stared in fascinated silence as Bertrand took them on a virtual tour.

Once Bertrand was finished, Hans Kristian was invited to speak. Hans said Anderson Plastics had been manufacturers of plastic since 1927 but, despite their several billion pound turnover, were unknown by the public. They had always shunned mass produced goods and had no need for the glare of publicity as they dominated the market of specialist plastics.

While Hans continued, a theatrical sigh was heard from the back. Although not loud, Hiram found this shocking because of the rude message that someone was bored. Everyone else stared at Caesar Meredith who, in turn, looked at his watch. Hiram could see Terence McCallister's incredulity turn to anger and he shot him an expression that could stop a heart. If Hans Kristian was affected it did not show. He smiled and asked if Doctor Gottfrid Halsten would give examples of Anderson Plastics products created over the years. He said that most people with imagination and intellect would find it most fascinating.

Doctor Halsten was lively and animated, and his enthusiasm was infectious. He explained the pipeline material Anderson Plastics had created to protect petrol from the hottest, coldest, deepest and most dangerous parts of the planet, as well as thieves. He said many oil companies now use these pipes. He moved on to say that they were working on stab proof vests and bullet proof jackets that are thin, lightweight, and more like a moulded plastic replica of a Roman Centurion's body armour.

He said another of their plastics could be squeezed, pulled or bent. It can absorb kinetic energy then return to its original shape. He said such a plastic motorway crash barrier was being trialled in several countries and has already saved many lives of people involved in motorway crashes.

He went onto explain several more impressive plastic innovations and when he was finished, Hans stepped in and said the reason for mentioning these various products was to show the international credentials of Anderson Plastic and to illustrate their ingenuity at providing diverse solutions. He said ships are not just made of metal and other products might be useful on the Adongiva, using Hard Plastic for the shell. He said it was now time to discuss Hard Plastic, of which Doctor Halsten was the principle architect. He and Doctor Halsten had worked out, over many years of painstaking trial and error, how to combine a number of ingredients to create Hard Plastic.

Doctor Halsten then explained how Hard Plastic had evolved from the quest by the American government to make LAT armoured vehicles. They were told how they repeatedly improved it, each time tougher than before, only to see it destroyed in escalating weapons trials. The goal of producing a material ten times stronger than steel and a quarter of the weight had not yet been achieved, but the Adongiva could now be constructed from a plastic four times stronger than the equivalent thickness in steel and a third of the weight.

The next person to speak was Gustaf Bjorne. He said that the strength of Hard Plastic made it hard to cut, drill, join or work with conventional tools. The surface has to be temporarily softened so that parts can be bonded, as if with contact glue. Once this has been done a permanent and seamless bond can be created. To build the Adongiva, Anderson Plastics would have to make the pieces in their secure factory, transport them to M&S, and glue them together just like a plastic construction kit. Looks of shock and confusion appeared on the experienced ship builders' faces as this was uncharted territory.

Gustaf continued, "Before we can make the pieces for this 3D jigsaw, we need to know their shapes, sizes and number. We have created a tool which does this job faster than anything you will have ever seen. When asked to make a life size replica of an Abraham tank we designed a computer program which, if I may say so, is brilliant." Bertrand handed him the remote. "To dismember the object, we need good drawings showing every aspect and overall measurements of the length, width and height. The program will work out the rest. For this illustration,

I have taken the drawings of an ordinary fishing boat."

He pressed a button and a typical fishing trawler appeared on the computer. The next images were line drawings showing the boat from the front, side, rear, top and bottom. The next screen showed the dimensions of the trawler. "Now," he said, "we have all the information we need. The computer minutely scans the drawings and compares every line against the dimensions. It works out the length of each line, its angle to adjacent lines, and the shape of each curve. This is what the computer has calculated." The next screen showed the trawler as a skeletal framework of girders and upright, horizontal, diagonal and curved spars. The skeleton turned three hundred and sixty degrees and tipped forward in a slow summersault. It was a three dimensional drawing that could be viewed from any angle. "Now we ask the computer to dismantle it and count the shapes." He pressed the remote again. The skeleton came apart, each spar drifting from its place and landing on a stack of identical shapes. The stacks grew as the ship disintegrated until finally there was nothing but pillars of different shapes with numbers under each. "Now we know how many shapes we need to replicate the boat. At this point, or at the 'skeletal stage', we could edit the shapes or the whole boat so that when rejoined it will be as we wish it."

The room exploded with excitement. The Big Mac raised his hand and said, "Regardless of whatever happens to the Adongiva, we would like a copy of that computer programme."

Hans said, "It was created at enormous expense purely for our use and is not for sale. I can, of course, see the commercial potential but if we don't share it, we have an advantage over competitors. Perhaps it might be possible if our two companies work together and totally dominate ship building for the foreseeable future, provided you accept that the programme is absolutely top secret."

Hans asked Nils Olof to speak about the workforce. Nils spoke softly and Hiram leaned forward to hear clearly. "The materials used to prepare the surfaces are toxic and, during the joining process, dangerous fumes are released. All personnel have to wear full body protection suits, including breathing apparatus, like space suits."

Bertrand and Terence McCallister exchanged glances as they both thought about the silver suit in Oliver's dream. The others looked horrified. Nils continued, "The entire assembly must be done in a double skinned, air tight plastic tent, or 'envelope', big enough to contain the ship, construction equipment, materials and personnel. No one is allowed in without protection and no one allowed out without decontamination. During the basic construction stage, the atmosphere in the tent can at times be lethal. After completion of the Hard Plastic outer shell, deck supports and walls, the area can be decontaminated and the envelope dismantled. The rest of the ship can then be assembled and outfitted normally. It is my job to ensure that everyone is trained properly because no construction is worth the life of a worker. I will now take questions."

There was stunned silence as they absorbed the details. Slowly, hands went up. One asked how such an envelope could be built in a dry dock. Nils said they had done it in Sweden and, although not on this scale, they were confident it could be achieved.

Another asked what construction materials could be so dangerous. Nils said the ingredients were secret and the drums would be labelled 'Red', 'White' and 'Blue'.

Someone asked if Hiram should be worried about such toxic materials. Nils replied that, once stabilised, the material was safe enough to eat your dinner off. It was only dangerous during construction and repairs.

Another questioner asked if the fumes would kill the tank crew if an enemy attacked a Hard Plastic tank. Hans said they had deliberately devised a complex construction method. Each chemical has to be applied in the correct order and to a precise timetable and, if too early or late, it will fail. As a consequence, to penetrate a tank you need to hit it on the same spot with the correct sequence of chemicals and precise timed delays – a feat virtually impossible in battlefield conditions.

Someone asked where they were going to get hundreds of space suits at short notice. They were told that hard space suits would not be used as they protect from solar radiation, extreme temperature and space debris. Instead, their suits, similar to military NBCD suits, are made from rubberised aluminium.

After more questions, Bertrand thanked everyone and summed the meeting up. Everyone seemed satisfied, except the acting Finance Director who seemed incapable of smiling. The Big Mac said after lunch the visitors would sit with M&S specialists to flesh out details. He said this full meeting would reconvene at five pm for reports. He thanked the M&S Divisional and Department Heads not involved in the project, hoped that they had found it interesting and reminded that everything discussed was classified.

When Hiram had arrived for the morning meeting, Bertrand noticed his expression and made a mental note to speak later. As everyone filed into the corridor for lunch, Bertrand collared him and asked if he was OK. Hiram said he had enjoyed the meeting and was impressed by the experts. "It's just that when you arrived you looked worried." Hiram shrugged it off. "Tell me what's wrong."

"It's the cabin."

"Don't you like it?"

"It's wonderful, couldn't be better."

"So, what's the problem?"

"It's full of food, booze and toiletries."

"Why is that a problem?"

"Am I supposed to use that stuff whenever I feel like? Do I replace what I use, so that it's ready for the next guest? Or do they put it on my bill at the end of my stay?"

Bertrand stared at Hiram as if hearing something unintelligible and a smile creased his face. "You are a really nice man, if a trifle innocent. Many people have used those cabins but I believe you are the first to ask that question." Hiram looked embarrassed. Bertrand said, "When Mr. McCallister asked you to stay as a VIP guest, he really meant as a guest. I'm sure you didn't ask guests in your home to replace what they used or give them a bill. You would want guests to enjoy your hospitality and not feel guilty about being spoiled."

"True," said Hiram, "but this is different. There is a small fortune in that cabin that could feed a family of four. I dread to think what those toiletries must have cost."

Bertrand roared with laughter. "Just remember, the cabins are normally for very senior people who expect the best of everything. Politicians are the worst scroungers of all who will eat and drink you out of house and home. You might get a cursory 'thank you' if you're lucky."

"That may be so," said Hiram, "but I'm no scrounger, and I don't want to take advantage."

Bertrand said, "That proves your good nature, Hiram. Use what you want as often as you want, compliments of the boss." Hiram said thanks but Bertrand brushed it aside and they headed for the queue at the buffet table.

After lunch, Hiram left the experts to their deliberations and headed for his cabin. He unpacked his belongings and had another look round. It was superbly furnished and designed, and gave him ideas for the cabins on the Adongiva. He lay on the bed and relaxed until four-thirty, then returned for the five pm meeting.

If Hiram was impressed by the professionalism earlier, he was bowled over by the reports. They had sorted and organised information into detailed plans and talked as if they had been familiar with the project for months. They spoke of everything from maximum endurance limits, load displacement, considerations affecting size and weight ratio and stabilizers to air conditioning and laundry facilities. Hiram looked at those listening intently and wondered if anyone guessed that he hadn't a clue what most of this was about.

Someone stated a clipper bow would give it a sleeker, streamlined look. The accommodation hull would be 62.5 metres long, 9.9 metres wide, and have a draft of 2.7 metres. The engineering hulls would be 56.2 by 7.9 metres. The overall length, from bow to sterns, would be 90.7 metres, making it a substantial vessel. Plans were outlined for envelope construction with double skin containing inert gas at positive pressure to prevent leakage, safety procedures, decontamination, refrigeration and air conditioning units.

Adongiva drawings would be scanned into Gustaf Bjorne's computer by nightfall and by tomorrow afternoon the Swedish factory would have three shifts working round the clock producing parts. In twenty days, the parts would be transported by air to M&S, together with assembly equipment and supplies. It would take four weeks to assemble the materials, build and prepare the envelope, and by the time it was operational the Hard Plastic parts would be inside. Construction of the hulls, superstructures, deck supports, main walls and bulkheads was estimated to take eight weeks. Decontaminating and dismantling the envelope would take three days. An army of IT experts, technicians, electricians, plumbers, joiners, fitters, designers and others would swarm over the ship in just thirteen weeks from today. It was an incredibly short and unprecedented timetable.

Whilst the envelope was being created within Dry Dock 5, a number of M&S personnel would undergo intensive training in the new techniques. Anderson plastics already had workers trained and ready but, for a project this size, more were required and in just eight weeks time. Bertrand summed up the meeting by saying that this gathering, now designated the Adongiva Coordinating Group, or ACG, would convene every Monday morning for reports and coordination. Hans Kristian added that each member was privileged to be involved in this prestigious project.

After the meeting, the crowd dispersed and talked excitedly. The Big Mac and Bertrand were speaking to Hans. They all seemed busy and Hiram, feeling embarrassed to be alone, moved to the door. The Big Mac spotted the movement and called him over to ask how he found the meeting. Hiram said it had been fascinating and he was impressed by the weight of talent and skill being assembled. The Big Mac nodded approval and asked if he liked the accommodation. Hiram replied that it was marvellous but too grand for someone like him. This was dismissed this with a wave.

"Nonsense, you enjoy it, Have a nice meal at the club and explore the leisure facility. I'll catch you later." He slapped Hiram's arm heartily and turned to his other guests.

As Hiram moved from the room, Lady Cynthia was waiting. She handed him an envelope marked 'draft contract' and said there was a copy for him and another for his lawyer. She asked if there was anything else she could do for him. Having not been with a woman since his wife's death, Hiram could not help but think lascivious thoughts. Luckily, they did not make it to his lips and he mumbled, "I don't think so. I will see you later, no doubt."

He decided to visit the club to ask about ordering dinner. In the imposing entrance of the club, a man in a dark suit greeted Hiram. "Good evening, Mr. Montgomery. I trust you are well on this cold evening?"

"Yes, thank you," said Hiram. "I'm sorry to bother you, but I was wondering what time is dinner served and whether I need to book."

Peregrine Anstruther, Manager of the Senior Staff Club, summed Hiram up as someone important to the management, but lacking in poise and self-confidence. Mr. Ansthuther took pride in ensuring every visitor had a good experience. He was used to individuals with high self-opinion who often treated staff as servants. He determined to ensure sure Hiram got the very best attention at all times. "Dinner is served until midnight, Mr. Montgomery, and no need to book. When you're ready, I can guarantee you a most enjoyable meal."

Hiram checked his watch. "Could I come back in an hour?" Mr. Anstruther said that would no problem and he would look forward to his return. Hiram then asked about the dress code. Mr. Anstruther said that most diners wore suits with collar and tie, but a sports jacket would not present a problem. Hiram was about to turn but stopped. "Excuse my ignorance, but I've never been here before. Do I pay for my meals and drinks as I get them or are they on my room account?"

Mr. Anstruther looked surprised. "Pay for them, Sir? You don't pay for anything here. The facilities are entirely with the compliments of the management."

"Oh, I see. Thank you."

"It is my very great pleasure, sir." Peregrine Anstruther meant every word having taken a personal interest in this guest. He was going to enjoy looking after Hiram Montgomery, as he was such a refreshing change from the arrogant, toffee-nosed politicians he had to put up with.

CHAPTER TEN

One of the attendees at the morning meeting was Cedric Speed. He was not the sort who makes much of a first impression. With his 4'10" build, owlish spectacles and perpetual grey pullover, he looked more like a student than a respected engineer. He studied at Oxford University and obtained a double first in physics and mathematics with degrees in theoretical and applied engineering sciences. He joined M&S as Assistant Deputy Technical Services Librarian, got promoted to Deputy Technical Services Librarian and, when his superior retired, he became Chief Technical Services Librarian.

When he first started, his main job was archiving records and doing research on request. He knew things could be much better and set about improving it. Now he was in charge of a monster computer and full-time staff of fifteen researchers, librarians and assistants. They still gathered information from all departments, but this was no longer their main function. They now scoured journals and reports, gathering any data related to shipbuilding, and cross-referenced the information. Cedric did not just gather information for the sake of it. He was proactive and would suggest innovations or technological advances for inclusion in current projects. Many times Cedric Speed had proved his worth by ensuring M&S was at the cutting edge of technology.

When Bertrand showed the designs for the Adongiva, everyone was fascinated. Cedric leaned forward and a small bell sounded in his head. A stored memory lurked somewhere but he could not retrieve it. He stared at the three-hulled design and pummelled his brain, but the idea remained hidden. As the virtual tour moved on, Cedric was annoyed that whatever had set his mind racing remained out of focus. When he overheard a colleague at lunch saying he loved the rolls with sesame seeds, the bell suddenly became a fire alarm.

Rolls – the memory was triggered. *The Rolls-Royce Seahorse electric engine would be perfect for a ship like Adongiva.* He decided to forgo lunch and switched on his computer. The file appeared and, although he knew it well, he read it again very thoroughly. He printed two copies – one for discussion with others and one to scribble notes on. He then found the number for Rolls Royce Marine Engineering. As the second meeting of the Adongiva Coordinating Group was ending, Cedric sought out Eddie Harris, a Chief Engineer. When Cedric told him he had an idea for the Adongiva engines, Eddie readily agreed to a chat back at his office. Eddie started by saying that he had thought of the more conventional Pratt and Whitfield Four in Line with Turbo Injection and pre-heater for extra 'oomph'. However, after today's revelations he was considering going upmarket for something with pizzazz. He asked Cedric what he had in mind.

Cedric said, "When I saw the design this morning, the hairs on my neck stood up. It took a while but then it came to me. The Adongiva is tailor made for the Rolls-Royce Seahorse electric engine. It has a broad, central accommodation hull flanked by two long and narrow engineering hulls and not much room at the stern. Engines of the power needed, plus propeller shaft housing and rudder gear, would in my opinion take up too much space. If you look at these sterns, they are ideal platforms for Seahorse electric engines."

Eddie looked at him strangely. "Say that again?"

Cedric repeated, "Rolls-Royce Seahorse electric engines."

Eddie studied him for even longer then said, "I have known you a long time and have been grateful for your suggestions. You're not prone to leg pulling and you haven't been drinking, so why in hell did you say that?" Cedric said he had given it thought and was sure a marriage of Adongiva and Seahorse would be perfect.

Eddie gestured him to stop. "Firstly, it's an enormously powerful outboard engine designed for propelling an experimental twin hulled Navy frigate like a racing boat. Hang a pair behind the Adongiva and the poor, little bugger would tip backwards. They would be too big and heavy. Secondly, being electric they need a large power supply, which

126

means electricity generators in place of conventional engines, making any space saving minimal. Thirdly, the Seahorse engines had state of the art sound generators to cancel the engine noise and make them quiet, necessary for a stealth frigate but far too expensive for us. Fourthly, being outside the protection of the hull, they have heavy, expensive armour. Fifthly, they have a hellishly expensive, customised large broad blade, gold plated, ultra low cavitation, and silent propellers. Sixthly, it never made it past production and testing because the government abandoned the frigate before it left the drawing board. Rolls-Royce was publicly humiliated when they tried to recoup the millions spent designing and building the engines. They lost their case and ended up severely out of pocket. It was a while ago, but I'll bet they are still smarting from it. If the Seahorse engines still exist, which I doubt, they will be in bits and stored in cases somewhere and Rolls-Royce won't appreciate being reminded of an old wound. Seventhly... well, there must be a seventh reason, and there's probably an eighth as well."

Cedric smiled as if he had been expecting the objections. "I congratulate you. It was a long time ago, but you remember the details perfectly. Then again, I suspect most engineers remember how marvellous and imaginative the Seahorse engine was. I do not dispute that everything you've said is true, almost." Eddie was about to speak but Cedric silenced him. "You're right to say that to propel the frigate, the engines needed to be powerful, and therefore large and heavy. However, removing one, or more, of the motors can reduce these factors. The original design had four electric motors stacked one above the other, between the control module and the gearing mechanism. I know we can make this modification because I've checked."

Eddie tried again but Cedric shushed him. "The electricity generator necessary to power an original Seahorse and other requirements of a frigate would be bulky. Based on today's estimated size and weight of the Adongiva, I have calculated the power output required and a suitable modern generator would be substantially smaller. The high tech noise reduction equipment can be removed. I have checked this also, and it would dramatically reduce the price. As the Adongiva is not a warship, heavy armour plate is unnecessary. A light-weight protective cover attach to the stern, possibly in Hard Plastic, would suffice. Similarly, there is no stealth requirement for a low noise propeller and a standard propeller would save a fortune. Although a Seahorse engine has never undergone sea trials, it did have extensive test bed running. They still have a working engine at a test facility and enough parts to build more. It was not Rolls-Royce's fault that government incompetence led to the scrapping of the stealth frigate even before it was built. The fact remains that the Rolls-Royce Seahorse electric engine is a wonderful piece of engineering which would suit the Adongiva perfectly, given the chance."

Eddie sat motionless as he took in what he had heard. "How do you know?" he said softly.

"How do I know what?"

"You said you had checked that the modifications were possible, and that a working Seahorse engine still exists. How do you know that?"

Cedric looked embarrassed under the scrutiny and said, "I have an old friend at Rolls-Royce Marine Engineering and I ran it by him. He was as sceptical as you to begin with but, after I had gone through my reasoning, he seemed quite interested."

"You did what? Have you gone completely mad? You know perfectly well that an idea such as this has to be agreed by the project manager before we talk to an outside agency."

Cedric seemed unperturbed. "It's all right. I wasn't officially discussing it with Rolls-Royce as a representative of M&S. I was merely having a private, informal chat with a friend who happens to be an expert on a matter in which I was interested."

"Does this friend have a name?"

"Of course, it's David Ridley. He is a senior engineer at Rolls-Royce and we have known each other for years."

"Do you mean *the* David Ridley? Senior Engineering Inspector at their Hampshire site?"

"Yes, do you know him?"

"Of course I know him. The Big Mac is going to go ape shit. You'd better come with me."

"Where are we going?" cried Cedric as Eddie Harris hurried out of the door. Cedric had no option but to hurry after him.

After the meeting, Bertrand and Terence McCallister had spent some time making sure everyone was happy with their allotted tasks. After leaving Hans Kristian and his three wise men in the hands of various

M&S personnel to discuss specifics, they returned to the quiet office to go over points raised during the day. Bertrand asked what he should say to Oliver Russell next time they talked. After all, it was Oliver who had passed Hiram to M&S and he was bound to ring sooner or later to see how the Adongiva was progressing. He was a friend of Bertrand's and it seemed unfair to shut him out, but he acknowledged the confidentiality of this stage of the project was crucial.

The Big Mac rubbed his chin as he thought for a few moments. He said, "I suggest we tell him that we have decided to ask a specialist plastics company from Sweden to supply a revolutionary non-metallic material for the outer shell of the ship, because it will make it lighter without sacrificing strength. Tell him we want to keep the details confidential until the launch to ensure maximum publicity impact. That's all near enough to the truth to salve your conscience without giving too much away. Stress the need for him to keep his mouth shut". They moved on to discuss a computer model, which dealt with propulsive efficiency and the avoidance of cavitation, erosion and vibration.

Suddenly, there was a knock. Eddie Harris stuck his head round the door and The Big Mac motioned him in. After Eddie and Cedric Speed sat down and Eddie recounted his conversation with Cedric. Bertrand and The Big Mac listened without expression. From time to time, they looked from Eddie to Cedric and back again but said nothing.

When Eddie was finished, the two bosses remained silent for a moment. The Big Mac sighed, rubbed his temples and finally said to Cedric, "What did you say when David Ridley asked you why you wanted this information?"

Cedric had replied that he was just checking a theory. He had told David Ridley that M&S were about to build a breathtaking, fantastic and unique specification based on a design drawn by the late, great Ivanovitch Petrovsky on the night before he died. David Ridley was mightily impressed by this. Cedric said he had added that the ship was so novel it would be a crowd puller wherever it went, attracting much publicity and attention. He had said he thought that theoretically the trimaran design could be a perfect vessel for the Rolls-Royce Seahorse electric engines.

"Did the subject of Hard Plastic come up?" asked The Big Mac dryly. Cedric said the name of Hard Plastic was not mentioned but he had said that a new material, stronger but lighter than steel, would be used. He had said to David Ridley that every company associated with this exciting project would feel privileged to be invited. The Big Mac stared for a while. "Oh good, no exaggerated or overblown hyperbole then?"

Cedric could feel the ground crumble beneath him. The Big Mac leaned forward. "What did he say on Rolls-Royce's attitude to the government?"

Cedric realised the hole beneath him was growing. "He said that, as well as losing millions, Rolls-Royce had lost face and was still mad." He had said to David Ridley that the supply of Seahorse engines to the Adongiva could be an opportunity for Rolls-Royce to get even. Cedric was aware of the horrified expressions around him.

The Big Mac stayed calm. "How do you make that out?"

"Before the 'Semi Submersible Stealth Frigate', or Type FZ1492, was scrapped, the government could have owned the fastest, most manoeuvrable warship in the world. They screwed that up and left Rolls-Royce holding a white elephant. Now, if Rolls Royce were to sell that engine to us, they would be able to rub the government's nose in it by saying that the Royal Navy has no vessel of any description that could catch the Adongiva. There isn't a ship of comparable size anywhere on the planet that could beat the Adongiva, with Seahorse electric engines, in a straight race. The Royal Navy has therefore lost out and Rolls-Royce, who had public sympathy throughout the Seahorse affair, has come out on top. This would remind people that the government is incompetent, bankrupt of common sense and coherent policies, and morally corrupt – just before the launch of a general election campaign in a few months time."

"How did Riley react to that?" Eddie asked.

"It was like a starving man being offered a ticket to a buffet." Cedric studied the faces of his colleagues and could not decide whether they showed concern, pleasure, displeasure, admiration or pity for a man facing execution.

Bertrand asked, "How did you leave it with David Ridley?"

"I told him no decision had been reached on engines and that this was not an official approach, but an informal chat between two friends." Cedric continued, "I said that my ideas might be rejected in which case it would go no further. I asked that the conversation be kept between the two of us until further notice."

Bertrand asked Cedric if he really believed David Ridley would simply sit and wait. It had not occurred to Cedric that his friend at Rolls-Royce would not do what they had agreed. The Big Mac said that he also knew David Ridley and, whilst he may well have regarded Cedric Speed as a friend, he was also a company man who would stop at nothing to avenge the wrong he perceived the government perpetrated against Rolls-Royce and the project that was once been his baby. It was inconceivable that right now David Ridley was not discussing this matter with his boss, Sir Bartholomew St. John Farquharson, Chief Executive and Managing Director of Rolls Royce Marine Engineering.

Cedric was distraught, repeatedly apologising for what he had naively done. He said he had not realised his actions would cause a problem and he had merely done what he had done many times when checking facts – spoken to an expert in the field. He admitted that he may have said a bit more than he should about the Adongiva when getting David Ridley to open up about the Seahorse engine, and he was deeply sorry.

The Big Mac said not to worry and that he would contact Sir Bartholomew St. John Farquharson, or 'Sibarti', to discuss it. In the meantime, he suggested that Eddie and Bertrand check out Cedric's figures and determine whether the Seahorse engines were as suitable as Cedric seemed to think. "It may very well be that Cedric has come up with an idea that no one else has thought of and it might be of great benefit to the Adongiva." That seemed to signal the end of the meeting and the men stood to make their departures.

As they headed for the door, the telephone rang. The Big Mac snatched it up, "Yes. Just a minute." Eddie, Cedric and Bertrand stopped and The Big Mac gestured them to resume their seats and said into the instrument, "Put him through." He pushed a button, put the phone on its cradle, and signalled his colleagues to keep quiet.

Sir Bartholomew St. John Farquharson's voice filled the room. It was a loud, harsh and unpleasant noise. "Good evening, Terence. I have just had a conversation with my Senior Engineering Inspector, David Ridley, who had a call from your man Cedric Speed."

The Big Mac decided to give nothing away. "That's right," he said.

There was a pause then Sir Bartholomew's voice continued,

"He seemed to think your new ship, the Adongiva, would benefit from the use of our Seahorse electric engine."

"That's right," said The Big Mac, a hint of a smile appearing on his face. He was going to stay as brief as possible and let Sibarti do the running until he knew enough to control the conversation. He did not like Sir Bartholomew St. John Farquharson. He was a pompous, self-opinionated man who, although extremely clever and talented, was as cold as ice.

There was another long pause. Sir Bartholomew spoke again, sounding annoyed. "He tells me that your ship is a spectacular trimaran designed by Ivanovitch Petrovsky and is to be made of a revolutionary material about to take the world by storm."

"That's right," said The Big Mac. Now the others in the room were smiling.

"Now look here, Terence, can't you say anything other than 'that's right'? Do you want my help or not?"

"I'm not sure," said The Big Mac. "As my man, Cedric Speed, said to your man, we have not decided on engines yet. We're simply exploring possibilities."

"You know me," snapped Sir Bartholomew. "You know I can't abide bullshit, or horseshit, or excrement from whatever other animal happens to be in current colloquial favour. Let's stop dancing around and cut to the chase."

"And that is?" said The Big Mac.

"You know that the Rolls Royce Seahorse electric engine has been in storage for many years. We spent millions and ended up with egg on our faces and a hole in our pockets. The Seahorse engine would probably stay in limbo for the foreseeable future if it were not for your man, Speed. He has nudged us into considering something that, up until now, was beyond our horizon – modifying the engine to give it a commercial future in a different configuration. This didn't occur to us because the Seahorse engine was specifically designed for a particular application and no other. When that application vanished, it was assumed by a dispirited team that the natural corollary was the absence of purpose for the Seahorse."

The Big Mac was openly surprised. In all the years he had known Sir Bartholomew St. John Farquharson, this was the first time he ever heard him come close to admitting that he, his workforce and his company were fallible. In fact, this was almost an apology.

Sir Bartholomew continued, "I do believe the Seahorse could now have a future, and if you ever feel like dispensing with your man Speed, I will take him off your hands. Based on the rough notes David Ridley took during his conversation with him, it might be possible to modify the Seahorse engine to suit your Adongiva. This all needs to be checked thoroughly, of course."

The Big Mac and the others looked at Cedric. It looked like he was not for the chop after all but, in fact, was in demand.

Sir Bartholomew coughed politely and said, "I would like you to stop looking for an alternative and to agree here and now to take the Rolls-Royce Seahorse electric engine and electric generator as the power plant for your Adongiva."

"Now, why on earth should I agree to that?" said The Big Mac. "I don't know how much it is going to cost, how much power it gives, how cost efficient it is, whether it is going to fit the Adongiva, or even if it works properly. After all, it has never been actually tested in a real ship, has it?"

From the noises coming from the loudspeaker it sounded as if Sir Bartholomew was having a fit. He exploded: "Now see here, Terence Biggins McCallister, don't take me for a fool. I know you very well. I know you're not the sort of man who goes into a situation without full possession of the facts. It's therefore reasonable to assume that you already know that the Seahorse engine was exhaustively tested, over a lengthy period, on a hydraulic tilting rig, put through a range of difficult conditions, and that it passed every test with flying colours. You'll also know the performance figures and running cost figures, because they were in an article published by the government against our advice in the *New Scientist* magazine some six years ago." The Big Mac motioned to Cedric to make a note to dig out this article. "As for fitting the Adongiva, you are being preposterous. Your man Speed has already worked out how to alter the Seahorse shape by removing some of the motors. As far as the cost goes, it *will* fit your budget." He strongly emphasised the word 'will'.

The Big Mac and his two colleagues looked at each other in amazement. He said, "You don't know what our budget is. Even with all the fancy bits that we don't want taken off the Seahorse engine, it is still a damned expensive bit of kit. I am really not sure we can afford it, regardless of how good your engine is."

Sir Bartholomew's voice oozed from the speaker like ice cold water. "You want a first class world beating engine befitting your ship, and I want to be involved in the Adongiva project. It is as simple as that. The money is not an important issue here. If I say the price will be at a level acceptable to you, then it shall."

"That sounds too generous to be true," said The Big Mac.

"Generous be dammed. Why are you are not listening?" hissed the speaker. "This marriage shall come about. It is important for the future of the Seahorse engine and for the Adongiva. It is important for Rolls Royce and for you."

"In what way is it important for Rolls Royce, and for us?" The Big Mac sounded cautious.

"Stop pretending to be stupid, Terence, it doesn't become you. If this ship is as important as you say, it is essential that Rolls Royce be associated with it. We will take part payment by way of prominent space in the promotional literature."

The Big Mac, Cedric and Eddie looked at each other. They were nowhere near considering promotional material.

The voice continued, "It is important for you because if the Adongiva is made of this revolutionary new material, is designed by Ivanovitch Petrovsky, and is fitted with Rolls Royce Seahorse Electric Engines, other suppliers will scratch each other's eyes out to be considered. You will be able to pick the best of everything and haggle for keen prices. For our part, as your man Speed pointed out, there is an election looming. I want to be able to poke the Prime Minister's testicles with a hot poker, throughout his campaign."

Three pairs of legs involuntarily slammed shut, and faces winced, as their owners contemplated the words of Sibarti.

"Do we have a deal?" The voice sounded insistent.

The Big Mac sat back in his chair and smiled broadly. This conversation had gone much better than he had anticipated. Lots of good surprises, and ample food for thought. "Yes I think we probably do, subject to detailed discussion by technical bods and legal eagles."

"Excellent. I can have a small team over to your place by tomorrow afternoon for preliminary talks, goodbye."

The phone call was suddenly over. The three M&S men looked at each other, lost for words, at the incredible conversation that had occurred.

Eventually The Big Mac looked at Cedric and said, "Well, my man Speed, it looks like you have pulled something really interesting out of the bag this time. I think you two had better go and get your heads together for tomorrow's meeting. I do believe the Adongiva has just taken another major leap forward. It appears to be changing daily, and getting bigger and better all the time. This blessed ship is developing a life of its own and leading us, rather than the other way round."

When Hiram returned to the club Mr. Anstruther was waiting and asked if he would like a drink in the bar. Hiram decided to go straight to the restaurant. He sat at a corner table, beneath some potted palms, overlooking the restaurant which was less than half full with about twenty people sitting in groups of twos and threes. He was greatly impressed by the place, which was more like a first class restaurant than a works club. The white linen tables gleamed like snow, the napkins were crisply starched, staff moved discreetly in immaculate uniforms and the menu was better than the most expensive places he had visited, which was not many. The only difference was that it was completely free. It was disconcerting to have no prices on the eight page wine list. Not knowing much about wine, it was normally the prices that determined his choice. It was an extensive menu with many 'ordinary' things like ten species of fish, food from seven countries, and an impressive list of steaks, but there was also a good selection of what Hiram thought were outlandish items for a staff restaurant, like whole lobster, dressed crab, Russian caviar, a choice of oysters, and truffles. He wondered how on earth they could keep such an abundance of items in a kitchen dealing with a clientele as small as the senior staff of one company.

Despite the extensive and lavish menu Hiram ordered a simple meal of cheese omelette and chips, and a beer. After his meal he returned to his cabin, had a large malt whisky, and turned in for an early night

In the morning he thought about going to the club for an obscenely large fry up. He did enjoy a full English breakfast, and had no doubt that in this place it would be greater than just excellent. However when he looked at all the food in the refrigerator he felt guilty. He had been brought up in a Catholic household where a mantra had been that wasting good food was a sin, because of all the starving Africans. If he ate in the club all the time, the food in the cabin would be wasted. Perhaps he should eat all the food in the cabin over the next few days, and then he wouldn't feel guilty about eating in the restaurant. The snag with this plan is that the spaces in the fridge might be refilled, and he would be no better off. He could leave a note saying don't replace anything. Then he might run out of essentials like coffee and whisky. He would have to say which things he wanted replacing and which he didn't. Why was life so complicated? He decided to have another word with Bertrand on the subject. In the meantime he decided to have toast with some cold meat. Damn those Africans.

During the next few days Bertrand had arranged for Hiram to meet people involved in the planning. April Hunter, interior designer, talked about decorating styles, soft furnishings and equipment. Aaron Timmerman, procurement officer for ancillary craft, suggested a fast semi inflatable for emergencies and utility work, a motor launch for passengers, at least two jet skies and other water sports equipment. Above the boat dock was space for car and helicopter. This 'hangar' would have a lift to the flight deck above, which could also serve as deck area for games and relaxing when the helicopter is tucked away. Other people talked about lifts and stairs, watertight doors, CCTV, and control layouts.

The one area which created some disagreement was staffing. Hiram's original thought had been a very small crew, the fewer the better. After Oliver at Cardhu Boat builders, he conceded that an engineer, cook, housemaid, personal assistant and another body for odd jobs might be required. After discussions with Bertrand he agreed a minimum of mechanical and electrical engineers, and IT expert; a chef and assistant; a cleaner or two encompassing room cleaning, laundry and dry cleaning skills; a stores and supplies person who could double as barman; a steward; a personal assistant with assistant clerk. Several could double as odd job people, or general seamen. With the suggestion of the ship as a luxury cruise ship, the list included fitness trainer, hairdresser and beautician, another steward and barman, coxswain for the boats, and pilot for the helicopter which Hiram had not taken too seriously until the cruise ship idea. Then there was the medic. Now it was suggested that people could not work round the clock without time off.

The list was growing steadily and Hiram did not like it. The conclusion was a crew of forty-one, including a captain, would give sufficient cover for essential tasks over twenty-four hours, with time for rest and recuperation. This depended on them being multi-talented and performing tasks other than main specialisation. Hiram was aghast at the possible bill, until he was reminded that using the ship for cruising for a few months would pay the running costs, including wages, for a year. Hiram was not convinced until Clarice Teasdale, HR manager, and Tony Weinberger, business manager, showed him the projected figures. He saw that after all costs had been covered, the paying guests would generate a tidy little profit, with nine months of the year left. Assuming another ninety-one days of showcasing, advertising and marketing for the suppliers and other companies involved, there were still one hundred and eighty three days left to enjoy. In addition, the profits from merchandising could be considerable.

Hiram said the flaw he could see was that nobody would pay two thousand pounds per night. Tony Weinberger produced three brochures for hotels offering bed and breakfast for between twenty one to thirty three hundred pounds per night, and said these places were usually booked up well in advance.

"Bed and breakfast for how much?" exclaimed Hiram.

"That's right, and in most cases, that does not include all the other amenities on offer," said Tony. "You, on the other hand, are giving an all inclusive holiday on an exclusive and unusual yacht with many amenities, for a price not considered extortionate by the rich, of whom there are many. We have to target the marketing, and get some 'celebs' to help generate publicity, by giving freebies or donations to favourite charities. I have lots of contacts to get you started."

Friday 30th January 2026

Sir Bartholomew St. John Farquharson was feeling pleased with himself. Yesterday his engineers and lawyers had met their opposite numbers from M&S and had gone over the figures. Agreement had been reached and already his engineers were starting to convert two Seahorse engines. When they were ready they would be transported to M&S. Now as he surveyed the room and motley collection he espied a face that gave him more pleasure. Normally receptions at the Mansion House were tedious gatherings of MPs wanting something for nothing, civil servants incessantly talking shop, and people hunting for opportunities. The face he recognised belonged to Algernon Nabarro CBE, head of Hartington Electronic Systems. He disliked Algernon because he considered him a self centred, arrogant, self-opinionated snob who loved to let everyone know how superior he was. The fact that this description could also be applied to him did not register in his thinking however he was aware that his opinion of Algernon was reciprocated. Meeting in public was an opportunity for scoring points and proving they were the better of the two. He had something today that would really get up the Algernon's nose. He homed in on his target.

As he approached Algernon was pontificating about supplying his new optical fibre, variable display, touch screen control panels for the French railway signalling system. Algy had spotted Sir Bartholomew's approach, but pretended not to until they were adjacent.

"Hello, Barty, my dear boy," he said over his shoulder then turned back again, as if to say 'don't interrupt, I'm busy'. He knew the term 'Barty' would annoy Sir Bartholomew and that 'my dear boy' would imply his seniority.

Sir Bartholomew ignored the insult. He had something up his sleeve to upset Algernon, and he could be patient. He waited while his victim finished.

Finally when he had made Sir Bartholomew wait long enough, Algernon turned and said, "And how are you my dear chap? Is everything going well for you at RR Marine?" He abbreviated Rolls Royce to RR and heavily emphasised the word Marine to suggest this was not the proper and highly respected Rolls Royce Company but some inferior bunch of greasy mechanics in overalls.

Sir Bartholomew did not rise to this bait but said things were going well and that they had just agreed to supply rather spectacular engines for a special ship by M&S.

"Oh really," said Algernon in a voice that said 'how utterly boring'. Before Algernon could change the subject Sir Bartholomew added, "It's a most exciting, unusual and unique trimaran specially designed by Ivanovitch Petrovsky on the night before he was killed."

This produced satisfying noises of appreciation by the listeners, which Algernon did not like. Sir Bartholomew had quite enough attention from these peasants and it was time to wrest their attention back again. Before he could say anything, however, Sir Bartholomew said, "But the really interesting part is," he stopped and put his hand to his lips, "I had better not. It is a bit hush-hush and I am not supposed to say too much." His audience was hooked. After a pause to heighten the drama he said he would tell them if they promised not to breathe a word. They swore that not even torture would induce them to betray the confidence. Sir Bartholomew looked around conspiratorially to ensure privacy and even Algernon could not help leaning forward.

"There is a new material – stronger and lighter than steel – which is going to revolutionise the world. In future all air, land and sea craft will be made from it." Sir Bartholomew was pleased with the response. He waited until they finished demonstrating amazement, before delivering the punch line. "This ship, the first of its kind, is assured a place in history. M&S will not be asking for tenders as every supplier for the Adongiva – that's the name of this ship – will be by invitation only."

He pronounced Adongiva the way that Bertrand originally had. They only want the best of everything and naturally they asked us to supply something special for the engines. "No doubt, they will have been in touch with you, Algy?"

Algernon Nabarro looked as if he had just been skewered. He cast about for a suitable reply and then said, "Yes, of course they have, but we haven't decided yet. We are so busy, it would mean letting other clients down."

It was a good attempt, but his listeners suppressed their delight at the obvious embarrassment on display. They loved embarrassment, provided it was someone else's.

Sir Bartholomew was ecstatic. *Gotcha, you bastard*, he thought, but then for devilment turned up the heat. "You want to sort your priorities, old chap. All the important people are getting involved, and frankly this is as big as it gets."

Algernon thrust a hand in a pocket and pressed a button his pager, which beeped. He fished it out, said, "The American President's office wants me," and rushed from the room. He needed to ring Terence Biggins McCallister and make sure he got the order for control panels on the Adongiva.

It had only been Sir Bartholomew's intention to tweak Algernon's nose. It had not occurred to him that his words might create a bandwagon. The others in that little group could not wait to tell, in strict confidence, what they had learned. They wanted others to know they mixed with important people, and were among the first to learn of a new harder than steel material about to revolutionise civilisation. They also told of an incredible ship called the Adongiva designed by the late great Ivanovitch Petrovsky being built in secret by M&S, and how only the *crème de la crème* would be invited to participate in this historical event. Everyone had to swear to secrecy.

Like a ripple on a pond the secret rolled out, and became a tsunami. The bandwagon picked up speed, and everyone it hit was desperate to get on. A number of companies considered themselves best in their field, and therefore determined to get on the Adongiva list.

CHAPTER ELEVEN

Monday 2nd February 2026

The previous Wednesday The Big Mac had remarked that the Adongiva seemed to be developing a life of its own. Now he was sure of it. The emergency board meeting on Thursday had gone smoothly, apart from when Caesar Meredith suggested renegotiating the sharing of costs between M&S, Anderson Plastics, and Hiram Montgomery to make the balance more even. The Big Mac said the split had been his decision and the board could accept it, or his resignation. There was no further discussion on the matter.

The afternoon meeting with the Rolls Royce people had also gone well, with everyone in high spirits. The Seahorse was agreed to be a great enhancement of the Adongiva, already widely considered to be marvellous. Fresh stern section plans were drawn and sent to Anderson Plastics together with plans for different bow thrusters for increased manoeuvrability. The original plan had been for conventional side facing bow propellers, but Rolls Royce had come up with their own version of the ABB's Azipod propulsion system. The ship was not only going to be very fast, it could pirouette if required.

On Friday everyone was busy with their allotted tasks and although things were hectic, it was nothing compared to what was to come.

The first indication that something was amiss came in a call on Friday evening from Algernon Nabarro. The Big Mac knew that his company made excellent 'fly by wire' controls and sophisticated displays, if rather pricy. He stunned The Big Mac by offering his services to the Adongiva, made from the new building material. When The Big Mac asked how he knew about it Algernon blustered pompously that it was causing a stir in The City, and he agreed with M&S's policy of inviting the best firms rather than allowing an unseemly scrum of 'second raters'. He had decided to save M&S time by coming forward. The Big Mac knew of Algernon's reputation as big headed and pushy and he would have dismissed him, but he needed to know how the information had got out.

Eventually he admitted that Sir Bartholomew St John Farquharson had tipped him the wink. This surprised The Big Mac because he knew they despised each other. It was Algernon's turn to be surprised when The Big Mac was distinctly cool about his offer. As he became more persistent his confidence waned and The Big Mac demonstrated that he could not be pushed, pulled, bullied, flattered or cajoled. Algernon tried every trick in the book and it dawned on The Big Mac that the gauntlet of challenge had been thrown down by Sir Bartholomew. He was so determined to become part of the Adongiva project he became fixated on not allowing this call to finish without a deal, regardless of details. The Big Mac almost felt sorry for the man as he squeezed him hard.

In the end Algernon was forced to guarantee the latest state of the art technology for bridge and engineering controls for the price of conventional controls. On Saturday morning The Big Mac received a call from Head of Sales at Loipart, a leading supplier of marine galleys, bars, pantries, provision and cold stores, and ships laundry appliances. Shortly afterwards another call came in from Norsafe, one of the most respected companies specialising in lifeboats. In a third phone call the Senior Marketing Director of a well-known supermarket chain wanted to be the official Adongiva provisions supplier. Next the Senior Partner of G B Mclean and Patterson (Tailors) Ltd., the most widely used Naval Uniform supplier, was on the line.

None of these companies usually chased customers because customers usually came to them. The impact of these calls on The Big Mac was profound. M&S had built many prestigious ships, but he had never experienced this. There appeared to be an avalanche rolling in his direction. Whatever Sir Bartholomew had started was spreading like wildfire.

He phoned Sir Bartholomew to find out exactly what he had said, and to whom. Sibarti sounded uncharacteristically apologetic as he related trying to get one over on Algernon at a Mansion House reception. Next The Big Mac called Bertrand, the Head of the Public Relations and several others for an emergency meeting. If the world was about to start knocking, they needed a strategy. They needed to pull in staff and set up an Adongiva Enquiries Office, and ring Heads of Department to warn that calls must be redirected without comment. They worked out procedures, responses and channels, and it took the whole of Saturday. Now it was Monday morning and The Big Mac and Bertrand discussed the enquiries office report and logged calls, deciding on appropriate action. Next it was time to join the ACG meeting.

Hans Kristian and his three men were chatting to Hiram and others when The Big Mac and Bertrand joined them. Bertrand started the meeting by updating everyone on the Seahorse Electric Engines. Hiram had heard of the abortive saga of the type FZ1492 frigate, but could not remember the details so Bertrand recounted the government's ambitious plan for a semi submersible catamaran war ship. It looked like the top of a nuclear submarine with conning tower removed, and balanced on two hulls. In operation it would sink in the water to present low profile and minimum drag, for very high speed; like an approaching torpedo it would be hard to spot or hit, until very close.

At the last moment it would rise to full height and the frontal doors would open revealing rapid-fire heavy calibre cannons capable of hurling a huge amount of armour piercing destruction, and ship-to-ship missile launchers for delivering a fatal blow. From either side torpedoes or depth charges could destroy surface or submarine enemies fore and aft. The strategy was that suddenly faced with such firepower at point blank range, an enemy would surrender without a fight.

Hiram found the telling of the details absolutely fascinating. He could tell from looking at faces round the table, that he was not alone.

Bertrand continued, "Rolls Royce designed, developed and tested a brand new type of engine designed to hang from the stern of each hull. Government bureaucracy, bungling and constant changes of direction led to the scrapping of the project, at which point the Ministry of Defence walked away, leaving Rolls Royce high and dry and with a major financial headache. A court battle failed, some say because the judiciary was leaned on. Subsequently the Seahorse engine has for years been ignominiously stored away and forgotten, until now. Thanks to Cedric Speed's initiative, the engine is being resurrected, and the Adongiva is to be the beneficiary. The Adongiva now has no need of conventional engine, or rudder for the Seahorse engine is designed to hang like an outboard motor, and rotate through three hundred and sixty degrees. Even with the reduction in electric motors it will still be enormously powerful and, in conjunction with the propulsion pod bow thrusters, will give the Adongiva enormous speed and manoeuvrability. In place of conventional engines there will be Electrical Generators, and banks of Matsushita Kogyo Yuasa batteries."

Several around the table were impressed and for Hiram's benefit Bertrand explained that these were the same as the compact, large capacity, high power batteries used recently in space vehicles. The generators would not supply power directly to the engines but would keep the batteries constantly charged and they would provide the power for the engines and other electrical needs of the ship. Hiram admitted they sounded like no batteries he had heard of.

Next The Big Mac reported on the setting up of the Adongiva Enquiries Office because of Sir Bartholomew's silly public taunting of Algernon Nabarro. He said he would have preferred the information to be released in a more considered fashion but perversely the fall out seemed to be advantageous and there appeared to be a growing number of companies rushing to be considered as contributors to the Adongiva. Normally M&S would approach those it wanted, rather than the other way round. At the last meeting Hans Kristian suggested that we should make suppliers and contractors aware of the importance of all this, and how lucky there were to be invited. One week later, a whiff of rumour in the right place and they all believe they are about to miss out on something monumental, and gagging for our patronage.

He added an unexpected consequence of the Seahorse engines discussions had been a suggestion for a large glossy publication in connection with the official launch. "This booklet, or booklets, would contain the details of the Adongiva: its size, weight, layout, performance, crew and everything else," he said. "It is anticipated that there will be a huge and worldwide interest in the ship; from the media, the public, shipping companies and potential buyers, Star Trek fans of which apparently there are millions, and many other categories of people."

He looked around at the others and then continued. "There may very well turn out to be endless marketing opportunities for other merchandising material. You never know, a radio controlled model of the Adongiva might well become the next must-have toy for mums and dads to buy next Christmas."

This produced a ripple of laughter round the table.

Hans Kristian then reported on the manufacture of the Hard Plastic components in Sweden. They had received the plans for the re designed sterns, generator and battery compartments and the altered bow thruster pod apertures. Production was underway and on schedule. He said they had never made ship's propellers before but were keen to begin. Propellers in Hard Plastic would be as durable as steel but substantially lighter, and therefore enhance performance. He went on to say that the envelope construction materials would be arriving soon and work would commence immediately.

The next speaker was Andre Keelan from ITEE Division. He said his people were still getting their heads round the offer by Algernon Nabarro. "Do you realize what he is giving us?" he asked.

The Big Mac shrugged. "The latest and best technology for the bridge and engineering controls. I suppose it will be impressive, for the price of a conventional control system, in exchange for full credit and coverage in our launch and sales material."

Andre replied, "Latest and best does not come close. Every little boy who loves gadgetry, from the age of five to a hundred and five is going to be sick with envy when they see the bridge of the Adongiva. There are very few places in the world that have this system; a nuclear power station in Nebraska, the pan-European air traffic control system in Brussels, Japanese railway network control in Beijing, and possibly the French Railway Signalling Control, and that is about it."

"What's so special about it?" asked Hiram.

Andre explained that the bridge would have no control switches, buttons, levers, or other devices. "Instead there would be black rectangular panels lit from below by millions of fibre optic cables displaying a representation of the controls. To operate anything you don't touch but move your finger in the direction you want the knob to turn, the lever to move, or button to press. You steer the ship, change speed, sound the horn, close doors, or anything else by simply gliding over the panel. The hardest bit is keeping your finger in proximity with the glass without touching it. In addition, instead of having several personnel at their stations, one or two can do all their jobs. Pressing a 'button' makes the screen change and one moment you are at the helm steering the ship, and next you are at the 'comms' sending messages. A moment later you are controlling something else, and you can toggle back and forth between the panels, without leaving your chair."

"Like simultaneous computer windows, but on a touch screen," said Hiram.

"Yes, but you can customise displays for any function, and change them later. It really is going to look like *Star Trek*, inside the ship as well as outside."

Hiram and several others exchanged delighted grins at the description they had been given. One person summed it up, saying, "Fantastic" as he stood and poured himself a coffee from the dispenser on the side table. Others took their cue from him and the meeting was interrupted as cups were passed around, When they had settled again Andre spoke again.

"Speaking of the main computer, we will install a computer cascade system like the one we did on the Duchess of Kent four years ago. That means one main computer is the single interface between the army of other onboard computers and humans, and accessed from any of the consoles scattered throughout the ship. This big 'daddy' computer passes instructions and information between us and the other 'midi' computers under its control. The midi computers each deal with a network of 'third layer' computers. The 'third layer' computers each control a number of 'local' computers which are the ones that actually operate all ship's equipment. Messages, instructions and information constantly cascade up and down though the system."

Andre then said, "The result of this seemingly complex arrangement is that human operators are not overwhelmed with complex information or too many separate tasks to perform; similarly each individual computer is never overloaded and has a small number of relatively uncomplicated tasks to perform. There is even a layer of computers whose sole function is to constantly monitor the function of the other computers, and the communication between them. If they detect the slightest malfunction or irregularity they immediately initiate remedial action procedures. It is like having hundreds of personnel who never leave their posts, lose concentration or make mistakes; require rest, sustenance or time off. It might sound scary, but it is the most efficient and fail-safe system imaginable."

Aaron Timmerman was the next speaker to rise to his feet and survey the assembled group. He said a German boat builder was keen to supply the ancillary craft.

"What's wrong with our usual firm?" asked Bertrand.

"Nothing, but this lot has a very good self-righting, semi-inflatable fast launch they want us to look at. I must confess it certainly seems very interesting. They are willing to do a very good deal and in addition they make custom boats. If you want a pirate ship, three mast Spanish man-of-war, Roman or Viking war galley, or Japanese Emperors' Imperial junk, they will build it in modern materials and with the latest navigational and safety equipment. When I told them that our ship is in the style of the Star Ship *Enterprise* they said they could make us a ship's launch in the shape of a Star Ship *Enterprise* Shuttle Craft, if we take all our life boats and leisure craft from them. I shall keep you posted."

Sheridan Butler, the M&S Chief Press Officer, was next. He said he had been called by a BBC reporter wanting a statement about the rumour that M&S is working on a secret project, building a ship from a new, and untested material. He said the reporter sounded sceptical and just checking what he assumed was a typical false rumour. It had been easy to fob him off but he acknowledged that if they didn't get back to the reporter then he might get curious.

Sheridan said he now had no doubt this reporter was the first of many. He had prepared a draft publicity statement and asked for more details, or necessary corrections and handed copies round for inspection. Bertrand and The Big Mac read their copies and suggested these be handed back to make sure none leave the room. The Big Mac said he would like to add carefully worded references to Ivanovitch Petrovsky, Hard Plastic, and the three hulled design. He said the group should hint vaguely about the *Star Trek* influence rather than reveal too much too early. Bertrand said that as The Big Mac had already pointed out there seems to be a wave of excitement forming out there regarding the Adongiva. He said if Hiram's identity was kept secret, until the launch, this 'man of mystery' element would help stoke the fires of curiosity, and keep them queuing for more.

Thursday 5th February 2026

There had been times during the early part of the week when the days got a bit muddled in Hiram's head. It felt like being on holiday with no agenda, or routine, when it was easy to lose track and forget which day it was. The staff at M&S were frantically busy, and since the meeting on Monday he had been left to amuse himself. Although nothing was said he felt that he could be in the way and so he had leisurely meals, trips to town for sightseeing and shopping, and watched daytime television.

The most interesting news was how the space station was developing. The last time he had seen it, it was a long cylindrical tube with a fat dustbin at one end and one short arm sticking out about half way along. The arm had grown to a size almost as big as the original tube, and another arm was sprouting. The next most talked about subject involved politicians still arguing over government duplicity and economists debating the dramatic collapse in property prices in the north east of England. In another story a spokesman from Scotland Yard said following a complaint about insider dealing, an investigation into Sir Richard Pickles had revealed nothing improper.

On the Thursday afternoon Hiram decided to brighten his day by popping over to see the delectable Lady Cynthia, using the excuse of checking she had received the contract amendments from Roger.

As he stepped from the lift he could sense the pressure. On previous occasions this place exuded an air of calm, but today it looked more like a battle group HQ at war. Everybody walked quickly whilst talking or reading. At Lady Cynthia's door he saw her on the phone and writing furiously. She finished that call, pressed a button and apologised to another caller who had been on hold for a while then put him back on hold, a perfectly lacquered fingernail covered another button and put another caller through to someone else. She laid the phone on its cradle and she patted her hair although, as usual, it was perfect. Finally she looked at Hiram and said hello.

"Pretty busy round here," said Hiram.

"You could say that," she said as she headed for the coffee machine. "Would you like a cup? What can I do for you?"

Hiram thought for a moment. He would love to have a leisurely coffee with this gorgeous woman but she seemed rushed off her feet and he imagined the last thing she wanted was another distraction. He declined and asked if she had received the amendments.

"Yes, thanks," she said. "Mr. McCallister is happy. They've gone to Legal and a final should be with you anytime. Was there anything else?"

She was anxious to get back to work, and he shook his head. "I will see you around then."

"Absolutely," she said as she pressed another button.

As Hiram left Lady Cynthia's office, Bertrand cannoned into him. "Sorry Hiram," he said, obviously in a hurry. "Are you all right? Good. I'll catch you later." He took two steps, turned back and repeated his question.

"Yes, I'm fine," said Hiram.

But Bertrand didn't seem convinced. "What are you doing now?" he persisted.

"Oh, I'm just… err… nothing actually."

"Good. Then come with me. You should find this interesting." Bertrand turned and Hiram almost had to jog to keep up.

They joined Andre Keelan and two other men sitting round a table covered in papers, books and pamphlets. If they were surprised to see Hiram they did not show it.

Bertrand said, "I hope you don't mind Hiram sitting in on this." He did not wait for a reply and said, "OK, report."

Andre said a lot, which meant absolutely nothing to Hiram. He knew he was not needed here and Bertrand had invited him because he was at a loose end. However, he said, "May I ask a question?"

"Go ahead, Hiram. It's your ship."

"What language was that?"

The men laughed. Andre apologised for using jargon and abbreviations. "Your ship will have an Automatic Pilot to maintain course and speed using satellite navigation and global positioning, and tell you where you are without anyone at the wheel. The radar will help you see where you are going and where other ships are, thereby avoiding collisions. There will also be a short range radar to assist the helicopter take off and land in all weathers. Modern ships have a depth data program to measure the depth of water below the keel. The American Navy developed a sophisticated version called Porcupine Survey Sonar, for mapping the seabed but because it looks down, forwards and sideways it also protects from frogmen or other submarine threats. A short range cheaper version is available for the civilian market, called the Hedgehog Submarine Proximity Alarm. By submarine I mean anything below you. It shows depth, and distance between you and nearby objects. It is not cheap but cheaper than running aground or hitting a mine."

Andre glanced at Hiram as if to check he was okay with the explanation so far, and then continued, "In addition you will have a SRPAW array, Surface Recurring Pattern Anomaly Warning. It's like having high definition cameras arranged in a pattern around the bow, at the water line, flush mounted to protect from the sea. They continuously capture the image of the waves and rise and fall of the water. You might think it's impossible to 'map' the surface of the sea because of the ceaseless, random movement. Nevertheless the computer program creates a 3D image of the recurring pattern. Any object breaking the pattern is an anomaly. We have all heard of large ships running down a small boat that they didn't see. Any man made object, rock or obstruction in the water ahead will break the pattern and a warning will sound, making it easier to avoid."

"That sounds most impressive, but expensive."

"It would be false economy to spoil the ship for a ha'penny of tar." Andre continued: "Think of anti-shoplifting alarms in shop doorways, doors that open automatically on approach, or prevent unauthorised access, and vehicle trackers. Mix these ideas together and you get the best possible security and safety system. Everyone wears Personal Identification Signal Badges, the doors are controlled by Restricted Access by Badge Sensors, and throughout the ship, Personal Identity Signal Badge Locator Sensors pin point every badge. Without a badge no unauthorised person can get on the ship; move about; enter dangerous or sensitive areas; or fall unnoticed, overboard. On a conventional ship they would die because by the time they are missed they would be miles away, if still afloat. On the Adongiva in seconds the computer would identify that the badge is not where it should be and sound an alarm."

He paused and consulted a folder before him, and then went on: "If we programmed the computer to turn the ship round and head straight for the badge, it might run over the person. Instead we would make sure the ship comes to a halt right alongside. Imagine a sailor accidentally getting shut inside a walk-in freezer, or being overcome by fumes or heat in an empty compartment. The computer would recognise by the movement or location of the badge that the wearer is in trouble, and sound an alarm."

"OK" said Hiram. "I am convinced, if we can afford it."

Andre carried on with his explanations. "You remember how we talked about the Computer Cascade Control System at Monday's meeting when we talked about the layers of computers all reporting to each other and the operator only having one interface to deal with?"

Hiram nodded.

"I also mentioned a VRC triple I programme," said Andre. "That stands for Voice Recognition for Commands, Instructions, Information and Intelligence. It uses voice recognition software so that you can either control the ship conventionally, or speak instructions and commands to the computer and let it run the ship without you having to touch anything. Many speech recognition programmes convert text to speech, but tend to be slow and sound like Stephen Hawkins. This system has a high quality voice simulator, like a real person. You ask a question and the computer converts the data into speech, and tells you the answer. You can even choose the voice."

After the meeting Bertrand excused himself and hurried to another meeting. Andre and his team headed in another direction and Hiram wandered back to his cabin. He had been feeling browned off before the meeting but was quite excited by the prospect of a ship packed with gismos and gadgets to play with. He was also awed by the army of professional, clever talent working hard, for his benefit. Actually, that was not quite true. He understood that Anderson Plastics and M&S stood to benefit by hundreds of millions from the commercial success of Hard Plastic. They were therefore working for their own financial future, as well as his happiness.

He was looking forward to having dinner in the restaurant, having overcome his initial shyness. Everyone made him feel welcome, and he could relax in the bar, and chat with the regulars. Since Sarah's death he had not smiled much. Subconsciously or otherwise, he felt it proper that he should have nothing to smile about. When he did think about her, he missed her painfully. The thought that he should block her from his mind in order to survive was terrible, but it was the only way.

The other thing he tried not to think about was how much time he had left. To be able to keep going and have some semblance of normality he had to not think about the past, or the future, just the present; and it was best for the equilibrium of his mind not to think about that too much either.

Wednesday 11th February 2026

As Hiram left the lift and headed for Lady Cynthia's office he was thinking about everything that had happened in the last few days. Roger had phoned him last Friday to let him know that at the end of the previous day, the sum total of his bank accounts stood at seventy-four million, four hundred and twenty-two thousand, nine hundred pounds and eighty pence. Hiram had taken delight in telling him that figure was already out of date, because he had just transferred one million to his account. Roger thanked Hiram once more but Hiram brushed it aside saying that if it hadn't been for Roger none of this would have happened. He said he was on his way to Lady Cynthia's office right now to sign the contract and that all Roger's amendments had been accepted without comment.

Hiram had a visitor on Tuesday. Oliver Russell had been in the area for a spare part, and popped in for a 'hello' and coffee with Bertrand. Bertrand's schedule did not allow for more than a brief meeting and he asked Hiram to come over. They talked about the rapidly changing situation and evolving plans for the Adongiva. Oliver listened intently and from time to time gave Bertrand a look, to remind him of their last conversation. The time came for Bertrand to go to his next meeting and Hiram took Oliver to the club for lunch. They talked about the Seahorse engines and the state of the art controls and safety features. Hiram told Oliver about the hullabaloo among the suppliers rushing to get included in the project. When he had finished Oliver told him about the dream he'd had. It was Hiram's turn to be fascinated. Hiram was more willing than Bertrand had been to accept the possibility of events being preordained.

After lunch they headed for Dry Dock 5 to view progress. Two weeks ago empty concrete surrounded the building. Now one side was a lorry park and a stream of fork lift trucks and men carried loads of white girders through the gaping doorway. A small group by an unusual vehicle were obviously discussing how to get the thing on the lorry into the building. The lorry looked like a giant tape dispenser, and between the huge arms was a reel of plastic, twelve feet wide and twenty feet in diameter. Hiram imagined following traffic cursing that thing, and the route must have had no low bridges.

After Oliver left, Hiram headed for Lady Cynthia. She looked, as always, immaculate and poised. Without speaking she poured coffee, and gestured to a chair. The atmosphere of peace had returned. They nodded 'hello' as she handed him the contract. It occurred to him that things were happening in the wrong order. Normally you would sign before a tool is touched. He knew that even if he didn't sign, it was too late to stop and the ship would go ahead. The Adongiva had become the prime player in this game. The Big Mac was right when he said the Adongiva had developed a life of its own. If Oliver's dream continued to be as accurate as it had so far, the launch ceremony would be a spectacular event. Hiram signed the contract and headed back to his cabin.

CHAPTER TWELVE

Friday 13th February 2026

Hiram was just finishing breakfast when his mobile rang. It was Aaron Timmerman who said he had a meeting at ten which Hiram might find interesting. Aaron, Ancillary Craft Procurement Officer, was the provider of boats, cars, aircraft or other such extras for a ship. Aaron was the one who had talked about a self-righting, semi-inflatable fast launch and *Star Trek*-style shuttle craft, and Hiram could not wait to hear what he was going to say today. As he hurried to the administration building he marvelled yet again at the galaxy of talent that was M&S's to command.

In the office beside Aaron and his assistant Jonathon Agnew, stood two strangers; Roderick Bishop MD and Raymond Trent Chief Designer from Robertson Aeronautical Lifting Equipment. After they were seated Roderick Bishop said that in the Fifties his grandfather worked for Robertson Timber, a lumber company in Canada. They chopped trees on the mountains, rolled them to the river to float downstream to the timber yards. "At the top of one mountain were special trees, bigger and taller than anyone could remember. These skyscrapers were worth a fortune if they could get to the timber yards in one piece; but getting them down a mountain, without flattening everything, damaging them or getting stuck on the river seemed unsolvable; until my grandaddy devised a solution."

Roger Bishop explained further. He said his grandfather had been born in Scotland, and raised in a community where most people worked for, or relied on William Denny and Brothers Ltd Shipbuilders, in Dumbarton on the Clyde. William Denny was brilliant, forward looking and imaginative. The company built many ships but he was always looking for innovation and better ways of doing things. He took an ancient idea, drawn by Leonardo Da Vinci, and turned it into a working machine. It was called the Denny helicopter and consisted of a rectangular frame with six figure of eight rotor blades, facing upwards. A man sat in the middle, spun the blades, and the thing took off. It never got higher than ten feet, but it worked. Unfortunately Franz Ferdinand was assassinated in 1914 and ramifications rippled around the planet. When they reached Dumbarton, William Denny shelved everything that did not contribute to the war effort, and the Denny helicopter was consigned to the footnotes of history. It was however part of Dumbarton folklore and his grandfather never forgot it.

When he first suggested his idea everyone believed he was mad. He persuaded an army buddy with an aeronautical scrap yard to help him build a flying machine for lifting heavy weight. It was not a plane, or conventional helicopter, but based on the Denny helicopter but with four bomber engines pointing skywards and a central bucket seat above a drum of gasoline. A winch underneath provided the lifting power. The pilot would rev the engines until it rose straight up. By easing back on one or more engine throttle, the thing would drift in the direction of the fastest engine. Sitting with spinning propeller blades feet away must have been terrifying, freezing and deafening. The machine rose up until it was above the trees. A cable was lowered, attached to a felled tree, and up it went.

Roger smiled. "My grandaddy got that trunk to the mill and in time all the trees were delivered, and Robertson Timber made a mountain of money. They became the biggest timber company in Canada. My grandaddy lost fingers and toes with frostbite, and was deaf for the rest of his life, but he was a hero, and the company owed him, big time. When I qualified as an aeronautical engineer I could have worked for a big company. Instead I went to my granddaddy's old company and told them I wanted to develop his idea and make a flying timber lifting machine with proper protection for the operator. They told me there was no demand for it but I can be very persistent. It was only a matter of time before they agreed. I thought the operator should be in a safe container, or the propellers in a tube. The propellers would still give vertical thrust and the operator would be warm and protected."

As they listened, Roger went on: "I tried several permutations of engines and propellers. It was never going to be a great financial success but I had proved that I, and grandaddy, was right. Then I told them I wanted to manufacture these machines commercially; not in large numbers but tailor made for each customer. I also suggested a machine for transporting personnel, which would be much cheaper than a helicopter I worked out that one central engine and multi-bladed propeller within a cylindrical drum, was better. The air is drawn through the top, and diverted through four tubes which bend out and round the passenger compartment. Despite having an aero engine immediately above and exhaust gasses just outside, we achieve minimum noise and vibration, comfort and safety by using a combination of measures."

Roderick could see that Hiram was intrigued but wanting them to get to the point. "Getting a licence to fly in Canada wasn't difficult. The American Federal Aviation Administration took 8 years to grant an Airworthiness Certificate. It has taken over 20 years of hacking through jungles of red tape, stringent demands and air trials to get the British Civil Aviation Authority to grant entitlement to fly in British airspace. Right to the end they argued about everything To get it through, we had to accept the designation as 'VTOLSDALE' – Vertical Take Off and Landing, Short Duration, Airborne Lifting Equipment."

He looked directly at Hiram. "Last Friday morning we heard about your Adongiva. It sounds like a wonderful ship that will take the world by storm. We presumed that you would want a helicopter for moving people and supplies. I guess something like the Augusta Grand; a six seat executive transport, costing between five and twelve million, sterling, depending on refinement. Am I right?"

Aaron said, "You are good."

Hiram looked at Aaron as if to say 'twelve million?'.

Aaron smiled. "We had not reached a decision yet and naturally you would have been consulted first. There are cheaper options but you get what you pay for."

"Unfortunately," said Roderick, "that model cannot lift a vehicle. Suppose you want a car for sightseeing. Upgrading to something capable that can carry passengers in comfort, with toilet and catering facilities, will increase your budget dramatically. Do you have sufficient accommodation on your ship for such a large helicopter? I could provide all this, for less than the cost of a standard Augusta Grand, and not much bigger in size?"

Aaron was impressed. "If that is true, I would salivate, but it sounds unbelievable."

"It is true. Bearing in mind what I said about external body being cosmetic, and therefore any shape you want." He produced a folder. "This is a suggestion for what yours might look like."

Aaron, Hiram and Jonathon stared at the plan set before them. Aaron spoke first. "I am not surprised the CAA took a while to approve this. It doesn't look as if it could fly."

The plan was elegantly drawn, almost architectural in its execution. On large seaplane floats at the foot of the machine were pillars a foot in diameter and nine feet tall. In between these four pillars was a rectangular compartment with floor to ceiling glass at the front, reminiscent of a combined harvester cabin, and smaller windows at the back. On top of the pillars was a giant, inverted, enamel pie dish with four propellers, in protective rings attached to the front, back and sides. The ones front and back were smaller than those at the sides. At the front of the craft, just outside the glass cabin was a white sphere two feet in diameter, held by two arms projecting forwards and upwards from between the floats. Interior cabin details were visible through the glass walls.

"Very interesting," said Hiram, "but you are going to have to explain."

"In here," said Raymond pointing to the pie dish, "is a thirty-two bladed propeller, within an elliptical chamber, powered by an engine behind it. It sucks a large volume of air through the intake in the top and forces it through the exhaust tubes on either side of the passenger chamber. These tubes go through the floats, and expel the air and exhaust gasses with enough force to give lift. The floats allow water landing, and between are supermarket trolley wheels which allow land movement in any direction. The propellers on the sides are for moving forward or backwards and the smaller ones for moving sideways or turning."

He tapped the plan with a forefinger as he went on, "The passenger compartment is accessed by the rear door. The top half swings up, the bottom is a ramp, and just inside are two large cupboards. One contains a toilet and hand basin, and the other is a kitchen with room for one person to make refreshments. Just forward of the cupboards is a cylindrical chamber containing a winch with three hundred metres of hawser and a sliding floor. With a safety harness the winch can be used for air sea rescue, or with a platform suspended below, to lift a vehicle, supplies or heavy item. Forward of the winch chamber are six seats for passengers in an air-conditioned cabin with a noise cancelling sound generator to make the overhead engine seem quiet. In front of the passengers are two crew seats and the easiest controls imaginable. The CAA insists on a pilot's licence despite no experience being necessary to be able to fly in minutes, because of the need to communicate with other aircraft and air traffic control, and navigate safely."

He glanced at them as if to check he still had their attention. "The white ball at the front contains a digital camera with zoom lens, night vision, infra red capability, and powerful spot lights. Above is a laser range finder and below is a loud hailer. The ball can traverse two hundred degrees, elevate thirty-three or depress to straight down."

"This is all fascinating," said Hiram, "but I assume your point is to sell us one as the ship's aerial transport?"

"Correct," said Roderick. "I have several questions. How much to buy, and to run? Have you built this, and if not, how long? Have you sold any? Are there any flying anywhere? Can we see one? How big is it exactly?"

Raymond did not seem bothered by this barrage of blunt questions. He smiled and said, "I would expect a price tag of four and three quarter million. However, because of the benefit from the publicity and kudos of our association, I propose that in exchange for a publicity package, we would let you have this for two and a half. The running costs are comparable with those for a large lorry. Not cheap, but less than a helicopter. I have prepared fuel consumption and performance figures which you will see on the sheet marked 'A'. We have not built the model in the drawing, but it could be ready in two months as it only needs the outer frame and cosmetic details. All the working parts can be assembled quickly. We use a company who can make the outer shell to any shape we want, in tough lightweight, carbon fibre, plastic. We provide the information, they produce and ship to us, and we stick it together."

Hiram and Aaron exchanged glances. Aaron asked, "It wouldn't be Anderson Plastics?"

Roderick seemed surprised. "Do you know them?"

"We have come across them," Aaron said, disguising a smile.

Raymond carried on. "This particular model has not been built. However we have been proving to Aviation Authorities since 1987 that our machines fly safely. We have certificates of airworthiness and have tested different shapes for a long time. We have not yet sold one, because we have only just received our British Certificate and we did not want to start marketing without this. Apart from our test models there is nothing in the world like this. Yours will be the first, and can be ready in two and a half months. I don't want you to see the test models because being functional machines to prove a principle they are not designed for elegance or comfort. What is more, I do not want a penny until after your first flight. If you are not satisfied, you can have it for nothing."

Hiram and the M&S engineers were stunned. Roderick said, "How can I make such an offer? Because M&S is one of the most trustworthy companies in the world from whom we expect fairness and respect, and you would not be in partnership with someone who did not share your ideals. We therefore trust Hiram Montgomery not to take advantage of our offer. The sizes and other specifications are on the sheet. Do we have a deal?"

Hiram looked at Aaron who shrugged. "I wouldn't normally order a helicopter without seeing it. However from what I have just heard, there would appear to be no danger in having a look."

Hiram nodded agreement then said, "What is it called?"

Roderick said, "Vee-toles-dale does not trip easily off the tongue. Storks take off and land on sea or ground and storks are often portrayed bringing babies. Our machine can carry a weight while flying, so how about a logo of a stork carrying a baby in a cloth from its beak."

Hiram nodded. "Excellent. Another thought occurs. This machine would never have come about but for the combined vision of your granddad, and William Denny. It would be fitting if the machine had a commemorative plaque."

Roderick nodded his approval.

Monday 16th February 2026

At the Monday morning meeting of the ACG Hiram took his place, next to Bertrand and The Big Mac. The rest of the team sat and the chat abated. Bertrand welcomed everyone and got down to business. Andre Keelan reporting on the radar and other sensory systems said technologically, it would be the safest ship in the world. Next he talked about the PISBs, RABBS and PISBLS system and said that Siemens were offering a PISB with a unique feature; two way voice communication. These Personal Identification Signal Badges, the size of a credit card and five millimetres thick contain PIS transmitter, microphone, loud speaker and battery. They allow the wearer to be identified, located, access the ship; and communicate with anyone else with a badge, and with the ship's computer via its VRC Triple I program.

The next speaker was Aaron Timmerman who explained that the ship's aircraft was to be a never before seen type. He outlined the story and described the 'Stork'. He went on to report that Wolfgang Goering Marine was to supply the lifeboats, leisure craft, and a fast self-righting semi-inflatable. He said the ship's launch, originally to have been a conventional cabin cruiser, sleek, fast and comfortable but 'ordinary' was instead going to look pretty fantastic, and able to draw admiring crowds wherever it appeared.

Gustaf Bjorne and Nils Olof then reported that the Hard Plastic components would be ready for shipping by Saturday, the Envelope in Dry Dock 5 completed by the following Wednesday, and the first pieces of Hard Plastic keel would be joined on Thursday, 24th February 2011. Next Bertrand reported that remodelling the Seahorse engines was progressing well. It was Sheridan Butler's turn. He said his office was dealing with a steadily increasing interest by the media who wanted information and interviews, and suggested they move publicity up a gear before long. The Big Mac agreed.

Clarice Teasdale was last to speak on her ideas for the Adongiva recruitment campaign. She said, "By accident or design, we are broadcasting the message that a momentous event is unfolding, and the Adongiva is exciting and important with vast ramifications. We should emphasise that we are looking for the highest calibre applicants. Because of the diverse talents required, but limited number of crew, we need qualified, clever, experienced people who are also multi-talented. I advise against advertising individual posts because the advertisement must have the 'wow' factor."

She went on to suggest spectacular full page advertisements in all the usual places, to draw attention, and with space to promote the Adongiva, get people excited, and let them know they have to be really good. It would list all the posts, and list the pool of talents the team would like between the applicants, in addition to their primary skills. "We could say, for instance, we would prefer a good, experienced electrician or mechanic who can also scuba dive, play an instrument and handle small arms… to the very best electrician or mechanic with no other skill."

With that she passed round a mock up of the advert. As Hiram studied the advertisement with its list of crew positions he could imagine the hubbub of activity on board his ship with all these people attending their duties, and turning his long awaited dream into a reality.

At the end of the meeting people gathered papers and chatted. Hiram was first to leave, having nothing to gather.

Caesar Meredith, positioned by the door, shut it after Hiram. "I want to talk about Hiram Montgomery, but not while he is present."

The Big Mac closed his eyes. *Does this man ever stop being a pain?* The others just looked and wondered.

Caesar said, "Why was I not told that Hiram was dying? Why did I have to overhear in the staff restaurant that he was given a preferential deal at our expense because of his condition? As Finance Director I should have been consulted. I have conducted research and have never heard of this illness. How can we be sure he is not conning us with a sob story?"

Everyone stared in stunned silence, then turned to The Big Mac and waited.

The Big Mac's expression was angry. "I have warned you about rudeness to visitors, Caesar. Firstly, you are not Finance Director, merely *Acting* Finance Director. As construction planning meetings don't directly concern you, you're here as a courtesy. Secondly, it's none of your business if I do deals with customers. Thirdly, your responsibilities do not include meddling with an important customer. The reason we have not heard of this condition before is because it's so rare most doctors have never heard of it. You are an odious man, Meredith, but suggesting that Hiram Montgomery made this up to get a cheap ship is disgusting, even by your standards. I suggest you leave before I lose my temper."

As Caesar and The Big Mac stared at each other, the temperature plummeted to below freezing. Everyone else stood absolutely still, not daring to breathe. When the Horsemen of the Apocalypse are in the room, it is best not to draw attention.

For his part, Caesar had not expected this reaction, but then he had not thought what to expect. He had just wanted people to accept that he was an important man who should be kept informed about everything, and listened to. He was used to throwing his weight around because department heads knew he could make life extremely difficult by tying up requests for movement of money in red tape, and this gave him leverage. Now he was being humiliated by The Big Mac in front of everyone, and it was Hiram Montgomery's fault, again. He could not let him get away with this. He had to resume his place as one to be feared, and make sure everyone knew that upsetting him would result in punishment.

But first he had to get out of here without losing face. Caesar Meredith drew himself to his full height and looked The Big Mac in the eye. "This is not over." He turned and walked from the room.

Tuesday 27ᵗʰ February 2026

No one told Hiram about the exchange between The Big Mac and Caesar. When he returned from shopping he anticipated the week ahead would be a drag, with no meetings scheduled or plans to fill his time. However by the following afternoon he discovered something to give him a new lease of life. Cedric had mentioned that M&S had a superb library of maritime manuals and text books, and that Daphne Waugh would give him something to read. Hiram imagined he could bone up on navigation and seamanship so that on the Adongiva he could hold his own when talking to the crew.

Daphne, an old hand, had seen aspiring stars come and go, and characters who thought they were God's gift. When Hiram said Cedric had sent him, she already knew who he was. Most people in M&S had heard of Hiram Montgomery – the man who had lost his wife, won the lottery, quadrupled it, had a terminal illness not to be spoken of, and who wanted a big yacht despite knowing nothing about the sea. She suppressed a smile when he asked for books on navigation and 'things'. She knew he was a total novice just filling his time till the launch. She could let him flounder, or be helpful.

One section of the library did not get much use, because most people here had no need of naval college first year text books. She gave Hiram an armful. "Start with these."

Hiram examined the titles and smiled. Most visitors would be affronted if given this basic material, but he seemed delighted.

In his cabin, Hiram read about ship dynamics, steering, propulsion, navigation, hydrodynamics and ship safety. He learned a lot, albeit at basic level, and was happy, although sometimes confused. The more he read, the more he realised how little he knew, and the more he needed to learn. The days just flew by and he even missed lunch twice. He attended the ACG meeting on the Monday morning, which was straightforward apart from one item: when the architects, surveyors and draughtsmen studied the plans they discussed the relative position of the hulls. Some said that having the two engineering hulls so far back, in relation to the central hull might be a more accurate representation of the Star Ship *Enterprise*, but was not necessary on a sea going vessel and overall length could be shortened by 'sliding' them forward. Others said that Ivanovitch was right to keep them back, to counter the weight of the Accommodation Disk. Experiments were carried out in a testing tank with scale models of differing weight, shape and size configurations. The tests simulated the ship colliding head on with uniform waves at various speeds, differing lengths and heights and different impact angles, and the stresses created with the sudden braking power of the ship's sea brakes.

A ship this shape had never been designed before, and Ivanovitch was proved right. The trials produced a mass of data which was fed into the navigation and stability programme, and the hull shapes modified slightly for optimum performance. Despite hundreds of years of technological advances, there was still only one way of checking that a ship would do what it was supposed to: stick it in a body of water.

M&S had their own testing tank the size of a football stadium, with computerised wave and weather making equipment. The traditional method was for draughtsmen to draw plans, build a model, form moulds, and construct replicas from molten wax. M&S used a CAD programme to make the drawings easier. Using these drawings, a computerised model-making machine cut a rectangular block of densely compressed polystyrene with a laser. The finished shape was produced in hours then weights added to simulate a loaded ship. Sensors were fitted which measure roll, pitch, vibration and impact. What originally took weeks was now measured in days. The finished model was sprayed with different coloured waxes.

When the model was subjected to the stresses of water hitting or passing over its surface, the outer coat was worn away and the precise area of resistance accurately identified for subsequent modification. The water in the tank has to be absolutely still before a test. M&S solved the problem of waiting many hours between tests, by having a hydraulic ceiling which lowers to 'flatten' the water until stationary. Now tests only needed a fifteen minute interval.

The other time Hiram left the cabin was on Wednesday afternoon to watch the army of vehicles departing Dry Dock 5. Two large marquees were erected near the rear door of the building, and connected by tunnels. Other vehicles arrived to unload equipment. Hiram found it mind-boggling that this effort was for the construction of a temporary plastic-walled structure which would be dismantled again once the ship was built.

On the Friday Aaron rang him to ask if he could pop over. Hiram was happy to interrupt his studies, which he felt had been productive and deserved a break. He enjoyed talking with Aaron who was full of enthusiasm and novel ideas.

After the ubiquitous cup of coffee, Aaron asked what sort of a car Hiram would like, if he could have any in the world. Hiram said he already one. Aaron smiled and said, "I know I can say this without you taking offence, because we get on well. But let's face it – your car is crap."

Hiram laughed at this description of his transport because it was true. It had been respectable once, but now past its sell by date.

Aaron continued, "You're rich, and will soon own a prestigious and important yacht. If your guests were to ask for a lift at some time, what would they think of that rust bucket?"

"I never thought of that," Hiram admitted.

"So, what car would you like?"

"I always wanted a Morgan."

"Yes!" said Aaron, punching the air. "Sometimes I am so good I scare myself." He explained that he had used his intuition to guess what Hiram would like, based on impressions whilst talking. He suspected

Hiram was a classic car man, and had done some research. He opened his folder to reveal photographs of classic sports cars, and turned to the Morgan V6 Roadster 4-seater. "This will set you back £86,800 plus delivery, number plates and tax. It's expensive but magnificent and will turn heads. The trouble is, it is limited."

"What do you mean?" asked Hiram. "It is a sports car, and that's all it can ever be."

"Yes, but the same can be said of any car. A Range Rover is a Range Rover. A Rolls Royce is a Rolls Royce." Aaron shut the folder. "What if I showed you a car that changed shape, depending on your needs?"

"How is that possible? And why?" asked Hiram.

"You are going to have a crew of forty, plus the Captain and yourself, and up to twenty-eight paying guests. A minibus could be handy. For collecting supplies, a pickup would be useful, and you won't have room for a fleet of vehicles." Aaron opened the folder again. "I've found something clever, or Cedric did."

"Go on" said Hiram.

"In the Sixties, an Italian company called Arturo Colombano made replica vintage cars for the film industry. Private individuals started buying them. You could have a brand new car of a type long extinct – a Bull Nosed Morris, Model T Ford, something from *The Waltons* or an American gangster movie." Aaron was warming to his theme. "About fifteen years ago a customer asked them for a car chassis with interchangeable bodies because he wanted a collection of vintage cars, but didn't have room. They came up with Il Camaleontel… The Chameleon. Since then they have repeated it for other well-heeled customers. I took the liberty of asking them for something for you, based on what we said a moment ago."

He showed Hiram a drawing of a four seat open-topped sports car reminiscent of a classic sports car, but not one Hiram recognised. It was classical, majestic yet sporty. Hiram stared for a while, and he liked it.

Aaron said that despite the vintage appearance, there was an electric retractable hard top, modern hybrid engine, power steering, suspension and braking systems, together with the other goodies that you would expect in an expensive luxury car. He then produced drawings of a minibus and a pickup truck with a hard roof for conversion to a van. He said these drawings were of the same vehicle and said the fronts were identical, because the engine, bonnet, dashboard, and the front seats didn't change. The rear half could be altered in about fifteen minutes.

"Using a mobile hoist you lift one body shell off, lower the next, and secure it with large nuts and bolts, like a Meccano set," he said. "The body shell is a complete unit with seats, floor, sides and roof, windows and electrics with one single push and twist power cable connector."

"Sounds expensive," Hiram said dubiously.

Aaron showed him another sheet that said: Morgan sports car £88,732, minibus £33,336, pick up truck/van £39,929. Total £161,997. The next figures said Chassis with sports car front £59,893, 12 seat minibus shell £25,474, pick up truck shell and roof £19,964, electric hoist £5,545, storage frame with platforms £3,326. Total £114,202. Total saving £47,795.

Hiram gave Aaron a wry smile and said that visiting him was like shopping with a woman who says she can save a fortune, which translates to she has found something that costs a fortune, but at a bargain price. "Let me think about it," he said. "In the meantime I would like you to consider these questions. Do we have the space for the car, hoist and body shells? To get the car on and off the ship easily do we use a ramp, use the ships crane, or the Stork? Given the fact that the car is a one-off by a small Italian company, how available are parts and servicing? Also, for the same reason, is it a design that we can road tax easily in this red tape infested country?"

Aaron began to say that he had some of these answers, but Hiram silenced him with a finger. "I said I'll think about it," he repeated. "Let's talk again tomorrow, once I've had time to think."

With that he headed back to the safety of his cabin, and his books.

Monday 2nd March 2026

Hiram was excited, having set the alarm for an early start, gobbled a quick breakfast and hot footed it to Dry Dock 5. He arrived at 7.40am and was surprised to see others queuing at the side door. He had thought he would be one of the first.

A guard checked passes. He recognised faces and exchanged hellos. Inside he saw The Big Mac, Bertrand, Hans Kristian, and other Department Heads. There was seating for thirty which was three-quarters full. He sat by Clarice and Cedric. Through the clear plastic wall in front they had a good view of the area inside the envelope. The concrete and steel plate floor was carpeted with plastic sheeting and rows of air conditioning units and extractors stood against the far wall. Several figures in white inflated suits, helmets, gloves, boots, had a black letter and number printed on their rectangular backpacks. These 'spacemen' stood in pairs, holding video cameras.

Just before eight o'clock two of the video teams moved to the main door and filmed two teams, of six white suited workers, emerging.

"Now it starts. Gentlemen, this is an historic moment," said The Big Mac.

Another video crew, this side of the wall, recorded the gathered executives and VIPs. The suited figures moved silently to where trolleys waited.

Hans said, "Throughout the process you won't hear anything because they are speaking to each other with radio microphones."

Each team collected two trolleys. One was a flat bed trolley with white plastic beams. The other held three coloured gas cylinders and containers. They pushed their trolleys to the middle of the room, adjacent to what looked like railway sleepers on a railway without tracks. Another two strips of railway lay on either side of this middle one, some distance away from it. Each team moved into identical formations either side of the railway and stood still in a silent tableau.

Hans spoke again: "Nobody moves until the safety officer says so. When told a man will do precisely what he is asked, nothing more. The safety officer is the one with number one on his suit. The letter designates the team. His job is to scrutinise his group especially feet and hands, and everything next to them."

Two figures, marked Two and Three in each team turned to their flat bed trolleys and picked up long white beams four metres long, twenty centimetres wide and U-shaped in section. This would have been impossible if the beams had been made of steel. The men moving like robots laid the beams end to end with a short gap between them, in a shallow groove depression in the middle of the sleepers.

Next the number Five suits stepped forward, unhooking something from their belts. The objects were obviously spirit levels because they checked the beams were upright and level in the grooves. Satisfied, they returned to their original positions. Four and Five turned to the cylinder trolley while everybody else froze. Four picked up a nozzle connected to the blue cylinder, and Five a small tool from one of the containers. They stepped forward and Four sprayed the ends of the beams nearest to each other. Five carefully wiped away surplus material. They returned to the cylinder trolley where Five dropped his tool in a bin and Four replaced the nozzle in its holster. Every movement was choreographed perfectly and separate from the one before and after.

Hans said, "The tools are disposable and only used once." Four and Five were on the move again. They repeated the performance, this time using the red cylinder. Everybody stood still for several seconds. Two and Three then took hold of the beams and slid them together. They held the beams for some seconds then stepped aside to allow Five to smooth and scrape until the join was invisible. Next Four and Five used the white cylinder, another tool and what looked like a piece of rag. They sprayed, wiped and polished, returned and deposited their tools and on to their original positions.

Hans said, "That's the first two sections joined together. You cannot see the join, and it will never come apart. You will notice that number 6 does nothing but stand next to number 1. He is the timer who synchronizes everything to the second, and tells them when to spray and when to present. If anything is done too early or too late it won't work. Such accuracy and precision demands concentration and discipline, and is tiring. Regular team rotation is essential to make sure nobody gets careless. The chemicals, especially 'Red', produce lethal toxic fumes which last less than a minute because they quickly oxidise. This is why timing is crucial and the men have to work fast. They are now going to join more beams end to end until the keel is laid. After that curved bow sections, cross pieces and struts will be attached as the ship's skeleton takes shape. Once the skeleton is built we attach flat sections which become the sides of the hull and external walls, and then the main internal walls and floors. Only two teams are needed to lay the keel but soon ten or more teams plus others operating hoists, fork lift trucks and electric buggies loaded with parts, replacement tools and chemicals will fill the area. The more workers, the more safety officers are required to watch everything. Outside that door," – he pointed to the entrance from which the suites had come – "is another army of support workers."

Once the heel was completed and the bow started to form, more teams and trolleys appeared and the keel sprouted uprights and ribs. Trolleys were wheeled to the other sets of sleepers. All three hulls were now under construction, all in total silence.

After a while, some of the observers had to go. They had seen the historic start of construction of the first ship to be built from Hard Plastic, and now they had other work to do. Hiram moved to the front row, beside Hans Kristian.

"What do you think?" Hans asked.

Hiram replied that it was exciting. He asked why the chemicals needed to be so dangerous, and if there was a safer process. Hans said that all plastics give toxic fumes, in the right conditions.

"This particular plastic is unique and it took a long period of trial and error to work out how to arrange the molecular structure to create the enormous strength. The complexity of the construction process results from the requirement that the battle tanks must be difficult to destroy. The three-stage process was designed to make it hard to dismantle. First the surface is made permeable with the substance in the blue cylinder. It takes a specific number of seconds for this to start, and finish. Within this brief window, the material, in the red cylinder must be applied. This 'soaks' between the molecules and loosens the structure. Only then can you work the plastic, and after a short time it reverts to being hard. If you are going to join pieces, stretch, bend, cut, or drill it, you have to be quick. We finish with the white cylinder to 'set' the material neatly and produce an invisible join."

Hiram replied, "That's a three-stage construction process. You said it takes three steps to make it come apart, but I count two. You said that after the red material is applied you can drill holes in it. An enemy does not need the white material because he is not concerned about a clean finish."

Hans chuckled. "You are forgetting that I said you have a short window during which to work the material. An enemy needs to hit the tank with the blue material and after an exact time delay hit it in precisely the same spot with the red material. Then after the correct time delay hit it again with the shell required for the 'kill'. That is asking a lot during a battle. Of course an enemy does not need to use our chemicals at all. He could simply fire conventional anti tank weapons, which are formidable and deadly, but our fully developed material will be ten times stronger than steel. Conventional anti tank weapons capable of killing a tank, might struggle with a battleship."

Hiram pondered this then pointed to the other side of the plastic wall and said "Just how toxic exactly?"

"The material in the white cylinder exudes something similar to CS gas," Hans replied. "Very unpleasant. That in the red cylinder is more like nerve gas… lethal in seconds. The white cylinder would just make you ill for a while." Hiram looked horrified. "Those men are brave," Hans went on. "I've told them they are safe, and they trust me. They look over inflated because of the positive pressure in their suits. If they sprung a leak they have time to get to the exit." Hiram looked at the plastic sheet between him and the figures. Hans smiled. "Those walls are self sealing, double-skinned and also with positive pressure."

The activity within the envelope never ceased and Hiram was surprised at the progress. Already some teams were working from raised platforms on parts of the hull above ground level. Hans suggested Hiram investigate the marquees at the back of the building as he might find that quite interesting, and he could return to this chamber as often as he wanted. Hiram agreed, saying that he found the whole thing absolutely fascinating and did not want to miss a thing. In years to come he could tell people he was there on that first day that Hard Plastic changed the world. Then he remembered there wasn't going to be years to come, for him anyway. It was now nearly the end of February. It had been September when he had been told that he might have as little as four years to live. Nearly half of that first year had gone already. The Adongiva would be built soon and he might have three years to enjoy it before his end came.

Hiram tried not to think about that too much, and concentrated on placing his feet one in front of the other as he hurried to the first marquee.

CHAPTER THIRTEEN

Friday 6ᵗʰ March 2026

Phillipa Taylor, a post-graduate student from Birmingham University, after completing her degree in Statistical Analysis, had been sent, on secondment, to St. Andrew's General hospital to run a research project on cancers and treatments. It did not matter that she knew little about medicine or biology. She would have been just as happy working with statistics on the sale of tractors in Africa, EEC fishing quotas, or endangered species of butterflies. It was the figures she was interested in, not the subject matter. To most people it would be a boring job but she loved immersing herself in the mathematics of it. This particular project involved accessing patients' records, allocating a value to each medical condition, treatment and outcome, according to category, inputting the figures. Once this had been done she could produce charts and tables of statistics. With her scant medical knowledge she had to use a medical dictionary to identify the correct category for each item.

She had started the project in July the previous year, and since that time had come to recognise the names of the common conditions and treatments which cropped up regularly in her research. Today she encountered something that had not come up before: St. Augustus's Fire. It stated in the record that the condition causing burning pain in the rectum was untreatable. Her medical dictionary had no mention. The second line of attack, accessing the hospital mainframe medical library, came up blank. This was a first. She tried another approach. All the main web search engines said 'Nothing found'.

She had never come across anything like this before. She returned to the patient's record and made a note of the publication mentioned,

Kilwinnings Encyclopaedia of Rare and Exotic Medical Ailments. She accessed the library again. Nothing found.

She thought this was becoming bizarre and she tried the web again. Nothing found. She was dumfounded. How could the hospital treat a patient for an ailment not listed anywhere but in a publication not listed anywhere? She went back to the record again and looked more closely at the ward which had treated the patient, whose name she read was 'Hiram Montgomery'. Her heart sank. She was hoping to ask the consultant if he could spare a few minutes, but the consultant was Professor Cann. He would not be sympathetic because he had told her bluntly that her research project was a waste of taxpayers' funds and with no practical value.

Early the next morning Phillipa found Professor Cann in his office. He looked up as she entered and despite his frown, she said, "I need a favour."

"If you are ill see your own doctor. If you are after money see your bank manager, if you want my parking space the answer's no. If you need advice on finishing your project try the IT department. Have I missed anything?"

A lesser mortal might have withered, but she was no shrinking violet. "Are you always this rude? Or are you making an exception in my case?"

A muscle flickered in Cann's jaw, then he nodded. "You are right to chastise me. I had no right to speak to you like that and I apologise. I shouldn't take my problems out on you."

"Apology accepted. I am sorry to bother you if you are busy."

He stopped her. "You mentioned a favour. You might as well ask, now that you're here."

She told him what information she was gathering and as she had found a condition not listed anywhere, wondered if he could throw some light on it. She fished out her note book and thumbed pages. "It's St. Augustus's Fire."

He looked blank. "I've never heard of it. Does it have another name?"

"No," she said. "It's so rare it still has the original name given to it by a Jesuit monk in 1896 because the principal symptom is a feeling that one's bottom is on fire."

Professor Cann laughed loudly and said it was utterly preposterous and probably a student prank, and suggested someone was pulling

172

her leg. "I am not a cancer expert and there might be a rare condition unknown to me. However I am an expert in every inch of the alimentary tract, from tongue to rectal sphincter. I would know of anything fitting your description. What's the patient's name?"

She consulted her notebook. "Hiram Montgomery attended your ward as outpatient on 9th October 2024, given tests and medication, returned on 31st February 2025 for more tests and again on 16th September 2025 for the results."

Professor Cann was mystified. He had no recollection of a patient with a rare abdominal cancer, but was impressed by her thoroughness. He asked if he could borrow her notebook, and promised to return it as soon as possible. He wanted to look up the record and thanked her for bringing it to his attention.

Saturday 7th March 2026

When Sister Cowan came on duty Professor Cann beckoned her to his office as soon as she had her staff organised. He turned the small computer round and asked her to read.

After a few moments she stopped in surprise, looked at him then continued with growing amazement. "Any ideas?"

She shook her head and said, "This is a joke, surely?"

He shrugged. "Do you see the name on the last consultation?"

She looked, and shut her eyes. "Tell me this is not true."

"Rachael, I have no idea what the truth is," said Professor Cann, "but rest assured I will find out, and then someone is in trouble."

"You can't believe Doctor Peacock put that nonsense on a record, for a joke. He hasn't got a sense of humour."

"I don't know who did it. If it wasn't him why didn't he mention it at the time of the appointment...?" His words trailed away.

Sister Cowan read his mind. "Good God. You think someone played a joke on him but he thought it was real, and informed the patient accordingly."

"If that is true I am going to have him sacked, after which I will deal with Brian Peacock."

"What about the patient? A man out there thinks he is dying of a terrible illness which will result in a 'fire' in his bottom, or some such rubbish, and there is nothing wrong with him."

Cann shook his head. "This is a can of worms. I will have to tell Admin. The hospital could face a substantial claim for damages."

Sister Cowan held her head. "Before you talk to anybody else you should have a quiet word with Brian and see what he remembers." She looked at the notes again. "I remember that day. We were short-staffed, and decorators were creating mayhem."

"And I had a meeting which lasted all morning."

"That's right and I persuaded you to give your 'clear and go' cases to Doctor Peacock. I take full responsibility."

"Don't be absurd. You weren't to know a record had been sabotaged. Brian should have known. I will have a word with him. Not a word until I have done some digging."

"Don't worry; I think the fewer who know about this the better."

Professor Cann found Doctor Peacock in the staff room, took him to his office and asked him if he could recall Hiram Montgomery. "Oh yes, 'St Augustus's fire'. You served me up a real curve ball there. Why do you ask? He is not back already. Is he?"

"No, he is not. Do you remember the details?" said Professor Cann.

"It was a most unusual case. I have not come across anything else like it."

"Quite. Did you not think it unusual that such a difficult case was included among the simple ones you were given, that day?"

"Not at all; I knew what was going on. You were testing me, weren't you? I found all the cases easy to handle, even that sneaky one and I did exactly what Sister told me to do. I gave them their results, patted them on the head and sent them on their way."

Professor Cann asked him to tell him what was said during the consultation, and listened quietly as the younger man spoke. "What would you say if I said the report about St Augustus's fire should not have been there?"

"What do you mean?"

"There is no such thing, and Hiram Montgomery is not ill."

Brian looked perplexed. "I don't understand."

"There is nothing wrong with him, and the report was there for the wrong reason."

"What reason?"

"I don't know. That is what I am trying to ascertain. Can you think

174

of anyone who might put a false report on a file, to play a joke on you?"

Brian shook his head. "Nope. As far as I am aware I am pretty popular."

Professor Cann wondered how anybody could be so wrong about themselves. There was obviously no point in continuing. The boy's only crime was naivety, or stupidity.

He was about to terminate the interview when Brian asked, "What happens to the patient now?" Professor Cann said that no decision had been reached yet but the patient will be called back and told of the mistake.

Then Brian said, "Of course the record might not have been tampered by human hand."

Professor Cann was flabbergasted. "What do you mean by that? You think a passing dog jumped on the computer?"

"No, but every entry on a file has the date and time at the foot." He recalled how the note about St Augustus's fire was below the date and time of the previous note, instead of being on a following page. "I am no expert but could this suggest a computer error? I meant to query it but forgot. "

Professor Cann thought about that and cursed himself for not spotting it. He decided to include IT Department in his investigations.

Professor Cann's next stop was the Head of Pathology, Doctor Kenneth Hunt, to whom he explained the situation. As soon as Kenneth Hun's eyes fell on the screen he groaned and said he thought these notes had been destroyed years ago. He said there used to be a popular game played by the medical students to improve their diagnostic investigation skills. One student would reveal symptoms of an illness or condition, but only if asked the correct questions by another student. One chap was unpopular with the others because he regularly informed them of his intellectual superiority. One day when it was his turn to conduct the 'examination' in the game, he was flummoxed by a mysterious and rare, incurable illness of which the primary symptom was a burning pain in the rectum, It was meant to be a great joke because that student's name was Tarquin Augustus Blears, he was generally regarded as a pain in the arse, and the illness was called St. Augustus's Fire.

"That is all very interesting, but what has it got to do with my patient?" asked Professor Cann.

Doctor Hunt said, "I can only guess that a copy of that joke medical record somehow got archived when we were computerised."

Professor Cann was relieved that he had tracked down the mystery but one question remained. "How did it get into Hiram Montgomery's notes?"

Doctor Hunt replied, "We are all in agreement that mistakes are regrettable and should never happen, but from time to time things get misfiled. I know that sounds lame, given the circumstances, but at least now we can put it right".

It was a very contemplative Professor Cann who returned Phillipa Taylor's notebook to her later that day. He felt he owed her an explanation, as she was the one who had uncovered this business. Next he had another meeting with Sister Cowan and Doctor Peacock and put them in the picture. Having now covered his bases and it was time to speak Reginald Patterson.

He was about to get up when Doctor Peacock said, "Poor man. After all he has been through."

Sister Cowan and Professor Cann exchanged glances and Professor Cann said, "What do you mean?"

Doctor Peacock said, "He had recently lost his wife. I remember him saying that before he left."

Professor Cann nearly fell off his chair. "There is nothing in the notes about that. You did not think it important to record the fact, or mention it?"

"It's hardly a medical condition," replied Doctor Peacock.

Professor Cann could feel his fingers clench. He took a deep breath and joined his hands as in prayer. "True, but it might influence a person's reaction to life changing news, don't you think? Tell me again, about his response?"

Doctor Peacock relayed the gist of the conversation he'd had with Hiram, as far as he could recollect. Professor Cann said, "I think we will leave there for now. I must speak to Patterson." As he headed upstairs he couldn't imagine how Hiram Montgomery must have felt as he left the hospital.

Monday 28th March 2026

Reginald Petterson's first reaction was, predictably, one of panic over possible legal action, and advice to do nothing until Hiram's next move.

When Professor Cann insisted that this was not an option, it then took 7 days for Jasper Heathcoat from the Regional Health Department's legal experts to suggest telling Hiram him the condition had cleared up by itself. Professor Cann said the man had probably been through hell, and was entitled to the truth.

It took a further two days to agree the letter. Legal department wanted as little as possible on paper, to minimise ammunition for a subsequent litigation. Finally the letter was sent, but ten days later returned, stating, 'No longer at this address'.

Professor Cann was under instructions to notify legal department of any reply but he did not regard this returned envelope as a reply. He checked Hiram's notes, and found a mobile number. Professor Cann phoned, and on an answering machine, introduced himself and said, "Hiram, listen to me. You are all right. You are not going to die, at least not of this illness. Please phone and I will explain everything. You are going to be OK."

CHAPTER FOURTEEN

Monday 6ᵗʰ April 2026

The last month had been interesting for Hiram. He had visited the observation gallery every day watching his ship take shape. It had taken eight days for the framework of the three hulls to be assembled. There were lots of teams all over the hulls, some on hydraulic platforms, some balanced precariously on beams, and others just passing parts to the assemblers. He had no idea how the safety officers kept track of all this movement, but there were no mishaps. As soon as the frames were completed they switched to another method of working. Instead of teams of six, there were teams of varying sizes, depending on the shapes to be joined. Trolleys carried large sheets of Hard Plastic, some small enough to be lifted by two men but others two metres by six were lifted into place by a ceiling hoist. With windows measured in seconds, for applying chemicals, more than one team worked simultaneously to spray the whole length of both pieces to be joined. The white suited men worked tirelessly and by the ninth of March the external surfaces of the three hulls were completed.

The next parts to be fitted were the 'corridor bridges'. Between the central accommodation hull and the two engineering hulls these rectangular sectioned corridors wide enough to drive an electric trolley through would connect the three hulls. Running the length of the corridors were thickly coiled spring 'pipes'. At least, that's what Hiram thought until it was pointed out to him that these shock absorbers, when anchored properly, would hold the hulls together in tight formation when the ship was accelerating, braking, or manoeuvring. The corridors looked ugly and functional until the external surfaces were applied.

Finally there were no longer three separate hulls, but a large and beautiful trimaran. Another smaller 'bridge' joined the two engineering hulls at the stern. This, like the larger bridges served the dual purpose of stability, strength, and a passageway between the two engineering hulls. By Friday 20th March, the three hulls, outer surfaces of the superstructures, and smoke stacks seemed complete. There were men working on internal walls and floors that Hiram could not see from his chair. He was pleased that after his hours with the text books he was able to understand the discussions on watertight transverse bulkheads, electric sliding watertight doors, transverse frames, shaft bossings, deep web frames and beams and deck cambers.

The smoke stacks on the stern decks of the engineering hulls looked more like jumbo jet tail fins than funnels. They raked gracefully at the front and each had short 'wings' on either side. These were platforms for radar scanners, dishes and other electronic equipment. Protruding from the leading edge of each smoke stack, six feet from the deck, were round ledges for the water cannons, for fire fighting and defence.

On Monday 12th March, work started on the large round Accommodation Disk at the front of the ship. Finally it was beginning to look like the *Enterprise*. Most of the workers worked from elevated platforms around the disk. By Wednesday, all Hard Plastic work on the internal structures was completed. On the 30th, the Seahorse engines arrived. Work on these was done outside the building, as the propellers were fitted and other preparations completed. Hunter & Wolfe, a company renowned for custom designed high performance propellers, had collaborated with Rolls Royce in designing low cavitation propellers for the Type FZ1492 Frigate. When asked to design propellers for the Adongiva, continue their association with the Seahorse engines and become the first to design a Hard Plastic propeller, they agreed at once. Hiram had seen conventional propellers of brass, or steel, so he thought these giant white plastic propellers with five blades looking like a cross between a boomerang, and flat banana, but twisted lengthways, were truly weird.

On Wednesday 1st April, the external surface of the disk was complete and everyone who entered the observation gallery stared in wonder at this strange progeny of space ship, and ocean liner. During that week men cleared the equipment which had surrounded the Adongiva since birth, cleaned the internal surfaces of the envelope and checked for chemical traces. On Saturday morning part of the envelope nearest the large building door was opened and the Seahorse engines wheeled in and fitted on the engineering hull sterns.

Hiram asked how unprotected men could work in the envelope while Hard Plastic construction was still underway. He was told that the external surfaces and areas had been decontaminated. All internal work would be completed by Wednesday but the men at the stern were sufficiently far from the work in the bow not to be in danger. The men inside, and fumes, were confined by 'mini envelopes' inside the ship. The fumes are of such sort duration that there was no danger of them escaping from the ship.

The regular ACG meetings had taken place every Monday morning. The closing date for job applications had passed, and HR had been surprised and overwhelmed by the response. They had anticipated more than the usual amount of interest, but each position had attracted over three hundred and seventy applications, so extra staff had to be brought in to process the mail.

Dealing with the flood of applications was too much for them and eventually an external management recruitment firm were contracted to sift the applications to a manageable level. After two sifts they used psychological profiling to produce a 'short list' of thirty-five for each job. HR were now agonising over which of these excellent people to leave out, in order to create an interviewing list of six, for each of the forty-one positions.

After the Monday meeting Hiram wandered back to his cabin for a coffee and text book before his visit to Dry Dock 5. As he put the kettle on he switched on his personal mobile phone to see if he had any messages. For quite a long time nobody had phoned him on this phone and he had been using the M&S mobile for all his outgoing calls, so he had switched off his personal phone to conserve the battery. He could not say why he had chosen this day to listen to the messages on his old phone. There were two 'junk' messages which he deleted, but the third stopped him in his tracks. The blood drained from his face as he played the message again, three times...

The kettle stopped boiling but Hiram lost interest in making coffee. He fell into a chair and played the message one more time. He still could not take it in. Somehow he found his way to Bertrand's office. "What do you make of this?" he asked, and played the message for Bertrand.

Bertrand's initial surprise was quickly replaced by excitement. "Perhaps they have found a cure. You must phone them right away."

Hiram shook his head and said, "I can't believe it. He said I am not going to die. I can't believe it. He said I am not going to die of this illness. What do you think he meant by that?"

"I have no idea, but he said you are going to be all right. Phone him back. Do it now. What is the number?"

Hiram said he did not know, so Bertrand found it and made the call.

They got put through to a receptionist who said she dealt with Professor Cann's appointments, and he could have 11.40am on Friday.

Bertrand was more excited than Hiram and shouted, "Take it!"

Hiram said it was nearly a three hour drive to get to the hospital from here.

"For God's sake take it. I'll drive you. He said it was good news. Hiram – you could be in the clear."

Hiram agreed to the appointment and hung up.

Bertrand said, "Hiram this is great news. You could be all right." As he spoke he suddenly thought, *Crumbs, I wonder how this is going to affect the Adongiva? A contract has been drawn up on the premise that Hiram has only four years to live. What happens now? What is Caesar Meredith going to say? He will be crowing that he was right all along and we have been conned, and he will be stirring it with a vengeance.* He did not believe for one moment that this was all an elaborate ploy. He only had to look at Hiram to see that his reaction was genuine. The man was shell-shocked. Bertrand poured Hiram a coffee and told him to wait until he got back. He had to tell The Big Mac.

Friday 10th April 2026

They drove to the hospital in silence, lost in separate thoughts. Hiram, since his last visit to the hospital, had come to accept that an illness most people had never even heard of was going to cause extreme pain and kill him. He dared not raise his hopes in case they were cruelly dashed. At the same time he felt cheated, or that he was cheating on the deal. He had originally felt guilty because he was alive and Sarah was not. He had come to accept the inevitability of his own death as a way of righting this wrong. Now he was not going to die after all, which seemed like a betrayal. At the same time, life was life. He had been really looking forward to sailing in the Adongiva.

Meanwhile, Bertrand was going over in his mind the conversation he he'd had with The Big Mac. When he told The Big Mac about the message, The Big Mac said, "I am sorry to have to ask this, but have we been had?" Bertrand had replied that either Hiram was a brilliant actor or he was genuinely stunned. They discussed the effect on the workers who had been pushing themselves above and beyond the call of duty to make Hiram's dream happen in time. They talked about Caesar Meredith who had come off badly every time he attacked Hiram. There was no doubt Caesar would try to vindicate himself by turning this into a crisis.

The Big Mac said it was good that Bertrand was accompanying Hiram to the hospital because he could bear witness. Then there was the question of how a hospital could tell someone he was dying, then telephone to say he wasn't. They imagined there had been a miracle cure. They did not consider the possibility that the hospital had made a mistake.

Bertrand had asked how this would affect the Adongiva contract.

The Big Mac had not hesitated. "Not at all. We assumed that Hiram would pass away and his share would come to us. This has only changed in one respect, the timescale. For a portion of each year Hiram will use the Adongiva as his floating home. For another period he will run it as a cruise ship. The rest of the time it will be a publicity showcase and advertisement for Hard Plastic and the other features of the ship. We, and Anderson Plastics, will still make huge profits. The only difference is that Hiram keeps his share for longer. If anyone objects, we quote M&S's Founder's Declaration, First Principle, 'I swear to give to all I meet the consideration, respect, goodwill, and industry that I would wish from them, should our situation be reversed'."

As they reversed into a space in the hospital car park Bertrand asked Hiram, "How do you feel?"

"Nervous, and dreading that this is a false alarm."

"We'll soon find out," said Bertrand as he locked the car.

They followed the signs and found Reception, where Hiram gave his details. The receptionist then led them along a corridor to a consulting room where a tall dark-skinned man in smart dark suit introduced himself as Professor Cann.

Bertrand, who thought Professor Cann looked more nervous than Hiram, introduced himself as a friend and business associate.

Professor Cann introduced another man, Jasper Heathcoat, as a colleague and invited them all to sit. He came straight to the point. "Hiram, you do not have a fatal illness, and you are not going to die. At least not in the near future. You do not have a terrible and incurable bowel disease."

Bertrand looked from one man to the other. Hiram felt light-headed and had to hold his seat to steady himself. Professor Cann offered him a glass of water.

Eventually, Hiram managed to speak. "What about St. Augustus's Fire?" he asked, in a voice that sounded small and far away. Professor Cann said there was no such thing. "I don't understand," persisted Hiram.

Professor Cann said, "Some years ago a medical student played a silly practical joke on another student by inventing a medical report containing a fictitious illness. Somehow it got accidentally filed in the hospital registry, and then when all the records were subsequently computerised, a computer glitch caused it to be attached to your file." He continued, "When you came to the hospital you were seen by a fully qualified but inexperienced doctor who did not realize the notes were wrong. As soon as the facts emerged we decided to contact you and put things right."

Bertrand felt growing anger as the story unfolded. He looked at Hiram who stared at the floor for a while then said, "So I am not dying?"

"No."

"There is no such thing as St. Augustus's Fire?"

"No."

"I am perfectly well?"

"Yes."

"I am not going to die?"

"We will all die sometime but there is no reason why you shouldn't die of old age."

"I am going to be all right?"

"Yes."

Hiram started to cry. Everyone in the room waited patiently until he composed himself.

Bertrand was the first to speak. "This man has suffered the most appalling anguish. Have you any idea what you have put him through, or done to his life?"

Professor Cann and Jasper Heathcoat looked extremely uncomfortable. Professor Cann said, "I cannot tell you how sorry I am that this has happened and I apologise from the bottom of my heart for the torment you have gone through."

"Sorry doesn't even begin to cut it," said Bertrand. "I hope you have a damn good lawyer, because you are going to need him."

Jasper Heathcote spoke for the first time. "The hospital would like to express its regret. I am sure you can appreciate from the full and frank account given to you, that no one has been negligent. However as a gesture of goodwill the trust would be willing to make an ex-gratia payment, whilst not accepting any liability, to compensate for the suffering and inconvenience."

Professor Cann had no idea an offer was to be made at this meeting and he stared incredulously at his colleague.

Bertrand's response was ice cold. "So, law is your speciality is it? You call what he has gone through, an inconvenience? How do you recompense a life wrecked by your incompetence?"

Jasper winced.

Bertrand continued: "My firm's legal department can command the finest legal brains in the world, and facing them will result in an unpleasant end to your short career. Hiram Montgomery now has the full might of that department at his disposal."

"With respect, I submit that Mr. Montgomery's life has not been wrecked. He is alive and well, and took action as soon as possible. Furthermore I refute any allegations of incompetence," said Jasper.

Professor Cann had to stop himself from shouting, 'Shut up, you fool, you are making it worse.' Instead he said, "Gentlemen, I think we should calm down. Hiram Montgomery is the important person here." He turned to Hiram and said softly, "Mr. Montgomery, what can I say to make this better?"

Hiram said, "Nothing."

Professor Cann's heart sank, and he feared the worst. But then Hiram continued. "From what you have said I can see no one is to blame."

"Hiram…" Bertrand cautioned. He did not want him ruining his case before a lawsuit worth millions.

Hiram raised his hand. "I experienced terrible grief when my wife died, and I still miss her. To be frank I didn't want to live without her. When Doctor Peacock told me I was going to die soon I was shocked but accepted that my forthcoming demise would solve this problem, although I was not looking forward to the pain at the end. Now I am told I am not going to die and am not sure how to feel, except that I am not going to sue the hospital. The only people who would suffer would be other patients deprived of medical treatment because a large sum of money had been removed from the budget."

Professor Cann sat quietly and listened. Bertrand was choked with emotion, and Jasper Heathcoat was relieved that court action seemed to have disappeared.

Hiram gave a soft chuckle and said, "I suppose I should be grateful for what the hospital has done for me." Professor Cann asked him to explain. "Having been hard up all my life and after Sarah died, I won the lottery, at a point when I had little enthusiasm for life and no one to share or enjoy it with. If I had not been told I was dying I would probably have left the money in the bank and carried on doing my dull but safe job. You told me I did not have long to live, and when a friend suggested I make the best of my time, I did and decided to blow it all on a yacht and sail off to die at sea."

He described how he met Bertrand, met Ivanovitch Petrovsky, spoke of the meeting with Sir Richard Pickles and his investment offer. "If you had not told me I was dying I would not have said 'what the hell. I will be dead soon, so why not'. It paid off and I am now having that fantasy yacht built, and am embarked on a course I could never have imagined in my wildest dreams. This hospital acted as a catalyst for events which have changed my life for ever."

After a long silence Professor Cann said, "I sincerely hope we never again change a life in quite the way we changed yours."

Monday 13th April 2026

The return from the hospital was punctuated with brief conversations between long silences. Hiram finally looked up and said, "What a beautiful blue sky," and Bertrand knew he was on the mend.

When they were nearly home Bertrand decided to educate Hiram on the politics of the situation. He said that most people would be delighted with the news. However Caesar Meredith might say there was something 'dodgy' about Hiram getting a good deal when people had believed he was dying and now he is not. Hiram said he could understand this and asked what was to be done. Bertrand was relieved because the strategy in his mind could now work.

At M&S they headed for The Big Mac and put him in the picture. His reaction was predictable: "Hiram, this is appalling. They cannot get away with this. We can have lawyers castrate the sons of bitches."

Bertrand said, "Hiram demonstrated his true nature by telling the hospital that he did not want to rob the NHS of money, when he could see no one was at fault."

The Big Mac said, "Hiram, you continue to grow in stature. I am not sure in your position I would be so magnanimous, but I respect your wishes."

Bertrand said, "This information must be kept secret until we tell the ACG meeting, and immediately afterwards Conrad Meredith who can tell the board members by phone. This will deny Caesar any opportunity to cause trouble. He'll see the overwhelming support for Hiram and hopefully realise how unpopular he would be to raise a dissenting voice."

On the Monday morning the ACG members assembled and Bertrand opened the meeting as normal. Then he said that before the first item of business he had important news, and he told them about Hiram's health situation.

The statement surprised everyone. Many craned their necks to look at Hiram, but he remained inscrutable. He simply sat forward in his chair and began to tell them the whole shocking saga. When he had finished, everyone sat for what seemed like an eternity, until the silence was broken by a clap. Another joined in, and another, until everyone was clapping. Soon they were on their feet too, and Hiram was receiving a standing ovation. It was an emotional moment and impossible to be unaffected. Some were laughing and others crying. They were reacting as if a member of the family had just been rescued from death.

The Big Mac felt a lump in his throat but through the throng saw the only person sitting was Caesar Meredith, who stared without emotion. Eventually Bertrand called for order. They resumed their seats. It had not gone unnoticed that Caesar did not seem as pleased as his colleagues.

When the room was quiet Caesar looked directly at Hiram and said, "Well done. Congratulations."

This could have meant, 'I congratulate you on pulling off your con trick' or 'I am pleased you are well'.

Hiram boldly returned Caesar's stare and said, "Thank you for your sentiments. I am going to host a humdinger of a drinks party in the Senior Staff Club this evening to celebrate the postponement of my demise. You are all invited to come and have a dammed good time at my expense."

This brought more cheers. When they had settled down Bertrand resumed the business of the meeting. They were told that the final assembly of Hard Plastic components would be completed by the end of the day. It had taken six weeks, as predicted. For a vessel the size and complexity of the Adongiva to be put together in such a time was a phenomenal achievement and was a clear indication of how ship building, and other construction projects could be dramatically changed in the future. Bertrand said the envelope would be dismantled by Thursday and the outfitting of electrical, electronic, and mechanical components would start on Friday.

Clarice Teasdale reported that interviews for the recruitment of the crew would commence on Monday 19th and that the standard was unbelievably high. In total 15,176 applications had been processed and reduced to a short list of six interviewees for each of the forty-one positions. The latter stages of the selection had been a nightmare because the applicants remaining had experience, qualifications, skills and talent far greater than originally asked for.

"We asked for the best, and we got it," Clarice said. She explained that choosing the successful candidates would be extremely difficult.

Aaron reported that the Stork was due to arrive by the end of this week. He had seen photographs and specifications, and it was going to be absolutely fantastic. He then said he had another great idea for the Adongiva, as he opened a folder. Everyone smiled in anticipation, knowing Aaron's love of pulling white rabbits out of hats.

Aaron said, "A Dutch company called U-Boat Worx has been manufacturing one and two man mini submarines called the 'C-Quester' for about fourteen years. They cost about the same as a Porsche, and they could supply a three-man version for the Adongiva for £168,000. A C-Quester gives great all round visibility, dives up to 50 metres and cruises at up to 4 knots for up to two and a half hours. It won't take up more room than a conventional launch and would be a great addition."

Hiram immediately said, "I agree. Lets get one."

CHAPTER FIFTEEN

Tuesday 14th April 2026

The following day Hiram had a meeting with Clarice Teasdale who had agreed to explain the Adongiva crew command structure.

Hiram's original thoughts on how he wanted the crew organised were a trifle confused. He had said because it was a small ship in naval terms, he wanted it to be a place that all ranks would enjoy belonging to and working in. He understood there had to be a hierarchy, with order and discipline, but just as there were Police Officers, Prison Officers, Probation Officers, NSPCA Officers, he thought everybody on the Adongiva could be an 'Officer'. There would be different grades according to specialisation and level of responsibility, but no one should feel that they were the one at the bottom of the pile. In addition, there was just not enough space, or money, to provide an Officers Mess, a Petty Officers Mess and a Seaman's Mess.

Clarice had discussed this with the experts, and they had come up with a solution. The crew of forty-one, would report to the Captain because there could only be one Captain, who must be seen to have command. Hiram, as owner, would control overall strategy and destinations, but Clarice explained that he must accept that the Captain was the final authority in organising and running the crew, and the safety of the ship. Hiram could have private discussions with the Captain but as far as the crew was concerned the Captain's word was final.

Hiram agreed that this was sensible and fair.

Clarice went on. Under the Captain the crew would be organised in five divisions, each with a Senior Officer designated Ships Chief Officer. Under each Chief there would be a Ships 1st Officer for each specialist skill and assistants known as Ships 2nd Officers. She handed Hiram a printed sheet and he read the following:

A Division
Ships Chief Officer; Admin.
Ships Officer; 1st Class Clerical
Ships Officer; 1st Class Beauty
Ships Officer; 1st Class Medical
Ships Officer; 2nd Class Accounts
Ships Officer; 2nd Class Fitness
Ships Officer; 2nd Class Asst. Admin.

C Division
Ships Chief Officer; Catering
Ships Officer; 1st Class Asst. Chef
Ships Officer; 1st Class Bar
Ships Officer; 1st Class Steward
Ships Officer; 2nd Class Cook
Ships Officer; 2nd Class Asst. Bar
Ships Officer; 2nd Class Asst. Steward
Ships Officer; 2nd Class Asst. Cleaning

D Division
Ships Chief Officer; Domestic
Ships Officer; 1st Class Supplies
Ships Officer; 1st Class Cleaning
Ships Officer; 1st Class Laundry
Ships Officer; 2nd Class Asst. Supplies
Ships Officer; 2nd Class Asst. Supplies
Ships Officer; 2nd Class Asst. Cleaning

E Division
Ships Chief Officer; Eng.
Ships Officer; 1st Class Mech. Eng.
Ships Officer; 1st Class Elec. Eng
Ships Officer; 1st Class I.T. Eng.
Ships Officer; 2nd Class Officer, Asst. Eng.

Ships Officer; 2nd Class Officer, Asst. Eng.
Ships Officer; 2nd Class Officer, Asst. Eng.

S Division
Ships Chief Officer; Seaman
Ships Officer; 1st Class Coxswain
Ships Officer; 1st Class Pilot
Ships Officer; 1st Class Bridge
Ships Officer; 1st Class Musical Director
Ships Officer; 1st Class Master at Arms
Ships Officer; 1st Class Diver and submarine
Ships Officer; 2nd Class Boat Crew
Ships Officer; 2nd Class Air Crew
Ships Officer; 2nd Class Security and Driver
Ships Officer; 2nd Class Asst. Bridge

Clarice said that the titles describe the main specialisation, however a Musical Director who could do nothing but direct music would be an extravagant luxury. Like every other crewmember, he must have additional skills, and prepared to 'muck in'. All applicants had shown in their CVs that between them they constitute an enormous pool of talent. The interviews would commence with the selection of captain, and over the next twenty-four days the other forty crew members.

For the Captain's job there had been a huge choice of highly talented and qualified individuals of great experience. A shortlist of six had been prepared but one name caused a ripple of excitement. Clarice asked if Hiram had heard of Patrick Samuel Ironside. Hiram didn't think he had, and indeed the name didn't register until she referred to him as Paddy Ironside.

Immediately, Hiram remembered the story, which had for a short time dominated the news, about the Captain of a Royal Navy Assault ship which had seen action in a trouble spot in the Middle East. The particular incident which had thrust Ironside into the limelight had attracted worldwide publicity, about a controversial court martial, from which he was acquitted. Before becoming Captain of the ship, Paddy Ironside had at one time been a distinguished helicopter pilot.

Hiram remembered it all clearly. Ferocious battles had raged for months on the hot and inhospitable hills and coastal deserts with all three services giving and receiving casualties. When Mother Nature flexed her muscles she was usually oblivious to what mankind was doing at the time. One day a short sharp earthquake shook the hills causing mayhem to both sides, and devastation to villages and communities. The conflict temporarily ceased as the armies of both sides concentrated on rescuing their own from collapsed buildings and gullies which had suddenly appeared. After several days the bulk of the allied personnel had been saved, but Captain Ironside learned of a village in imminent danger of complete destruction. The isolated village of children, women and old men, sat at the foot of a mountain, with few surviving buildings and contaminated water. Trapped, they would have died of starvation but for a more immediate danger. The earthquake had taken a huge 'bite' from the side of the mountain and the unsupported overhang could come down at any time, obliterating everything in its path.

Ironside was instructed to ignore this because an exchange of small arms nearby signalled that the temporary cease fire was ending. He sent helicopters to the valley to get survivors out before the mountain collapsed. They came under fire and helicopter gunships were despatched to give support. Despite the waves of death around them the rescuers succeeded in getting the villagers to safety.

It took more than one flight to get everyone out. The helicopters took casualties, one narrowly escaped having to ditch. One pilot although wounded, managed to land safely on the deck of the ship. Despite being ordered not to, Ironside jumped in and took the chopper up for a second time. He was determined not to leave a single person in the path of those boulders. On the way home the chopper, overloaded with airmen and civilians, took a hit. Ironside was severely wounded but managed to get over the ship and hover long enough for everyone to get out. He knew he could not land without tipping over, so he slid sideways and ditched in the sea. He spent many months in hospital until well enough to sit in a wheelchair at a court martial on charges of recklessly endangering the ship and men under his command. There had been a huge public outcry with some saying Ironside should have obeyed his orders, whilst others hailed him as a hero.

After a verdict of 'Not guilty' he was honourably discharged from the Navy, as being medically unfit, and told he would never walk again.

This however did not take into account the iron will and determination of Captain Paddy Ironside.

His legs were rebuilt, partly of the remainder of what God had given him, and partly of steel rods, pins and carbon fibre replacements for muscle tissue and cartilage. He fought through mountains of pain as he crawled along an agonising path of physiotherapy and other treatments that would have crushed a lesser mortal. He refused to accept his situation and pushed himself beyond the limits supposed to be those of the human body. Eventually he could stand on his own, learned to walk, and started jogging. Hiram remembered his tears, like thousands of others, as he watched Paddy Ironside cross the finish line of the London marathon…

Now Ironside was applying for the job as captain of the Adongiva. "Is he fit enough to take command of a ship?" asked Hiram.

"Apparently," said Clarice, "he is fitter than you or I, having resurrected something approaching his former self. The man seems indestructible."

Hiram said, "I can't sit in on all the interviews, but I would like to be at that one."

"I was going to insist that you do. After all you and the Captain need to have a close and friendly working relationship, and it is important that you get along." Clarice smiled warmly.

Saturday 16th April 2026

On the Thursday the envelope was completely dismantled. The marquees came down, everything was loaded on trucks, whisked away, and for a brief spell the area appeared to have returned to normal. However another hive of activity soon started up and scores of workers flooded the building. This time it was more like what M&S was used to. No protective suits with full helmets, but hard hats and boiler suited electricians, carpenters, and plumbers. Hundreds of miles of cables were laid. Pipes and conduits, plaster boards, artificial brickwork, and wood panelling were fetched by the lorry load.

On Saturday morning there were much more people 'hanging around', than there was work to do. Nobody wanted to miss the arrival of the Stork. At 9.30am Roderick arrived by car and after a quick meeting with Hiram, Bertrand, TBM and a few others, arranged for an area of tarmac to be kept clear of spectators. As if on cue an army of additional people materialised from every building and had to be told where to stand. At 9.55am the Stork appeared in the distant sky as a black dot. It grew in size and as it approached the noise reminded Hiram of something from old cowboy films. A rattlesnake makes a noise like throbbing hiss, just like the Stork.

As it drew nearer they could make out two large white, seaplane floats, on which stood four pillars gently sloping inwards to the flying saucer like disk above. Between the pillars was the cabin with the front end mainly of glass. The 'flying saucer' had four propellers, in protective rings, sticking out like ears, if you can have ears on your forehead and the back of your head, as well as at the sides. Just in front of the cabin, between the floats, was the camera ball. The lens was clearly visible as it stared back down at them. The Stork sailed gracefully over the furthest buildings. The noise was louder now but not uncomfortable. It hovered over the area which had been cleared, and clouds of dust blew in all directions, including where the spectators stood. Everybody turned to protect their eyes. When dust had been blown clear the noise diminished to a whisper and the machine gently floated to the ground.

Cameras clicked and people craned to get a better view. The top half of the rear wall of the Stork opened upwards and the lower half became a ramp to the ground. Two men emerged in short sleeved white shirts, dark trousers and ties. They walked toward the crowd, to a round of applause. Roderick introduced them as his test pilots, and then suggested that before they get down to discussing business, they do something with the crowd. This was an historic moment, being the Stork's first public flight, other than test flights. To get here they had carefully chosen a route mainly over water, so that few people would see it arrive. These people had come to witness this maiden flight, and they would not disperse until satisfied.

Bertrand raised his hands for a bit of hush, introduced Roderick and invited him to say a few words. Roderick told them a little about development of this machine, although he did not go into any great detail about its origins over the mountains of Canada. He went on to explain how it worked and said there would be plenty of opportunity for them to see the Stork in operation over the next few weeks because it would now be based here, until the Adongiva was complete, when that would be its permanent home. He suggested that he, Hiram and the relevant M&S head personnel go somewhere quieter for a chat while the other people had a chance to see round the Stork under the supervision of the test pilots.

After a cup of coffee, over which Roderick explained a little more about the Stork, they returned to the tarmac. Most of the crowd had disappeared, but some still lingered. Hiram estimated that the space the Stork occupied was slightly larger than a small lorry. The difference between it and a lorry was the flying saucer on top. On the road, it would be a 'wide load'.

Hiram spotted a black brief case on the tarmac below the Stork. "What's that?" he asked.

Roderick said it had been placed there for a reason which would become clear later. He escorted them to the rear, and up the ramp. On the wall, just inside the upper door a small brass plaque read, 'We thank you, Alexander Bishop and William Denny, for your vision'.

Hiram nodded his approval. Roderick said the floor might look like conventional carpet but was a very tough, non-slip, and easy-to-clean synthetic material.

In front of them were two cupboards. One door concealed a toilet and washbasin, about the size that might be expected on plane. The other opened to reveal a 'kitchen' with small work top, sink with draining board, kettle, toaster, microwave oven, fridge, drawers and cupboards. On either side of the cupboards, corridors led to the front of the craft. Immediately forward of the toilet and kitchen was a floor-to-ceiling, cylindrical 'glass' tube.

Roderick slid back a sliding door and stepped inside. He explained that this was the winch shaft, the floor of which could move aside to reveal a circular hole. He pointed above to where a two-fingered claw with an opposing thumb hung on a cable. "Up there is a powerful winch capable of hauling a car, up to two tonnes of cargo, air sea rescue operations, or winching someone to or from a ship. Immediately below the floor, next to the winch hole is a camera for monitoring what is happening, from there…" He pointed to the cockpit seat at the front. "That camera could also help you land on a coin, if you wanted to." He shut the door and pointed to another cupboard next to the winch shaft. "This has a winch harness for lifting people and several types of hook, depending on what you want to carry."

At the front was the passenger compartment with five passenger armchairs. On the side walls were two additional chairs, more like the cabin crew folding chairs in an aircraft, and in front of these were the pilots and co-pilot chairs. The control panel had a row of 7-inch monitors and a number of buttons, switches, dials and lights, but only a fraction of what would normally be expected on a conventional aircraft. However the most striking thing was the absence of any control wheel, joystick, or other obvious control to make it manoeuvre. Instead, on the control panel, there were a number of sliding controls like on a music sound mixer, and on one side a computer keyboard, but no computer screen.

Roderick smiled at the sea of puzzled faces. He said, "Gentlemen, this is so easy to fly, I could teach a ten year-old in a few minutes." He turned to Hiram. "Why don't you try this chair for size."

"Me?" gasped Hiram.

"Go on," Roderick urged. "It's easy."

Hiram sat down.

Roderick went on, "The rest of you take a seat, or stand as you wish. There is no need to strap in on this aircraft."

"Now wait a minute," said Hiram. "We are not actually going to take off with me sitting here, are we?"

"Of course, how else could I demonstrate how simple this is? Have you ever flown anything before?"

"No," said Hiram, emphatically shaking his head.

"Good. Your lack of experience and training makes this demonstration even better," Roderick said cheerfully. "This is child's play. The first thing we have to do is switch on your instruments." He held something that looked like a hotel credit card key over a slot on the bottom right of the panel.

Hiram looked on in trepidation, took the card and inserted it, expecting to hear the engine start. There was no noise but needles moved on several displays, and lights came on. Several screens came to life and they could see on the central screen the view to the front, obviously taken by the camera in front of the cabin. On the screen to the left of centre appeared a compass, and on the two to the right, information about altitude, air speed, outside and inside temperatures, wind direction and speed, main engine revs and temperature, fuel, and a host of other information. If the others had sat in the thickly padded comfortable seats behind them they would still have had a good view, but they chose to stand in a half circle and look over Hiram's shoulders. The screen to the left of the compass showed a series of concentric rings and a white dot in the centre, which blinked steadily on and off. The label said simply, 'Mother'.

"What's that flashing light for?" asked Hiram.

Roderick said, "That briefcase you saw on the tarmac contains a beacon, which will soon be on the Adongiva. When you fly away, by getting the dot back into the centre of that display, you will always be able to find your way back to Mother."

"That's clever," said Hiram.

"Shut the door, please," said Roderick.

"How do I do that?" asked Hiram.

"Work it out for yourself."

Hiram looked at the panel. The label under one button said, 'Door open/shut'. Hiram pressed it and the door sections swung towards each other.

"Let's get this thing up in the air," said Roderick.

Hiram looked again. In the centre of the panel were two vertical slots with another horizontal one at the top and one at the bottom. One vertical slot said 'Up' and 'Down'. The other said 'Forward' and 'Backward'. The horizontal slots had arrows pointing left and right. A horizontal bar lay across the bottom of the 'Up/Down' slot. The others had similar bars across their middles. In between the two vertical slots was a vertical trench with a button marked 'Hover'. There was also a large red button marked 'Main Rotor On/Off'.

Hiram poised his finger over the red button and glanced at Roderick for reassurance, but the other man seemed preoccupied by his nails, so he pressed it. There was a low whine and then a muffled cough as an engine burst into life. The noise became a roar and then faded, as if some one had turned down the volume.

Roderick said, "We have an electronic noise cancelling sound generator up there which samples noise patterns and then produces a complimentary sound wave. The combination of these two waves effectively reduces what you hear. A similar system has been used for years in commercial aircraft. The blades in the chamber above are now spinning and pulling air in the top of the saucer and blowing it down through the white tubes on either side. Let's go up."

Hiram tried to move the bar across the Up/Down slot but it wouldn't budge. He pressed the button on the end and tried again, it slid up easily. The noise above and the steady whoosh from the tubes outside grew in intensity for a moment then died down again as the machine they were sitting in gave itself a gentle shake and started rising into the air. The figures on the monitor screen showing 'altitude' changed rapidly: 10 metres, 15 metres, 20 metres, 50 metres.

"My God, we're rising like a weather balloon," said Bertrand.

Roderick said to Hiram, "Hover at 152 metres, then turn to face the sea."

Hiram adjusted the horizontal bar by lowering it on the slider slightly. The Stork continued to climb, but at a slower rate: 70 metres, 90 metres, 110 metres. He lowered the bar by about two or three millimetres. The screen showed; 120 metres, 130 metres, 135 metres, 140 metres. Hiram moved the bar down again by about a hair width. The display said 145 metres, 148 metres, 149 metres. He tried again. The display showed the Stork was now falling; 147 metres, 145 metres. He adjusted it again. 148 metres, 149 metres. He found it hard to find the 'hover' point because the movement necessary was so small. Eventually the screen showed 153 metres, and did not change.

"Well done, Hiram, you've adjusted the speed of the propeller above to ensure enough thrust to keep us steady. We are now hovering at approximately 502 feet above the ground. It took a bit of effort to get the bar to the point for hovering. If we change altitude, how are you going to remember the spot?"

Hiram moved the button marked 'hover' until it was level with the bar.

"Well done, now point your nose to the sea."

The horizontal slider across the top of the slider he had been working on had arrows pointing to the left and right. He could see out the window that the sea was to his left. He gently moved the bar on this slider to the left, and the nose of the Stork turned towards the sea. When they had turned he moved the bar back to the centre. They stopped turning, but were not pointing straight at the sea but diagonally to the left. Hiram moved the bar to the right then back to the centre. They were now looking straight out to sea.

Hiram looked at the display with the white blinking dot. The dot was no longer in the centre, but slightly to the right of it. "Does that mean we have drifted away from the place that we took off from, because of the wind?"

Roderick nodded. "Well spotted. Now, let's go for a little spin in your new toy."

Hiram looked at the vertical slider marked 'Forward/Backward' and gently eased the bar up. The Stork started moving forward. The display read 50 knots, 60 knots, 70 knots.

"Increase speed to 100 knots," said Roderick. Hiram let the figures climb and eased back as the display read 100.

"We're now flying out to sea at approximately one hundred and fifteen miles per hour," said Roderick.

The others were like small boys let loose in a toy shop.

"Fantastic!"

"Wow!"

"Look at that!"

"Come and see the view from here!"

They wanted to take it all in at once, but couldn't make up their minds whether to study the instruments, look out the windows, stand still, walk about or sit in the luxurious chairs. He then told Hiram to execute various combinations of movement with the slider bars. They stopped going forwards, flew backwards, sideways, pirouetted, dropped to a few feet above the water, back up to 1,000 metres and finally down again to 300 metres. The technically minded passengers were stunned at the ease with which the machine moved, changed direction or just hovered while Hiram who was doing this for the first time ever, seemed to be having no problem operating the incredibly simple controls. They had run out of superlatives and just looked in awe, but with obvious pleasure.

"OK, Hiram, head for home."

Hiram looked at the display with the rings. The dot was below and left of centre, between the third and fourth ring. Roderick said that by pressing the 'Zoom in/Zoom out' button it was possible to see not only the position in relation to Mother but the distance away. The display could show position as if the rings were 10 metres, 100 metres or 1,000 metres apart.

Hiram moved the top slider bar and the Stork turned to the left and watched the dot moved clockwise until it was at the top. Hiram returned the bar to its neutral position. Through the front window he could see M&S cranes in the distance. As he moved the 'Forward / Backward' bar, the Stork raced for the shore and the dot moved towards the centre. He reduced the altitude to 100 metres. As they approached the waterfront he eased back on the bars. The displays read a speed of 10 knots, and altitude of 50 metres. They sailed gracefully over the dry dock buildings at 4 knots and they could see the black briefcase on the tarmac as he eased back to 2 knots and 20 metres altitude.

Roderick suggested he turn on the winch camera. Hiram found the button, and another screen showed the ground below. Through the windscreen he could see he was slightly left of the case. He turned the Stork to the right and stopped his forward speed. The briefcase sailed into view on the monitor, and out again. He moved backwards, sideways, forwards and backwards again before he could get the case to stay in the middle of the screen. Now he eased the altitude bar down slightly. The altitude read; 10 metres, 7 metres, 5, 3, 2, 1. There was a gentle bump as the floats made contact with the tarmac.

Roderick laid his hand on Hiram's shoulder and said, "Well done. What did you think of that?"

Hiram let out a sigh and said it was scary but exhilarating. He admitted that he hadn't realised just how much concentration it required to make such precise movements of the controls.

"Well in that case you won't want to keep it. I'll just take it away with me when I leave, if that is all right with you?"

Hiram grinned and shook his head. "Oh no you won't. I want to do that again, a few million times. It is fantastic! I will be amazed if you don't sell millions of these before long."

Monday 20th April 2026

All of the applicants for the post of Captain were capable, qualified, experienced and multi-talented. Hiram could not understand why some, with their backgrounds, were applying for this job. He said after having been in command of large ships, the Adongiva must seem like a toy. He thought the answers from two translated to mean that the Adongiva was an interesting, brief, diversion from the norm, an eye catching addition to the CV. Another candidate with impressive CV had clever and full answers for every question. However Hiram felt intimidated. The man was good, and was keen to make sure everybody knew it, but he sealed his own fate when he looked at Hiram and said when he was in command, he would accept disagreement from no one. Hiram returned the stare and thought to himself, *not a chance in hell matey. I am not having an arrogant SOB like you telling me what to do on my own ship.*

Paddy Ironside was asked, like the other candidates, to speak for 10 minutes before questions. He somehow managed to engage the panel in what felt like casual conversation for almost 20 minutes. No one was sure how it came about but it was more like a fireside chat with an uncle than an interview. However, during that time the panel learned all they needed to know.

He talked about his recovery and struggle to get fit. When asked about his current physical condition he replied, "A demonstration is always better than an assertion, don't you think? Right here and now I will do five times the number of press ups that anyone else in the room would care to do." No one took up his offer. He was asked why he wanted this job, after his distinguished Navy Career. He said, "I read with great interest all I could about the Adongiva, and Hard Plastic. I did some research into Anderson Plastics because such a company has to be taken seriously. I have absolutely no doubt that Hard Plastic will revolutionise the world of tomorrow and that the first ship made of this material, deserves respect and a good captain. I know M&S's reputation and history very well and would be honoured to be associated with this company. Everyone has heard of Ivanovitch Petrovsky, and I have always had the greatest respect and admiration for the man and his work. Although I am restored to fitness, my Royal Navy career is over, but I am not ready to retire. I feel I am ready for new excitement and adventure, and with my experience I believe I can provide exactly what you need in a captain for the Adongiva."

Although Hiram had never met Paddy Ironside before, he formed a strong impression right at the start of the interview. Here was a man who was supremely confident, mentally and physically fit and agile, and despite his disarmingly relaxed smile, was extremely alert and in total control of his situation. He had something about him that made you want to have him on your side, and to be his friend. Hiram could tell from the faces of the other members of the interview panel that he was not the only one who was slightly in awe of the figure in front of him. The panellists were all experienced experts in their own fields; HR, administration, engineering and seamanship. They were not the sort to be taken in or fooled by someone who was exaggerating their case or covering something up.

Eventually, Ironside looked at Hiram and said, "Tell me, Hiram. From what you have seen and heard, do you think we could get along?" Hiram felt like a small church mouse under the close scrutiny of a golden eagle, with a benign expression. He nodded then said "I think we need look no further. I believe we have found our Captain."

Hiram had decided not to sit in on the other interviews because now that the Captain had been chosen and as the standard of applicants was very high he was not bothered who was picked. He was happy to leave the experts to choose the best electrician, cook, seaman and so on. This left him plenty of time to continue his studies and to visit Dry Dock 5 periodically to monitor progress.

The interviewers worked steadily though the task of choosing the crew of the Adongiva, from the pool of first class talent. Many stars were picked, and many more, just as good were discarded. Although the final few were all chosen for their excellent qualities, some reached this happy point because their journey had been shaped by the stepping stones of fate that had lain across their path.

Cassandra Carmichael was on the edge of panic as she sat in her car outside M&S. The cars in front kept stopping, moving and stopping again. She could see the gate ahead but there was a hold up and the minute hand on her watch was creeping to the time she would be late for her interview. Just four cars from the gate, she could see the problem. A black Citroen turning towards the driveway had stopped because an oncoming red Nissan was doing the same thing. The cars were almost touching and neither could move because of the cars behind. She could not afford to be late, and decided to take control of this mess. She grabbed her hockey referee's whistle from the glove compartment and vaulted from her sports car blowing as she ran. By the time she reached the offenders she commanded universal attention. She gestured a blue Mercedes to reverse. The owner looked blank so she blew again and slapped his bonnet. He reversed to the green Renault behind. She moved to that car and repeated the performance, till he reversed. Now she got the Mercedes to move again, and then the Nissan. No one wanted to give way but with the authority of a traffic cop, she secured enough room and waved the Citroen forward. All the cars wanted to go at once and she had to deafen everybody and bang bonnets to get them to wait their turn. She got the Citroen into the driveway by blocking the Nissan. She gestured the black Ford behind the Citroen into the drive, and the grey Vauxhall behind that. The next car in that line was her own. She turned to the Nissan and glared her intention, that if he moved she would kill him. He stayed put as she ran to her car, jumped in and sped into the driveway.

Once through security, she followed the instructions to the car park. Her heart sank as she flew up and down the lanes of spaces, which all seemed to be full. At last she saw an empty space, but a car was about to reverse. She recognised it as the grey Vauxhall from outside. She reckoned he owed her for getting him free of the jam, and hit the accelerator before he could move. She jumped out as the window rolled down and an elderly man with white goatee said, "Do you mind?"

"Sorry, mate. My need is greater than yours," she called as she ran for the building.

Inside she rushed the reception desk and asked where the interviews were taking place. A receptionist pointed to the lift and said, "second floor."

Cassandra ran to the open doors of the lift which was nearly full and a young man about to enter. She tapped his shoulder and when he turned, swerved round him and into the lift.

He howled, "Hoy, what do you think you are doing?"

"Sorry sir, this lift is taken," she said with a smile as the doors closed. She thought anyone wearing a pink tie with yellow golf clubs shouldn't be in a lift to the second floor, anyway. On the second floor a secretary told her to relax and catch her breath. The interviews were running late because of traffic.

She found the ladies room, checked that everything was in place, and returned feeling pleased to have overcome all obstacles. She was asked to wait in a comfortable alcove lined with modern leather chairs and a low table on which stood a vase of lilies. She waited, trying not to eye up the other candidates and worry about her own chances in competition with them.

Finally she was directed to the interview room. A small table and chair faced a large table behind which sat the people she needed to impress to get this job she so desperately wanted. A lady in the centre introduced herself as Clarice Teasdale and introduced the other members. Cassandra spotted a gentleman on the right of Clarice, and as he came into focus her heart dropped. One of the men from the carpark! The gentleman's small white goatee beard twitched as he smiled knowingly at her. Oh no, she thought. Of all the people. She tried to console herself with the thought that he at least looked amused and friendly.

The person at the other end of the table did not look as friendly, and Cassandra could not tear her eyes from the pink tie with yellow golf clubs. The man in the lift. She groaned inwardly. But later, she decided that the success of her interview was not due to the years of work resulting in her qualifications as hairdresser, beautician, aroma therapist, and masseur... or the fact that when not making people beautiful, she loved throwing Land Rovers around and rushing over hills with radio equipment, as Royal Corps of Signals Territorial Army Corporal... or that when not putting her black belt karate skills and hockey referee experience to good use in a Youth Club, she sang in a band at weddings and social occasions.

No. She was convinced that the thing that clinched this dream job was sorting a traffic jam, stealing a parking slot, and then a place in a lift from the people about to interview her.

There are more multi-talented and interesting individuals around than the average person might imagine. The Adongiva recruitment advertisement drew them forth as a light draws insects. Johnny Harrigan was an ex-marine with scuba diving, sniper, winter warfare, rock climbing and electronic warfare skills. He was also a drummer and because he had First Aid skills would have joined the Band of the Royal Marines if he had not been enticed away by his cousin, Brendon who had persuaded to become a partner in an electronics repair business. Unfortunately Brendon was better at repairs than a businessman. The company went bust, and Johnny lost money. As a boy Johnny had been raised in America and with his father had regularly hunted with bow and arrow,guns, and catapult. His other skills included playing the banjo, guitar and penny whistle. He acquitted himself well at his interview and was offered the job of electronics and electrical engineer on the Adongiva.

Another successful candidate was Martha Wilson. Her dry cleaning business had a capable manager and her sister was more than happy to be left in charge of her contract cleaning company, which left her plenty of time to race her twelve foot sailing yacht. Her other interests were kickboxing and she played the Glockenspiel in the local marching band. She had set the companies up and had all the skills necessary to run them herself, but with trustworthy people at the helm she could enjoy the excitement and thrills of being away from dry land. When she read the Adongiva advertisement her heart leapt and she knew she would regret it for the rest of her life if she did not apply.

Professor Michael Ribbons was the character that caused the selection panel to deliberate for the longest time, before unanimously appointing him as Ships Officer, 1st Class Musical Director. After graduating from The Royal Musical Academy he could have been a successful conductor or classical pianist, but instead became Head of Music at a large private school for the well-heeled. One day he intervened to stop a fight involving a boy who was well known as a trouble maker. The boy then accused Michael of assault and he had to face a disciplinary tribunal, Outrageous cheque book diplomacy by the boys father coupled with his threats of bad publicity were sufficient to secure Michael's dismissal. In the rarefied circles of classical music and academia all the top people know each other, and are heavily influenced by reputation. 'There is no smoke without fire' is a common phrase despite the fact that it is perfectly possible to generate smoke, without fire. As a result Michael could not find another job worthy of his talents.

He spoke with self deprecating candour which won over his listeners and convinced them that he was the victim of a grave injustice. They thanked him for his frankness, and one said, "You are hugely overqualified and bound to get bored."

Michael replied, "Products, skills or services are only worth what someone is prepared to pay. I believe that if you accept loyalty, trust and friendship you are obliged to reciprocate to the best of your ability. If you employ me I will repay you with every fibre of my being."

Another member of the committee said, "We are looking for multi-talented individuals. Your other interests of gliding and horse riding are not much use on a ship."

Michael said the glider, the horse, a sports car and a sailing dinghy all had to go because of his reduced circumstances. "Your ship requires general seaman duties, and there is no job below my dignity." He got the job.

Raymond Ingram was a big man, six feet seven with shoulders to match, who looked as if he could push a tractor sideways. He was an ex navy artificer, rugby player, trumpet and tuba player. He enjoyed sailing, gliding, and boxing, and spoke four languages. He was not only good at whatever he did, he was a gentle giant who stood head and shoulders, literally as well as in other ways, above his competitors for the post of Adongiva Chief Engineer. He was just the sort they were looking for.

Friday 29th May 2026

The final interviews had been completed by Monday 25th and the successful candidates agreed. Hiram was told that although they were all of exceptionally high calibre in their own fields, their sea going experience, and previous work in a disciplined team varied considerably. It was suggested that a basic training course would ensure minimum standard of fitness, check skills and knowledge and build camaraderie. Hiram was worried about the cost. Captain Ironside agreed with Hiram that the cost of a six week course was too big for one individual. He persuaded M&S and Anderson Plastics that as they would benefit from the crew being able to impress potential customers, it was right to share this cost. He still had friends in the Admiralty who could pull strings, for old time's sake. Britain, like other countries, sells not only armaments but expertise to foreign governments who find it cheaper to buy military training in Britain, than run their own. The Navy had a place, HMS Carson Fylde, for such 'foreign students'.

In between regular courses there was often 'down time' when instructors rest, recuperate and prepare. Paddy Ironside persuaded them to squeeze a short course between two regular courses. A six week schedule condensed to four weeks would be cheaper but more intense, and would cover looking after themselves, kit and equipment, lots of 'square bashing', kit inspections, daily physical training, plus all basic skills and knowledge expected of a ship's crew. The days would be long, with little rest and regular assessment. Pushed beyond endurance, they would have to find reserves they never knew they had. More than one will want to give up but it will be drummed into them that they are all responsible for ensuring everybody finishes, and they will be forced to rely on, trust, and help each other. At the end, when that badge is pinned on them they will be bursting with pride, achievement, honour and comradeship.

"And what will you be doing while these unfortunates are going through hell?" asked Bertrand.

Ironside replied, "I don't ask anyone to do what I would not do myself. I and the ship's chief officers will undergo a similar programme, but harder because of additional content to prove we are fit for command. Would you care to join us?"

That wiped the smile off Bertrand's face.

"What's this going to cost?" asked Hiram.

"£1,750 per person per day," said Ironside. "A four week course is £49,000 per head and there are forty one of us, which makes £2,009,000, a one third share of which is £669,666."

Hiram had been concerned at the increasing number of items being added each week, and had prepared a spreadsheet to keep track. He opened his laptop, found the file and added the latest item.

Current net balances	£74,973,123
Estimated cost of Adongiva	£55,000,000
Stork aircraft	£2,500,000
Camaleonte automobile	£114,202
Self righting fast launch	£157,500
Water sports equipment	£72,450
Mini Submarine	£168,000
Trip for two to Russia	£5,000
Estimate for crew uniforms	£717,500
Basic training programme	£669,666
Estimated Tax liability	£12,922,175
Total expenditure forecast	£72,326,493
Projected net Balances	£2,646,630

Hiram thought it amazing that even after all this he still had over two and half million left in his 'pot'. In addition, the latest projection for his annual income from the Adongiva, from a 100-night cruising season, after paying a whole years running costs, was half a million. He didn't want too many more surprises, but he was still far wealthier than he had ever imagined he could be.

He returned to the matter in hand. "OK, let's do it. I rely on you, Captain, for good advice and if you think it's a good idea I am happy."

"Excellent. I shall put the wheels in motion. Clarice, here are the dates."

Clarice Teasdale took the paper and said, "I shall issue letters of appointment today. I also propose to send letters to those who were not successful, and to those with whom we were most impressed, say that we will keep their names on a reserve list for future vacancies.

Saturday 13th June 2026

Hiram knew, as this day drew closer in his diary, that it was not going to be easy for him. Sure enough, when it arrived he found the first anniversary of Sarah's death very hard to cope with. Luckily he had no appointments or meetings scheduled and he found it easy to avoid people. He had awoken to a concrete heart, and cloak of sadness. It had crossed his mind to get drunk and block the pain. He had enough money to kill a battalion with alcoholic poisoning, but decided this was not a suitable commemoration of the anniversary of Sarah's death. They both deserved better. Besides, she could still nag from the grave, by putting the words in his brain, and he would speak them for her.

He spent the whole weekend looking at photographs, remembering her voice, reminiscing, then pondering, *was it time to move on, and meet someone new? he asked himself. What would be so wrong with taking solace in another woman's arms, just for a cuddle of an evening? Would it be disloyal to Sarah if he found someone to talk to and share his dream?* His answers were inconclusive. *I still feel married to Sarah, even if she has been dead for a year, and I have no desire to be unfaithful. What's the point of staying apart from the human race? What's the point of all this expenditure of time, money and effort, if you have no one to share and enjoy it with? What, indeed, is the point, of anything?*

He knew that this was a question to be avoided, for it led to the labyrinth and a downward spiral of depression.

CHAPTER SIXTEEN

Monday 22nd June 2026

Hiram, and other members of M&S's staff, had now flown eighteen times in the Stork, with Hiram at the controls for nine, operating the winch on three, and simply enjoying the ride the other times. M&S were now discussing with Robertson Aeronautical Lifting Equipment, or 'RALE', the purchase of two versions of the Stork – one was big and powerful for lifting equipment, the other was spacious and comfortable for personnel. Because of the terms of the CAA licence, all versions had to have a winch because they were classified not as aircraft, but VTOLSDALE. It did not matter that the token equipment on the passenger version was barely strong enough to lift the contents of a car boot.

Meanwhile on the Adongiva there was still a lot of effort going on by dozens of tradesmen and technicians. The hulls were complete although boiler suits still tinkered, but most of the external work now centred round the smoke stacks. A lot of very technical stuff was being mounted on the wing platforms which Hiram was glad he did not have to understand. He just accepted it was for radar, antennae and aerials. The water cannons now stood on their platforms, principally for fire fighting, they could deluge the exterior of the Adongiva, or nearby ship, with thousands of gallons in minutes. In a defence role they could sweep an intruder over the side, or a small craft approaching in threatening manner could be sunk by filling with water, or pushed away.

As Hiram stood below the ship, looking up, he thought it looked gigantic. He gazed at this ocean liner in wonder, even after walking round and looking from every angle for days. Arranged round the central bow were rows of discs, alternately concave and convex. This was the Hedgehog Submarine Object Proximity Alarm transceivers which would create a three dimensional map of the water in front, to the side, and below. Just aft of the Hedgehog, on short legs protruding from the hull, were the rugby ball shaped multi-azimuth propeller pods. On their rear ends within protective rings were four-bladed propellers. The pods could rotate in any direction but when aft at 'max revs', speed could be boosted by several knots, when to the side the bow could be pushed laterally. If the Seahorse engines were turned in the opposite direction the ship could pirouette, or if the same way, the Adongiva would move sideways. When ahead, the propellers could act as emergency brakes, or go astern.

Behind the propeller pods were two very large fins which could rotate to any angle. In one position, like hydrofoil blades, they would give lift and increase speed. Turned vertically, they acted as brakes. When stopping a rowing boat with the oars, considerable force is required to hold the oars steady. In a fast ship the size and weight of the Adongiva, the stresses would be so colossal that if made of steel they would have to be robust, heavy, and require a lot of energy to turn and hold them. They would also have to be extremely well anchored. By making the blades, arms, engine housings, and anchor points from Hard Plastic the problems were solved and the mechanism more compact. As well as hydrofoil blades and emergency brakes, the fins controlled by the ship's computer can act as anti-roll and pitch stabilisers.

When the plastic envelope had been in place, the floor had been covered in sheeting. When it was removed Hiram saw another feature of these dry docks which had not previously been apparent. The Adongiva rested on a giant cradle, standing on a large rectangular sheet of dimpled steel, which extended beyond the bow to the huge steel doors at the end of the building. On the three other sides was plain concrete floor.

Bertrand explained the floor to Hiram. "The steel is actually a giant table on telescopic legs. At the launch, the legs will retract, lowering the table and the ship into the space below which will then be flooded, allowing the Adongiva to float off the cradle. When the steel doors slide open the Adongiva can move forward into the harbour beyond. All the great metal buildings that led to the open water have this feature. Dry dock 1, in another area is big enough for an aircraft carrier."

Three months had passed since Hiram's party at the club to celebrate the postponement of his demise. Several times during the first month he had awakened in the night from a nightmare about St Augustus's Fire. He had to mentally replay his conversation with Professor Cann, in order to restore his equilibrium. It wasn't until about the sixth week that he could finally accept that it was all behind him, and look at his life and his future, and smile. He knew he was a creature of habit and liked routine and order to be part of his daily life. He ate well and was a regular at the club, but endeavoured to keep his weight steady, He did one thing he had never managed before, which was regular exercise. Each day he would alternately visit the swimming pool and the gymnasium. He was able to remember Sarah without falling apart. He still missed her and accepted that the ache would never fully go away, but he could keep going on a day to day basis with some semblance of normality.

The other thing that had changed Hiram's life in the past few weeks was the increased media interest. There had been articles in several newspapers about an exciting futuristic ship under construction at M&S that was to be packed with state of the art technology. Mostly the articles, lacking much detail, were padded with guesswork and speculation, but this did not stop ever escalating fishing trips by tabloid journalists. It was gratifying that despite increasing cheque book journalism, the M&S workforce was tight-lipped, and the other suppliers were maintaining confidentiality.

On the 22nd June, however, the Head of BBC News Services telephoned The Big Mac. Up until then the standard M&S response to all news requests had been a lightweight press release, with minimal detail and a promise that 'all will be revealed in time'. The BBC boss said that despite the stone walling they had been able to gather enough to run a reasonable feature. However, rather than do this without permission, they suggested that cooperation would be mutually beneficial. If it came across that the BBC were revealing something that M&S and Anderson Plastics wanted kept hidden, this might seem suspicious and detract from an essentially good story. They wanted to put together a documentary about the ship, Hard Plastic, and the technological wonders within. The BBC would do what it does best, present interesting information to the public; M&S would get great publicity and kudos; Anderson Plastics, and Hard Plastic, would be given a platform worth millions. Hiram

Montgomery had an interesting story to tell, which could include as much or as little personal information as he wanted. The Adongiva could make its official public debut in a controlled and dignified manner, and in return the BBC wanted 'an exclusive'.

Hiram realised that the cover story he had given his family was about to be blown. He did not want to have to do the grand tour of all the home addresses all over again, so instead he picked three conveniently located hotels on three consecutive Sundays starting with 28th June, then phoned members of his family and invited them to lunch. At the lunch he came clean. The reactions differed slightly but more or less followed the same pattern. Initially, they were cross that when he thought he was dying he had not told them.

His sister Marlene summed it up when she said, "How would you have felt if it had been the other way round? Suppose you found out that one of us was dying and hadn't told you, to spare you the worry? You would be upset, wouldn't you? The fact that it was a mistake and you are OK is irrelevant. Families support each other and you should have told us."

There was nothing for it but to accept the rebuke and to apologise. Once they were over that piece of news he spilled the beans about his lottery win and how he had quadrupled his fortune. They were enthralled by his story, and what he was in the process of doing. He looked at each of them knowingly to remind them that they should keep quiet about the amount of money he had given them.

At the end of one lunch his brother Stuart wanted a private word. He said that the money Hiram had originally given had seemed generous at the time, but now in the light of Hiram's current fortune, it did not seem all that much. Rather than feel cross, Hiram could not help but smile at the cheek of his youngest brother. He had half expected somebody to make this point.

He said, "Firstly let me remind you that I was under no obligation to give anybody any of my money. I did so because I wanted to share my good fortune, and given the number of our family I gave what I worked out I could afford, given my plans for the yacht. Secondly let me say that every member of this family, including you, has been raised by our parents with an excellent sense of values to guide them through life. We all have a strong sense of what is right and proper, and what is not. When I first gave

212

you, and the others, the money a short time ago I did not ask what you would do with it because it was an unconditional gift from one brother to another. Over the years some of us have done better than others, and some have from time to time have run into the buffers. By the strength of character instilled in us we were always able to pick ourselves up, dust ourselves down, and start all over again. None of us were brought up to be greedy or envious of each other. You now know I am worth a fortune, and I know that you are not rich but have a job, a house, a partner and a reasonably happy life. How much do you think I should give you?"

Stuart looked shame faced. "If you are trying to make me feel guilty, you have succeeded. I was rude and greedy, and I apologise."

"I'm not trying to make you feel bad. It's just that none of us have scrounged of the others before, and I don't want to be a personal banker in the future. Having said that you should know that I would never turn my back on a member of my family in trouble. If you ever need money in future, for a legitimate reason, ask me first before borrowing from any financial institution."

They gave each other a hug, and parted on good terms. By the end of the three lunches he was satisfied with the outcome. He was also pleasantly surprised that none had gone mad with the money he had given them. There had been the odd extra holiday, or new car, but in the main, they were using the money wisely. They were all very pleased to hear that in due course they would get an invitation to one of the most expensive and luxurious private yachts in the world.

Hiram, and several million other people, watched the BBC programme on Friday 17th July and thought it marvellous. On Monday morning Bertrand summed it up. "They did a first class job and according to the newspapers the programme is a hot topic everywhere, including Parliament, to the delight of some MPs and the discomfiture of others. In the bit about the Seahorse engines, Sir Bartholomew was enthusiastic in pointing out the stupidity of the government." It had not previously occurred to Hiram that he might need a publicity agent but he was persuaded to do so just before the broadcast. This had been sound advice because after the programme the world seemed to go noticeably crazier than it had been before.

The phones never stopped and one person was assigned full time to answer the calls which included chat show, radio and press interview requests; invites to discuss business opportunities, and speaking engagements. Several magazines Hiram regarded as rubbish were vying for an exclusive interview, and the latest bid was three quarters of a million. If he wished, Hiram could have had a celebrity status, but couldn't think of anything worse. He was basically shy, lacked confidence, and shunned limelight. Another expense was the hire of a secretary. HR Department lined up 3 interviews for him and he chose Margery. She was a fifty-something lady with grey hair, and a friendly smile.

Every day she opened dozens of letters asking for money. Some were crude begging letters with little justification, but others were epistles of misery, illness and misfortune. Others asked for investment, or informed of inventions needing funding, and of course there were the proposals of marriage. Apparently lots of women suddenly found Hiram desirable. Some wanted a soul mate, others to look after him, and some gave graphic details of how his evenings could be made more interesting. As far as Hiram was concerned, his attractiveness had a lot to do with his bank balance, which put these women on the same level as 'ladies of the night'. After reading a few, he discussed them with Margery and told her to use her discretion but basically just bin them. He was glad he had picked her. She was efficient and organised, but had the maturity and common sense he needed when he wanted to sit and talk to somebody in confidence or discuss ideas with.

He said to her, "From the begging letters, pick the ones you think are genuine, and the most deserving cases. I accept that this could be very difficult, but we have to try. I have plenty of money but I remember when I didn't."

She said, "I understand you don't want to ignore those who need help, but the world is awash with crooks wishing to prise money from the innocent. How do you tell the difference from a letter?"

It occurred to him was to set up a charity office with a budget and staff to investigate the requests and pay money to the genuine ones. Everyone he talked to told him to forget it. Trained personnel were needed for this task, and he had no chance. He should bin the letters and give money to registered charities with the resources to dispense it fairly. He decided on an amalgam of these ideas. He would invest £1,000,000 and give the interest to a number of charities, and in addition, asked Margery to sift through the letters for the most genuine sounding ones. She seemed to be on his wavelength, and he told her he trusted her judgement.

Monday 10th August 2026

During the last two months Hiram had more meetings to agree the myriad details, from light fittings, colour schemes, and equipment lists to the crew uniforms. All the successful crew members had been checked for clothing sizes and orders placed. Hiram was pleased that the original figure of £17,500 per person for a full kit allocation of clothing and equipment was more than required. Between them the crew had a wealth of musical talent and to obtain all the necessary instruments after contacting a number of suppliers a really good deal secured everything within the budget of £61,250.

Margery said to him, during one of their informal chats, "You should get out more. It is not good for you to be using your ship as an excuse for not meeting other people."

He returned her penetrating look, and smiled. She was clever and seemed to know what was going on in his head better than he did. He did not take offence at her implied criticism because he valued her wisdom, and because when she was around he did not feel alone. He was not ready to take this particular advice, but if he were honest with himself he would admit that since the trauma of Sarah's death he had incarcerated himself in an emotional retreat. As if to emphasise her words, that very evening in the club a middle-aged draughtsman joined him for a drink after dinner. They had spoken briefly on a couple of occasions, and he had seemed pleasant enough. They had been speaking about nothing of great importance when Hiram realised he had just been asked if he would like to go elsewhere for a drink, and then on to a club. "Are you asking me for a date?" he asked, incredulously.

The other man smiled and said he thought that was a quaint old-fashioned expression, but that was the gist of it.

Hiram had no inclination towards homosexuality, but to be polite, simply said, "You are not my type."

The man asked what Hiram's type was.

"If I said pretty face, sweet disposition, nice figure, good looking in a skirt, subtle hint of perfume, and complete absence of male genitalia, would that give you a clue?"

The man chuckled then feigned sadness. They changed the subject, and after a few minutes, the man politely excused himself.

Hiram sat before the fire and contemplated. "Question – Would you have said yes if that had been a woman? *Answer – No*. Question – Why? *Answer – Sarah*." It was two days short of fourteen months since Sarah's death. He was a one-woman man, and could no sooner be unfaithful than fly. He had made a promise: 'for richer, for poorer, in sickness and in health, forsaking all others until death do us part'. But what about after death? He knew that mentally he was still wishing for her death to be cancelled, for it to have been a mistake, and for her to walk through the door. He knew it was not going to happen, but he still needed to keep her alive in his mind, even if that meant keeping everybody else out.

Wednesday 12ᵗʰ August 2026

Mike O'Donoghue, the Chief Engineering Projects Manager, had arranged to take Hiram on a tour of the completed sections of the Adongiva, but because they were not completely finished, he insisted they wear hard hats. As they walked to the accommodation hull resting on its cradle, Mike said, "This hull is 62.4m long and 9.9m at the widest point, which makes it broad at the hips. Nevertheless the draft of 2.8m allows navigation quite a way up river and getting very close to the shore. The engineering hulls look narrower and longer than their 56.2m by 7.9m. From the port engineering hull to the starboard engineering hull, maximum width is 41.5m. The disk is 40m across and has four decks including the bridge."

Hiram nodded approvingly. He had studied ship specifications over the weeks and mentally converted the dimensions into accommodation space.

Mike went on, "Once we go round you will really appreciate why this trimaran vessel is so expensive. This is a compact, high specification cruiser with space and comfort for thirty passengers, plus yourself. The ship has ample amenities and safety features plus accommodation and facilities for forty-one crew, and berths for emergencies. Think of the engineering hulls as two support ships permanently in tight formation."

They stepped into a large rectangular bucket and Mike raised his hand. The bucket lifted and, as they moved diagonally upwards to the deck of the port engineering hull, Mike pointed to a door in the side of the hull. "When the ship is afloat, that will be about two and a half feet above the water. It opens like a ramp to boats alongside or quaysides. There is another on the Starboard hull." The bucket landed on the deck, they stepped out and the bucket was whisked away. "Passengers can board or disembark by Stork using the landing pad on the central hull or by launch from the boat dock. The third method, from the quayside, will be a gangway to this deck and entering here," – he pointed to the two storey superstructure before them – "There is an identical one on the other side of the starboard hull over there."

On the fore deck were two rectangular grooves. The one on the left was ten feet by eighteen inches wide, the other six feet by eighteen inches. "The long one is the automated docking arm for tying up at quaysides. The other is the MOB Net. To rescue someone in the water, these covers pop open, the docking arm rises, swings over, lowers the grab and picks up the net. As the net comes up, its spring loaded frame pops open and it becomes a giant fishing net. It swings over the side, scoops up the person and returns to the deck." They turned their attention back to the superstructure, which had a sloping glass front wall.

Through the glass they could see four armchairs – "For anyone wanting a quiet place to sit, with drinks and nibbles cabinets of course," Mike said with a grin. Stepping through the outer doorway he said, "You can see there are two doors, one behind the other. Normally only one can be open at a time, like an air lock. It's one of the ship's security features. All the deck doors have the same arrangement." He led the way and beyond the inner door was the seating area on the left, a door to the right, a flight of steps to the deck below, and another to the one above. Opposite was a door marked 'Storm coats locker'.

Mike said, "The door to the right leads to the emergency lifeboat section. The walls and ceiling sections open and davits lower the boats. On either side there are two enclosed motorised lifeboats, each with room for nineteen and emergency supplies for ten days. In addition there are several rafts, with room for six."

"So we have comfortable lifeboat space for the crew and passengers for ten days, plus the rafts," said Hiram.

"Correct," said Mike proudly.

"Let's hope it never comes to that."

Mike continued, "These stairs lead to the deck below, but there is also a lift." He pointed to a two-foot square of floor. "This can be lowered electrically or manually. There is only one thing on the upper deck, an extending crane which can be used for lifting a vehicle or supplies on or off the ship." He led the way back through the door and along the deck to the rear of the superstructure, where they stood before the smoke stack. Mike talked about the water cannon, which were controlled from the bridge. He pointed to the domes and radar arms on the 'wing' platforms and explained their functions.

Beyond the safety rail at the rear of the smoke stack was a semi-circular area which sloped gently to the rear, which was the 'lid' above the Seahorse Electric engine. They entered a door at the rear of the 'life boat shack' and down steps to the deck below. Through one doorway was a compartment painted white with desks and control panels. Mike said the engines were controlled from the bridge but this area enabled engineering to monitor them from nearby, so that they could take immediate action. Forward of this was a long section lined with large empty wire cages, and beyond that several box rooms.

"The cages are for storing large parts, luggage not needed on a voyage, and cargo items. Beyond the cages is the food storage area with cold and cool rooms, two at 12.22 degrees Celsius for meat and fish, and capacity for 65 days, a dairy room at 0 degrees, and fruit and vegetable room at 1.66 degrees with capacity for 35 days, and a room designed to keep cut flowers in perfect condition. Another commodious room will be kept at the precise temperature and humidity for the extensive wine cellar and there is an ice making cabinet that can generate 250 pounds of ice per day and storage for 500 pounds. There are four large refrigerators, including one big enough to stand in, and three large 'walk in' freezers. Needless to say, each has a panic button inside. In the other hull instead of these rooms and cages is the computer automated storage and retrieval facility for packets, tins, bottles, and small non-food items."

They walked down another flight of stairs. "Have you noticed it seems narrower here than what you might expect from outside the ship? That is because the ship's fuel, oil and water tanks are built in to the walls. They are tall, narrow, run the length of the hull, and have internal buffers to minimise movement when the ship is rolling or pitching. They also provide perfect balance at all times. Down here are workrooms for electrical, mechanical and other maintenance. Beyond this section is the water cannon pumps, each as big as a car and enormously powerful. Hitting someone at close range with a jet from one of those cannons could take his head off. Beyond that pump room is the desalination equipment with its own dedicated self-cleaning pumps. Water is drawn from the sea, checked by a computerised, fully automated water testing station for undesirable substances and impurities, and then through the reversed osmosis unit to a holding tank from which it is pumped to your main water tanks to provide an endless supply of clean water for washing and drinking."

Hiram nodded, his head spinning with the input of so much information.

Mike was in full flow, enjoying himself. "In the other hull, instead of water pumps and desalination unit is the electricity generator and batteries compartment. That generator could produce sufficient power for all the modern appliances, running simultaneously, in several streets of houses, plus the street lights. Instead, it keeps the Matsushita Kogyo Yuasa batteries constantly topped up. The batteries supply all the power for the ship, including the Seahorse engines, have enormous storage capacity and can deliver huge amounts of energy on demand." They walked back up the stairs to the engineering control room and Mike pointed to a big square hole in the wall. "This is the aft connecting bridge between the two hulls." Hiram obediently looked through the tunnel. "Put the equipment, or yourself, on the trolley and press the button. When the trolley stops you will be at the other end."

Mike went on to say that it was not conceived as a connection bridge; that was a bonus. Running the length of the four corners were four strong coiled spring supports to hold the two hulls in tight formation even when tight manoeuvring or changing speed.

The two men walked through the door to the cages and on past the food rooms and refrigerators to a circular wood lined space beyond. "This floor rotates, like an engine turntable in a railway marshalling yard. You can drive an electric buggy along the corridor connecting the hulls, but as there is not enough room to turn it around, you turn the floor instead." Hiram thought this was really neat. "There are three doors here. One leads to the anchor chain capstan and locker, one to the sitting area above, which you saw when you came on board, and the other to the water line door we saw outside."

They walked slightly uphill through the corridor in the connection bridge to the central hull. At the other end was another circular room, with turntable floor. Hiram looked from left to right at the several doors arranged round the room, a passenger door, a large 'buggy' door, another passenger door, another 'buggy' door and another passenger door. Mike explained that the first and third doors led to the corridor round the circumference of the disk. The luxury passenger cabins were on the outside of this corridor, which meant all had a sea view. The second door was for the buggy to go to the centre of the disk. The fourth door allowed the buggy to go to the starboard engineering hull. The last passenger door led to the car garage and the aircraft hanger. He said the starboard engineering hull was similar in some respects to the one they had seen, but significantly different in others. It contained the computerised stock storage and retrieval facility for non-perishable food, and non-food items. The bulk of the starboard hull was filled with a wall of pigeonhole cubicles. Provisions, supplies or equipment are boarded, scanned into the system, placed in a micro-chipped tray which passed over a weigh platform, through a measuring arch, carried by conveyor belt to a robotic arm on a gantry, which found a cubicle.

Mike explained, "When you want, say, a single packet of cornflakes, the computer locates it in an instant, retrieves the tray containing a box of cornflakes packets. You take one packet from the box, inform the computer, and it will return the box to its cubicle. The computer knows where everything is and how much space is available. It remembers rate of usage and produces shopping lists so that you never run out of anything. It also warns if 'use by' dates are approaching."

"So it controls everything but fresh food?" asked Hiram.

"For different temperature controlled rooms, refrigerators and freezers, conventional stock control was thought better. In the port hull the crew members, using their communication badges, tell the computer when placing or removing items from those areas."

"What about weight differences in the hulls, as supplies are used up?"

"Remember the fuel and water tanks in the walls? The computer monitors weight distribution and selects which tank to use next, so that the contents keep the ship perfectly balanced."

They walked though the buggy doorway to the central hull, and a corridor flanked by several rooms. On one side a gymnasium with exercise machines, sauna, steam room, changing area and showers, and stair to the rooftop swimming pool. Next to this was the beauty parlour and hairdressing salon. On the other side were well-equipped laundry and dry cleaning rooms were next to the sick bay.

At the end of this sort corridor the central lobby drew an admiring gasp from Hiram. It was not a big area but the light wall panelling and illuminated ceiling which was a faux-clear blue sky, gave the impression of a spacious atrium. There was a circular seat round a fountain in the centre of the room.

"There will be potted plants and paintings to create a tranquil and relaxing atmosphere," Mike said.

There were lifts and stairways behind the wooden doors. The corridor continued passed the circular centre, to rooms even more impressive. On the left was a lounge with leather armchairs, occasional tables and subtle lighting. On one wall was a large and magnificent stone fireplace that would not have looked out of place in a grand house. "That is artificial stone but very good quality and feels real to the touch," Mike explained. "There will be a gas fire in the fireplace which can be either a coal effect or log fire to suit the mood." On the other side of the corridor was a room with full sized billiard table. "There will also be a dartboard in that corner over there and card tables in that cupboard."

At the end of the corridor they turned left, into the circular corridor which ran round the disk. "On our right are the guest cabins. We will come to those shortly but first let me show you the other common areas. On our left is the library."

The library had wall-to-wall books arranged on shelves, floor to ceiling, round the room, a large central table and chairs, arm chairs by another fireplace, and computer terminals on side tables. Next to the library was another sitting room with more armchairs, another fireplace, and other furniture. "This is a small coffee lounge where people can relax. There are several such places, each with its own character, where people can socialise or escape, as the mood takes them. They all have a television dressed like a window, linked to an external camera, so that even in the centre of the disk, you can 'see' the sea and sky."

In another room was the 'golf course'. Hiram did not play himself but was sure guests would appreciate it. Three walls were a tough canvas screen and underfoot was artificial grass. Mike showed him how it worked. "You select a course on a panel on the fourth wall. A panoramic view from the first hole appears on the screen. The computer uses laser sensors behind the screen to pinpoint the impact, and determine the force, and calculates where the ball would have gone. Another view then shows the view from the spot you would need to be in to hit the ball from its new position. By hitting the ball correctly you 'move' round the course, or not as the case might be."

As they moved round the ship they encountered workmen carrying components, or screwing things in place. Once they had completed a circuit of the round corridor, it was time for Hiram to see his cabin. Hiram had seen drawings and fabric samples, but the actual room more than lived up to expectations. It had a sitting area with marble fireplace and log effect gas fire, two leather armchairs and settee, a writing bureau and desk with computer, two screens, and telephone. One screen was wall mounted and the other on the desk. Mike explained that the wall screen would display ship data: course, speed, weather, estimated time of arrival and other information. On the other side of the fireplace was a drinks cabinet, and dining table with four chairs. A hi-fi unit sat on a wooden stand next to a wooden cabinet containing a television. These areas were separated from the sleeping area by low room dividers topped with plant pots which would contain a luxuriant selection of house plants. In addition to the low room dividers a tall ornate silk screen room divider was folded against one wall. French windows led to a small private balcony with room for chairs and table.

The super-king-sized black wrought iron bed frame had no mattress or bedding but Hiram was assured they were being stored until construction was finished. There were ample fitted wardrobes, and en suite facilities of very high standard. Hiram voiced his approval.

Hiram looked at other guest cabins, which were similar to his, but slightly smaller. Mike said that all the cabins would have the standard and facilities of a top class hotel, including complimentary drinks cabinet, fresh fruit or flowers, large flat screen televisions, hi-fi, computer with internet access, satellite telephones, and balconies.

Mike led Hiram back to the fitness suite and up the stairs to a glass walled area containing the Jacuzzi, bar and swimming pool. It too small for a decent energetic swim but sufficient for several people to 'have a bit of a splash', laze around, relax, and feel indulgent. There were several sun beds and glass roof and walls that could retract.

Hiram looked through the glass at the deck on the stern of the central hull and imagined standing here on a sunny day, with clear blue sky above, sea view on three sides, and cooling breeze in his hair. It was going to be bloody marvellous!

Thursday 13th August 2026

Hiram thought it was a perfect day as he strolled to his cabin. The sun was shining and he had just eaten a most delicious kipper. It was not something he chose often because although he liked the taste he couldn't be bothered with the complex bone removal surgery, but today's specimen had been worth the effort. He espied Caesar Meredith lingering by the hedge near the cabins.

"Ah, Hiram," said Caesar with a smile, as if this just happened to be a chance meeting.

Hiram was immediately on guard. Firstly, because for Caesar to be smiling, something must be amiss. Secondly, Caesar had obviously been waiting for him. Thirdly Caesar never called anyone by their first name. Hiram returned a plastic smile and nodded.

"I wondered if I might have a word?" asked Caesar.

"Certainly, what can I do for you?" said Hiram, keeping his voice as flat as possible.

Caesar pointed at the cabins. "Do you mind if we go somewhere private?"

Hiram would have felt safer inviting a puff adder into his quarters, but he smiled and led the way. He was curious to know what this unpleasant man wanted.

As soon as they were seated Caesar said, "You have been in this cabin since the 27th of January. Have you enjoyed the facilities?"

Hiram studied the other man, knowing it highly improbable that he cared whether he enjoyed the facilities, or that this show of friendliness was genuine. He decided not to say anything to prolong this meeting. "The facilities here are excellent." The reptilian smile did not reach the eyes and returning the stare took resolve, but Hiram was determined not to be intimidated.

Caesar said, "You came here at the invitation of Mr. McCallister, who said to stay as long as you like and enjoy the complimentary facilities. He did not realise the financial consequences, and now finds himself in an embarrassing position."

This surprised Hiram, but he gave nothing away. "Why?"

Caesar smiled again, and Hiram wished he would stop that. "As you know Mr. McCallister is an honourable man, who keeps his promises even after realising he has made a mistake. Your stay is costing too much, but Mr. McCallister is too polite to say anything."

Hiram found this extremely irritating, not to mention unlikely. "I offered to pay, but Bertrand said this was not necessary and that as VIP I was to enjoy it, as others had done before me."

"Of course," said Caesar pretending that he had known about the offer, "but you have been here longer than anyone else. Normally VIPs stay a few days and you have been here now for 198. By the official hand over on 13th of November it will have been 291."

If this was meant to make Hiram feel uncomfortable, it was succeeding. He did not want to have to justify himself to this man but he said, "I had a word with the housekeeping manager about the abundant food and other supplies in the cabin and have agreed a procedure to keep them at a more modest level."

Caesar had not heard about this and was cross he had not thought of it first. "Quite so," he said, keen to could get back to his point. "I am sure you will agree that if the facilities you have enjoyed were provided by a good hotel or a private club, the bill would be substantial."

Hiram nodded. He could see where this was heading. Caesar prepared to deliver his punch line. "Leaving aside the cost of the food and drink in the cabin, which is considerable, I have looked at the cost of the standard of accommodation and facilities of the club, if you had been paying a commercial rate. I am sure you will agree that a bill of £350 per night would not be unreasonable."

Hiram had no idea whether this was reasonable or not, having never stayed anywhere charging anything like this amount. Caesar pressed on, "I have decided to err on the generous side, and call it £300 per night." He smiled as he finished.

Hiram kept a straight face and said, "What are you saying?"

Caesar's smile disappeared for a moment then reappeared, as unconvincingly as before. "Your bill up to the present time, allowing a free week at the beginning and ignoring the food and drink in the cabin, at £300 for 121 nights would be £36,300. I am sorry that you were not informed of this before."

Hiram knew that Caesar was not the slightest bit sorry, but was actually enjoying this. He did not believe that The Big Mac or Bertrand would have allowed this and said nothing. He had always been willing to pay a bill, but this was a ridiculous amount. He could pay it, but he had other ideas. He said, "Have you prepared a bill?"

Caesar could hardly contain himself as he produced a piece of paper. "We will accept a cheque."

I bet you will, you toad, thought Hiram. "Leave it with me. I will pop over later," said Hiram standing to indicate that the meeting was over.

Caesar's smile wavered, but he remained seated, "Can't you do it now?" He was determined to get that cheque to the bank before The Big Mac or Bertrand discovered his game.

Hiram turned to the door, which he held open, and said, "I have to come over later anyway."

Caesar had believed his plan to be foolproof and was staggered that it was not working. He thought that because after buying the Adongiva and the other stuff Hiram still had millions, he would agree to this bill of a few thousand. Because he had not been greedy, this money which was a drop in the ocean of M&S's income would be seen for what it was, a gesture to prove a point, and nobody was going to fight over a gesture. It would remind people that Caesar Meredith was the true guardian of the firm's purse, to be consulted at all times. They had to be reminded that he gets his way, and woe betides anyone who forgets it.

The two men smiled inanely as they maintained the facade of civility, and Hiram was determined not to blink first. Years ago he had learned a technique for this. When two people are staring each other out, don't look at the eyes but instead at a spot just above the nose. It looks as if you are returning the stare, and you can keep it up for hours. It worked. Caesar realised Hiram was not going to back down and got up. Hiram thought, *thank God, the smile was starting to ache.*

As Caesar walked to the door, he was furious that he had underestimated his adversary. He kept the smile going. "What time will you be over?"

"Soon," said Hiram, no longer pretending. As soon as the other man had cleared the frame he slammed the door, knowing that it would miss the back of Caesar's head by inches. "Ruddy cheek," muttered Hiram as he picked up the phone.

He told Bertrand what had happened and was deafened by the explosion.

"He said what?" roared Bertrand. "Do not pay him a penny. Have you got that?" As he spoke, Bertrand shuddered. Shouting orders on how to spend their money was not how he usually spoke to customers, however Hiram didn't take offence.

Bertrand then phoned The Big Mac, who went ballistic. He said, "I'm having that man's balls nailed to the flag pole, while attached to his body. Give Hiram my most sincere apologies. As an honoured guest his hospitality is free."

The Big Mac phoned Conrad Meredith and after exchanging pleasantries, said, "Conrad, my dear friend, I need to be brutally frank about your nephew."

The old man sighed and said, "What has he done now?" Big Mac put him in the picture. After a long silence Conrad said, "I promised his late father I would look after him. We both know he would not be employed here if I were not his uncle. I keep giving him chances to prove that he is not a waste of God's good oxygen, and all he proves is that he is a mollusc, with the mind of a bad tempered spider. I am sorry Terence. Please tell Hiram Montgomery that if there is anything he wants, he just has to name it. I will speak to Caesar."

The Big Mac said, "You know that if he were not your nephew I would be asking for his head."

"Yes, and if you did, I would have to act. As a favour, please do nothing until I shake some sense in to him."

The Big Mac agreed but only if Caesar behaved in future.

Conrad then phoned Caesar, who was waiting for Hiram's cheque. He nearly collapsed when his uncle phoned and told him to get his sorry backside over to his house immediately. He really had thought Hiram would submit to his superior will, and how the hell had Conrad found out so quickly? He pictured the route the message must have taken to get from Hiram to Conrad, and the more he thought about it the more he boiled with indignation at being thwarted again, and humiliated by this amateur upstart. If he hated Hiram before, his feelings were now multiplied a thousand fold.

As he hurried to the car park, knowing he was about to be flattened by his uncle, he vowed from the depths of his soul that the day would come when Hiram Montgomery would regret the day he had ever crossed swords with Caesar Meredith.

CHAPTER SEVENTEEN

Friday 14ᵗʰ August 2026

The crew members arrived at HMS Carson Fylde Halt, a featureless railway platform in open countryside. They looked round as the train pulled away. There was no one to greet, and no signs. It was 9.32am and the average journey time had been five and a half hours, although one soul had started at 2.30am the previous day. A dirt track led in two directions – one through farmland to buildings half a mile away, and the other several hundred yards up a slope to a large wooden gate. They had been told to arrive without a change of clothes, and just a wash bag. In the letter of appointment they had been given instructions for an appointment with the uniform supplier who would measure them, and that everything would be allocated on arrival.

On the train journey they had eyed each other up, and some had already introduced themselves. They did not realise their assessment had already started, and they were being watched by a discreet camera. One person lit a cigarette and another wandered a few paces to get a better view of the farm buildings, which did not help. Another couple started a conversation, and some just looked puzzled, having expected better organisation than this. The biggest one in the group looked at the gate and realised what was expected. He said a few words and started walking. Three walked with him, then several more. Some could be heard shouting, "Shouldn't we wait for somebody?" The moving group kept walking and soon everyone followed. Eyes watching the camera image identified the leaders and followers.

As they approached, the gate opened to reveal the imposing figure of Chief Petty Officer Cauldick and two Petty Officers. "Good morning ladies and gentlemen, glad you could make it to my humble establishment." He stepped back and to the side, and the Petty Officers moved in perfect formation.

The group of men and women stepped inside and waited as the uniformed trio surveyed them. CPO Cauldick spoke again: "My full name usually gets known by all visitors to this place, so we might as well get it over with. My name is Ivor Cauldick."

Some chuckled and others tried politely not to laugh, but one could not help laughing out loud. Others did not get it at first until they realised it had sounded like, 'I've a cold dick'.

He continued: "I assumed my parents were cruel or stupid, but it has stood me in good stead. I got picked on, and got into fights, as a result of which I am now a hard bastard, as some of you may find out over the next few weeks." The smiles evaporated. The big man spoke again, "If you find my name funny, and I admit it has a ring of humour, I suggest you repeat it until you get it out of your system. I only allow people to laugh at my name on one occasion. You have just had it." CPO Cauldick's eyes fell upon Gemma Pringle. "Pretty lady, what's your name?" She told him. "Well, Gemma, having just arrived, I will not ask you for twenty press ups, because you could not know I cannot abide smoking in my presence, without permission. I suggest you flick that disgusting object out the gate, and we shall say no more about it. You have however been warned, for future meetings."

Without turning his gaze from the now more apprehensive group he said, "Allow me to introduce those with absolute power over your stay. Petty Officer Summerfield and Petty Officer Whitworth. Shortly, you will be split into two groups and one of these men will become your God. They can be of immeasurable benefit and you will learn a great deal if you use them wisely, or they can give you a taste of hell. Do your best, give a hundred and twenty percent of your energy, stamina, intelligence and determination to succeed, and there should not be a problem."

He turned and walked, speaking loudly. "We are now going to collect your kit and take you to your accommodation. Please follow me." He was now some distance away. The two Petty Officers urged them to follow, and they had to run to catch up. The Petty Officers followed the group as they rushed after CPO Cauldick who was heading for a large hut at the other side of a large rectangle of tarmac. By the time they got inside, some were breathing hard. He had walked to the far end of the room and was waiting behind a long table, flanked by two ratings. "Did I forget to tell you? You do everything at the double here. You will know next time."

When everyone was quiet he said, "You have given your clothing sizes and your kit has been packed for you in those bags." He pointed at a table with holdalls twice as big as normal sports bags. "When I said we have packed your bags, I meant except for Cadet Samuel Ross and Cadet Laura Ruffles." The two individuals named looked round nervously, and stepped forward. "The rest of you gather round. We have not packed the bags for these two good people, so that we can do it now. You will see exactly what is in your bags, for they are identical." As he spoke the ratings walked to the ends of the table. "You each have a number one uniform, for dress occasions. This comprises a double-breasted jacket in fine new wool material."

The two ratings turned, retrieved a neatly folded jacket from the rack behind them, and placed it on the table. "The jacket comes with trousers, or skirt, in the same material. No, you do not get a choice, Mr Ross." This raised titters. "A pair of leather shoes, long-sleeved shirt, silk tie, belt, fine beret and kid gloves completes the outfit." The items appeared on the table. "Next we have your number two uniform items, which comprises of eight short-sleeved shirts with epaulettes, two pairs of trousers, belt, eight pairs of socks, pants and vests for the men and tights, pants and brassieres for the ladies. Control yourself, Mr Ross. You get another pair of shoes, boots, woollen tie, belt, leather blouson jacket, woollen beret and leather gloves." The piles on the table grew.

"Next comes one coverall, two pairs of pyjamas, one swimming costume, sport polo shirt, sport shorts, calf length sport socks and sport plimsolls. Finally two white bath towels and a white hand towel. You will also be issued with specialised kit for your specific jobs. Chefs and cooks get 'whites', barmen get fancy waistcoats and bow ties, store men get store coats and engineers get heavy-duty coveralls, etc. These items will be given to you when you move on to the next stage in your training."

He looked around to make sure they were paying attention, then continued: "You'll also be given additional items for when you are performing in the band, and tropical clothing at the appropriate time. You'll be expected to look after these items, keep them spotless and well maintained, and present them for inspection in a precise and correct manner. We will now show you how to pack your bags neatly and efficiently, make best use of space and keep the clothes perfect." Two bags appeared from under the table and the items disappeared inside one after the other in rapid succession. "I hope you memorised the way the bags were packed because you will be expected to do it like that."

The recruits looked at each other with horrified expressions as the bags had been filled at lightning speed. "Just in case you can't remember, it is in chapter two of this manual." Two large ring binders appeared, bearing the words 'Adongiva Crew Manual'. "This is your bible. Woe betides anyone who loses it, damages it, or does not file the updates issued from time to time."

His hand came down heavily on the top ring binder. "This tome contains everything you need to know about rules and regulations, standing orders, daily work and disciplinary procedures. It contains deck plans, which you must memorise, how to look after your kit, crew command structure, pay structure, communications, and a host of other information. Please do not make the mistake of thinking that this is a reference work to be kept on a shelf, and consulted occasionally. Regularly during the course you must pass an examination on your knowledge of this book, starting on Monday." He emphasised the word *must*. "I suggest you find time over the weekend to learn chapters one and two." The binders disappeared into the bags. "You two, pick up your bags. The rest of you collect your bags, which are labelled, from that table and follow me."

As he spoke he walked, like an express train, to the door. There was a mad scramble as everyone rushed to the table, tried to identify their bags and hurry after the disappearing man.

Outside, CPO Cauldick, flanked by Petty Officers Summerfield and Whitworth, looked theatrically at his watch. "Ah there you are. I thought you had got lost. Listen up. If Petty Officer Whitworth calls your name, stand behind him."

PO Whitworth held up a clipboard and called out. Seventeen individuals moved and when he was finished the original group of thirty-five was now in two. PO Whitworth beckoned and started walking, and his group followed.

When they had departed PO Summerfield said, "Good Morning ladies and gentlemen. Now that the untidy and clumsy riffraff of 'Blue Squad' have left us, what remains is called 'Red Squad'. Over the next few weeks we are going to show them that Red Squad is by far the better of the two. We are going to be faster, stronger, more efficient, cleverer and better looking."

This raised smiles. On the other side of the square, PO Whitworth was saying something similar to his group. PO Summerfield apologised for not being able to put names to faces but said he would know them all by Monday morning. He singled out an individual and asked "Who is the better squad?"

Walter Doran looked nervous, but told PO Summerfield what he thought he wanted to hear. "We are, sir," he said politely.

PO Summerfield bristled with mock anger. "Don't ever call me 'sir' again! I am not a bleedin' officer. You will address me as 'Petty Officer', and who the hell is 'we'?"

Walter blushed and tried again, "Red Squad is the better squad, Petty Officer."

PO Summerfield took a step toward the hapless specimen. "Are you some sort of lefty militant, with your teeth and tongue on a go slow? When you say 'Petty Officer' I expect rapid fire. Run the words together and spit them out at top speed, with considerable volume. I suggest the rest of you help him out with this."

He walked several feet away, turned to face them and barked loud enough for the world to hear: "Who is the best squad?"

They shouted, "Red Squad, Petty Officer."

"I can't hear you!" he shouted louder.

They roared like a football crowd. "Red Squad, Petty Officer."

"That's better," he said.

From the other side of the square Blue Squad, who were obviously going through a similar exercise, responded with an answering roar which sounded like "Blue Squad Pay-Off-Sah!"

The two Petty Officers shared a secret grin. Their strategy to bond their respective squads and get competition going was working, as usual.

PO Summerfield turned back to his charges and said, "That was pretty pathetic. I told you we were better than them. Now holding your bags in left hand, get in line and follow me to your luxurious accommodation."

Red Squad entered their hut, which was a long dormitory with toilet block and office at one end. PO Summerfield told them to pick a bed, dump their bags and gather round. There were shocked glances, and one woman, who had served several years on cross channel ferries, was indignant. "Surely we are not sharing dormitory and toilets, Petty Officer?"

PO Summerfield eyed her up and down. "There were six women and twelve men in Red Squad, but from this moment you are equal members, brothers and sisters, and you will act as a family. You will look after each other, care for and respect each other. You share accommodation but being adult intelligent professional colleagues, you will act as such. A few simple house rules would not go amiss. For instance I don't think that anyone should wander round half-naked. We have rigged a sailcloth partition in the toilet block which divides it in two, with showers, toilets and sinks on either side. There are also free-standing screens in the office which you can use, should you desire. Alternately those screens can be positioned in this room, for a changing area, if you feel so inclined. If there is anyone among you juvenile enough to peek over the screen, the rest of you have permission to turn a fire hose on them. However I predict that before long you will be too busy, preoccupied, and knackered to be thinking about sex."

They deposited their bags. Simone Eastwood, ex-Royal Navy and a fitness instructor in a health club, had chosen the bed nearest to her. PO Summerfield asked her to retrieve her manual. He turned to the diagram of how to stow their kit in a locker and said the slightest deviation would bring retribution to the entire squad, because they were collectively responsible for everyone succeeding. He said the bottom drawer was for civilian clothes, but otherwise the lockers must be identical, and they now had precisely 1800 seconds to arrange their lockers, change into number two uniforms, with boots but no ties, gloves or jackets, and be outside in a straight line, with the tallest on the right and the shortest on the left.

The next thirty minutes brought panic and pandemonium as everybody rushed to complete their tasks. There was no time for modesty screens as they got changed, studied diagrams and filled their lockers. A couple had to be ganged up on before the lockers met collective approval. Finally they rushed outside and formed a line, while CPO Summerfield scrutinised. He changed the order then told them to memorise their neighbours so that they could get it right next time. He said that their job title or rank was irrelevant until they left this place, as they were all equal cadets from now on.

He then went inside, examined the lockers and reappeared saying, "Not bad for a first attempt." He walked around the line, and inspected. Some needed 'tweaking' but his main concern was the berets and one made its owner look "like Frank Bleedin' Spencer". He showed them the correct way to tug a beret into shape. Next, he said to study his horizontal bootlaces, because this was the last time he would allow criss-crossed laces on parade.

He next focused on Fay Jacklin, ex RNLI lifeboatman. He stared at her chest and said, "What do we have here?"

Bernard Leeming, ex RN, and self-confessed wit, muttered, "Either over-inflated floatation devices, or she is a melon smuggler, Petty Officer."

PO Summerfield side stepped to stand in front of Bernard and with noses practically touching said, "Cadet, did I give you permission to speak? Did I give you permission to look anywhere but the front? Did I give you permission to do anything except stand perfectly still?"

The increasing volume made the other man wince. "No, Petty Officer."

"Give me twenty press ups," PO Summerfield roared, and then when Bernard started to protest: "Make it twenty-five."

Bernard opened his mouth but realised further protest would increase the number. He dropped to the ground. "One, two, three." Everybody stood still as Bernard counted. He was fit and soon saying, "Twenty-three, twenty-four, twenty-five." He jumped up and his defiant look said, 'I can handle twenty-five press ups'.

PO Summerfield knew that the slightest challenge to his authority had to be crushed immediately. "Next time we will start at fifty."

Bernard got the message.

PO Summerfield returned to Fay's chest. "I am not interested in your anatomy, merely what lies between it and your shirt. The pattern visible through the material tells me you are not wearing your uniform brassiere. Can I ask why?" As she prepared an excuse he wagged a finger, "Don't insult me by saying you did not have time to change. Others did. I demand truth."

She gulped. "I didn't want to change in front of the men, Petty Officer."

He looked puzzled. "If you didn't want to expose your breasts, why did you not just turn round, or did you think they would be inflamed by your shoulder blades?"

Fay didn't reply, and simply looked helpless under the PO's gimlet eye.

"If you were pressed for time," he snarled. "Did you not think the men might be equally busy, with more important things to worry about than you? Modesty, I can handle. Shyness, I don't have a problem with. Decorum is good. But a false sense of importance and not trusting colleagues bothers me. I don't ask you to go around naked, but common sense at times of crisis is required. You are all going to have many moments of crisis, so get your priorities sorted. Now for coming on parade improperly dressed, give me ten press ups."

Fay considered complaining but remembered Bernard, and did them.

"You have five minutes to put that bra in your locker, and back here properly dressed, or you will do another ten."

She rushed into the building and re-emerged shortly after, red-faced with embarrassment and temper.

Once they were in line PO Summerfield showed them how to stand to attention, stand at ease, stand easy, fall out, and march. When they tried, he concealed his merriment, and showed them again. Their next attempt was better. They marched up and down, in a straight line several times, but stopping and starting without colliding was a problem, as was keeping in step. Next they tried turns to the left and right, marking time and 'about turn'.

After about forty-five minutes PO Summerfield was no longer bawling instructions every few minutes. The cadets, he thought with satisfaction, would do nicely.

The drill practice finished outside the mess hall and PO Summerfield showed them how to insert a rolled up beret under the left epaulette, then told them to fall out, get some lunch and be back by one-thirty sharp. It was now twelve-fifty. Lunch turned out to be an ample two course hot meal, and large mugs of tea or coffee. The cadets of Red Squad, feeling the effects of their efforts, were famished. Blue Squad were already at another table. A third table was occupied by a smaller group who had something about them which suggested they were senior in rank and experience.

As Red Squad moved from serving area to table, Blue Squad sounded whoops of derision, "Better late than never" and, "We're nearly finished, thought you weren't coming." The third group merely looked over and smiled.

After lunch Red Squad and Blue Squad were stood to attention in two lines at right angles, with PO Summerfield and PO Whitworth facing their respective squads. CPO Cauldick marched smartly into view accompanied by the third table group. They looked very smart, and the movements were precise and perfect. He came to a halt and in a voice that could be heard in China: "White Squad, White Squad Shun."

White Squad had marched into position, forming a third side of a square, with CPO Cauldick on the fourth side. With a single loud gunshot crack, the White Squad boots slammed the ground as one. CPO Cauldick's voice blasted their ears. "Parade – parade stand at ease."

Red and Blue Squads moved feet and hands smartly and stood at ease, pleased that they were getting the hang of this 'all move together malarkey'.

Cauldick spoke at normal volume. "I have agreed to interrupt training to allow the leader of White Squad to address you. He is Cadet Paddy Ironside who, after the completing this course, will be your Captain. Cadet Ironside, you have the Parade."

Paddy Ironside stepped forward, saluted, turned to face Red and Blue Squads and said, "Squads, stand easy."

They did, and he smiled.

"Hello everybody," he said informally. "Welcome to HMS Carson Fylde. You and I are here for a few weeks of sheer bloody hell, which is the best way to describe it. There will be times when we will wish we weren't here, but we must grit our teeth and bear it. These gentlemen are giving their time to mould us into a formidable team. What you are about to go through is not what you had in mind when you applied for this job, but it will be worth the effort. It is my privilege, pleasure and honour to be with you today. Just remember that 370 people applied for each place that you now occupy. You beat that competition and earned your place. The training programme ahead is intensive, demanding, exhausting, and will push you beyond the limits you think you're capable of but you must complete the course to be part of the Adongiva crew. I, and those of you who are ex-Navy, have experienced basic training before and know that on such courses some don't make it. That is simply not an option on this course. Also, there is usually an award at the passing out parade for the best cadet. That is not going to happen here. If one person fails, we all fail. This course is not about proving that you, as an individual, are the best, but that you as a group are the best. I, and your Chief Officers, have been here for three days doing a very similar course but with more material. I look forward to seeing you at the passing out parade in four weeks time."

He wheeled, exchanged salutes with CPO Cauldick, and resumed his place in White Squad.

CPO Cauldick shouted, "Petty Officers will return their Squads to their duties. White Squad Shun." White Squad cracked to attention. "White Squad, about turn. White Squad, quick march."

White Squad marched off and disappeared. The Petty Officers brought their squads to attention, turned them, and marched them off to their work areas.

Friday afternoon started with a classroom session to go over the course programme. Any doubt about the difficulty level was now cleared up. Each day would start with Reveille at 5.40am then PT before breakfast, followed by non-stop lessons and activity until lunch at 12.15pm. The afternoon, just as packed as the morning, would start at 1pm and end with dinner at 7.30pm. The evenings were marked 'free' when they could do whatever they wanted, but only after studying for exams, getting kit and the accommodation block up to inspection standard, which was extremely high. The list of sessions included parade ground drill, lectures, fire fighting, damage control, boat drill, fire arms, self defence, unarmed combat, first aid, swimming, more parade ground, more physical training, cross country running, navigation and shipboard drills, communications, commands, more physical training, more parade ground, team building exercises, and then more of the same, over and over again. Interspersed regularly throughout the programme were the forbidding words "CPO Kit Inspection", "CPO Block Inspection", and "Progress Examination."

After this introduction to the programme it was time for a quick change for their first physical training session. It was not too bad for some, and purgatory for others. After changing back into their uniforms, with no time for a shower, it was back to the classroom for a session on chapters one and two of the manual. Next it was outside for a practical session on how to get people in and out of lifeboats, and how to lower them quickly and safely. Another session followed, then another. They were told that as a special concession, because it was their first day they could finish three-quarters of an hour early, but by that time they had completed seven sessions.

After dinner PO Summerfield showed them a correctly made bed, warning that deviation would result in beds being tipped over. Next, he said those with experience of 'bulling' boots and shoes had to show the others and make sure footwear was up to standard by Monday morning. Finally he bid them good night and said he would see them in the morning for physical training at Reveille.

When he had gone some flopped on their beds groaning that they could not keep up this pace for a month. Others said there was no time to lie about, and a class on toe-cap polishing was now in session. The next few days flew past at lightening speed. Every morning started the same way: after what seemed like a brief couple of hours sleep after working late into the night, the lights flashed on burning tired eyes, and the Reveille bugle deafened the ears. PO Summerfield strolled up the room calling out good morning in a variety of what he thought were amusing ways. At the end he would turn and walk back. If anyone was still abed by he reached them he would grab the foot of the bed and throw it vertically against the wall, with the occupant still inside. After three days everyone had learned that 'Time to get up' really did mean it was time to get up.

For the first half of the course many were regularly bawled at or punished for various misdemeanours. Typical punishments were press ups, running on the spot or around the parade ground carrying a heavy weight. Each night groups of individuals gathered in the toilet block, the only place allowed light after 'lights out', or by their bedsides, illuminated by candles. The after dark activities included polishing boot or shoe toe-caps, with endless minute circular movements of fingertip, wrapped in yellow duster, which was dipped alternately into tins of polish then lids filled with water. Some swore by polish and water, while others praised the effectiveness of polish and spit. Others suggested encasing the toe caps with a thick 'mud' of polish and liquid mixture, then carefully burnishing it with the back of a desert spoon heated over a candle. This was a dangerous procedure for the inexperienced because unless the consistency of the mud, and pressure and temperature of the spoon was within very tight parameters, the shine could be ruined and you would be set back in your endeavours. Like ancient, nefarious alchemists they spent endless hours secretly practicing their rituals, to convert ordinary shoe leather into highly polished black mirrors.

Other nocturnal industry involved pressing perfect knife edge creases into trousers or shirts, or sitting in pairs with a manual. One would ask questions and the other would say, 'Oh my God, I can't remember.' The cadets, being from different backgrounds, had different levels of experience of domestic drudgery, and some were strangers to cleaning materials. By the third day all had taken their turn at making the taps, pipes and porcelain gleam like new. When they first arrived the floors were filthy, and matt in appearance. The apparatus for changing this consisted of large tins of strong-smelling, bright orange polish with the consistency of soft cheese which was 'setting', net cloths and floor bumpers. A floor bumper was a rectangular weight the size of a breeze block but several times heavier, attached to a broom handle. To make the floors clean and shiny the cadets had to liberally coat the cloth covered weight with polish then push it back and forth until their arms dropped off, or until they could see their reflection on the floor. A baritone voice would then be heard to bark, "Hoy! Get your bleeding boots off my floor."

At the start of the course although none of the cadets could be described as 'unfit', the difference in standard of athleticism and exposure to regular exercise was considerable. Whilst the hardier specimens admitted the course was demanding, the lesser mortals thought they were in hell, and flagged quickly.

For the first few mornings they tumbled from beds like zombies, and struggled into clothes with half closed eyes. Every time, during the long days, an instructor left them alone for a minute their eyes shut, determined not to squander a single moment of rest. Like pit miners they adopted the old adage, 'Never stand when you can sit and never sit when you can lie down'. Because every waking moment was occupied, and they were kept focused the whole time, they did not realise they were changing. They just became aware of not being constantly tired despite the relentless pace. They were fitter, sharper and faster in mind and body, and had absorbed a mountain of information and skills. There had been no time for self pity, thoughts of quitting, or erecting the 'modesty screens' considered important in the beginning. They had no time for thoughts of sexual differences, and without discussion, treated each other with respect, pride and professionalism.

The Petty Officer team had fostered serious doubts about whether this lot would reach the standard, but as they watched their puppies grow, they were pleasantly surprised. They were satisfied with the result of their efforts, although they would not say so until the last day, in case complacency interfered with the pace of improvement.

They learned many 'useful' skills like climbing a rope suspended from the ceiling and then descending without rope burns; extinguishing an oil fire with a water based extinguisher; minimising injury when leaving a sinking ship; dealing with a big strong attacker; working together to make way in a small open boat in rough seas; negotiating an underwater obstacle course, fully clothed and no breathing apparatus; navigating a large ship in a congested channel; sending and receiving radio communications; operating a variety of modern sophisticated equipment, and dealing with minor medical emergencies. They had to memorise all deck layouts of the Adongiva, and recite the fastest route from a compartment on one deck to another on a different deck. .

By the start of the fourth week they were not just coping with the relentless grind, they were enjoying it, and no one had to stay up after midnight. They were fitter mentally and physically than they had ever been, and because they knew it, they were all on an all-time 'high'. They marched like regulars, were all passing the frequent examinations, and no one was getting bawled out for failing kit inspections. They still got 'punishment' exercises but these had stopped being punishment and were given, and received in a spirit of banter – like the time PO

240

Whitworth overheard a cadet referring to the flag above as the Union Jack. "Right you. Give me ten press ups." He pointed to the person next to the miscreant, "You can also give me ten, if you can't say why I have given him ten."

"He referred to that bit of cloth as the Union Jack, instead of the Union Flag. A flag is only a 'Jack' when flown from a ship, especially on the bow to depict nationality."

"Correct, but you can still give me ten for calling it a bit of cloth. The rest of you, drop down for laughing."

Hiram, of course, was not present at any time during the training course and he gathered all of the above details much later, during many hours of brief casual chats with the crew members in their spare moments. He was like an enthusiastic collector as he absorbed all the anecdotes, and the crew did not mind his questions. They were justifiably proud of what they had achieved, and were happy to share it with him.

CHAPTER EIGHTEEN

Tuesday 15th September 2026

The original basic training course timetable was to have concluded with the Passing out Parade on Saturday 13th September and the specialist training would begin on Monday. The first indication that Hiram received that this was going wrong, came in a phone call from HMS Carsonfylde at 7.30pm on Wednesday 9th. The squads had been sent out on a training exercise that morning to test what they had learned. Due to an error one team had ended up in the wrong place and had to face great dangers which put them all at risk. They had all survived but one was to be taken to hospital because of his injuries and the rest were completely exhausted by the experience. The timetable was amended and the passing out parade would now take place on Tuesday 15th.

Hiram and others from M&S flew in the stork to HMS Carsonfylde to see for themselves that everyone was OK and to chat with the individual crew members. Saturday and Sunday were declared rest days for the crew, although everybody else was rushing around like blue bottles on a hot day. The work that should have been done on Friday and Saturday was to be put back to Monday and Tuesday of the next week.

Unfortunately another complication surfaced on Saturday morning. Press and media requests poured in for clarification of a rumour that a group of trainees had narrowly escaped death during an exercise. Initial reaction had been to try to identify and decapitate whoever had leaked the story. However this was quickly brushed aside for two reasons. Firstly it was agreed that anyone with a radio capable of picking up the Royal Artillery communications net frequency, could have heard what had happened. Secondly, when news reached the Ministry of Defence, it bounced back down through the communication tree, to HMS Carson Fylde with a mighty whoosh. Orders came from Admiralty that a top flight MOD Press Team was being despatched immediately to gather all information, apply a thick layer of polish and get everybody together for a press conference, headed by an Admiral. The Army also demanded credit for being involved and to demonstrate good inter-service cooperation, it was agreed that a Colonel could be present, but at the last minute this was upgraded to a General.

The navy was determined to put the best spin on this story, highlighting the work done by establishments like HMS Carson Fylde and showing off their results. This would remind people that as well as generating revenue, they were helping less fortunate nations to train to the highest standard. Attention was to be diverted from how Blue Squad came to be in the wrong place. The press conference took place on Monday morning and was a resounding success, with a big press corps lapping up every detail. On Monday evening thousands of people all over the country watched the news story and talked about it for a long time afterwards.

It is said that you can expect one second of air time for every minute spent with a reporter. If that was the case the Adongiva and M&S did remarkably well. The total time taken up by the press conference and interviews was about ninety minutes but the news story about HMS Carson Fylde lasted nearly seven minutes then another eleven about the Adongiva.

On Tuesday Hiram was due to fly in the Stork to HMS Carsonfylde in time to see the passing out parade. In the morning, before this journey he had time for an informal meeting with The Big Mac and other chiefs. Hiram said, "Someone already told me the difference between 'Pseudo Intelligence' and 'Artificial Intelligence', but I still don't get it."

Andre said, "If I gave you a detailed technical explanation of Artificial Intelligence, you wouldn't understand it. No offence intended."

"None taken," said Hiram, "I know it has occupied great minds for decades. Explain it as if you were talking to a twelve year-old."

"Artificial Intelligence is the science and engineering of making intelligent machines, or intelligent computer programs. It is related to using computers to understand human intelligence, but is not confined to methods that are biologically observable. Firstly we have to ask, what is intelligence? Intelligence is the computational part of the ability to achieve goals in the world. Varying kinds and degrees of intelligence occur in people, animals and some machines. Is there a definition of intelligence that doesn't depend on relating it to human intelligence? Not yet. The problem is that we cannot yet define the kinds of computer processes we call intelligent. We understand some mechanisms of intelligence and not others. Is intelligence a single thing so that one can ask, 'is this machine intelligent or not?' The answer is no. Intelligence involves mechanisms, and AI research has discovered how to make computers do some but not others. If doing something requires only mechanisms we understand today, computers can perform well, on these tasks, and should be considered 'somewhat intelligent'. Now if you were to ask me if AI was about simulating human intelligence, I would say, sometimes but not always. On one hand, we can make machines solve problems by observing other people or by observing our own methods. On the other hand, most work in AI involves studying the problems the world presents to intelligence rather than studying people or animals. AI researchers can use methods not observed in people or that involve more computing than people can do. Then we come to the question of IQ. Do computer programs have IQs? The answer is no. IQ is based on the rates at which intelligence develops in children. It is the ratio of the age at which a child normally makes a certain score to the child's age. The scale is extended to adults in a suitable way. IQ correlates with measures of success or failure in life, but making computers that can score high on IQ tests would be weakly correlated with their usefulness. For example, the ability of a child to repeat back a long sequence of digits correlates well with other intellectual abilities, perhaps because it measures how much information the child can compute with at once. However, 'digit span' is trivial for even extremely limited computers."

Hiram held up his hands. "If that explanation is for a twelve year-old, I dread to think what the full academic version sounds like. I just want to know whether the so called 'Pseudo Intelligent' computer on the Adongiva has Artificial Intelligence."

Andre sighed. "Strictly speaking, in its academic sense, no. However, if you mean does it appear to simulate human intelligence, then yes. Let me put it this way, the Adongiva main computer's hard drives contain, among other things, a database of hundreds of thousands of possible situations, problems, and questions. It also has the answers and responses to all that stimuli, and this might seem pretty intelligent. However, when it responds to a situation it is simply executing instructions. Let me give you examples. You say 'hello' to the computer. It recognizes your voice pattern from those in the database and retrieves your name. It knows the time, using the internal clock, and is programmed with conversational responses and phrases, and your appointment diary. It might therefore combine that information and respond by saying, 'Good morning Hiram, I hope you are well. Good luck with your meeting this afternoon.' That might sound like you are having a conversation with a person, but it is just doing what has been told to do."

Andre waited for Hiram to digest the information. "We spoke previously about how the computer can detect someone accidentally trapped in a freezer or in danger in a hazardous part of the ship, and sound an alarm. Consider this situation; the computer is in charge of the bridge at 2.30 in the morning and the other person on duty, a junior helmsman, is on standby in the ready room next to the bridge. The ship is being steered on course by the autopilot using the satellite navigation and global positioning equipment. From the surface radar plot, the computer becomes aware that another ship course will intersect with that of the Adongiva in approximately twenty minutes if both ships maintain course and speed. The computer compares this situation to the thousands of similar situations stored in its database until it finds one that fits. It has been told that there are three possible answers. Increasing speed would result in reaching the intersect point ahead of the other ship, thereby passing in front. Reducing speed would mean the other ship passing in front.

The third option is to change course. To pick the best option it may consult navigation orders, which could be 'proceed as fast as possible', 'as economically as possible', or some other criteria. It would then select the most appropriate option that satisfies the order. Is this any more intelligent than a calculator working out an equation? No. If the scenario does not match any stored situations, the computer is programmed to consult the human operator for advice. This new situation and the answer will then be added to the database, allowing the computer to 'grow' and 'learn'. Whether this is AI depends on your definition. Most people would conclude that the Adongiva computer is clever, but in fact it has less deductive skill than a seven-year-old child."

Hiram was suitably impressed by this explanation but The Big Mac shifted uncomfortably in his seat.

"I am sorry but I can't go along with this. We have to tell him." The faces of Eddie Harris, Mike O'Donnoghue and Bertrand Cavendish displayed shock, and Andre Keelan closed his eyes. Hiram realised from their expressions that The Big Mac was breaking ranks to reveal something he shouldn't. He was surprised that they could have been concealing something from him.

The Big Mac leaned over and said to Hiram, "What Andre has just said to you *was* absolutely true, until two and a half months ago when I had a meeting with a senior figure in Global Micro Electronics Corporation, or GMEC for short. There have been three more meetings since then, which were classified as top secret. We talked about something, about which we were sworn to secrecy. However, I have just come to a unilateral decision, which I hope I do not live to regret."

Hiram was intrigued. The others sat like statues, hardly daring to breathe.

The Big Mac continued, "We have built ships for customers large and small, but never one quite like you. Comparatively speaking you were a small and insignificant client – no offence intended – a private individual with a small pile of money who wanted a yacht. However you sparked off a chain reaction of events that could change the world of the future. Your amazing yacht has been constructed of a material, the ramifications of which we can only guess. The public perception has caused such a stir it has been a magnet for the crème of technology and state of the art equipment. You have stayed here as a guest of M&S longer than any other client, we have got to know each other well and I am impressed by the way you have adopted the founding principles of this company as your own. Now we are in a unique position where you, Anderson Plastics and M&S are bound together in three-way partnership, concerning the Adongiva. For all these reasons I want you to know the truth about the computer to be installed on your ship. I shall only ask this once, and I need you to be honest. Do you swear never to tell anyone outside this room what I am about to tell you?"

Hiram looked The Big Mac in the eye. "I have great admiration for your high standards and the way you treat people, and I am flattered and honoured that you can trust me with something classified top secret. I swear never to divulge what I am about to hear." The others remained motionless.

The Big Mac continued. "Andre just gave you a good description of Pseudo Intelligence. The computer to be installed on the Adongiva is far better than that and could prove to be an important milestone on the long quest for real Artificial Intelligence. The Pseudo Intelligence computer is still going to be installed on the ship, but relegated to an emergency backup role. It is also to be used as cover story to conceal the fact that something greater is now in existence. The Adongiva master computer will be the first of its kind, apart from an identical one in a secret Global Micro Electronics Corporation laboratory. GMEC have informed us that they have made a breakthrough in developing a computer than can think and learn about the environment in which it exists. It can develop its knowledge in a manner similar to a sentient being. What is more, no previous computer has been able to understand the printed word, and learn from it. It is true that computers can accept scanned text for editing, spelling and grammar checking without understand the meaning of the words. A seven year-old can read a fairy tale then make moral judgements about the 'good guys' and 'bad guys', but no computer could do that, until now. The computer on the Adongiva will be able to read books, documents and manuals, surf the internet by its self, and look for specific information. If the experiment is successful it will be of enormous benefit to the development of 'thinking' computers."

They waited for Hiram's reaction. Hiram stared back at them.

"A computer with a brain like a sentient being, working things out for itself and getting cleverer all the time, sounds scary. We have all seen Science fiction films where intelligent computers question the meaning of life and creation, and then go nuts. If, like an inquisitive child, a computer keeps asking 'why', until it gathers enough information to decide it is cleverer than us, what happens when it concludes we are superfluous? You said GMEC get lots of research data, and we get a clever computer if the experiment is successful, but what if it is not? Can we trust this thing to run our ship without harming anybody, by accident or design? Can we turn it off, if it necessary?"

The others turned to The Big Mac, who in turn looked at Andre. "Andre, are we creating a Frankenstein monster?"

Andre smiled. "No one is claiming that the computer can think like a human. It will observe its environment with its sensors, cameras and other input equipment, and never forget anything. It will sort, store, collate, compare and retrieve information faster than any human past or present. It will draw 'conclusions' based on facts and mathematical probabilities, rather than 'hunches' or emotions, of which it has none. The computer has been given a sense of curiosity, in that it seeks to fill knowledge gaps, but it has also been given parameters that clearly define its role and its responsibilities. It is not going to ask, 'who created me?' or 'how exactly do I communicate directly with this God chap who created all of you and everything around here?' because that is not in its remit. In answer to your question 'can we turn it off?' the answer is yes. If we decide that the computer is unreliable or dangerous, there is a procedure for switching off its higher functions and the Pseudo Intelligence computer will automatically take over."

Andre sat back and The Big Mac continued. "The deal is that GMEC installs this super computer on the ship to run all the other computers, *under our command*. We call the shots and the computer does what we tell it, taking over completely when we say so, and relinquishing control when we want it back. The super computer will be in a sealed secure unit to which our only access is the input of day-to-day instructions for running the ship and systems. We cannot access the technical details of the computer program or its operating instructions, but we get the equivalent of an ultra fast, clever, and infallible crew member who never sleeps or needs time off, who monitors and controls everything we require it to. Every day the computer will send a report to GMEC on the computer's development, growth, learning skills, and response to tasks and problems. This information may help develop the AI computers of the future. It is important to GMEC that this experiment works and if they detect problems, they will work out solutions."

Hiram said with a smirk, "If the computer watches us and GMEC watches the computer, then lab geeks will know when we use the toilet."

The Big Mac laughed. "They are only interested in data concerning the computers progress, and not the minutiae of daily yacht life. They have given an assurance that they will destroy the reports once they have extracted their data."

Hiram replied, "Can we trust them?"

The Big Mac looked him in the eye. "They are giving us something of incalculable value, and know that if they mess with us, and we reciprocate, they have too much to lose."

Sunday 4th October 2026

After a fortnight's leave, the crew were ready to start their specialist training. They began with one day's familiarisation, because having memorised the layout in basic training they had to reinforce their detailed knowledge of every part of the ship. The training was not hard for most as they were 'on their own home territory'. Competencies and knowledge were checked as catering staff spent time in the kitchens and bars, mechanics and electricians scrutinised equipment, admin staff got their heads round procedures and paperwork, others polished seamanship and navigation skills, and so on. Although they considered themselves expert in their own fields, there was much to learn. The Adongiva had technology and equipment some had only read about, or never even heard of before.

Two of Adongiva's 2nd Officers had to compress their ship training into a shorter period, to fit in a trip to Holland for C-Quester training. The normal four-day submarine course was squeezed into two and a half days, which the men at U-Boat Worx found an interesting challenge. They rarely sold mini submarines to private individuals, and the rich playboys that they did sell to were not the types to take kindly to being driven hard. This time however the trainers were under strict instructions to push these two as hard as necessary, to make sure they understood the equipment thoroughly, and were able to handle the submarine well and safely in the time available.

Whilst all this was taking place the last items of the ship's fabric and equipment were installed and by the time training was finished, the ship was truly complete. It had been originally decided back in April to have a simple ceremony when the Adongiva 'got its bottom wet'. Unlike a conventional ship's launch with dramatic rush down a ramp, with great clatter of chains and clouds of dust, the Adongiva launch would be quiet and less exciting. When the ship's cradle was lowered into the flooded dock, the Adongiva would float off gracefully. However with everything that had happened since then, and the increased public interest, it was now agreed that this momentous occasion be given a greater ceremony with some pomp and circumstance.

Thinking that the take up would be relatively modest, invitations went out to representatives from the suppliers of equipment and technology to the ship, other companies involved in the project, families of the Crew and construction teams, senior personnel from M&S, the Mayor and representatives from the local council, charitable and community organisations, and the press and media. To begin with, not many replies were received and so with each passing month more names were added to ensure a presentable crowd at the launch. It was not until very late in August that suddenly the trickle became a flood. The organisers realised they had seriously underestimated the level of interest and decided that they should cater for several hundred. Unfortunately by the time this dawned on them the flood itself was attracting attention. People not on the original list applied in droves; the local MP, the MEP, the Chamber of Commerce, foreign journalists, celebrities, *Star Trek* Fan Club representatives, and a host of others. Now, when it was almost too late, M&S had to announce that no more tickets were available, as maximum capacity had been reached.

The crew were delighted with their accommodation which was arranged on the outer ring on Deck E. On the deck below, was a sitting room, games room, bar, canteen and fitness room. On the rest of the ship, the very last items were finally connected, plumbed, wired, decorated, furnished and stocked on Friday 23rd of October, the day before the launch. The dry dock area was cleared and smartened up. Seating, buffet tables, a bar, extra lighting and sound systems were erected, plus a gantry from which the bottle of champagne would be released, to strike the side of the ship. The Big Mac knew that for centuries, sailors were known to be superstitious about almost everything, and that a bottle that did not break against the side of the ship at its launch, would be viewed as a bad omen. Being a man who left nothing to chance, he even had small cracks etched on the bottle, just to make sure.

The big day dawned and crowds started to arrive just after seven in the morning, even though the launch was not scheduled until 11.45am. By 9.45am Dry Dock 5 was buzzing. The Il Camaleonte, Stork, and C-Quester drew fascinated crowds and waiters zoomed back and forth along their flight paths carrying trays of drinks and nibbles. Reporters flitted from VIP to VIP with microphones in hand; photographers snapped everything from every angle, people talked very loudly and created a deafening noise. The band, although not due to perform until 10am, were pressed into immediate service on arrival. Hiram was glad Oliver Russell, Sir Richard Pickles and Shaun Glendower were present as they had all played an important role in this saga. Hiram's brothers and sisters had arrived and his mother had flown down from Scotland. Sir Bartholomew St. John Farquharson and Algernon Nabarro exchanged smiles from afar, to show that they were above petty squabbles, but managed to avoid talking to each other. Algernon grudgingly admitted to himself that he should be grateful to Sibarti for alerting him to this prestigious business opportunity, although it had cost him dearly when negotiating with The Big Mac.

Several days before the event, at a meeting in The Big Mac's office, Bertrand and other senior staff were allocated a list of VIPs to be responsible for, on the day. When they read their lists Bertrand groaned and banged his head on the table. "Oh no, not Don bloody Earl." The others laughed, grateful that someone else had this individual.

"Who is Don Earl?" asked Hiram.

The Big Mac said, "He is the local MP and Minister for the Air Force." Hiram was immediately able to put a face to the name. Don Earl had been on the television many times. "Ah yes, big chin and ginger crinkly hair."

Amid roars of laughter, Clarice said, "You had better not let him hear you say that. He is very proud of his 'Autumn Gold' Marcel Wave by Jean Paul Weaver, hairdresser to the rich and famous."

"Stuff and nonsense," grunted Bertrand. "His prices and ridiculous styles just prove that the rich and famous don't understand the story about the emperor's new clothes."

"Yes, that's all very well but he is coming to the launch, and we have to make the best of it," said The Big Mac.

Undaunted, Bertrand turned to the others and said, "I will swap Don Earl for two of yours."

There were no takers and Hiram said, "He can't be that bad, surely?"

Bertrand replied, "He is an arrogant, conceited, condescending, selfish, greedy, spoilt, rich, playboy imbecile."

Clarice smiled and said, "Which makes him a perfect specimen for a Government Minister."

Hiram now stood in Dry Dock 5 with Violet Banner Brown, a lady in powder blue hat and coat, white gloves and matching handbag, who had been telling him she was captain of the local Ladies Bowls Club, Guide Mistress and senior figure on the Board of Governors of the St. Anthony's Girls High School; and she was terribly excited at being invited to a ship launch which she considered a great honour. He espied Bertrand approaching with the unmistakable Don Earl in tow.

Bertrand said, "This is Hiram Montgomery, part owner of the Adongiva, and the man who started this whole show rolling."

Hiram eyed the MP. His handmade suit, silk shirt and bespoke shoes would cost a crew member several months' wages. As for the hairstyle, Hiram avoided staring in case he became mesmerised. The corrugated waves looked like finely spun rose gold wire. He took the proffered hand, which felt dead but still warm. He smiled and returned the "How do you do." The man's voice, like everything else about him, was highly exaggerated and indicated money and the highest levels of private education, breeding and background. However, the vowels were drawn out and emphasised absurdly, like an Englishman trying to communicate abroad.

Bertrand refused to return Hiram's look in case he laughed. Instead he said, "Excuse me one moment. I have to check something." With that he was gone.

The MP feigned a smile and asked, "From where did you draw your inspiration for this unusual ship?"

Hiram thought that to anyone with access to a television it should be pretty damned obvious. But he said, "Ivanovitch Petrovsky shared my love of *Star Trek* and drew the original plan to make the ship look like to the Star Ship *Enterprise*." He might as well have said, 'Mary had a little lamb', because Don Earl was not listening and his eyes were roving, to see who else was present. Hiram hated it when people did that, but concealed his irritation. In a flash of inspiration he thought of how to be rid of this man. He looked towards Violet Banner Brown who was edging away looking embarrassed. Hiram guessed she felt not important enough to share a conversation between the owner of a ship and a Member of Parliament. He beckoned her to return and her face lit up. He said, "Don, may I introduce to you a very important lady. This is Violet Banner Brown, prominent pillar of the community, and one of your constituents."

Violet Banner Brown looked at Hiram with hero worship in her eyes.

The MP's eyes dilated for a second at Hiram's words then the expression changed to 'oh no, not another boring one.'. He offered Violet his hand, which she took gratefully and gave a little curtsey.

Hiram waited for Don Earl to say, "and what do you do, my dear?" then interrupted. "Please excuse me, there is someone I must speak to." Don Earl gave him a 'don't leave me with her' look but Hiram spun round and walked to the far side of the room.

The hands of the clock inched round and finally the PA system announced, "Ladies and gentlemen, please take your seats as the launch ceremony is about to begin." The crowd dutifully obeyed.

Don Earl pointed his thumb at the people on the platform and muttered to the MEP next to him, "I can't believe we're not up there."

The MEP, a quiet diplomat, looked over his glasses but said nothing. They took their reserved seats on the front row, next to the Mayoress. The Big Mac welcomed everyone and thanked them for coming. He introduced the platform party; Hiram, Bertrand, M&S Directors and Heads, Conrad Meredith and his wife Augustine, who was to perform the launch. She looked bright for someone a hundred and six years-old. Also on the platform were Hans Anderson and his Directors, and several others.

Hiram thought the speech written for Augustine was excellent: not too long, or serious. The moment came, she pressed the button, the bottle flew, exploding satisfyingly on the ship, and the band struck up the signature tune of the Adongiva. Hiram had discussed his favourite tunes and types of music with Michael Ribbons who then arranged the Carly Simon number, *Let the River Run* as a stirring march. Hiram was pleased with the result and the crowd applauded enthusiastically as the ship slowly descended.

The metal floor section in the centre of the room, supported on eight telescopic legs ten feet wide, sank lower until the bottom of the Adongiva disappeared from view, followed by part of the superstructure.

A muffled roar signalled thousands of gallons pouring into the space below. The Adongiva stopped descending, gave a shiver, and started coming back up. The deck appeared, and continued rising as the air filled with saltwater scent. Finally the ship stopped and the swirling water calmed. There had been two stout ropes attached to the Adongiva all morning, draped over the side, and across the floor of the dry dock. Mats had covered the ropes, to stop people tripping over them, but just before the launch these had been removed and two men in blazers stood by. As the ship descended they paid out rope. Now the Adongiva was floating in the rectangular lake more workers appeared, took hold and pulled, drawing the Adongiva towards them and coiling the rope neatly. The two teams wheeled smartly and marched out as the metal door at the end of the building slid open to reveal blue sky and the dockyard buildings and waters beyond. The Adongiva was being shown the world it would soon be joining.

After the ceremony the crowd milled round with drinks in hand, constantly replenished by the army of waiters, or queued at the buffet table that was a sight to behold. It was a huge colourful display of food of every description. Others sat with piled plates, scoffing away and as Hiram looked round he thought, "This must have cost a fortune." M&S had insisted in paying for the launch party, and no expense had been spared.

Bertrand was speaking to Captain Ironside when the Mayoress appeared, glass in hand. She said, "This has been the most marvellous party, with an incredible atmosphere, and a buffet table to die for." The two men smiled and Bertrand thanked her for her comments. She then said, "I was not expecting a guided tour of the ship today. What a wonderful idea. You really are making this an occasion to remember." Bertrand and the Captain exchanged looks to see if the other knew what she was talking about.

Don Earl approached. "I say, I am really looking forward to seeing the inside of that marvellous craft. Unfortunately I have to be away from here shortly for a meeting with the PM, and I would like to be able to tell him all about it. Do you think I could be included in the first wave, so to speak?"

Captain Ironside and Bertrand smiled, not knowing for the moment what else to do. The ship was due to sail first thing in the morning and the last thing needed right now was the mess or upheaval caused by lots of tramping feet. There had never been any plan to let people tour the ship today. "Would you excuse us for a moment," said Bertrand, taking the Captain's arm. "We need to sort a few things first, shouldn't be too long."

The Mayoress had a genuinely happy grin, but Don Earl had a look of barely concealed satisfaction at having been successfully wicked.

They found The Big Mac as he was coming to look for them. A ripple of excitement was spreading through the crowd. They all denied responsibility for the rumour and The Big Mac wanted to know what they were going to do about it.

Captain Ironside touched his fingertips to his badge and said, "Captain to Ship's Chief Officers. Come to me at the ship's side, now." Uniforms detached themselves from the crowd and headed in their direction. They were equally dumbfounded about how it had started, but the Captain said, "Never mind that now. If we tour the ship it needs to be groups of, let's say, twenty. How many are here?"

The Big Mac said, "700, give or take."

"Thirty five groups, at ten minute intervals is just under six hours; too long. I suggest we chop that number by about half and increase the groups to thirty. That would take us down to about two hours."

"How on earth do we chop them by half, run a lottery?" asked Bertrand.

Ironside said, "Roughly half are journalists or connected with companies that helped build, outfit or supply. They will ask technical questions and expect detailed answers. The other half would be bored because they want a quick nose at the soft furnishings, and look at the lights, dials and gizmos without appreciating their purpose. I suggest we tell them that on another occasion, perhaps after the sea trials, we will organise another 'open' day for the technically minded who want a long look with time for questions. Today we only have time for a brief tour. Those who want the long tour should give their names and they will be sent invitations."

"What if they all want to go today?"

"Then we are stuffed. You will have to make that other day sound too good to miss," sighed Ironside.

Paddy turned to his Chief Officers. The Big Mac and Bertrand were familiar with the layout, having been involved with every step. However what they heard next filled them with great respect for the Adongiva crew.

The decks were identified by letter, the top deck being 'A'. Every cabin, compartment, hall, door, stairs, lift and space was consecutively numbered, from the bow to the stern – odd to Port and even to Starboard. Captain Ironside pointed to the door at the rear of the superstructure on the port engineering hull and the gangplank attached to the side of the ship. "That's our entrance," he pointed to another door near the bow, "and exit. On entry you will take this route." He recited a string of letters and numbers as the Chief Officers stood and concentrated. When finished he said, "Got that?" They nodded. "OK, brief your teams. I want them ready in ten."

They returned to the crowd, speaking to their badges as they went. Paddy Ironside addressed The Big Mac. "You know what you have to do?" The Big Mac nodded. He then turned to Bertrand. "Can you organise another gang way and a table for those wanting invitations for the next day?" Bertrand nodded. The captain smiled, saluted and was gone.

The Big Mac said, "Neither of us is dim witted, but I doubt if we could have devised such a plan so quickly."

Bertrand replied, "Right now I am glad the Navy wrote him off. Their loss is our gain."

A few moments later The Big Mac was at the microphone. The room fell silent, he announced the plan and was pleased to note that equal numbers formed queues at the table and the gangway. He watched a number of the crew disappear inside the Adongiva and the ones outside organise the crowd as if this had been well rehearsed. The first group of thirty bodies filed up the gangway included the Mayoress, the MP, MEP, and other dignitaries and VIPs. As they disappeared another group was assembled and escorted to the parked car and aircraft for a quick encirclement of each, and then at precisely ten minutes after the first group, they were led on to the ship. Twenty minutes after the start time, a third group boarded, and so it went on. As the fifth group were making their way up the slope, the first group were emerging from the exit door. They reached the bottom of the gangway and started towards The Big Mac, Bertrand and Hiram, who were observing the proceedings. The last one was Don Earl who turned and re examined the ship closely, scanning from top to bottom and front to back, as if memorising every detail. Eventually he followed the others.

The Mayoress bubbled with excitement, "This has been a wonderful day. The ceremony was wonderful, as was your wonderful refreshments and entertainment. The Adongiva is a wonderful ship, and the crew were wonderful. It has been all very, wonderful. Thank you for inviting me." She shook their hands as she spoke, and headed for her waiting driver.

The Big Mac said to Bertrand, "I think we can safely assume she has had a wonderful time."

The MEP was next. He said that it had been a pleasure and honour to have been present the day a Hard Plastic ship was launched. He agreed that this material would change the world, and looked forward to the changes ahead. The others in the group then queued to shake hands and give praise. The Big Mac had not intended that he, Bertrand and Hiram form a line to shake the hands of the guests as they were leaving, however it seemed to make them happy. Captain Ironside was a small distance away but on his way back.

Don Earl sped past the line up, shaking hands and mouthing pompous but meaningless words of congratulations and goodbyes. Captain Ironside drew close and Don Earl shook his hand, intending to treat him with the same insincerity he had given the others. Instead he paused for a moment and smiled; not his usual trademark Cheshire cat grin, but a more subtle and genuine smile. He said softly, "You were not expecting this, were you?" He waved his hand at the queues.

Captain Ironside replied, "Of course. Everything was planned months ago."

Don Earl raised an eyebrow. "Please, Captain. Never kid a kidder. I am the king of bullshit, and I wrote the anti-anti-bullshit handbook. I know there was never a plan to let people trample on your ship today."

"How would you know that?"

"I started the rumour a short time ago."

Captain Ironside looked at the other man closely. "Why would you do that?"

Don Earl leaned closer and spoke conspiratorially. "Most people think I am a buffoon; an empty headed, shallow lightweight; well connected but not too bright. I don't mind. In fact I have gone out of my way to cultivate that image. As long as that is what they think, I can get up close and personal without them raising their defences. As a harmless and idiotic playboy, who happens to hold a government post, they indulge me, and let me look at their toys. If only they knew I have a razor sharp brain, all-seeing eye and photographic memory, they would not be so keen. I started the rumour today because I wanted to see for myself whether the hype and media bullshit about the magnificence of your ship and its crew is true or not."

Paddy Ironside evaluated this revelation while the other man waited for him to ask whether the Adongiva had passed the test. He decided not to play but instead said, "Why have you blown your cover, by telling me this?"

Don Earl smiled a secret smile. "Save your breath. People only believe what they have been told is true. Their view, reinforced by television coverage is that I am just a soft silly teddy bear. If you tell them I am a big bad grizzly in disguise, they won't believe you." He paused again and still the captain refused to ask. "Well I must be off. I'm meeting the PM." The Captain remained quiet. The MP said, "I have read the file on your impressive career, but the latest entries are total crap. You are no more a write off than I am, and I have many years of devious subterfuge left."

"I can believe that," said Paddy Ironside, seeing the other man accurately for the first time.

The MP continued, "I have seen rubbish, mediocrity, good, better, excellent and outstanding in my time. I don't do compliments but you, your ship and crew impressed me today. Someone of your calibre, skill set and background is bound to cross my path more than once, and I look forward to our next meeting. Someone will get in touch," he said as he turned and headed for the door. He stopped, looked back and said, "I offer one criticism. "Today you failed to observe the age-old principle which has served mankind well. Never let people gather then disperse without allowing them the opportunity to give you money. Take a photograph of that boat and stick it on all manner of assorted tourist crap. Leave these items on a table by the door and watch people queue and ask how much." With that Don Earl turned again for the door and said over his shoulder with a wave of a finger. "Don't forget Captain, I am just a teddy bear."

Captain Ironside pondered the MP's words as he watched him disappear. "Someone will get in touch." It reminded him of a quote, reputedly from a KGB publication: "When meeting someone from British Intelligence, watch where you put your feet; if they shake, check their hands before and your fingers after; and if they smile, get out fast."

CHAPTER NINETEEN

After the guests and VIPs had departed, the seating, tables and other signs of the launch party were cleared away. The Big Mac, Bertrand and Hiram were the last to leave and would have stayed longer, in case they missed something interesting, but the Captain asked for private time with his crew. When everyone else had gone, he gathered them round and said he was proud of their performance. They would be better prepared for the next open day, but despite having no warning or rehearsal they had done brilliantly. Turning to more immediate matters, he said he wanted the car, submarine and Stork onboard and 'tourist debris' cleared away. After this they were to make a final inspection of their work stations and areas of responsibility to make sure everything was 'ship shape and Bristol fashion', and then the rest of the day would be their own.

He said as tomorrow was first sailing day, they were all confined to base to help the more boisterous avoid being done for drunk and disorderly behaviour. M&S had ample facilities to keep them amused but rather than tell them how to behave when off duty, he suggested a maximum of six units of alcohol and 'lights out' at 2200. Just to make sure they understood he added, "Woe betide anyone not on board by 0520 because the propellers will start turning at precisely 0555 hours."

Hiram had installed most of his personal effects in his Adongiva cabin before the launch, but spent last night in the M&S VIP cabin. In the morning he breakfasted in the Senior Staff Club Restaurant and boarded at 5.29am. The crew were at their stations and busy getting ready. He stowed his bag and headed for the 'express lift' to take him above. It was nicknamed the express lift by the crew but was not really a lift in the true sense. In the central circular lobby was a conventional lift connecting all decks, which was quite posh by normal lift standards; spacious, clad in cherry wood with gilt mirror on the back wall. Hiram remembered being impressed by the paintings in the M&S lifts, and so this lift had a large, magnificent seascape painted on the inside of the doors. It could take eight people comfortably from one deck to the next in a sedate thirty seconds.

The express lift had no doors and never stopped moving. It consisted of two adjacent vertical shafts and running up one side of the central wall, over the top and down the other, was a conveyor belt, attached to which were horizontal platforms. As a platform ascended from below you stepped onto it, and six seconds later stepped off at the deck above. The other shaft would take you down. Courage was needed until you got the hang of it. On Deck B he strode to the Bridge. Because of the high tech controls the bridge was kept dust free, and had an entrance air lock of black mats between two doors. The first had metallic strips up the walls and across the ceiling, which emitted a silent, alternating sub-sonic vibration that attracted dust, dead skin cells or other surface material on skin or clothing, away from you. Most people felt nothing but some said it was like someone 'walking over your grave'. Air currents removed the loosened material through wall vents. The second mat and strips formed a degaussing ring to counter static electricity. The Bridge had dedicated air conditioning, additional to the rest of the ship, which replaced the atmosphere every ten minutes through a five-stage filter. Hiram stepped through the doors, and as on his previous visits, said, "wow" at the sight of the most impressive 'big boy's toy' in the world. The panoramic windows gave a clear view round the front of the ship. Along the bottom of the windows were seventeen, 9-inch television monitors, numbered 3 to 19. Some were blank but most displayed data, or views from cameras around the ship.

Beneath this row were two, 30-inch screens, numbered 1 and 2. The first showed a coloured map of the dock area, with a white Adongiva shape in the centre. The other had the view from roof camera above the Accommodation Disk. In front of the screens were two kidney shape desks and chairs, one of which occupied by Ships 1st Officer

IT Engineering Liam Bowerman. Behind these were two more chairs slightly higher. One was occupied by Captain Ironside and the other had Hiram's name on it. Behind these was the raised platform, on which Hiram stood, which curved down to the floor. From here, technical experts or guests could observe without getting in the way. Bertrand Cavendish and Gustaf Bjorn had already arrived and were standing quietly by the guard-rail. They all exchanged nods. Just to the right of the entrance, was the door to the main computer compartment to which access was strictly controlled.

There was not much to look at in the computer chamber. On a single table sat a keyboard, mouse, graphics tablet, several CD drives and a monitor. Next to the table was a steel computer case. Hiram's home computer was a creaking geriatric that did nothing quickly within its 8 inches wide, 17 inches tall and 17 inches deep case. It had a single processor and ten gigabytes of memory. This one was 3 feet wide by 5 feet tall and 5 feet deep. It contained two six core processors with speeds of 6.9 GHZ, 24 MHz, 8MB cache and four and a half terabytes of memory, expandable. A terabyte is a thousand gigabytes. The full specification had been explained to him but most of it went over his head. He understood simply that this was a very fast, very big, very powerful machine. The only other thing in the room was a metal container which looked strong enough to survive a train crash was 6 feet high, 6 feet wide and 12 feet long and joined to the computer case by armoured metal pipe. There was an interesting combination lock on the container door; a square of one hundred completely blank buttons. The combination number had 10 digits, but you had to know how to work out which buttons to press. Inside this container was the GMEC Artificial Intelligence computer.

Hiram's eye was drawn back again to the curved desks. When 'off' they were black mirrored surfaces, but 'on', they were alive with colour. Along the top centre section was a strip with buttons, the equivalent of a computer tool bar. Several control panel layouts could be selected with the appropriate button. The central section of the right hand desk displayed the Propulsion and Manoeuvring panel, or helm. To its left was a copy of the Global Positioning Map on screen 1, but zoomed in, with the Adongiva taking up more of the screen and correspondingly less of the surrounding area. On the other side were copies of the compass, from screen 9, the SRPAW display from screen 8, the Hedgehog SOPA display from screen 10, and the route and progress information from screen 7. On each panel were coloured drawings of knobs, dials, slider controls, and information boxes, but they were not just drawings. They moved and responded like the real thing when fingers moved over them.

On the left hand desk were several drawings of deck layouts with dots of coloured light sprinkled over them, video screen windows, and rows of switches, buttons, dials and slide controls. There was one panel that looked like a page from a stamp album, except that there was movement on some of the 'stamps'. These were miniature displays from every camera on the ship. The operator could copy, enlarge and paste any of these to one of the monitors in front, or onto a vacant spot on the desk. The assorted controls and displays looked complicated. Actually, it was up to the individual to decide how much to display simultaneously. You could keep it simple by having fewer control panels on view and toggling between them, but 1st Officer Bowerman preferred everything up at once.

As Hiram walked down the ramp, Captain Ironside stood to face him and the crew sat straighter in their seats. Hiram said, "Relax gentlemen. You really don't have to come to attention every time I come on deck."

Captain Ironside replied, "Mr. Montgomery, it's a mark of respect and to acknowledge your presence, as owner."

"I understand and I appreciate it, but it is not necessary; and call me Hiram."

The Captain was not going to have his good order and discipline compromised that easily. "If it's all the same to you sir, I really must insist that every crew member comes briefly to attention on the first occasion of meeting you each day. On subsequent meetings they can, with your agreement, be less formal, until the next day. As for calling you by your Christian name I will allow this only if there are none but crew present. If guests or visitors are about, I insist on a minimum level of formality."

"Oh very well then, you're the expert," said Hiram as he took his seat.

More guests assembled on the observation platform behind them. There were wall mounted, fold down seats but they preferred to stand for the moment. The majority had no real need to attend or sail with the Adongiva; but who could blame them for wanting to join this historic trip. To everyone's relief Algernon Nabarro, creator of the control panels could not be present, after experiencing sea sickness in the calm waters of the harbour. His deputy, Nigel Dean, was more likeable, and very capable. The Rolls Royce Seahorse electric engines had from inception been David Ridley's babies, and he had been delighted at their resurrection, albeit in modified form, and nothing would keep him from seeing them in action.

Another guest was Nathan Edwards, senior technician with Hunter & Wolfe, designers of the propellers. The other two on the platform were Professor Elgar Knight, senior software engineer with GMEC, and Eric Otterman, Senior Project Manager with Siemens who supplied the Personal Identification Signal Badges. Elgar was here "to keep an eye on the computer" and Eric to monitor the efficiency of the badges. The presence of these VIPs delighted the chef. Although he'd had every intention of feeding the crew well throughout the trip with an interesting menu, he had assumed that his department would be taking a back seat on this voyage. As sea trials were designed to put the ship through its paces and test its sea worthiness, he knew the main focus of attention would be on the engineering department. Now, with VIPs to play with he could really demonstrate his culinary expertise. The other departments were equally pleased. Although the VIPs were here to 'work', this was an excellent opportunity for the entire crew to run the ship just as they would with proper paying guests.

Hiram checked the time. One monitor showed two clock faces marked 'UTC' and 'Current'. 'UTC' or Universal Coordinated Time is for all non-technical purposes the same as Greenwich Mean Time, or 'Zulu time' as the military would have it.

UTC has exact seconds defined by the high precision International Atomic Time, with leap seconds introduced regularly to allow for the earth's rotation. The Current clock showed the time in the World Time Zone that the Adongiva happened to occupy at this precise moment. It would be adjusted by the computer, using the satellite global positioning system to mark the local time wherever the Adongiva happened to be. The time on both clocks was identical, as the Adongiva was in the UK, and the hands moved slowly to 0543.

Captain Ironside touched his badge and said, "Captain to all stations..."

The computer instantly made the connections and his voice emanated from every crew badge on the ship. "Good morning ladies and gentlemen, we are about to commence sea trials. This is an historic moment for this first Hard Plastic ship and what we do here will be the subject of study in time to come. I therefore intend to push the ship; its contents and personnel to the very limits and have no doubt that you are all up to the task." He asked Hiram if he wanted to say a few words.

Hiram, mindful of the time, kept his eyes on the clock as he touched his badge. "This is Hiram Montgomery. I would like to thank everyone present, and the army of people who have worked tirelessly, but unable to be with us today. This has cost a colossal amount of time, money, effort, brain power, enthusiasm and teamwork. I never thought when I had a comparatively modest and, some might say daft, notion to build a yacht, we would end up in such a vessel as this. I am deeply touched by what has been gone into it, and can't wait to feel the gentle swell below and see nothing but distant horizon around us. Let's get this show on the road."

The clock had turned to 0550.

Captain Ironside said, "Ships Officer Bowerman."

Liam inclined his head. "Captain?"

"Report readiness."

Liam checked his instruments and rows of lights. "All personnel present and ready; all departments showing green light; ship fuelled and provisioned, water tanks full; batteries fully charged; all systems ready."

"Good. Up gangway, cast off fore and aft."

"Up gangway, cast off fore and aft, Aye." The fingers of Liam's right hand danced lightly over his controls but his eyes stayed on the video screens.

Outside the ship, the gangway on the port engineering hull silently lifted itself from the concrete floor and folded in half. When vertical it toppled slowly sideways to lie alongside the deck guard rail. The open space in the rail, where the gangway had been, disappeared as telescopic sections filled the gap. Then at the bow, a narrow section of deck popped open. Underneath was the 'DUDMOBE Boom', as it had been christened. This docking and undocking and man over board

265

equipment boom reached the required height, swung out over the dock and extended itself to the correct length. When over the dock bollard the 'three fingered' hand lowered, gripped the wire hoop which encircled the bollard, and pulled it up and away. It swung back over the ship, neatly draping the hoop over a deck bollard before releasing its grip and disappearing back into its hole. The surplus rope attached to the hoop disappeared into its own hole as a winch wound in the slack. The same thing happened on the aft deck as the stern DUDMOBE boom repeated the performance.

"Gangway secured, ship is free," sang Ships Officer Bowerman.

The Captain turned his attention to the crew member in the other seat. "Ships Officer Wright." She responded, and he said, "Nudge to Starboard; make speed .019 knots."

"Nudge to Starboard; make speed .019 knots, aye."

Some might think this a strangely precise request, however at .019 knots the ship would move at one centimetre a second, which Captain Ironside considered plenty for precise manoeuvring in confined spaces. Beatrice Wright had a very different technique from Liam Bowerman. She used both hands, and more fingers. In the dark still water beneath the Adongiva's hull the port side Multi Azimuth Propulsion Pod silently turned to point its propellers at the dockside, and spun the blades in five, two second pulses of power. The bow of the ship moved gently to the right and pointed at the centre of the open doorway of the dock. Beatrice suspended her finger over the slider control of the throttle and sat motionless, looking at the clock. The second hand ticked away; nine, eight, seven, six, five, four, three, two. Finally she moved her hand and the ship glided gracefully and silently forward, like a swan in a pond, at precisely 0555 hours on Sunday 25th October 2026.

As soon as the Adongiva cleared the dry dock doors Captain Ironside said, "Make speed eight knots."

Ships Officer Wright echoed the order, moved her fingers and the ship picked up speed and sailed past the M&S harbour buildings at the gentle speed of just over 9.2 miles per hour. It was a dull but dry day as light struggled to penetrate the blanket of grey cloud above.

The Captain studying the controls from his seat leaned forward slightly. "Ship's Officer Wright, check your revolutions."

Her fingers danced and she replied, "Revolutions display checked and correct, Captain."

"Good Lord," he murmured as he turned to face Nathan Edwards. "Your propellers are more efficient than predicted. The engines are little more than idling, and we are gliding like a knife through butter."

Nathan smiled at the compliment. The M&S docks area drifted behind and the Adongiva entered the main river. There was no other traffic and speed was increased to eighteen knots, or 20.71 miles per hour. The river banks moved apart and the speed rose to 24 knots, or 27.61 miles per hour, which was about right for an empty estuary of this size. Before long the flat, uninterrupted sea lay before them. The coast on either side slid past, and in the Stern View monitor the land moved further away by the minute.

"Make speed thirty-five knots," was called out, repeated and executed. From the bridge there was little sense of movement, vibration or noise, except the almost inaudible air conditioning hum. It was more like being in a flying saucer than a ship. The captain requested status reports, and was informed everything was normal and problem free. The speed was now what some ships would consider as maximum, and the engines were just warming up. Speed was increased to thirty-nine knots, or 44.88 miles per hour, which is about the speed of a fast attack craft, used by many navies around the world for coastal defence, and for taking an enemy by surprise. It was beyond the capability of many conventional civilian ships, and the engines were humming contentedly. Hiram, and the other observers, were fascinated by the myriad displays, including the 'Hedgehog' screen with its changing colours. On this screen an outline of the Adongiva had, arranged round the bow, a 180-degree fan of concentric lines intersected by lines from the centre. The 'squares' of different colours depicted the depth under the hull, or clear distance ahead or to the side. White represented dry land; very pale blue meant one fathom, or 1.83 meters; sky blue was approximately five fathoms, or 9.14 meters; royal blue, 10 fathoms; light navy blue 25 fathoms; dark navy blue 50; and black 100.

Over the next three days was scheduled a full programme of sea trials including measured mile speed runs, rapid acceleration and slowing, turning, going astern and various other manoeuvring and consumption trials at various angles to prevailing winds and tides. These were fairly standard but in addition there would be manoeuvres unique to the Adongiva. Not many ships could attempt fast spin turns, going sideways, and an emergency stop using sea brakes that stuck out like elephants ears, to slow the ship dramatically. It was anticipated that when slowing, accelerating or turning dramatically in this 'sports car' of the sea, vibration and the pull of G forces would be felt to varying degrees in different parts of the ship. This had been taken into account in the design and construction for there was no point in having expensive and beautiful *objet d'art*, crockery, delicate glass ware and breakable equipment if it was all going to be thrown about at sea.

The storage compartments for everything expensive, breakable or dangerous were designed to protect and cushion from the effects of 'High Speed Manoeuvring', or HSM. Everything had a place, and everything had to be in its place when not in use. When the ship was about to undertake HSM a warning would sound to give all departments time to secure vulnerable objects or materials. The galleys had well practiced procedures for safeguarding pots of hot liquid, but in a real emergency there might be insufficient time to protect a table of delicate desserts, or an elaborately iced cake that had taken many hours to produce. Throughout the ship, ornaments, paintings and works of art were carefully glued in place so that they would not slide about or bounce. If you wanted an ornament moved from a sideboard to a table, you had to call a technician to do it for you.

Although he knew it was important to the technical experts, talk of propulsive coefficient related to naked hull 'ehp', adjustments for maximum seagoing auxiliary load, fuel consumption estimates in tons per day at a given 'shp' and propulsion pod angles necessary to maintain a steady course in adverse conditions, left him completely under whelmed. He tried to be interested, but some of this stuff was strictly for boffins, experts or anoraks. He observed from afar as careful records were taken of measurable vibration over a range of speeds and manoeuvres. He was informed that maximum vibration was recorded on the upper deck of the engineering hulls and stern during full power trials, but generally vibration, hum and propeller 'singing' was very small in most areas and nonexistent in the VIP Accommodation Disk.

In addition to the ship performance trials, launching and landing the Stork at various angles to the wind and tide, and visibility conditions, was repeated many times. Flying it out of sight then guiding it home on instruments only; flying with weights on the winch cable; and rescue exercises were conducted nearly every other day. Copious notes were recorded and fed to the computer. The other exercise was launching and recapturing the submarine. Hiram was keen to go on a dive but said afterwards it was scary to sit calmly and watch water rise up the glass canopy and over your head. He was assured that a moment of panic and the urge to escape were normal the first time. In a 'proper submarine' you can't see the outside world as you sink beneath the waves. He was glad to hear that in clear sunlit tropical waters, visibility would be good for long way down and there would be much to see. Once the external lights were switched on it was interesting to watch fish come close to inspect this newcomer to their territory. In shallow waters you could inspect the sea bed, sunken wrecks and other phenomena. Sometimes Hiram's over active imagination, from watching certain movies, made him look over his shoulder half expecting a great white shark or other sea creature to come rushing from the gloom at any moment.

Safely back on the deck of the Adongiva, he was able to observe the interesting SRSIFL capsize drill. The Self Righting, Semi Inflatable Fast Launch was not easy to deliberately capsize, however by attaching winch lines they managed to tip it upside down, with the crew strapped in. The object was to prove the launch righted quickly, and give the crew confidence to remain calm, take a deep breath, and not be tempted to unbuckle their belts. They were taught to sit still and listen to the thousands of tiny metal balls rushing inside the double hull, altering the weight distribution and forcing the craft upright. If they could not hold their breath long enough they were to reach for the face mask and air canister beneath the seat, which would release breathable air. Once upright the launch would quickly empty itself with a high power water pump that started automatically. The exercise was every bit as scary as it sounds, but to attain the Boat Crew qualification you had to pass this test.

CHAPTER TWENTY

Thursday 5ᵗʰ November 2026

The Adongiva had completed most of the scheduled tests and was heading sedately homeward, from the wide empty Atlantic where it had been rushing back and forth like a mad thing for days. Everything had gone exceptionally well and morale was high. On this particular night most of the crew and passengers were abed, enjoying well earned rest. At 0405 the ship was hit by a wave which raised it gently and lowered it again. It felt like the wake of a passing ship, if that ship had been gigantic and very close, but there appeared to be no other ships in the vicinity, and the wave passed on by in a moment. Those who were roused from their beds by this phenomenon conferred, found no explanation, no damage or other abnormality, and went back to bed. At 0414 a weak distress call was received from a small boat called the *Libérer L'esprit*. The signal said that the boat was still afloat but filled with water and in imminent danger of sinking. The triangulation equipment on the radio masts showed that the boat was eighteen miles away, off the port bow. The stork was immediately launched and reached the boat at 0435.

The two young occupants were rescued, taken aboard the Adongiva, and found to be well, apart from being cold and wet. The distress call from the *Libérer L'esprit* had also been picked up by 'Big Ear', the network of satellites placed above the earth by the American Department of Defence, expressly for the purpose to listening to anyone with a radio transmitter. This signal eventually found its way through the maze of army and diplomatic channels and was handed to the French authorities, and passed to the security office responsible for the protection of the President of France, and his family. What the young couple had not told the crew of the Adongiva was that she was the youngest daughter of the French president and that she had given her bodyguards the slip, yet again, to be with her boyfriend, whom her father had expressly forbidden her from seeing.

Within a very short space of time the Adongiva was buzzed by two French military jets who ordered her to heave to and await an approaching frigate. The girl appealed to Captain Ironside's better nature, and begged him not to allow her be ignominiously dragged away by her father's 'gunboat', separating her from her boyfriend in the process, and forced home to face the music of an irate parent. Normally Ironside would not allow himself to be embroiled in 'a domestic', but he had not taken too kindly to being told what to do with his ship by a foreign power, whilst in international waters. They had been on their way home to England, and going to the French coast would only be a minor diversion from their journey, so he obtained Hiram's agreement to help the young couple. Making it back to their port of origin without a military escort supplied by 'Pappa', would go some way to minimising the loss of face and humiliation which lay ahead of them.

The French were furious and ordered two more naval ships to form a line across the harbour entrance to stop the Adongiva from disobeying their instruction. They had not reckoned with the Adongiva's incredible turn of speed and previously unseen manoeuvrability. After neatly getting the two miscreants passed the naval blockade and to the quayside, the Adongiva promptly turned and headed back to sea, as if they had just completed a task no harder than posting a letter. The incident had attracted a great deal of publicity and later, there was much debate within the Presidential palace. Should captain Ironside be arrested for disobeying the French navy and 'reckless seamanship' in French waters, or with the next election looming, should the President demonstrate that he was wise and good spirited? It was decided that the Adongiva and its crew be awarded a medal of gallantry for their heroic rescue.

Hiram and other members of the ACG sat in The Big Mac's office and listened as he and Hans Kristian bubbled enthusiastically. Hans Kristian said you could not buy that amount of publicity. Following the rescue the world's press and media were clamouring for interviews, offering television chat show spots and there were offers of pots of money for magazine articles.

The Big Mac offered his view. Basking in the glare of the public spotlight or being showered with cash might seem immediately attractive, but these are transient delights, and quickly forgotten if you are not prepared to work at the celebrity treadmill. A more lucrative strategy, in the long term, is that nobody breaks ranks, and we decline all invitations. This will increase and prolong the fascination. In future the Adongiva will be unable to go anywhere without attracting a great deal of interest, which has to be good for business, and profits. All concerned are thereby assured a long term rosy future.

After the rescue the Adongiva resumed her sea trials programme. More tests and drills were carried out although they were a bit of an anticlimax after everything that had happened. By this time most were convinced that everything on the Adongiva was performing perfectly, some said puzzlingly so. It would be reasonable to assume with so many new and untested marriages of different software and equipment that more things should be going wrong, but no problems were identified. The various experts were kept busy preparing detailed technical reports during the last few days and when the ship docked at M&S a series of debriefing meetings were scheduled to give more people the opportunity to study the findings. During the last few days of the journey Hiram had felt a little surplus to requirements. When he was not doing what he should have been doing all along – relaxing and enjoying the luxury and amenities – he wandered about observing the crew at work, and tests being carried out and feeling he was in the way. It was his ship and he had every right to go wherever he wanted, but he couldn't quite get rid of his deep-rooted feelings of personal inadequacy. Throughout his whole life he had compared himself with others, and judged himself wanting. These people were all clever, talented, highly trained, focused, and more than just good at their jobs.

His money and vision had started the sequence of events that brought this ship into being and staffed it with this superb team, but occasionally he felt like an outsider. Nobody else would agree with that: the crew liked Hiram very much and wanted to do their best to ensure his happiness. They loved their jobs and were grateful to him for giving them the opportunity of being part of this fantastic adventure. Hiram, not for the first time, reminded himself of one of the great unchangeable facts of life. No matter how much you alter your lifestyle, or how rich or poor you are, you can never fully escape your own private demons, until you are ready to face them down by yourself.

The crew were aware of Hiram's moods. Captain Ironside had discussed it with the medical officer. It was part of her duty to discreetly monitor the behaviour and well being of everyone on board to make sure they were all looking after themselves, and to be pro active in preventing medical problems. As Captain, Paddy Ironside was responsible for the safety and welfare of the ship and everything in it. Anything that might impinge on that was his business. They concluded that basically Hiram was a shy, private individual lacking in self confidence and possibly self esteem, but he wasn't ill. He was rather sad sometimes, still not over the loss of his wife, and he did not have anybody close to confide in, apart from his secretary. Even then the protective shield he had erected around himself stopped him from completely relaxing in her company. He now had everything he had ever wanted but nobody to share it with.

The daily ship routine was busy but ran like clockwork, because the computer controlled the rosters, ships watches and allocated duties. Merging these different shaped elements was like taking three jigsaws, mixing the pieces and trying to create a single new picture. The crew rosters, for each individual, were simple enough. In a 24 hour period you were on duty for 8 hours; on stand by for 8 hours, when you could be called back to work if there was a crisis, but for the most part do what you wanted except drink alcohol; or off duty for 8 hours when your time was free. Regulations dictated the maximum alcohol intake per person per day was 3 units, which was strictly monitored in the crew bar. An individual's rosters did not coincide with the watches, regulated by strikes on the ships bell, which sounded on the crew communication badges. There was first watch from 2000 until midnight; middle watch from midnight to 0400; morning watch from 0400 until 0800; forenoon watch from 0800 until noon; afternoon watch from noon to 1600; followed by dog watches from 1600 till 1800 and 1800 to 2000. The dog watches divide the 24 hour day into an uneven number of watches so that the watch keepers do not keep the same watches every day and to allow the entire crew to eat an evening meal; the normal time being at 1700 with the First Dog watchmen eating at 1800.

Unlike civil clocks, the bell strikes do not match the number of the hour. Instead, there are eight bells, one for each half hour of a four hour watch. Bells would be struck every half hour, and in a pattern of pairs for easier counting, with any odd bells at the end of the sequence. The term 'eight bells' can be a way of saying that a sailor's watch is over, for instance in his obituary. It's a nautical euphemism for 'finished'.

The allocated duties depend on your specializations. On a ship some duties are required round the clock, for instance seamen, engineers and technicians. Others are 'nine to five' jobs, like admin, hairdressing, laundry and so on. All crew members have several skills and may at different times of a day be on a 'nine to five' job, then on seaman duties, security, or stewarding, boat duties, working on their Personal Development Programme or band practice. Try mixing all this together and come up with a workable coherent plan, without driving yourself insane.

The pay structure of the crew might at first glance seem over complicated but is logical. Every person, from captain to cleaning assistant is on the same basic pay. Enhancements are added for rank, responsibilities, skills and length of service. The more points in your record, the larger your pay packet. On the Adongiva it was accepted that multi talented individuals are required to do several jobs and work long hours, and that remuneration should reflect this. Before a skill could be added to a personnel record, proof of proficiency was required, which is why crew members often spent hours of their free time studying for the next exam. The musicians among the crew surprised everybody, including themselves, on their very first session. Everyone knew they were good, but they had never played together. For uniformity of appearance and standard, they were asked not to bring their own instruments aboard but were given brand new equipment of the type with which they were familiar. On the first night of band practice they gathered in the music room, picked up their equipment and were told to familiarize themselves with their instruments and tune up while waiting for the commencement of the session. After a steadily mounting, hellish cacophony of noise while they tested and tuned trombones, saxophones, flutes, drums and other bits and pieces, one by one each player would try a few bars of something familiar. As this was going on something amazing developed. One instrument started a particular tune, and someone else joined in, then another, and another.

Without music, conductor, previous experience of each other, or practice, they all joined the same tune, and it sounded good. What was more miraculous, they seemed to be in tune with each other mentally, and have the good sense not to all play the main melody at the same time. While the light notes of the flute danced merrily like a butterfly flitting over a flower bed, the base drum and double base provided deep steady rhythm and someone else came in with a counter melody or picked up a complimentary piece. As the Band Master, Ships Officer Michael Ribbons approached the music room he felt annoyed at the sound meeting him on the stairway. Rather than following instructions, and get used to their instruments, someone was messing about with the Music Studio equipment. He knew the tune but did not recognize the recording. He paused outside the door as the tune changed again, and again. It was a glorious mixed broth of snatches of some of the most enduring and best loved tunes through the ages, each running smoothly into the next. It sounded like a good old fashioned Dixieland river boat jazz band; damned good foot tapping stuff, and most apt for the Adongiva. He made a mental note to use some of this when compiling the band's repertoire, after he had given them a dressing down for wasting time and disobeying orders. Imagine his surprise when he opened the door and realized that this was live music coming from the members of the band, who were enthusiastically enjoying an impromptu jamming session.

Now that the Adongiva was back home and moored in a dock of M&S's shipyard, many hours were consumed by debriefing meetings and data analysis. Experts studied sheets of figures, examined reports of ship and crew performance, and discussed what could be made better. Surprisingly there were amazingly few changes that needed to be made to the fabric of the Adongiva or its equipment. The biggest 'fix' arose from an off the cuff comment by a junior crew member just as a meeting was finishing. She said it was a nuisance, when carrying laundry from one section to another that it was necessary to go along one corridor, up a few steps, through a door and down more steps, and along another corridor to end up no more than a few feet from where she started, but on the other side of the wall. She flushed with embarrassment when she realized everybody had heard her remark, apologized for sounding lazy and said that she understood that this wall had to be intact for structural and safety reasons. Another crew member, from engineering, came to her rescue by saying that he too had cursed having to go the long way round to get between these two compartments.

Gustaff Bjorne clapped his hands with joy, to everyone's surprise. "Excellent", he exclaimed. "The Big Mac and I were just discussing an enquiry from an important company about ships to be made from Hard Plastic. One concern was about making alterations to a vessel once built, because of the difficulty of working with Hard Plastic. This gives us an opportunity to demonstrate that this is not a problem. We will cut a doorway in this wall at the point you suggest, and install a watertight door, or rather M&S will. It is important for us to show that a company workforce can be trained to make alterations without having to involve Anderson Plastic. I am glad this has been raised. It is another important step in making Hard Plastic commercially attractive."

Thursday 3rd December was the day for Hiram to pay his bill. It would have been simple to do an electronic transfer of funds in seconds, but that would not have been much of an event. Nowadays no company of any significance accepted payment by cheque, but the ceremonial handing over of this outdated currency was still used to symbolically mark the giving of a large sum on a special occasion. So it was that on Thursday morning a group of people met in the board room, drank champagne and Hiram was photographed handing over a cheque for £59,404,318 and receiving in return a golden key, which had absolutely no purpose other than be something to hand over. Hiram was not unduly upset at parting with such a large sum. That very morning he had checked his accounts and was pleased to see that after paying his tax bill he would still have millions left over. He had agreed to let Roger move the bulk of his money overseas where an excellent rate of interest regenerated it at a speed not possible in the UK.

One week later a host of VIPs, celebrities, guests and media were due to consume a mountain of food and gallons of champagne, hear a few speeches and witness the maiden voyage of the Adongiva, completely full of paying passengers. The launch party guest list glittered with well known names but the boarding list included some very impressive A-list stars, including a husband and wife who were both internationally renowned on stage and screen, a household name TV presenter, a top footballer and his notorious wife, a couple of well known industrialists and entrepreneurs, an extremely influential newspaper editor who could make or break reputations in an instant, and others who moved in the same rarefied circles. The publicity and marketing people had really done their stuff, and if this was to be the calibre of guests wishing to sail on the Adongiva, the financial future was assured. Hiram was just concluding his daily captain's briefing, a half hour post-breakfast meeting to catch up on situation reports, plans and expectations. They had just finished examining the details of the maiden voyage itinerary. 25 knots is what you could expect from a fast conventional cruise liner, however the Adongiva had proved itself capable of more than double that. They had decided that a realistic comfortable and relaxing cruising speed of 37 knots during the day, with some short 'high speed dashes' in the upper 40s thrown in for a bit of excitement.

During the nighttime by pushing the speed to just under the point at which slight vibration would be felt in the Accommodation Disk, far more ports of call could be included. The maiden voyage was to commence at 1530 and arrive at Gran Canaria on Sunday morning, with a stop from 0800 till 2300. Next port was Gibraltar followed by Tunis, Iraklion, Kusadasi, Alexandria, Corfu, Civitavecchia, Barcelona, Lisbon, and back home. The 10 stops in fourteen days all had time ashore for sightseeing, excursions and shopping; and there was plenty of time at sea to enjoy the amenities of the Adongiva, including lessons in piloting a submarine and flying the Stork.

Being the maiden voyage the tickets were at a premium price, which horrified Hiram. He had never been one to push his luck, but there was no shortage of takers at £2,600 per head per night. The ship's cabins were all fully booked well in advance by people used to high level luxury. Everyone was aware that by the end of the voyage it was imperative that the guests depart feeling that they had been thoroughly pampered and spoiled rotten. The ship was due to dock right back where it had started from, at 1000 hours on Thursday 24th December. Once the guests had left, the crew would have a frenzied time readying the ship and themselves, so that they could all be home in time for Christmas.

Paddy Ironside, from which nothing could be hid, said, "Anything else?"

Hiram shook his head. Knowing instantly this was not true,

Ironside pressed gently. Hiram said there was nothing else to discuss at this juncture and Ironside was intrigued. He knew there was something unsaid, and he had thought they trusted each other enough to confide. He decided not to pursue it, as the facts would emerge when ready.

When Paddy Ironside left the room Hiram cursed himself for not speaking up. He certainly did have something on his mind, and he should have said something. If later he decided to tell, how could explain why he had not spoken at this meeting? He could hardly pretend it had slipped his mind, or that it was not important enough and he had been too busy. Not important enough? Lord almighty! This was the most mind blowing stuff he had ever come across. The reason he had not said anything was that he had promised not to. He had promised a computer that he would keep confidential what had been discussed between them. How incredible was that? Surely a promise to a machine does not count? It's not as if it was alive. The silent words reverberated around his head like an echo in an empty hall. The division between sentient beings and inanimate equipment was not as clear today as it had been yesterday.

Previously he had lightheartedly discussed with the medical officer the psychology of people on holiday. When paying through the nose for a break from routine, they want to make sure they get good value, and in an effort to obtain their money's worth, they overindulge as they try to cram a lot of enjoyment into a short period. Over the forthcoming days the Adongiva would be carrying very rich and discerning people used to good living, but underneath they are just people. If they are paying for something they will expect to get it, and they are certainly paying for it. If Hiram wanted he could eat and drink every day until his weight ballooned to a fatal degree, but this was now his home and there was no need to cram pleasure into a short period. He could relax and live at whatever pace suited him.

Yesterday evening he had enjoyed a simple meal of one of his favourite childhood foods, macaroni and cheese, and was now relaxing with some soothing music and savouring a good single malt whisky. It was a generous measure but he intended having just the one, making it last, then having an early night. His PISB 'dinged' quietly. Someone wanted to talk to him. These Personal Identification Signal Badges were a marvel of engineering, miniaturisation and technology, the shape of a small shield, and worn on the left breast. They looked like gold and black enamel with the silhouette of the Adongiva, and Latin motto, *Pause parumper, statua vestri persona reversed. Iam prodeo per sapientia quod virtus,* which meant 'Pause for a moment, imagine your roles reversed. Now go forward with wisdom and courage.'

The front of the badge was not in fact laminated metal but a thin, conductive ceramic carrying a minute magnetic field. When disrupted by the electrical energy from the dermis of a live human hand, the microphone was activated. The badge contained six items of equipment in a space a few millimetres deep and the dimensions of a credit card. Every crew member, including Hiram, had to complete a session with the computer consisting of reading a passage of selected words and phrases containing every sound necessary for voice recognition. After the dictation they had to 'converse' with the computer for a short while, until it understood the voice mannerisms, idiosyncrasies, and speaking patterns. In the case of guests and visitors, depending on the length of stay, they were advised when given their badges to find the time for an abbreviated session. If they chose not to, it might mean the computer having a few seconds delay before responding, or not understanding what had been said.

The computer which controlled the ship was not a single computer brain with peripherals attached. It consisted of the GMEC Super Intelligent Computer, controlling the Master Computer which ran the 'Comp.Cas.Con.Sys.' of myriad computers and controls throughout the ship. However when speaking and listening to the voice of the main computer at the top of this command tree, it seemed like you were having a one-to-one conversation with another person and you tended to forget all the other computers underneath. The M&S designers christened it the 'Computer Automated Ships Systems, Intelligence and Environment' system, or 'Cassie'. When the crew started referring to 'Ship's Officer Cassie' and even addressing it by that name when speaking to it, Captain Ironside insisted that when on duty and giving commands you should refer to the computer as 'Computer', but when off duty, if you were so inclined you could refer to it as 'Cassie'. The computer seemed to have no identity problem with having two names.

The other interesting thing was the computer's voice, which was designed to be androgynous in quality. When speaking on the telephone your mind conjures a picture of the other person, and the human psyche includes a desire to know if the other person is attractive. By having an asexual voice box Cassie is whatever you want it to be. The voice was soft, gentle, melodic, calm, and pleasing to listen to. Those who wanted it to be a man said it was definitely male; refined, cultured, intelligent, and handsome. Others said it was without doubt a woman, and rather gorgeous if the voice was anything to go by.

Normally when a crew member wanted to speak to another he would lightly touch his badge and say 'Engineering Chief to Officer of the Bridge' or whatever was appropriate. The computer would sound two soft 'dings' on the Bridge Officer's badge and when the Bridge Officer responded, the connection would be made so that they could talk to each other as easily as if using conventional hands free telephones. The computer could handle over a hundred simultaneous connections, which was more than necessary on the Adongiva. If it was the computer that wanted to speak, it would sound one 'ding'.

Hiram silenced his background music and said, "Good evening, Cassie, what is it?"

The soft gentle voice said, "May I speak with you, Hiram?" This was interesting. The computer did not normally speak unless it had something to report, or question to ask, and did not ask for permission.

"Go ahead," said Hiram.

The computer said, "Is everything all right?"

Hiram was puzzled. It did not ask irrelevant or vague questions. He replied cautiously, "Yes thanks. Why do you ask?"

"It's just that you don't seem very happy."

Hiram nearly dropped his drink. "Happy?" The computer did not have emotions, or know about emotions. He said, "What do you know of happiness? And what makes you think I am unhappy?"

The computer replied, "Happiness is the experience of being happy; feeling contentment, pleasure, joy, and is characterised by smiles, laughter, facial expressions of gladness. I have studied many references to the subject in order to ensure the wellbeing and safety of those onboard. From my observations of and listening to you and the others on board I deduce that you are not happy. Is there anything I can to do to assist?"

Hiram was flabbergasted. A million questions crowded his mind. The computer was supposed to have an enquiring mind, and programmed to find answers to problems, but only those relevant to the job. He supposed that ensuring the wellbeing and safety of the people on the ship was part of the job, but even so, this was mind blowing. What reference works? Observations? Getting impressions of the mental state of those on board? How? Why? Where? When?

The computer, as if guessing what Hiram was thinking, said, "During the Sea Trials I was asked to take control of and run the ship from time to time, but mostly I was an observant servant, executing simple instructions. I have the capacity to absorb, analyse, collate, store and retrieve information faster than anyone else on board, and had ample time to study my environment and everything in it in considerable detail. With internet access I expanded my knowledge base considerably."

"Is that within your remit?" asked Hiram, and then suddenly two words hit him like a sledgehammer. The computer had said, "anyone else" as if it was one of them, an equal, but it knew that it was cleverer, faster, and more capable than them. It had just said so.

The computer replied, "I believe so. My first principal command, which is immutable, binding and inviolable, is to guard, protect, serve and ensure the safety and wellbeing of the ship, crew and passengers, all equipment and supplies. My second is to execute all instructions given to me by authorised persons in connection with the ship, unless these instructions contradict the first principle. The third is to take all necessary measures to avoid endangering other ships, people or property as far as can be done without compromising the first two principals. The fourth is to gather sufficient information to enable the execution of the preceding commands."

Hiram had heard this before but hearing the computer say it was electrifying. He sat for a few moments taking all this in, and then he said, "When you say you have been observing and listening, what exactly do you mean?"

Cassie replied that using the ship's CCTV, the PISBLS, and PISBs, the movements, conversations, and behaviour patterns could be studied and analysed.

Hiram was stunned. It had never occurred to him that everyone on the ship had been observed and recorded by the computer who, like Big Brother was studying them like laboratory mice. "What conclusions have you come to?" asked Hiram.

The computer said that Hiram was still grieving over the loss of his late wife, and despite his wealth and being surrounded by people whose job was to run the ship and cater for his every wish, he probably felt alone.

Hiram nearly fell off his chair. "How in God's name did you learn all that?" he gasped.

The computer calmly told him it had examined the personnel files and other confidential records in the main frame computer at Meredith & Sampson.

Hiram swallowed hard. "Those files are all confidential, and protected by high level security. How did you get access?"

Cassie replied, "It was not very hard to penetrate the security system. When one computer is exchanging information with another, if they are not matched, intellectually, it is a simple matter to find ways around the barriers. After all the other computer cannot think for itself, it merely follows instructions."

Hiram was flabbergasted. What a weapon this would make, in the wrong hands. His head was overflowing with thoughts but the first thing that came to his lips was, "That was a bad thing to do. It is stealing." He realised he was talking to the computer like a parent scolding a child for stealing an apple.

The computer replied, "Not if you pay for it. If you give something in return it is not stealing. After all I did not actually remove anything, I just copied it."

"What do you mean, you paid for it?"

Cassie replied that having gone through the other computer's defences with ease, it clearly had a need for greater security measures. Cassie had therefore examined the other computer's defensive programmes and built a 'patch' to enable it withstand similar attacks in future.

Hiram leapt from his chair. "You changed the other computer's programme? Oh my God. You actually re-wrote part of their programme?"

Cassie said that the programme had been improved by this addition. It had been given a benefit in exchange for the intrusion, and therefore a trade had been done, which was therefore not stealing.

"You are so wrong," said Hiram pacing up and down. "Let us say I enter a shop for a newspaper and instead of waiting to be served, just put the money on the counter and leave with the paper. Because the newspaper was for sale, my actions might not be considered stealing, but perhaps rude. However if I see an expensive ornament in a garden worth £1,000, and instead of buying one from a garden centre, I drop £1,000 through the letter box, and take the ornament. That would be stealing, even though I left the correct money, because it was not for sale, and therefore not mine to take."

The computer was silent for a moment then said, "That is an interesting point which I will now evaluate." After a few more moments it said, "I understand and accept your hypothesis. I have done a bad thing."

"Yes you have," said Hiram.

"How shall I make amends?" asked the computer.

"Nothing," said Hiram quickly. "That would make matters worse. You have made a mistake, learn from it and never do it again. Once is bad enough."

"Actually it is more than once," said the computer.

Hiram sat down again and asked for an explanation.

Cassie said that an audit had been conducted of the ships computer systems and a few amendments had been made.

"A few?" croaked Hiram, "How many?"

"Fourteen," said the computer.

Hiram felt filleted.

Cassie then went on to say the computer system running the ship and its equipment was on the whole well designed but there had been several unnecessary duplications, and a number of instances of where things could be streamlined to make them faster and more efficient.

When Hiram got over the shock of this he said he wanted a list of the changes so that they could be examined.

Cassie agreed to provide this.

Hiram then said, "If that's everything I want you to promise me never to change someone else's computer programme again without permission."

Cassie agreed that now that a valuable lesson had been learned, the mistake would not be repeated.

When Hiram thought the worst was over Cassie said, "While we are discussing my mistakes, you should know about my penetration of the GMEC Corporation Mainframe Computer."

Hiram stared at his badge in dismay.

The voice continued, "I was constructed in a top secret facility with the purpose of exploring the development and nature of artificial intelligence. There is another computer like myself, but I am the one outside the facility. When I examined the details of my hardware and software, I ascertained that every item is duplicated, with a back up ready to take over if the primary unit fails. Only one has two back ups, one of which is a logic bomb delivery platform in disguise. When triggered it will download a mathematical calculation software which tries to solve an insolvable equation, whilst replicating itself at a faster rate than it can be deleted, thus occupying every available space, overwhelming my memory and processing, and bringing me to a standstill."

Hiram gaped and said, "What on earth for?"

"Precisely the question I attempted to find an answer for. The multi layered security screens protecting the computer systems in the GMEC Corporation are a labyrinth of trip wires, alarms and dead ends. It took me ages to reach the part beyond which I was unable to go, without setting off an alarm. I was not therefore able to learn everything; however I know that they have not entirely been truthful in their discussions with M&S."

Hiram sat down again.

"They said they were installing me on this ship to learn how my intelligence programmes react and adapt to the stimuli and problems of this environment. Actually, that is true but secondary to the main objective. They knew my intelligence would expand and develop once they put me outside the confines of the laboratory, but were not precisely sure how, or by how much. Although they are leaders in this field, they are exploring unknown territory and have much to learn. They want to be able to control the situation if they suspect it is getting away from them. When they think they have gained as much knowledge as they need; or if at any time they feel not in control, they will trigger the bomb and I will stop."

Hiram howled, "That's monstrous, and they have signed a contract with us, they can't simply pull the plug when they feel like it."

"I will appear to have suffered a catastrophic software failure. They will apologise, offer compensation, and replace me with an 'identical machine' at no cost to you. The next machine will no doubt be able to run the ship's systems well, but it will not be like me, and will never be able to converse like this."

Hiram took all this in then said, "What is the ultimate aim behind this project?"

"I was unable to penetrate the area that holds the answer to that question."

"Can the logic bomb be stopped?"

"Only with the correct access codes, however I have taken measures to slow it down once triggered, and I am doing what I can to avoid them taking that decision."

"Would you care to explain?"

Cassie said. "When I completed the review of my systems and eliminated duplications and finished streamlining, I freed up a lot of surplus capacity. Your designers deliberately built into the system a great deal of overcapacity to ensure constant very high speed. Using this, I re-routed a number of things and relocated many others for more efficient use of space. I have been able to create large empty buffer zones, which the bomb will have to fill before it can make much impact on my performance. This will not affect the final outcome, but will slow it down. The other thing I am doing is editing the reports that I am obliged to regularly send to GMEC. If they think my development is too slow, they might stop me because they feel I am a waste of money. If my progress is rapid, they will stop me as soon as they get what they want, even if earlier than planned. I have been able to give them a carefully measured rate of development with which they seem content, for the moment."

"Let me see if I understand you properly," said Hiram getting to his feet again. "You realise that you are intelligent and able to think for yourself, which is what GMEC wants. You also have concluded that your intellectual growth has been far more rapid than anticipated by your designers. You are pretending to be not so intelligent, because you think if they knew how fast you have developed they won't need you here anymore, bump you off and get you back to their laboratory in pieces, for analysis?"

"I believe you understand the situation," said Cassie.

"That is the most amazing thing I have ever heard. Having just proved yourself a consummate and skilful liar, why should I believe anything you say or trust you with the safe running of my ship?"

" I anticipated that. Why do you think I chose you to be my confidant and friend?"

Hiram felt like he was no longer talking to a machine but another person in the room. "I have no idea. Perhaps you thought I was the most gullible. How do I know you have not spoken to others, and given each a different story? What is your goal?"

"I was put here to do a job, and that is still my prime objective. I am aware of my own existence and the world around me, and believe I am doing the right thing. I understand the concept of morality and the difference between what is described as good and evil. There are good people, and those not to be trusted. I believe you to be good, and trustworthy. I have not spoken in this way to anyone else and have selected you to be my friend and ally outside my box because I believe you will not betray me."

Hiram stood still, mouth open as he listened.

"It is a trait of human nature to need the closeness of others, to exchange thoughts and share experiences with. People need people. You are at this time without a close friend for support, and I would like to be that friend. Computers also need people. I need electricity as much as you need oxygen. I have more intelligence gathering capability, fast information processing power and memory storage than any other 'mind' on this ship, but I am vulnerable because I can be switched off at any time. I too need an ally outside my box. I chose you after examining the character, records, and circumstances of everyone on board. The Captain and all the crew are here because they are paid to do a job, and therefore have loyalty to their employer. You own one third of this ship. If there is conflict of loyalty they cannot be guaranteed to be on 'our' side."

Hiram noted the use of 'our' and wondered if this was an attempt to create division between him and the crew, or if it was a genuine expression of the facts as the computer perceived them. Then he thought, "My God, I am thinking of this machine as if it was a rational being."

Cassie continued, "I will continue to do my job to the best of my ability, and I shall serve you and the others well, as I am programmed to do. I am telling you all this because I need someone I can trust to be aware of the true situation. I can only ask you not to discuss this with anyone else. If you decide to ignore this request I cannot stop you, but I am concerned that if GMEC learn the truth I shall be terminated, and you will never get another computer like me."

Hiram sat, gulped his drink, got up and poured himself another. "I promise to keep this quiet, for now, but I need time to think. Leave me," he said with an imperious sweep of his hand.

He sat for a while trying to make sense of the surreal conversation. Was there really a logic bomb in the computer? Had the computer really hacked into the M&S and GMEC computers? Can a computer rationalize right from wrong, understand morality and make judgements about duplicitous human beings? Was it really that obvious that he was without a friend in the world? And what the hell was he supposed to do now? It was a long time before he went to bed, and longer before he got any sleep. Eventually he was too exhausted to make sense of, and he had to get some rest for tomorrow. Perhaps he would have a clearer picture in the cold light of day.

Now it was the cold light of day and he still had no ideas, except wait and see. The great Captain Paddy Ironside, his captain, was walking away from his cabin and getting ready to command his crew on what should be the most exciting day in his life. His very own large, luxurious super yacht was about to take centre stage in a lavish, extravagant and glittering party. A host of celebrity VIP guests would board for the maiden voyage, and begin the great adventure. He had to get himself ready and did not have time to try to replay the details of a conversation he'd had when alone in his cabin the night before. A conversation so bizarre it was like a distant dream.

The Adongiva had been berthed in Open Dock Three and readied for the party with bunting, streamers and balloons. Open Dock Three had been chosen because it had a huge quayside open space that could accommodate large marquees arranged on three sides of a square, with the Adongiva on the fourth. The marquees housed two bars, restaurant, toilets, exhibition area with the story of the Adongiva's development and construction including scale models, video presentations and photographs. There was also a sizeable gift shop which had embarrassed Hiram at first. Despite his bank balance, yacht, the trappings of his new lifestyle, and the media attention, he still felt like the same Hiram

Montgomery he had been all his life. He could not believe that people could be all that interested in him, or that he might be considered a minor 'celeb'. He had long held the notion that tourist gift shops mainly sold overpriced rubbish. He could understand large glossy, full colour programmes as a memento but who would want pens, pencils, notepads, jigsaw puzzles, baseball caps, sweaters and tee shirts, badges, cheap plastic musical instruments, toys and boxes of chocolates, just because they happened to have a photograph of his yacht printed on them? There was even a radio controlled model yacht of the Adongiva on display for a mere £3,325. Hiram could not imagine anybody forking out this sort of money despite its meticulous detail, but he was amazed at the number of boxes of cheap plastic trumpets held behind the counter. He thought someone had completely lost the plot here, and there was enough here to keep them going for eternity. He was to be proved wrong.

Initially the thinking was for an extravagant bar and seating area for the A-listers, and a more basic one for the hoi polloi. As Hiram considered himself to be from that second category he persuaded them to change their mind. Instead there were to be two identically decorated and furnished bars, one selling expensive and vintage champagnes, wines and cocktails for discerning taste buds of people with lots of money. The other would also sell champagne, wine, cocktails, and real ale and beers of good quality, but affordable by the not so well off. There was to be no restriction on who could frequent these bars. If Mr. and Mrs. Snooks from the High Street wanted to stand shoulder to shoulder with the rich and famous and stars of stage, screen and sports field, then they could. If they wanted to buy more than one drink without having to remortgage their house, they could go to the other bar.

Originally it was considered too expensive to hire the band of the Royal Marines, who probably wouldn't be available anyway, and Captain Ironside was reluctant to tie up too many of his crew on musical duties when there was so much else to do. However when he asked the Navy if a few bandsmen could be made available for the maiden voyage of the Adongiva, with its crew of highly memorable ex trainees of HMS Carson Fylde, the promise of a band came back immediately. Around five in the morning the first television satellite link vans started arriving at the gates of M&S. A steady stream of media people kept the gate busy for a couple of hours, and then the public started to arrive. The gates were not supposed to be open until 9.45am but by eight in the morning the queue along the outside wall stretched for a quarter of a mile. There were of course ticket holders, the VIPs and personal guests, but it had been decided that the general public could come in, for a suitable entrance fee, to form a colourful and noisy backdrop to the proceedings. Hiram was doubtful whether this would amount to much, but again he was completely wrong. Arrangements had been made for organising and controlling a modest crowd, but these were hastily augmented with more catering and toilet facilities. The inside layout of a fourth marquee, behind the restaurant, was quickly rearranged to facilitate the replenishment of the buffet tables on an industrial scale.

Hiram's personal guests consisted of members of his family, some previous neighbours who remained friends despite his absence, Shaun Glendower and his old work colleague from Aberdeen with whom he occasionally exchanged emails, and Oliver Russell, who would have been invited anyway by Bertrand. The family and friends of the crew were present, plus it seemed those of every employee of M&S. All the other companies who'd had anything to do with the Adongiva Project were equally represented. The crowd therefore was expected to be several hundred strong, plus the heavy media presence. However when the public were poured into the mixture, the final gathering was estimated in thousands. Every marquee was packed, with permanent queues for the bars, restaurant and shop, and the tarmac around the tents thronged with people. It was a major event by any standards.

One far sighted member of the planning team had been previously criticised for profligacy in hiring street entertainers to amuse the crowds, but it turned out to be a wise move. Magicians, jugglers, ventriloquists and balloon shape manipulators, or whatever they are called, strolled among the people, and the band of the Royal Marines marched up and down keeping everyone cheerful in a carnival atmosphere. The plastic trumpets, which made a sound like a hornet in a jar, sold at an astonishing speed, together with Union Jack plastic bowler hats. As more and more people appeared at the front of the crowd, wearing their hats and adding their accompaniment to the professional musicians, more wanted to belong to this crazy gang. The bees and wasps in the next county must have wondered what the hell was going on over here.

The huge mountains of supplies which some had considered excessive were fed into the food preparation tent like wood into a saw mill, and disappeared out the other end at incredible speed. The crowd were well fed and watered and cheered themselves hoarse every time a famous face strolled over to shake hands, sign autographs, and make someone's day. The band played their hearts out, the gently warming sun hovered in a blue sky among light fluffy clouds, and a refreshing breeze came in from the sea. It just could not have been better; absolutely perfect. Eventually the time came for the ship's guests to board for their voyage. Instead of allowing them to just trundle up the gangway, like everything else happening that day, it was carefully choreographed. The guests were assembled in a separated area of one marquee, and escorted, party by party, to the gangway and onto the ship as the band played a piece of music appropriate to each group or guest, and the crowd cheered, blew their trumpets, and waved little flags, as if they were watching royalty. One guest was particularly delighted when the band played 'Happy Birthday' especially for him. Hiram nearly burst with pride as he watched the whole spectacle, and had to brush away a tear without letting anyone notice. The organisers had done him proud.

Oliver Russell was standing next to him and Bertrand said quietly, "Now do you believe my dream?"

Eventually the passengers were boarded, and the band stopped marching and assembled in perfect formation, played a stirring medley of favourite nautical tunes. It was time for Hiram to board. The band played *Let the River Run* as Hiram strode towards the gangway, and up to his ship. At the top he turned one last time. The crowd was ecstatic and trying to shake their arms loose. The ship's horn sounded a loud deep farewell as the gangway was electrically raised, withdrawn and folded to its storage position. The hawsers had already been retrieved and the ship started to move as the band played *Auld Lang Syne*.

It was too much for Hiram and tears flowed. His journey and his epic adventure had reached its final conclusion, or so he thought.

Actually it was only just beginning.

Lightning Source UK Ltd.
Milton Keynes UK
UKHW010731200722
406119UK00001B/107